BOGEY SPADES

JACK STEWART

Severn River Publishing
SevernRiverBooks.com

This is a work of fiction. Names, characters, businesses, places, events and incidents are either the products of the author's imagination or used in a fictitious manner. Any resemblance to actual persons, living or dead, or actual events is purely coincidental.

ISBN: 978-1-64875-609-2 (Paperback)

ALSO BY JACK STEWART

The Battle Born Series
Unknown Rider
Outlaw
Bogey Spades
Declared Hostile

To find out more about Jack Stewart and his books, visit
severnriverbooks.com

For Tre, William, and Rebecca,
Who gave me reason to fly.

1

Miramar Reservoir
San Diego, California

Corporal Adam Garett shifted the thirty-year-old Jeep Cherokee into park, then lifted his smartphone from the cup holder in the center console. A cool evening breeze rushed in through the cracked windows, circulating the cab's dank, stale air, and he listened to the silence echoing across the parking lot while trying to ignore his pounding heart. After unlocking his phone, he opened the Tapatalk app and selected the Mustang forum he subscribed to, then scrolled to a thread listed under "1979-1993 (Fox body)". It was ironic, since Adam knew next to nothing about cars—let alone forty-year-old muscle cars—but he spent more time scrolling that particular thread than doing anything else.

SSP Coupe Suspension Specs?

Adam hadn't the faintest clue what an "SSP" was, but it might as well have been the shackle keeping him bound to a world he couldn't seem to escape. He took a deep breath and scrolled to the bottom, looking for the reply a regular user had posted earlier that evening. There was no text, just a picture showing something Adam suspected was an obscure component in a car's suspension. He wouldn't have been able to tell the difference between a coilover and a carburetor, and he sure as shit wouldn't know if it belonged on a Fox body. The picture was labeled with a string of seemingly random numbers, but he knew better.

01052330329191211709721.jpeg

First week of the month, on the fifth day, at thirty minutes to midnight. He looked at the clock on the dash and saw that he still had twenty-five minutes until the appointed time, but the coordinates were on the opposite side of the reservoir from the parking lot. He sighed and opened the door, stepping out into the crisp fall evening just as a flight of two F-35C Joint Strike Fighters flew overhead bound for the Marine Corps Air Station.

Adam watched the strobing anti-collision lights retreat into the distance, then set out on the road winding its way around the man-made lake. Leaving the water treatment plant behind, he was surprised by the lack of joggers or bikers on the path. But then he remembered it was almost midnight. Most sane people were at home, preparing for one final day of work before they could enjoy the first day of the weekend downtown in the Gaslamp Quarter or at one of the more popular watering holes at the beach.

Not meeting a Chinese spy in the dead of night.

Why am I even here?

But he knew why. Once you made a deal with the devil, you were stuck. And that meant continuing his relationship with the Chinese Ministry of State Security and feeding his new handler just enough information to remain alive. But not so much that he ended up in jail.

But whereas his first handler had rewarded him with the pleasures of her body, his new handler was less accommodating. Shi Yufei was a squat, stern-faced man with a permanently etched sour expression. He was firm and unbending like a shoot of bamboo, contrasting starkly with Chen's supple and sexual femininity. Adam much preferred Chen's carrot to Shi's stick, but they hadn't asked his opinion on the matter.

As he followed the road east, he glanced across the reservoir and saw the faint twinkling of stars reflecting off its placid surface. A complete circuit of the lake was almost five miles, but it was less than half that to the appointed meeting place. He glanced at the glowing dials on his watch and muttered a curse. Why Shi had insisted on meeting in such an obscure place was beyond him, but he knew the spy would give him hell if he was late.

Feeding off the memories of forced marches at boot camp, he hinged forward at the waist and increased his pace. But a flash of light across the water froze him in his tracks after only two steps. A muted *pop* reached him a split second later. He reacted on instinct, dropping to a crouch behind the bushes edging the reservoir's shoreline. Adam peered through the tall blades of grass, straining to see across the water. Beads of sweat trickled down the sides of his face, and his heart raced with anxiety.

Flash. *Pop!*

If he had been uncertain following the first one, there was no question what he had just witnessed after the second. He could tell he wasn't the intended target, but he remained frozen and stared wide-eyed across the reservoir, waiting for another light or sound or something that might give him a clue what to do next. Should he continue with the meet? Should he abandon it and return to his barracks?

Adam pinched his eyes shut and hung his head in despair. Things had been so easy before. He had much preferred passing information to Chen through their covert communication device or, even better, while their naked bodies were intertwined under the sheets. But since her disappearance, everything had become more complicated. Coded messages, brush passes, dead drops, midnight assignations in remote locations.

And now, gunshots.

He lifted his head and peered across the water again, noticing the dark outline of a man walking on the opposite side. Again, he felt his heart rate spike as doubt flooded him. The silhouette could belong to anybody.

"Damn," he muttered.

Adam made no attempt to leave his hiding spot as he watched the lone figure walking around the lake. But if he didn't do something soon, the man would be upon him, and he would find out who the strange figure was whether he wanted to or not. He looked over his shoulder at the apartment complex up on the hill south of the reservoir, then at the distant glow of the water treatment plant and lot where his Cherokee was parked—just one among many.

"Damn, damn, damn!"

There was nowhere for him to go, and the man was inching closer. If Adam got up and made a run for it, there was a good chance the movement would draw the man's attention, and he'd suffer the same fate as the poor soul on the opposite shore. But staying in place wasn't a good option either.

Slowly, Adam backed himself deeper into the blades of grass, following the sloping ground toward the water's edge. The foliage was thicker in some places than others, but it was little more than tall grass where fate had decided he hide. He craned his neck to sight in the stranger walking toward him, estimating the distance between them at one hundred yards, then slinked further away from the road.

A thorn snagged the palm of his hand, and he suppressed a yelp. Another glance, and the man had closed to within seventy-five yards. The closer he got, the slower Adam moved. But he still felt exposed, too close to the road to remain invisible. He edged nearer to the water and froze when he felt moisture seep into his tennis shoe.

That's it, he thought, looking back at the man. *Fifty yards.*

Adam lowered himself to the ground, bending and contorting his body to slip in between clumps of grass and press closer to the earth. A few seconds later, he heard the soft plodding and scrape of a heavyset man walking with a limp along the road. He tilted his chin up slightly, catching sight of the figure as he closed to within twenty-five yards of his hiding place. Adam's heart pounded, but he took slow, silent breaths to restrain his fear and let his eyes follow the man from left to right.

Keep walking, he urged. *Please, keep going.*

The man didn't. He pulled even with Adam and stopped, then reached into his pocket. Adam held his breath and waited for the man to pivot and level the silenced pistol on him. He knew it was an appropriate fate for what he had done, but he didn't want to die. No matter how much he knew he deserved it for betraying his country, he didn't want the stranger to leave him floundering in the shallows like a dying carp.

"He wasn't there," the hushed coarse voice said.

Adam exhaled in silent relief when he recognized the object in the man's hand.

"I'll find him."

It wasn't Shi, that much he knew. The man wasn't even Chinese. But

Adam hadn't the faintest clue why he was circling the reservoir in the middle of the night.

Please, keep going, he thought.

Almost as if hearing Adam's plea, the man ended the call and continued toward the parking lot in his awkward step-shuffle gait. When he had gone a hundred yards, Adam let out a muffled sob of relief. He inched his way out of the bushes and back onto the road, torn between continuing to the meeting place, or retreating to his car and the safety of the Marine base.

Adam did what he always did.

He fled.

2

Special Agent Emmy "Punky" King sat in the parking lot behind the wheel of her 1999 Porsche Carrera cabriolet. It was hard for her to believe the car was old enough to be considered a classic, but that was exactly what the dealer had told her when she called about the listing. After her last foray with modern American muscle had ended with yet another wrecked vehicle, she decided to go with something different and opted for a German-engineered sports car. And the often-overlooked "classic" fit within her budget.

"What am I doing here?" she asked with a groan.

Nobody answered because she was alone, staring through the windshield at the Jeep Cherokee of a similar vintage. She guessed some probably considered it a classic too, but whereas the Marine's vehicle was purpose-built for off-roading and utility, hers was made for spirited driving and going fast.

Definitely not for staking out a parking lot in the middle of the night.

But, then again, she didn't have much of a social life. Sitting in the parking lot at the Miramar Reservoir while horny teenagers made out in the back seats of their parents' cars was probably the closest she'd come to getting any action on a Thursday night anyway. She looked to her left at the

Toyota sedan with fogged-up windows and figured Johnny Q Starting Quarterback was rounding second on the prom queen.

Hope you brought protection, kid.

Instinctively, she dropped her elbow and felt for the butt of the pistol holstered on her right hip.

I brought mine.

Though she was beginning to wonder if she even needed it. She had followed Corporal Garett from the Marine Corps Air Station in Miramar through the East Gate and across Interstate 15 before easily accelerating the Porsche northbound and merging with the sparse traffic. Less than two miles later, she followed the Cherokee as it exited on Carroll Canyon Road and eventually Scripps Lake Drive.

The reservoir's parking lot was closed after sundown, but as Punky pulled in, she noticed the chain had been cut—likely by an enterprising adolescent with more testosterone than good sense. She joined the smattering of cars parked there, each of which had left at least two vacant spaces between them, giving an illusion of privacy to the whole affair. Nobody would bat an eye when she parked in the back row, bordering the water treatment plant.

How romantic, she mused.

As unlikely as it seemed, she couldn't help but wonder if the Marine had only come for a tryst. It seemed even more unlikely when he climbed out of the Cherokee and made for the dark trail circling the water. She had been tempted to follow but figured she would either give herself away at best or walk straight into an ambush at worst. Neither outcome was very appealing, so she contented herself with sitting in the cramped Carrera while avoiding looking at the surrounding cars that occasionally rocked on squeaky shocks.

"What are you doing here?" she asked, again not expecting an answer.

As the minutes ticked by, she watched one car pull out, then another. The lot was far from vacant, but if the exodus continued at the same rate, it wouldn't be long before she was left alone with only the Marine's Jeep keeping her company. Would she stay and wait until he returned? Get out and go looking for him? Or would she leave to preserve her anonymity— regroup and try again another day?

Thankfully, before her anxiety forced her into taking action she might later regret, a shadow emerged from the trail. She leaned forward in her seat and stared through the darkness at a lone figure passing from underneath the thick branches hanging over the parking lot.

It's not him.

Whereas the Marine was best described as scrawny and cocksure, this man was thicker around the waist and walked with a limp. She leaned back with a huff, frustrated more with herself for throwing away yet another available evening than she was with the Marine who was doing God-only-knew-what in the moonlit darkness. But her eyes followed the stranger as he crossed the parking lot and climbed in behind the wheel of a dark-colored Mercedes S500 with tinted windows.

She watched the luxury sedan's headlights wink on, then pull out of its spot and make for the exit—not exactly in a rush, but not wasting any time either. She squinted through the darkness and scribbled down four of the license plate's seven characters.

It's probably nothing, she thought.

As the Mercedes disappeared, she returned her attention to the darkened trail where the Marine had disappeared. She was certain he had a connection to China's Ministry of State Security, and she was bound and determined to discover what it was. If she could identify his handler, then she could begin a coordinated surveillance effort that might lead her to *KMART*. But, at the very least, it would give her a more complete picture of the Ministry's network.

A dark shadow moved briskly from the trail toward the parking lot. Again, Punky leaned forward over the leather-wrapped steering wheel and narrowed her gaze.

"There you are," she breathed, recognizing the Marine's silhouette if not his gait.

But something about it seemed off. He wasn't limping or showing any other outward sign of distress, but he was walking faster than normal in a stuttered, almost jittery fashion. His head whipped left and right to scan the parking lot—*What are you looking for?*—and she slinked lower in her seat as his gaze passed the Porsche. After several uncomfortable seconds, Corporal

Garett opened the Cherokee's driver's door and climbed inside. A few seconds after that, he was gone.

Punky waited for the SUV to leave, then opened her door and climbed out of the Carrera. She was dressed in her normal evening attire—a University of Southern California hoodie, pulled down to cover her pistol, and a pair of faded jeans that tapered at her black and white Vans. To the casual observer, she didn't look any more out of place than the other young adults who frequented the park, but she was far more than a pretty face. She had long, raven hair and blue eyes that practically glowed in the moonlight.

But those eyes saw things others missed, making her one of the most talented counterintelligence special agents in the Naval Criminal Investigative Service.

Punky crossed the parking lot and ducked onto the walking path before pulling a penlight from her front jeans pocket and clicking it on. The brilliant beam splayed across the asphalt, and she kept it trained on the ground ten paces ahead of her as she paralleled the shoreline to the east. She listened to a symphony of crickets and other critters performing over the soft lapping of water against the shore. It was eerily quiet.

She walked a hundred yards before stopping to sweep the light across the trail and the foliage on either side—not sure what she was looking for —then over her shoulder at the parking lot still visible around a bend in the trail. If the Marine had come to the reservoir for a clandestine meeting, she knew it wouldn't have been in that spot. It was too exposed to the parking lot and the homes on the nearby hillside. Sure, it was dark, but she had more respect for her adversary than to think they were stupid enough to arrange a meeting somewhere so public.

She glanced across the water, barely able to make out the opposite shore. "That's where I'd go," she said.

Returning her penlight's beam to the walking path, she lowered her head and resumed walking. She tuned out the evening's sounds and listened for movement in the bushes on either side of the trail. But the silence was almost overbearing, and her pace slowed when she reached the other side. Punky scanned the foliage on either side of the road, looking for clues that might reinforce her belief that a meeting had taken place, then shone her penlight onto a narrow finger of water that jutted north from the reservoir.

"This is it," she said. "This is where they met."

She wasn't sure how she knew. But she knew.

Punky chewed on her lip and swept the light across the ground in gentle arcs, looking for evidence to support what she knew in her gut. It was more than just the secluded location or the way the sloping terrain on all sides seemed to funnel the surrounding noises to that one spot. More than the tall grass along the edge of the walking path that had been flattened in places.

Her beam stopped and she squinted to make out what she'd spotted.

"Is that . . ."

She clicked off the light and fumbled for her phone.

3

In Li Hu's line of work, one didn't often get an opportunity to correct past mistakes. But as he squatted on his haunches high on the hill above the reservoir, he couldn't believe his luck. When Mantis had activated him to provide overwatch for Shi Yufei during his meetings with the Marine, he hadn't expected to ever run into one of his former targets.

But there she was, standing in the tall grass at the edge of the water behind a flashlight's dancing beam.

His heart racing, he pulled the night-vision monocular away and stood, careful not to expose himself to the streetlight's glow from over his shoulder. He stood several paces down the slope from the cul-de-sac where multi-million-dollar homes with multi-million-dollar views sat perched atop the hill. As he had been many times during his career, he was nothing more than a phantom in the night, floating across the topography like the early morning mist.

But the lone figure standing on the shore four hundred yards away kept him frozen in place. He reached up and massaged the scar on his left shoulder, remembering with sudden clarity the searing pain from the bullet that had narrowly missed his brachial plexus.

"What is she doing here?"

Shaking away the memory, he reached into his pocket for the encrypted phone and placed the call he had been reluctant to make. He had wanted to delay calling Mantis until after he had sanitized the location, carried away his comrade's body, and scoured the location for clues. But that was before he spotted *her*.

"Yes?"

"We have a problem," he said.

He heard Mantis moving around on the other end and knew she was probably getting out of bed. Breathless, she asked, "Is the Marine okay?"

Li Hu furrowed his brow at the odd question, then ignored it. "Somebody ambushed Shi Yufei," he said.

"What of the Marine?"

"Did you not hear me? Somebody murdered Shi Yufei!"

His statement hung in the air for a few seconds as he watched the flashlight's beam dance across the ground where the not-yet-cold body of Shi Yufei rested in the grass. He brought the monocular to his eye again and watched the woman remove a phone from her pocket and hold it to her ear.

Shit.

At last, she spoke. "What happened?"

"I don't know," Li Hu replied honestly. His shoulder throbbed where a bullet had pierced it, and he fought the urge to massage it. "But that's not the only problem."

"What else?"

He lowered the monocular and studied the hillside in either direction. He was still alone. "A woman just showed up."

Mantis let out an exasperated sigh. "What aren't you telling me?"

He winced with shame at the memory of a telephone pole racing closer as he bled out behind the SUV's steering wheel. "I've seen her before."

"Where?"

"She was with the pilot Chen sent me to eliminate—"

"You mean the one who killed your entire team and got away?"

He snapped his mouth shut and gritted his teeth. It was the pilot who had shot him and inflicted the greatest damage, but he knew better than to quibble. For an operator of his pedigree, tracking down and eliminating a pilot and his girlfriend should have been a simple task. But somehow the duo had turned the tables on him. And his men had paid the price.

"Yes, ma'am," he said.

"And the Marine?"

Li Hu shook his head. "What?"

"What happened to the Marine?"

"He never showed."

He couldn't be sure, but he thought Mantis exhaled with what sounded like relief. For whatever reason, she had taken a personal interest in seeing that the Marine was protected at all costs. As far as Li Hu could remember, she had never ordered one of his men to provide overwatch for meetings with low-level assets, and he had naturally assumed it was to protect Shi Yufei.

But it had become clear this asset was different.

"I need you to find him," she ordered.

Li Hu never questioned his orders, but something seemed off. "Why is he so important?"

If Mantis had been sleeping when he called, any trace of lingering fatigue was now gone. Her matronly voice sounded as hard as iron. "You will find him and report his location to me immediately."

He swallowed.

"And, Li Hu . . ."

"Yes, ma'am?"

"If you ever question my orders again, you won't live to see another sunrise. Am I clear?"

"Yes, ma'am."

The line went dead, and he slipped the phone in his pocket as he considered the strange assignment. As a special forces brigade veteran of the People's Liberation Army, he tended to think in terms of military objectives. Offensive and defensive operations, stability, support, and even psychological operations. But what Mantis had asked him to do was to ignore the closest and greatest threat. Somebody had ambushed one of her agents and killed him. She should have ordered Li Hu to uncover the assassin's identity. But instead, she chose to waste her precious resources on a low-level asset.

Why is this Marine so important?

With one more glance at the woman standing over Shi Yufei's body, he turned and started climbing the hill. He stepped over the guardrail at the end of the cul-de-sac and followed the sidewalk up the street to where he had parked the Volkswagen Jetta. His eyes never stopped moving, scanning the shadows for an invisible threat that hadn't existed before.

Somebody was hunting them. And no matter what Mantis said, he needed to find out who.

San Jose, California

Mantis ended the call, then placed her cell phone on the table next to her chair and stared vacantly through the front windows at the green space across the street. It had been a year since she sat there on a park bench and learned that her husband had deceived her and exposed their most precious secret to the Ministry. His admission put everything she had worked for at risk and further strained their already tenuous relationship. But she was determined not to let it derail her progress in expanding their West Coast network.

Glancing up at the clock on the wall, she noted the time—1:05 a.m.— and knew she would not be able to go back to sleep. Even if Li Hu found her asset and reported back to her that he was safe, the assassination of one of her agents still troubled her greatly, despite what the former Night Tiger commando might have thought. Probably even more so because he had been killed during an arranged meeting.

Mantis suppressed her rising anxiety and stood from the chair, then shuffled across the cool wood floors to the kitchen. She began most days the same way—rolling out of bed at five to complete ten minutes of stretching and calisthenics on her plush bedroom carpet before walking to the shower for a five-minute soak under scalding water. But Li Hu's late-night phone call had accelerated her morning routine, and she skipped straight to making her tea.

She heated the water just short of boiling and poured it over the dark, twisted leaves, steeping it for four minutes. After decanting, she was left with a beverage that had the fresh, clean flavor of green tea with the thick, luscious fragrance of black. The Da Hong Pao oolong from the Wuyi Mountains of the Fujian province was her favorite and was believed to have numerous health benefits, not the least of which was to support healthy brain function.

She picked up the teacup and carried it back to her chair in the living room, where she brought it to her lips and sipped delicately on the hot tea. She sat in the darkness, staring through the window as she patiently waited to hear back from Li Hu. She had other resources in the San Diego area she could use if he was unable to locate the Marine, but doing so might expose him to unwanted attention.

"What's wrong?" Her husband's voice startled her.

She looked up at his shadowed form standing in the hallway. "Nothing."

Everything, she thought. *Everything is wrong.*

"Why are you awake?"

She wanted to snap at him, to tell him it was his fault. But she didn't. Since he had confessed to her, she continued playing her role of doting wife and hadn't expressed the gut-wrenching disappointment that her own husband had betrayed her. "One of my agents failed to check in," she said, telling him only part of the truth and avoiding her real concern.

"And you can't reach him?"

She took another sip of her tea and looked away, letting his question linger. He grew tired of waiting for a response and turned back into the hall. When she heard their bedroom door close, she glanced down at her cell phone and silently urged it to ring while contemplating the larger problem. As Li Hu had alluded to, the greater concern was the unknown assassin who had taken out one of her agents.

Her phone rang, and she snatched it off the table. "Yes?"

"He has returned to the base."

She set the teacup down and leaned forward in her chair. "Bring him to me."

"Yes, ma'am."

4

Marine Corps Air Station Miramar
San Diego, California

Punky stretched her lithe frame inside the cramped confines of the Carrera and lamented the decision to use her personal vehicle to continue her surveillance. Not only was the arctic silver Porsche with blue soft top prone to draw attention, but it was too compact and lacked a place to put a steaming cup of coffee—something she desperately needed.

She stifled a yawn and glanced in the rearview mirror at the barracks, waiting to see what the intrepid Corporal Garett had planned for the weekend. It was Friday afternoon—less than twenty-four hours after Punky had found the dead body of who she believed was an operative from China's Ministry of State Security—and she once more found herself hopelessly entangled in her work.

This is getting downright sad, she thought.

The parking lot had slowly emptied of its stereotypical inventory of Mustangs, Camaros, Jeeps, and trucks of all makes and models. Everywhere she looked, she saw nineteen- and twenty-year-olds with high and tight haircuts, ripped jeans, and Ed Hardy T-shirts fleeing the barracks and the confines of the air station for the promise of alcohol-induced female companionship at one of the many bars, pubs, or nightclubs that turned a blind eye to being underage. Just as long as you had a military ID.

Punky reached over to the passenger seat and picked up her cell phone to check for a call or text message she might have missed in the two minutes since she last checked. Still nothing.

She was about to drop the phone in disgust when it suddenly vibrated and lit up with the name of her supervisor. She swiped across the screen to answer.

"What did you find out, Camron?"

"The victim's name is Shi Yufei," the senior agent replied. "According to LinkedIn, he's a scientist and the founder of Nanotech Innovations in San Jose."

"Sounds like bullshit to me," she said. Punky had first set eyes on Corporal Garett while conducting surveillance in the Willow Glen neighborhood of San Jose. And she didn't believe in coincidences. With its extensive united front networks, clusters of advanced technology, and undeniable electoral heft, the Bay Area was prime territory for Ministry operations.

"I agree. His curriculum vitae seems a little too polished to be legit."

Punky was about to launch into one of her typical rants about the pervasiveness of Chinese espionage activities on the West Coast when the barracks door opened. Corporal Adam Garett emerged with an olive drab duffel slung over his shoulder. His eyes darted nervously across the parking lot as if expecting a hit squad—or NCIS special agent—to leap out from behind a parked Jeep.

"Punky?" Camron said.

She shook her head to clear away her fatigue. "We don't have a file on Shi Yufei?"

"Not until now," Camron said.

"But you agree he was obviously a Ministry operative. Why else would he have been meeting with Garett in the middle of the night?"

"We don't know he was meeting with Garett—"

"Oh, come on."

"What about the other man you saw? The one with the limp?"

"I was there, Camron. I remember how I described him. Were you able to pull anything from the partial I gave you?"

"Yeah, but it's not good news. There are over forty-five thousand possible license plate matches."

"And how many are on new Mercedes S-class sedans?"

"We're working on it."

Not fast enough.

The Marine reached the dark blue Jeep Cherokee and tossed his duffel inside before climbing behind the wheel. Punky turned the key and fired up the 3.4-liter, six-cylinder engine, preparing to follow the Marine wherever he went. "Anything from forensics yet?"

She heard him shuffling papers in the background. "Just an initial report that indicates a bullet caliber between 7.82 and 7.91 millimeters."

"Seven six two?" Punky was far from a weapons expert, but she knew enough to know that if Shi Yufei had been executed with such a large caliber weapon, she would have heard the gunshots. "No chance, Camron. Not unless he was killed by a sniper."

The Cherokee's brake lights flashed on as the Marine started the engine, then winked off when he put it into gear and pulled forward from his parking space. She tapped on the button to put her phone on speaker, then dropped it back onto the passenger seat as she shifted the Porsche into reverse and backed out of her spot.

"It also looks like he was shot inside ten meters."

"So, not a sniper."

"Doesn't appear that way."

Punky shifted into first before she had stopped rolling back and quickly added gas to spur the Carrera onward. She didn't know where the Marine was going, but it was pretty obvious by the packed duffel bag that he didn't plan on returning anytime soon. She couldn't be certain, but she thought a bar was probably the last thing his plans included for the evening. It looked like he was going on the run.

"We need to figure this out, because I don't think he's planning on coming back."

"What do you mean?"

"Looks like he just packed up everything he owns into his Cherokee and is getting ready to beat feet."

Camron sighed. "Alright. Just stay on him."

The Cherokee came to a complete stop before leaving the parking lot, then turned onto Bauer Road headed east. Punky held back just far enough not to make it obvious she was following, but she didn't think twice before cutting off a slower-moving government sedan to keep sight of the classic SUV.

"Can we get some black-and-whites to make a probable cause stop? Get him in an interview room and make him sweat for a few hours?"

"Not without tipping our hand," Camron said. "And we don't have enough evidence yet for a warrant."

Punky knew it was just part of the job, but she wanted to scream in frustration. "So, being in the same place at the same time as a murder isn't enough?"

"For murder, yeah. But we need to take down his network. We'll know more when we get the complete forensics report back from the lab. Until then, just keep tailing him. See if he leads us somewhere good."

Punky eased off the gas as they approached the intersection with Mitscher Way, curious to see what direction the Marine would go.

"I'm on him," she said.

"I'll keep digging into the third person. Just hang loose and stay out of sight." He paused. "And, Punky?"

"Yeah?"

"Let's not get into any gunfights today."

Camron ended the call before she could rebut his statement. At the intersection, the Cherokee turned right and Punky followed, pressing hard on the gas pedal to cut in between a Toyota Tacoma pickup truck and Garett's Cherokee in the left lane.

5

Cajon, California

Adam knew he was in a shitload of trouble. For all he knew, the limping stranger had executed Shi Yufei, and now he was the Ministry's prime suspect. But even if he wasn't—even if Shi Yufei hadn't been killed—he had missed his meeting, and he knew they didn't take kindly to that. There would be consequences for his noncompliance. Staying in San Diego was not an option.

"Shit!" He slammed his palm onto the plastic steering wheel, then reached down and twisted the knob to find a station without static. He had exited Interstate 15 near Murrieta and driven north on the 215 toward March Air Reserve Base, before cutting through San Bernardino and rejoining the 15 at the Cajon Pass. "What am I going to do?"

It wasn't his first time making the trek through the Mojave Desert in his trusty Cherokee, but he wondered if it would be his last. He glanced over at the duffel bag sitting in the passenger seat and knew he probably wouldn't return to Miramar.

One way or another, his time as a Marine had come to an end.

His phone rang, and he grimaced when he saw the name on the Caller

ID. No matter how much he wanted to, he couldn't run from everybody. He swiped across the bottom of the screen to answer.

"Hi, Mom."

"Darling," she replied.

"Is everything okay?"

She rarely called, and Adam couldn't help but wonder if some ill had befallen one of his aging parents. Though they had always been in good health, he knew time was not on their side. He had enough to worry about already, and that was the last thing he needed.

"Everything is fine," she replied. "Do I need a reason to call my son?"

He shook his head. "No, of course not."

"Where are you? It sounds like you're in the car."

Adam chewed on his bottom lip. Growing up, he had learned early on that both his parents had the uncanny ability to sniff out a lie. Fortunately, he had learned that lesson while still young, and by the time he became a teenager, they trusted him and gave him far more freedom than most of his friends' parents. Telling her the truth had always been easy for him.

But somehow, this just felt different.

"Getting out of town for the weekend," he said. It wasn't an answer, but maybe it was enough to sate her curiosity.

"Is everything okay?"

Again, he wanted to tell her he was in trouble. He wanted to tell her he had made a terrible mistake and fallen into bed with a spy and found himself embroiled in a treacherous world fraught with danger. But his parents were traditional. They believed in things like honor and duty, and they would never understand how he could have betrayed his country.

"Everything is fine," he said, hoping his mom would drop it and move on to something he wouldn't have to lie about. "Work has just been stressful."

"Of course. Maybe you should go to the cabin. The fresh mountain air might do you some good."

His heart lurched into his throat. There was no way she could have known he was already headed there. But at least now he wouldn't have to lie about it. "I think I might."

"Good," she said. "Call me if you need anything."

"I will," he said, though he knew he wouldn't. He couldn't put his mother in danger and involve her in the mess he had made for himself. He had failed a lot of people, but he wouldn't fail her.

"I love you, Adam."

"I love you too, Mom."

She ended the call, and he tossed the phone back into the cupholder, disgusted with himself for deceiving the one person he could trust to always have his best interests at heart. He had made the mistake of falling into Chen's web of deceit, but he would spend the rest of his life finding his way back out. No matter what it took, he would become the man his mother had raised him to be.

Li Hu trailed the Cherokee by several miles, relying on the tracker he had placed on the Marine's Jeep during one of his scheduled meetings with Shi Yufei. Nobody had instructed him to do it, but he figured if Mantis had taken such an interest in this asset, it wouldn't hurt to have the ability to know where the Marine was at all times.

Now, he was glad he had.

But he still wasn't sure what to do about it. Since leaving San Diego, it quickly became apparent the Marine wasn't alone. He could hardly believe it, because the silver Porsche convertible was the last car he expected someone wanting to remain inconspicuous would drive. But turn for turn, the German sports car had followed the SUV and remained a predictable four or five lengths back.

His phone rang, and he pressed a button on the steering wheel to answer. "Yes, ma'am?"

"We intercepted a phone call to the asset," Mantis said. "He's going to Lake Tahoe. You can break off surveillance and resume there. I don't want you spotted."

As he crested the final hill in the pass, the interstate stretched out before him, and he had no difficulty spotting the blue Cherokee. Or the silver Porsche behind it.

"We might have a problem."

Mantis inhaled sharply, and Li Hu suddenly regretted his decision to tell her of the tail. He knew he could handle whoever had taken an interest in the Marine and didn't need any backup. He just wanted Mantis to know he would take care of it.

"What is it?"

"Someone has been following the asset since he left the base."

"Are you certain?"

He glanced down at the Jetta's odometer. "We're nearly one hundred and twenty miles from the air station, and the same car has been four or five lengths behind since the start."

"Is it the female agent?"

"I don't know," he answered honestly. "But I'll find out."

"It doesn't matter who it is," she replied. "But you need to intervene and ensure the Marine reaches his destination."

There were a few places on their route where Li Hu could set up a diversion and cause the Porsche to break off its pursuit, but none that would allow him to do so without attracting attention. "There will be risks," he said.

"Just do it," Mantis ordered.

The phone went dead. Li Hu floored the accelerator and strained the turbocharged four-cylinder engine as he slowly accelerated and closed the distance between them. Not that the Marine had been driving much above the speed limit, but the Jetta wasn't built for quick acceleration.

Leaving the San Bernardino National Forest, Li Hu saw mountains stretching across the horizon in the distance and knew he couldn't delay taking action. The longer he waited, the more likely it became that they would reach a populated area, which would make it difficult for him to escape. But, more importantly, if the driver of the sports car really was the female agent, this was his opportunity to remedy his past mistake.

He wasn't about to let her get away again.

Li Hu fixed his gaze on the silver Porsche as the Jetta's speedometer needle crept past eighty miles per hour. Though he hadn't expected a kinetic operation, he was still armed. He reached down for the pistol concealed on his right hip, pleased that he had opted to carry the Glock 19X —a compact 9mm pistol with a full-size frame that carried two more rounds than its smaller cousin. Though he always carried several spare magazines, Li Hu knew that if things went sideways, those two additional bullets could mean the difference between success and failure—between life and death.

The Jetta developed a slight shimmy at ninety miles per hour, but Li Hu was committed. He was less than four hundred yards behind the Porsche, and he could almost taste the sweet flavor of revenge.

Come on. Faster.

6

Punky sighed and scanned her mirrors again. After two hours on the road, she still didn't know where the Marine was leading her. She could have reached out to his command to see if he had requested leave or been authorized to travel beyond the approved liberty radius. But the last thing she wanted was for the Marine Corps to spook him. They could deal with him being AWOL after she got what she needed.

Descending from Cajon Pass into the Mojave Desert, Punky was thankful it wasn't the middle of summer. Though it was still warm, the early fall temperatures had dropped enough for the aging Porsche's air-conditioning system to easily control the climate of the cramped cockpit. And it was surprisingly comfortable. Unlike her father's old Corvette, the classic German sports car seemed designed around the driver's comfort.

"Gotta hand it to 'em," she said, her eyes tracing the curved lines of the car's interior. "The Germans know how to make a good car."

A flash of light drew her eyes up to the rearview mirror. Through the heat shimmering from the asphalt behind her, she caught the distorted view of a car quickly eating up the distance between them. Her stomach suddenly knotted with fear. Immediately, she thought back to the jarring impact of a car hitting her father's Corvette and spinning it out of control just before a team of Ministry commandos descended on her. She remembered playing chicken with a gunman on a motorcycle before he put several rounds into her bulletproof vest.

"Shit!" She stabbed her left foot into the clutch while reaching down to drop the Porsche into fifth gear. As soon as she let out the clutch and stomped on the gas, the RPMs jumped and provided an instantaneous boost in horsepower. The Carrera leaped forward.

But the approaching sedan kept coming. It weaved into the left lane, betting that she wasn't going to give up and allow someone to ram into the back of her Porsche. Punky glanced down from the rearview mirror and saw that she was quickly gaining on the Marine's Jeep in front of her. The last thing she wanted to do was blow by him and give up the advantage she had preserved for over one hundred miles, but she didn't see any other way around it.

Punky reached down and unlocked her cell phone, then dialed Camron's number and put it on speaker. She dropped the ringing phone onto the passenger seat as she flew by the Cherokee at almost one hundred miles per hour.

The gig's up now, she thought.

But losing surveillance on the Marine was still preferable to being rammed by a car.

Swerving back into the right lane in front of the Jeep, she half expected the Volkswagen Jetta to continue in the left lane and pass her by. Instead, it dropped in between the Porsche and the Cherokee, making it abundantly clear its driver's sights were set on her. For whatever reason, she was being targeted.

The call picked up and a tinny version of Camron's voice sounded from her phone's miniature speaker. "Punky?"

"Something's going down," she said.

"What?" His voice was tinged with fear. The last time she had made a similar call was right before a gunman on a motorcycle ambushed her in broad daylight, north of San Diego. And Camron had been there in the aftermath, when the paramedics loaded her into an ambulance.

"A car nearly rammed me, and I had to break off the tail," she said, shifting back into sixth gear and putting distance between her and the compact sedan.

"Are you okay?"

She looked beyond the Jetta and saw the Cherokee shrinking in the distance. "I'm in front of the target now," she said. "But it's not over yet. I think it's about to get worse."

Up ahead, Punky saw an off-ramp leading into what looked like an almost ninety-degree turn. If she wanted to be free from her pursuer and resume her surveillance, she needed to do something. And the Porsche had a distinct advantage over the Jetta in that *something* she had in mind.

"How much worse?" Camron asked.

"Exit 138 on Interstate 15," she replied. "Send the Highway Patrol."

"Punky. . ."

But she was no longer listening. She jerked her steering wheel to the right, and the nimble sports car responded without hesitation. A glance in her rearview mirror showed that she had guessed right, and the German sedan swerved onto the exit to follow. One way or another, she was going to put an end to the chase.

Punky was afraid she already knew how it was going to happen.

Without slowing, she passed a gas station on her right and spurred the Porsche around the sharp right bend. The off-ramp ended at a T-intersection, and she quickly downshifted to prepare herself for the tight turn back in the direction she had come. If things went the way she hoped, she might be able to lose the Jetta and resume her surveillance none the worse for wear.

But that hope was dashed with a quick glance in her rearview mirror.

"Shit!"

She jerked the steering wheel hard to the right and stomped the accelerator into the floor, but it wasn't enough. The Jetta had come careening around the corner, with no apparent regard for the hairpin turn, and slammed into Punky's right rear tire. Instead of launching up the road toward the gas station like she'd wanted, she was relegated to gripping the steering wheel as the world spun around her amid the soundtrack of broken glass and twisting metal.

Punky didn't have time to lament the destruction of yet another classic car or even brace for impact. She simply held on for dear life and waited for the world to stop spinning. When it did, she trembled behind the steering wheel and shook her head to clear away the cobwebs of confusion and inaction. After several moments, she snapped into action, unbuckling her seat belt with one hand while reaching for the SIG Sauer at her hip with the other. If her recent spate of vehicular mishaps was any indication of what was about to happen, this was about to turn into a gunfight. And she didn't plan on sitting back on her heels and waiting for the gunman to come to her.

That sonofabitch!

Punky opened the door and spilled out onto the uneven concrete, struggling to orient herself to her surroundings. She brought her pistol up and scanned beyond the front sight post at the gas station and off-ramp, cringing when she realized that the impact had spun her completely around. Her head throbbed from the impact and her vision was blurred, but she breathed through the pain and ignored the minor aches and pains she knew would only get worse.

"Federal agent!" she yelled.

But she was met with silence. Punky pressed against the car's body and inched back to use the crumpled engine as a shield. Though the Porsche's engine had fallen silent, she could still hear the Jetta's anemic motor straining as its driver attempted to flee.

Slowly, she pressed her body up and peeked through the Porsche's shattered windows at the German sedan. Its driver had intentionally launched the car at her like a missile, succeeding in spinning her out of control. But in the aftermath, it had become high-sided on the curb.

"Show me your hands!" she shouted.

The glare of the overcast sky on the Jetta's rear window made it difficult for her to see anything of the car's interior. She could just barely make out the darkened silhouette of the driver's head. But no hands.

Rising into a crouch, Punky lifted her pistol and aimed it at the Jetta, stepping away from the Porsche on unsteady legs. Her aim wavered, and she winced as a sharp pain radiated from her collarbone where the seat belt had dug in. But she gritted her teeth and refocused on the front sight post, keeping it pointed at the back of the driver's head.

"Show me your hands!" she shouted again. "Now!"

She side-stepped carefully to her left, keeping the pistol trained on the

Jetta as she moved from what little cover the Porsche had provided. She listened for the wail of sirens that might indicate Camron had succeeded in requesting backup from the California Highway Patrol. But other than the pounding of her heart and the *tick tick hiss* of the Jetta's ruined engine, she heard nothing.

She took a hesitant glance over each shoulder to make sure they were still alone on the side of the road, then continued circling around the front of the Porsche to approach the Jetta from the side. With each step, she felt more confident in her position. She had turned the tables on what had begun as an ambush, and now she was confidently in charge.

"Last chance," she shouted. "Turn off the car, toss the keys out, and show me your hands!"

The driver's head slumped forward in apparent resignation, and she felt the tension in her body instantly dissolve. She readjusted the grip on her pistol and swallowed back the lump in her throat, relieved that this wouldn't turn into a gunfight after all.

But that relief was suddenly eclipsed by the eruption of gunfire punching holes through the Jetta's door.

Punky flung herself to the side as bullets zipped through the air around her. She responded on instinct and squeezed her trigger repeatedly until she had emptied her magazine into the Jetta.

7

Eisenhower Executive Office Building
Washington, DC

Samuel Chambers reclined in his plush leather executive swivel chair with his feet propped up on his desk. He had just been given a bit of good news and was enjoying a celebratory moment of silence while he contemplated everything that news meant for them. The next year would be busy—chaotic, even—but that only meant that what they had been striving for all these years had finally come to fruition.

His cell phone rang, and he leaned over to look at the number. It wasn't listed in his contacts, but he recognized it immediately and wondered how *he* had heard the news so quickly. He scooped it off the table and answered.

"Business or pleasure?" Sam asked.

"Maybe a bit of both," Teddy replied.

Sam glanced at his watch. He was still hours away from being able to knock off work completely and retire to their favorite watering hole for happy hour. "Not really in the mood today, Teddy. If you have something you want my staff to comment on, just send it—"

"This is explosive," Teddy said, cutting him off. "It's only because of our friendship that I'm bringing it to you first."

Sam kicked his feet off the desk and leaned forward as a feeling of dread washed over him. He and Jonathan both had plenty of skeletons in their collective closet, but his response would be dictated by which one Teddy had uncovered. "I'm listening."

"Sam, you need to know this one literally fell into my lap. I wasn't trying to dig anything up—"

"Out with it already."

Sam had always believed that bad news didn't age well, and the wait was killing him. But he had faith in his ability to tackle any problem that came his way. He just needed to know.

"Does the name Aurora Holdings mean anything to you?"

Sam's stomach dropped. Of course he recognized the name. But Teddy was the last person he wanted to confirm that for. "Should it?"

"Sam, I'm only doing my job here."

"What is it you're asking of me?"

The Washington Post reporter sighed. "It appears that this company has been receiving regular payments from an account linked to your boss."

Sam saw his opening, and he took it. "He's just like any other American citizen, Teddy. You make payments to lenders, don't you? You're probably still paying off your first Dell computer."

Teddy laughed at the inside joke. "As far as I can tell—and I haven't done much digging yet—your boss is the only one conducting regular business with Aurora Holdings. This call is really a courtesy. You know I like you, but I have a job to do."

Sam knew he could stonewall his friend for a little while. But in the end, Teddy would have no choice but to run a story. That was his job. And it was Sam's job to make sure it was a story he wanted splashed across the front page of the Washington Post. He rubbed his temples while formulating a strategy in his mind. "Can you give me thirty minutes?"

"I need something, Sam."

"Thirty minutes, Teddy."

Sam ended the call and dropped his phone on the desktop blotter, amazed at how quickly his mood could shift with the currents of DC politics. But he didn't have the luxury of sitting and waiting for a solution to present itself, and he pushed himself up from the chair and strode across the room to the open door leading to the vice president's office.

He knocked and waited for his boss to acknowledge him before walking in.

"What is it?"

"We've got a problem."

Jonathan Adams looked up from one of the reports his staff had prepared for him and fixed his gaze on his longtime friend. "What kind of problem?"

"The kind we don't want in the Washington Post."

Jonathan leaned back in his chair and turned to study his chief of staff. "Okay. Spill it."

So, he did. In a matter of seconds, Sam briefed his boss on the conversation he'd just had with one of the least discerning individuals in Washington. It was part of the reason Sam had cozied up to him once they arrived in Washington. Having a reporter of Teddy's stature in their corner could come in handy, and it looked like that time had finally come.

"This isn't even about me—"

"I know Teddy," Sam said. "He's going to run with something. We just need to give him a scoop big enough to make him put this one on the back burner. At least for the time being."

Jonathan shook his head. "I know what you're thinking, but I gave the president my word—"

Sam held up a hand. "And I respect that. I do. But this will sink us, Jonathan."

The vice president steepled his fingers and brought them to his lips in obvious contemplation. His ability to look at problems from all different angles and make a decision based on an incomplete picture of the situation was one of his most admirable traits. Jonathan was rarely struck with paralysis by analysis, and he was always willing to make an unpopular decision if it was the right course of action.

"And you think this is the only way?"

Sam nodded. He wished it wasn't, but he couldn't think of anything else juicy enough to keep Teddy from sniffing up the wrong tree. "This will at least buy us some time."

"How much?"

He shrugged. "Honestly, I don't know. Months, maybe. Long enough to come up with a more permanent solution."

"You know this won't stay buried forever."

The two locked eyes and shared an unspoken sentiment that had been buried almost as long as Aurora Holdings. "I'll take care of it," Sam said. "You know I always do."

Jonathan pursed his lips and nodded. "You're a good friend, Sam."

Sam had been with Jonathan long enough to recognize when he had been dismissed. He nodded in agreement and spun back for his office, hoping the upcoming phone call with Teddy would be enough to sate the reporter's investigative appetite. If it wasn't, their good news wouldn't seem so good anymore.

He dropped back into his chair and picked up his cell phone as he mentally rehearsed how he planned on selling this. Teddy obviously hadn't dug deep enough into Aurora Holdings to learn that it was a shell company of dubious origins. So, he clearly didn't know the reason behind its existence.

Is this even going to work?

Sam took a deep breath and dialed. There was only one way of finding out.

"What's the verdict, Sam?"

He leaned back in his chair and closed his eyes. "The vice president has no comment on Aurora Holdings—"

"Sam—"

"Just hold on, Teddy. You're my friend, and you're valuable to us. He has no comment on Aurora Holdings *at this time*. But as a sign of good faith, he wanted to share a bit of news and give you the scoop of the decade."

"You want me to bury this," the Post reporter said.

"I want you to be patient with this," Sam corrected. "When the time is right, we'll have something for you. But, for now, it's no comment."

Teddy was silent for a moment, then sighed heavily. "This better be good."

Hook, line, and sinker.

Sam grinned. "Oh. It is."

8

Viper 1
Navy FA-18E Super Hornet
Eighty nautical miles east of Fallon, Nevada

Lieutenant Commander Colt "Mother" Bancroft slapped the control stick hard into his left thigh to come up on a wing and look down on the desert floor just north of Austin—a well-preserved example of an early Nevada mining town. But it wasn't the living ghost town Colt was interested in. It was the flight of two Navy F-35C Lightning II Joint Strike Fighters passing underneath him.

"Showtime One One, Jedi, merge plot, single group, bogey spades."

Colt grinned. The range training officer had just told the fighters a bad guy was in their knickers.

And this is where the fun begins.

"Ivan, Viper One, tally two," he said, letting the adversary air intercept controller know he had both fighters in sight. "Request elevator."

"Viper One, cleared to engage. Elevator approved."

Colt continued rolling the Super Hornet onto its back, craning his neck up to look down on the fifth-generation fighters. The JSF was a sleek stealth fighter with two sharply pointed inlets on either side of the fuselage that fed air to the single massive Pratt & Whitney afterburning turbofan. As one of the Navy's recognized experts, Colt still remembered what it felt like to fly the advanced jet. But at the moment he was looking forward to seeing it in the center of his HUD, or heads-up display, as he prepared to teach the pilots a lesson in humility.

Sometimes, experience trumped having the newest and baddest toys.

Colt let his jet's nose fall through the horizon and gently increased pressure on the stick, bringing his nose onto the closest of the two fighters. He knew in a real engagement, the fighters would have had the advantage of an entire suite of sensors and electronic countermeasures to prevent Colt from getting within visual range. But this training exercise was designed to test the pilots' abilities to look outside their cockpits and spot an enemy fighter with their own eyes.

The low warbling sound in his helmet gradually increased in frequency and intensity as the infrared seeker of the Captive Air Training Missile on his right wingtip latched onto the F-35's hot exhaust. As the range between their two jets rapidly decreased, the tone reached a crescendo, and Colt pulled the trigger.

"Smoke in the air, north fighter," he said.

The jets hesitated for a split second before the fighter he had targeted abruptly banked right and executed a high-G break turn toward him. "Showtime One One, tally one . . ." The fighter's radio call was punctuated by heavy breathing as the pilot performed an anti-G straining maneuver and fought to keep the blood in his brain. ". . . right four o'clock high."

"Showtime One Two, tally visual," his wingman responded, giving him peace of mind that he knew who the good guy was and who was the bad. Even though it was obvious—*JSF good, Super Hornet bad*—Colt appreciated their use of the standardized calls.

The nearest JSF brought his nose up toward Colt, and he adjusted his heading to take the fighter close aboard. "Right to right," Colt said.

"Right to right," the fighter parroted.

With the JSF pointed nose high and Colt pointed nose low, the two fighters made minor adjustments to merge and pass each other on their right sides. But Colt was already looking for his wingman.

"Showtime One One, standby single group."

Colt's eyes danced from his cockpit's displays at the dark gray fighter growing rapidly in relative size through his forward canopy. Without even consciously being aware of it, he was taking in an array of data points and processing them to adjust his tactics to win the engagement. Airspeed and altitude were of paramount importance and prominently displayed in both his HUD and Joint Helmet Mounted Cueing System, or JHMCS. But there were other factors at play as well, including the angles from his nose to both the merging fighter and his wingman, the lateral separation between them, and the distance to Showtime One One, who was trying to maneuver for a shot.

"Shoot shoot, Hornet," the merging fighter said.

"No shot," his wingman replied.

In a blur, the JSF raced by his right side and continued upward, while Colt immediately adjusted his nose to point at the wingman as he came around for a shot. Like a game of chicken, the two fighters pointed at each other and jerked their noses left and right as they jockeyed for the most advantageous position.

"Left to left," the wingman said.

"Left to left," Colt replied.

Unlike his first merge, this one would follow the standard American rules of the road as each jet cleared to the right for a left-to-left pass. In the three-dimensional world of aerial combat, it really didn't matter which direction they chose, but Colt understood the significance of what the wingman had done. By forcing Colt to look out the left side of his jet, he would be blind to Showtime One Two who was maneuvering on his right.

Well played, he thought.

As an instructor on the staff at NAWDC, the Naval Aviation Warfighting Development Center, Colt was responsible for ensuring the pilots who went through the training syllabus would be prepared to face off against real-world adversaries. The pilot of Showtime One One had demonstrated his competence in dogfighting by complicating Colt's ability to switch back to the first jet he had merged with.

Colt craned his neck forward, and his eyes darted to the mirrors affixed to his canopy bow. Even as he angled his Super Hornet toward the second

JSF, he scanned the reflection of the sky above and behind him for the other one.

Where are you?

A flash of light caught his attention, and he spotted a dark speck set against a backdrop of deep blue.

Gotcha!

Another blur, and Showtime One One raced past his left side. Colt head-faked a turn across his tail, then abruptly yanked the stick to his right to put the top of his helmet on the other fighter. Taking a deep breath, he braced himself for the rapid onset of G-forces, then pulled the stick into his lap while pushing his left hand forward and engaging the Super Hornet's afterburners. He knew he would only be able to keep them lit for a few seconds before the other fighter could lock onto the heat source, but he would need every ounce of thrust available if this was going to work.

"Switch switch, the bandit's coming to me," Showtime One Two said, recognizing that Colt had switched back to him after the second merge. "Showtime One Two is engaged."

A breathless voice responded. "Showtime One One is free."

Unlike the lead fighter, Showtime One Two had demonstrated his lack of experience in basic fighter maneuvering. Instead of trying to flatten out the merge, he had accepted being vertical and raced downhill toward Colt, who was bringing the Super Hornet up for his third merge.

That was a mistake, Colt thought.

He pulled his throttles out of afterburner as his nose came up to meet the descending Joint Strike Fighter.

"Right to right," Colt said.

The fighter echoed his call and adjusted his heading to make the prescribed merge. Colt felt a smile crack his face as he anticipated the early turn maneuver that would give him a concrete offensive advantage and land him squarely in Showtime One Two's control zone.

Check and mate.

His fangs were out, and he could taste blood. He knew he was selling everything to put the younger pilot out of his misery, but the engagement had lasted long enough. It was time to end it and return to base for the debrief.

The Joint Strike Fighter pilot seemed completely unaware of the mistake he was making. Showing no remorse, Colt counted to three, then rolled his jet ninety degrees and began pulling onto his back before even reaching the merge. His opponent suddenly recognized what Colt was trying to do. Thick clouds of vapor formed above Showtime One Two's wings as its pilot snatched the stick back to arrest his descent.

But it was too late. The Super Hornet's slower airspeed meant that Colt's turning radius was smaller. He could bring his nose around far faster than the JSF could.

Suddenly, a high-pitched oscillating tone erupted in Colt's helmet, and his stomach dropped.

"Showtime One One, fox three," the other pilot said. "Kill Super Hornet nose low."

Colt's shock turned to disappointment and embarrassment when he realized he had given the other fighter an opportunity to target him. While he had been fixated on executing a flawless low-to-high merge to punish the younger pilot, he had ignored the threat that still existed. And it had cost him the engagement.

"Copy kill," he said with disgust.

"Showtime, flow two seven zero," the triumphant pilot said, directing their formation to flow west. "Jedi, picture."

"Picture clean," the RTO replied.

"Bandits evaluate."

Colt glanced at his fuel before replying. "Bandits recommend terminate."

"Knock-it-off, knock-it-off. Fighters knock-it-off."

"Bandits knock-it-off."

The knock-it-off call signified the end of the fight. Colt hadn't put the exclamation mark on the hop like he had hoped, but there were still plenty of lessons that could be learned—from both the fighters' and adversary's perspective. It wasn't his first time being killed in a mock engagement, but this one stung. And he knew he would dwell on it the entire way back to the air station.

"Viper One, Showtime One One has the lead. You're cleared to join."

"Viper One," Colt replied through gritted teeth.

9

Silver State Club
Naval Air Station Fallon
Fallon, Nevada

Colt walked underneath a Tomcat speed brake mounted above the front door of a beige stucco building and slipped his khaki garrison cover into his flight suit's bottom right leg pocket as he entered the Officers Club. He was still chafed at having made such a bonehead mistake to end the section engaged maneuvering training sortie, but it salved his bruised ego somewhat to know that the fighter lead was also a former TOPGUN instructor.

Though it was late on a Friday, the Officers Club was still full of pilots in flight suits who had completed their training for the day but didn't want to venture across the hill to Reno. A few were sitting atop stools circling the bar, rolling dice and engaged in idle chatter, while others were crowded around a large piece of painted plywood as teams of two hurled dice through the air. The mood in the club was different when an air wing was in town. It was competitive and electric, reminiscent of the glory days of Naval Aviation.

"Colt!" a voice called out. "Why the long face?"

He smiled when he turned and saw Lieutenant Commander Bill "Jug"

McFarland hail him from the pool table. The two had been close during flight school but only recently reconnected after the Navy took them in different directions. "Because I'm still here and not at the Bug Roach mixer?"

"You going?"

"Of course I'm going." Aside from the years he had been deployed, Colt hadn't missed the annual Tailhook Association symposium since he earned his wings. He wasn't about to miss it now that he was again assigned to the base only sixty miles east.

There was no place Colt would rather be than in the Nugget Casino, enjoying a few cocktails at the Friday evening mixer named in honor of the legendary fighter pilot and landing signal officer, Commander John "Bug" Roach. The first Paddles Award for LSO excellence was named after him and presented at the 1990 Tailhook Convention. Only a year later, Bug was killed when his A-4E suffered an engine failure and forced him to eject off the coast of San Diego. Now, the mixer was an opportunity for fighter pilots —past and present—to gather and tell stories over a few cold beers. Some were even true.

"So, why you still here?" Jug asked.

Colt would have already been there if not for the cryptic message from the NAWDC Commander. "The admiral told me I needed to meet somebody before leaving."

Jug squinted at him, as if wondering whether Colt was yanking his chain. "Not because Cubby kicked your ass today?"

Colt's mouth fell open with a stunned gasp. Of course, he shouldn't have been surprised Jug already knew about it. Lieutenant Carlton "Cubby" Elliott had recently left as an instructor at the US Navy Fighter Weapons School for a training officer tour in Jug's squadron, and pilots tended to gossip more than adolescent girls. Colt wasn't surprised Jug had seized on the opportunity to give him shit.

Especially since Colt had tried shooting him down.

But he recovered from his surprise and shook his head. "I made a mistake. He capitalized on it. And no. I'm here to—"

"Hey flyboy."

Colt froze when he heard the deep baritone voice. He slowly turned and appraised the man wearing a short-sleeved button-down plaid shirt and a pair of blue jeans over Solomon trail running shoes. It was the last person he expected to find standing in front of him at the Fallon O-Club.

"Senior Chief?"

The SEAL smiled behind his thick beard. "Keep it down, sir, or they're gonna boot me out of here." He leaned close and added in a conspiratorial whisper, "But they made me a Master Chief."

Colt looked from the frogman back to Jug and saw an equally surprised look on his face. He might have thought the former test pilot had something to do with it, since the first time Colt had met Master Chief Dave White, he and Jug had landed their F-35C Joint Strike Fighters at the military airfield on San Clemente Island after almost running out of gas. But Jug's expression made it clear he was just as surprised to be confronted with a ghost from their past.

Colt turned back to the SEAL. "What are you doing here?"

Dave cocked his head to the side with a confused look. "I'm here to talk to you."

"Wait . . ." Colt was still trying to make sense of it. "*You're* the person the admiral sent me to meet?"

Dave nodded.

"Why?"

The SEAL shot Jug a glance. "Maybe we should talk somewhere in private?"

"I know when I'm not wanted," Jug said, then held up both hands and backed away. Like most in their line of work, he didn't take offense at being asked to leave a discussion covering a topic he wasn't privy to. It was just the nature of doing business in a world filled with secrets, sensitive compartmented information, and special access programs.

Colt gave him an apologetic look. "See you at Hook?"

The test pilot nodded. "I'll be there."

As Jug melted back into the sea of flight suits, Colt turned and appraised Dave with a dubious look. "You've definitely got my attention."

"Good. Follow me."

Without waiting to see if Colt did so, Dave turned for the door and stepped out into the late afternoon sunshine. Colt hesitated for only a second, then made his way across the street to where the SEAL was climbing behind the wheel of a lifted Ford F-250 Super Duty truck.

"Where we going?"

Dave grinned at him. "You'll see."

Colt sat in the passenger seat and appraised the senior non-commissioned officer as they reached the roundabout and headed south on Carson, passing both the NAWDC headquarters and the Fleet Training building. Dave looked relaxed behind the steering wheel, barely cresting forty miles per hour as they passed the approach end of the short runway and headed toward the Naval Special Warfare Ground Mobility Training Center.

But when Dave kept driving, Colt furrowed his brow in confusion. "Where we going?" he repeated.

Dave laughed. "Is there an echo in here?"

As Carson Road ended, Dave turned left toward the flight line and weaved through the side streets until they reached a parking lot adjacent to a dilapidated hangar. He put the truck in park and killed the engine.

"Come on."

Again, Colt hesitated for only a second before following the SEAL out of the truck and across the lot to a gate set in the perimeter fence. Dave reached into his front pocket and removed a thick plastic card that he swiped in front of the keypad next to the turnstile. After entering a four-digit code, the light above the gate turned from red to green, and the lock disengaged with an audible *click*.

"After you," Dave said, gesturing for Colt to proceed through the turnstile.

It was all very cloak-and-dagger, but it was hardly the first time Colt had been read into a top-secret program or required to navigate additional layers of security. If there was anything the attacks on the *Abraham Lincoln* or *Ronald Reagan* had taught him, it was that even when the world seemed asleep and at peace, war lingered just beneath the surface. He pushed through the turnstile and waited for Dave to repeat the process and join him on the other side.

"When are you going to tell me what this is all about?"

Dave paused. "I told you I'd be reaching out . . ."

"For?"

The SEAL's eyes twinkled with obvious amusement. Whether he enjoyed watching Colt squirm because he didn't know why he had been summoned to a secluded part of the base or because he was missing the convention kickoff in Reno, it was apparent Dave found the situation entertaining. "Let me show you."

Again, Dave turned and led Colt to a heavy steel door set into the side of the hangar. He repeated the process of swiping his keycard and entering his PIN, then held the door open and ushered Colt through.

Colt stepped inside and came face-to-face with a large mural of what looked like a squadron logo painted on the brick wall—the black silhouette of a horse rearing up on a field of red with parallel yellow zagging lines like an inverted seven, representing the flight paths of four attack aircraft. "What's this?"

"Welcome to the *Black Ponies*," Dave said.

Colt gave a little shake of his head. "What?"

"Light Attack Squadron Four," Dave said. "First established in 1969 to conduct surveillance and offensive operations to support river patrol craft and SEALs in Vietnam. Together, with the *Seawolves* of Helicopter Attack Squadron (Light) Three, the *Black Ponies* flew the OV-10 Bronco in combat over the Mekong Delta until their disestablishment in 1972."

"Yeah, I've heard of them. But that doesn't explain this."

Dave nodded and gestured for Colt to follow him deeper into the hangar. "In 2007, the Secretary of the Navy posed a question to special operations forces while touring the Middle East—what was it we needed but didn't have access to?"

He had heard this before too. As an instructor at TOPGUN, Colt had advocated for dedicated light attack and later volunteered to support its development. "A light attack aircraft configured for intelligence, surveillance, and reconnaissance that could integrate seamlessly with ground forces."

Dave looked over his shoulder. "Very good. So, you know that the Navy acquired a single EMB-314 Super Tucano and began testing the platform for interoperability under a program code-named *Imminent Fury*."

Colt nodded. "I also know that from the ground operator's perspective, it was a tremendous success and paved the way for a much larger joint operational test and evaluation with the Air Force."

"One you were a part of," Dave said, confirming that he knew more about Colt's past than he let on.

Colt was surprised, but he nodded. "Doesn't matter, because Congress canceled it."

They reached the end of a short corridor, and Dave opened the door and led them into another, longer hallway that ran the length of the hangar. "Well, the Special Operations Command doesn't like to take no for an answer. From 2010 through 2015, they funded the operational test of light attack capabilities using the OV-10 Bronco."

"*Combat Dragon II*," Colt said. "But they eventually scrapped that program too."

"Officially." Dave stopped walking and gestured to the window that looked out into the main hangar bay, where a single dark gray A-29 Super Tucano turboprop was parked prominently in the middle. "Unofficially, we resurrected the *Black Ponies*."

10

Hangar 7
Naval Air Station Fallon
Fallon, Nevada

Colt stood in stunned silence as he studied the plane. He had flown the Super Tucano during the Air Force light attack experiment but had never seen it painted in dark gray with a black pony rearing up on the engine cowling. That made it seem different somehow.

He turned to look at Dave, who had been quietly standing off to the side. "Is this for real?"

He nodded. "I've been part of the WarCom working group for several years."

"This isn't just another op eval?" Colt asked.

Dave shook his head, but it was a fair question. The F-35 Lightning II was a perfect example of how long it took the wheels of progress to churn in the world of government acquisition. In 1997, Lockheed Martin and Boeing were selected as the only two competitors for the Concept Demonstration Phase of the Joint Advanced Strike Technology program—later renamed Joint Strike Fighter. Lockheed Martin was declared the winner in

2001 and awarded the System Development and Demonstration contract. But the first F-35 didn't fly until 2006.

And the Navy didn't achieve operational status with the carrier variant until 2019.

Twenty-two years after the initial award.

"Okay. How's it work?"

"Well, I assume that fan-looking thing spins really fast," Dave said, pointing at the five-bladed Hartzell propeller.

Colt looked over at the SEAL and saw a mischievous smirk hidden underneath his beard. "Yeah, I got that part. I mean the squadron. What's its mission?"

Dave led Colt on a tour around the airplane, running his hand along its smooth surface. "Sea, air, and land, brother. Naval Special Warfare has always been pretty stacked with assets to support us in or on the water. Beneath the waves, we have teams operating and maintaining Mk 11 SEAL Delivery Vehicles and Dry Combat Submersibles. On the surface, we have Special Boat Teams operating different-sized combatant craft and riverine boats. But until now, we haven't had anything dedicated in the air. We've had to beg, borrow, or steal."

"What about the *Firehawks*?" Colt asked, referring to the MH-60S squadron based at Naval Air Station North Island that routinely worked with SEALs.

"Sure, for training and readiness," Dave replied. "But I'm talking about real-world operations. A force multiplier. Just like the original *Black Ponies*, we'll exist solely to support Naval Special Warfare."

"Under whose control?" Colt knew the devil was in the details. Even the best ideas fell flat if they weren't given the proper support.

"We're assigned to the JSOC task force in Virginia Beach. They have operational control."

Colt whistled. "Tier one stuff, huh?"

"Welcome to the big leagues, flyboy."

Colt ran a finger along one of the propeller's blades. "So, why are we here then?"

Dave stood and slapped Colt on the back. "Because nobody knows we exist. If we base the squadron at Naval Air Station Oceana and grow it to operational strength, there will be no way of hiding us." He turned and waved a hand at the mostly empty hangar. "But here . . ."

Colt knew what he meant. Fallon was in the middle of nowhere. Technically, Fallon was about twenty miles west from the middle of nowhere, but the base was isolated and out of the public eye. By contrast, the Navy's master jet base on the East Coast was in the middle of the most populous city in Virginia—just a hop, skip, and a jump from the DC beltway.

"I see your point."

Dave thrust his hands into his pockets and squared off against Colt. "What you really want to know is why *you're* here."

Colt nodded. "The thought had crossed my mind."

Dave narrowed his gaze and appraised Colt the way a parent might when trying to decide if their teenager was telling the truth about how daddy's Cadillac got a scratch in the door. "The skipper's an OG—one of the originals involved in *Imminent Fury*. Former A-10 pilot with a chest full of Distinguished Flying Crosses—"

Colt held up a hand. "Wait. He's an Air Force guy?"

"*Was.* Once upon a time. He resigned his commission when *Imminent Fury* was scrapped."

"Why?"

Dave shrugged. "Because he believed in the program. For *Imminent Fury*, it all came down to dollars and cents—they didn't have the dollars, and Congress didn't have the sense to fund them. Freaq was determined not to let the same thing happen again."

"Freaq?"

"The skipper—Andy 'Freaq' Wood. You'll like him. He's a lot like you."

Colt couldn't help but smile. He sure sounded like someone he wouldn't mind sharing a beer or ten with. But he knew the SEAL Master Chief hadn't plucked him from the Fallon Officers Club and driven him to a remote part of the base just to show him an airplane and tell Colt his boss wanted to meet him.

"Alright, cut to the chase."

Dave chewed on his bottom lip for a moment before answering. "Okay, flyboy. The squadron is going to grow to a fleet of six airplanes and ten crews made up of Naval Aviators with strike backgrounds and SEALs qualified as Joint Terminal Attack Controllers. You have experience in the plane and the mission, and we want you to help us pick the pilots."

The ride back to the Silver State Club was mostly silent as Dave allowed Colt time to process his invitation to become a plank owner in the *Black Ponies*. In the grand scheme of things, Colt knew he had received orders back to Fallon likely at the behest of Freaq. But the choice was still his to make. He could turn down the SEAL's offer and remain in his current role at NAWDC. No harm, no foul.

But he knew he wouldn't. It just wasn't in his nature.

"So, what now?" Colt finally asked as Dave steered the truck into the O-Club parking lot.

The SEAL came to a stop next to the main entrance and shifted into park before turning to Colt. "Now, you stop waffling and tell me you're in."

"I'm in."

The words came out easier than he'd expected.

"Good. The skipper and I will be flying this weekend, and I'll set up a time for you to meet with him on Monday. It might be in your best interest to bring a list of available candidates. Interviews start in a week."

Colt slipped his khaki piss-cutter garrison cap onto his head, then reached for the door handle. "What about me? I don't need to interview?"

Dave smiled. "I'd say your experience in the plane and what you did over the South China Sea qualifies."

Colt nodded. As much as the Navy had tried keeping the whole ordeal under wraps, it was common knowledge—among tailhookers at least—that Colt had shot down a Chinese fighter and attack helicopter while protecting Dave and his team of SEALs. They might not have all the details, but he knew that wouldn't stop his peers from plying him with alcohol over the course of the weekend to get him to open up about it.

"Guess I'll just wait for your call then?"

Dave shifted the truck back into gear. "I'll be in touch, flyboy."

"I really hate when you say that."

But Colt was smiling. He opened the door and hopped down from the lifted truck, focused on getting inside to see if he had already missed the big push across the hill to Reno. But his mind was swimming with thoughts of piloting the single-engine turboprop again, low and slow over a team of SEALs on the ground. He would have been lying if he said he wasn't excited about the possibility.

Colt was so engrossed in his thoughts that he barely looked up when he crossed the threshold into the bar with his garrison cap still perched on his head.

Ding! Ding! Ding!

But the bartender didn't miss much, and Colt looked up to see her smiling at him. As the thinning crowd of pilots turned to shout their thanks, he suddenly realized his mistake and snatched his hat off his head. He had violated the very first rule of every Officers Club.

He who enters covered here, buys the house a round of cheer.

11

Nugget Casino Resort
Sparks, Nevada

Two hours later, Colt descended from the hills east of Reno and exited Interstate 80, grinning at the throaty growl of the 302-cubic-inch V8 under his hood. He eased off the gas approaching the intersection and looked up at the hotel rising above the freeway. The glow of the word "Nugget" was clearly visible, and it drew him in like a moth to a flame. He knew there were generations of carrier aviators inside, tossing back drinks and swapping stories about their glory days.

But if things with the *Black Ponies* panned out the way Colt hoped, then his glory days were still ahead of him. He just needed to figure out who else was coming along for the ride.

Colt steered his lovingly restored 1969 Ford Bronco underneath the freeway and followed the road around to Nugget Avenue, paralleling the train tracks on his left. He pulled into the resort's parking garage and climbed out, already looking forward to the first of many cold beers at the Bug Roach Mixer.

After looking at the time, he elected to leave his duffel bag in the Bronco. He was already running late, and the last thing he wanted to do was miss out on even more fun by stopping at the front desk to check into his room. Colt left the parking garage and weaved through a throng of pensioners tossing coins into slot machines to reach the stairs leading up to the convention floor. As he neared, he could hear the din of his fellow pilots enjoying the revelry of the once-a-year event.

The moment Colt stepped into the exhibit hall, he felt right at home. Everywhere he looked, he saw a sea of green flight suits adorned with various patches—some from squadrons that only existed in history books. He saw young faces of freshly winged aviators and new tailhookers, weathered faces of veterans come back to share in the camaraderie, and everything in between. Men and women of every ethnic group were represented, and Colt smiled as he waded through the crowd to check in.

"Took you long enough."

Colt turned to see Jug smiling at him from a small group of pilots milling around the ship's store that sold all manner of merchandise adorned with gold wings and tailhooks. He almost waved off the invitation to join them, but when Jug held up a full bottle of Rogue American Amber Ale, Colt couldn't resist. He pivoted toward the crowd and accepted the outstretched brew.

Jug clinked his own bottle against Colt's, then took a sip. "I was just telling these young, intrepid aviators how their very own training officer brought the smackdown on the one and only Lieutenant Commander Colt 'Mother' Bancroft."

Colt took a long pull from his own bottle and stalled while his brain raced for something witty to say in reply. But instead of something clever to silence his friend, he opted for the truth. "Cubby's a good pilot. Probably one of the best. You guys would be smart to listen to him."

Jug's smile vanished when he realized Colt hadn't taken the bait. But the four gathered lieutenants nodded their heads and took Colt's advice to heart.

"Thanks for the beer," Colt said, lifting the bottle in salute before turning back to the registration desk.

As he stepped away, Jug darted forward and grabbed his arm. "You okay, man? I was only busting your balls."

Colt nodded. "I know, brother. Just got a lot on my mind."

"What did Senior Chief have to say?"

"You mean Master Chief?" Colt noticed Jug's raised eyebrow and led him to a semi-secluded patch of real estate on the convention room floor before continuing. "During your time in China Lake, did you ever work on any programs related to the Air Force light attack experiment?"

Jug gave Colt a blank stare as if he hadn't processed the question, then shook his head. "Not that I can think of. Why? Weren't you involved in that before they scrapped it?"

Colt nodded. "Yeah. It looks like the idea is alive and well."

Jug narrowed his eyes, trying to discern Colt's hidden meaning. "I'm a little removed from the test world these days, but I remember there were a few other Navy guys involved."

Colt felt a surge of hope that the daunting task of coming up with a list of ten names by Monday might not be that difficult after all. "Who?"

Jug took another pull from his beer. "Remember Bueller?"

Colt's hope vanished. Lieutenant Christopher "Bueller" Short had been a Navy Hornet pilot and TOPGUN graduate who volunteered to fly the A-29 Super Tucano during the second phase of Air Force testing. He died when the plane he was flying crashed over the Red Rio Bombing Range. "Yeah, I remember him. We lost a good one in him."

"Yeah, we did. He was perfect for the program."

Colt nodded. He couldn't have agreed more. "Now if I could find ten more just like him."

"I'm sure there are some young first-tour JOs who'd be interested in standing something like that up."

"Yeah, but they're all being sent to pointy-nose squadrons."

Jug's face darkened, then his eyes suddenly lit up. "Hey, why don't we ask the flag panel why light attack isn't a detailing priority?" It was an annual tradition to put a group of admirals onstage to field questions from brave—and hungover—junior officers who were frustrated with the direction of naval aviation. More often than not, it was just an opportunity to vent to leadership. But occasionally a good idea birthed there gained traction.

Colt shook his head. "I wouldn't do that."

But Jug didn't pick up on his meaning. "Come on. It'll be fun to watch them squirm under the heat of difficult questions. They bailed on *Imminent Fury* and *Combat Dragon II*—"

"I know what you're saying, Jug. But I don't think we want to draw attention to light attack right now."

This time, Jug seemed to catch the barest hint of a hidden message. "What *exactly* did you and Master Chief talk about?"

By the time Colt finished giving Jug the big picture of how the *Black Ponies* had been resurrected, he was almost certain he had found the first name to add to his list. He and Jug had been friends since being paired up during the Air Combat Maneuvering phase of training in flight school, but their friendship had been put on hold for several years when the Navy sent them to opposite coasts.

The events surrounding the attempted attack on the USS *Abraham Lincoln* had brought them back together in the most unlikely of ways, but not even their closest friends knew what had happened.

"Are you saying that because you flamed out on San Clemente Island, Master Chief thinks you're the right person to help stand up a top-secret squadron?"

Colt knew the question was asked tongue-in-cheek, but there was probably a shard of truth to it. On a whole, fighter pilots tended to be proud and arrogant, but even the most humble felt slighted when they weren't picked for a special project. Jug hadn't known the program existed, but Colt could almost see him mentally reviewing each of the career decisions that resulted in being overlooked for the job.

"To be honest, I think my previous experience in the plane had more to do with it." Then Colt lowered his voice. "But there are a few other things."

Jug tipped his bottle up once more, but pulled it away from his mouth in disgust when he realized it was empty. "So, there's truth to the rumors then?"

Colt knew it was only the first of many times he would be asked that question over the course of the weekend. But if there was anyone he could trust to know the truth, it was Jug. "Master Chief led a team of SEALs into a

non-permissive environment to rescue a captured Agency operations officer. I just happened to be in the right place at the right time to keep them
from being shot out of the sky."

Jug nodded. "Maybe when we're in the same squadron, you'll give me
all the details."

Colt studied his friend and saw a familiar twinkle in his eyes. "Are you
saying what I think you're saying?"

"I'm saying I want in."

"What about your department head job?"

Jug leaned to the side, and Colt turned to follow his gaze. Standing ten
feet away was the group of young lieutenants Jug had been mentoring
before he showed up. Colt understood right away what his friend was
thinking. He was a good leader who cared about his people and didn't like
the idea of abandoning his squadron or its pilots for the opportunity.

"They've got time to fill our spots," Jug said.

"*Our* spots?"

"Me and Cubby. You said it yourself. He's probably one of the best, and
he needs to be in on this too."

Colt admitted Jug had a point. If the smackdown the other pilot had
given him earlier that day wasn't enough to convince him he was perfect for
the job, Jug's recommendation was. "You know it's not my decision."

"Just put us on the list."

"Want to talk to Cubby first?"

Jug tossed his empty beer bottle in a nearby trash can and nodded.
"Let's go find him."

12

South Lake Tahoe, California

It was close to midnight by the time Adam pulled into the driveway of his family's cabin. Built in the early 1970s, it was a simple four-bedroom retreat on a quiet half-acre knoll with expansive views of the lake and surrounding mountains. With four separate decks, there was no question it had been built as a haven to escape the city and take in the fresh mountain air.

It was exactly what he needed.

Adam parked the Jeep Cherokee on the large pad in front of the garage and turned the key to kill the engine. He sat in silence, listening to the wind whipping through the tall pines and mentally running through his options. There was no way he could go back. Not to the Marine Corps that had used him up and tossed him aside like he was just another cog in the machine. And not to the Chinese, who had manipulated him and twisted him into a tool for their own devices.

As much as he resented feeling this way, he would have given anything to have his mom there. Growing up, she had been a steadfast constant in his life—always there for him to lean on in turbulent and trying times. She was soft-spoken and thoughtful, and he had always found it easy to talk to her. But how could he tell her about this?

With a grunt, he broke free from his silent brooding, opened the door, and climbed out of his four-wheeled prison. Looking up, Adam saw a tapestry of stars blanket the night sky with a view he always found breathtaking and humbling. He took a moment to appreciate the serenity of his surroundings and freedom from the Jeep's confines, then ducked his head back inside to snatch his duffel bag off the passenger seat.

Walking up the steps to the front door, his paranoia was on full display, and he whipped his head left and right with each snapping twig or rustling leaf. The sounds were normal for the mountains, but his overactive imagination twisted each one until they became the telltale signs of an approaching assassin with a limp, come to finish the job he had started at the Miramar Reservoir.

"You're being ridiculous," he told himself.

Just before reaching the front door, Adam bent down and felt for the loose stone where his mom hid the spare key. He had told her for years to upgrade the lock to an electronic one that could be actuated with a four-digit code or wirelessly through a smartphone. But she was old-fashioned and resisted change.

He wiggled the stone free and hooked a finger inside the cavity to fish out the key, then stood and unlocked the door. The panel on the wall to the right chirped at him, reminding him to disarm the alarm before it alerted police to a break-in. Now that he was officially Absent Without Leave from the Marine Corps, the last thing he wanted to do was identify himself to law enforcement.

Adam quickly entered the code—his birthday—then closed the door and locked it. He dropped his duffel in the foyer and stuffed the spare key into his pocket, then made his way to the stairs at the end of the hall. He knew there wouldn't be any food in the refrigerator, but he was almost certain he could find Pop-Tarts or some other sugary treat in the pantry to tide him over. All he really needed was a good night's sleep. He could figure out the rest in the morning.

Adam made his way to the kitchen and rifled through their meager supplies before finally giving up and heading upstairs to his bedroom. He didn't bother turning on the lights as he moved through the house, focused only on collapsing on the full-size bed to recover from his nine-hour drive. But even after kicking off his shoes, stretching out on top of the quilted comforter, and closing his eyes, he found that sleep eluded him.

After several minutes, his eyes snapped open.

He didn't move, but his mind raced to process the creaking and popping noises that were normal for a fifty-year-old house. Even the faint sounds of animals beyond the walls intruded on his peaceful sanctuary and pushed the notion of sleep even further out of reach. He had come to Lake Tahoe to escape civilization and find peace alone in nature.

But being alone and off the grid came with a different kind of anxiety.

Just go to sleep, he thought.

The memory of standing on the shore of Lake Miramar and witnessing a man being murdered came roaring back.

The man with a limp is coming for you.

A car passing on the street below cast long shadows across his ceiling, and he followed their movement with increasing dread. He had no idea why someone would be after him, but there was no denying what he had seen. He didn't know whether he had been the target or merely in the wrong place at the wrong time, but it didn't really matter. Dead was dead, regardless of the motivation.

He knows you're here.

Even his thoughts carried a panicked tone. But he tried countering them anyway.

"How? How does he know I'm here?"

Maybe if he said it out loud, it carried more weight. But the sick feeling in his stomach hadn't let up, and he knew it would be a restless night. He could either toss and turn and jump at his own shadow, or he could go someplace else. Someplace where he wouldn't be alone. Someplace where he wouldn't be an easy target.

With a grumble, Adam made his decision. He bolted from his bed and raced for the stairs, blowing through the front door and bounding down the steps for his Cherokee. He left the front door unlocked and his duffel bag on the floor in the foyer, but he couldn't stomach the thought of going back inside.

After all, it was just for one night.

The man pulled the night vision monocular away from his eye and grunted. He was pleased they had been right about the cabin being the Marine's destination, but he was surprised to see him flee the house only minutes after arriving. He reached down for his phone and tapped on the only number he had called.

"Yes?"

"He's here."

"Good. Alone?"

He watched the Marine climb into the Jeep Cherokee and pull out of the driveway. "Yes, but he's leaving the cabin."

This time, the voice on the other end grunted. "Where's he going?"

"I don't know. Should I follow him?"

"Yes. The team is already in Reno. All you need to do is give them the time and place."

He set his jaw. "It will be done."

"Very good."

The call ended, and he put the Mercedes sedan into gear and pulled away from the curb. The Marine's Jeep was snaking its way down the hill, and he quickly accelerated so as not to lose him at the intersection with Pioneer Trail. When the Cherokee turned right and headed north past Heavenly toward the lake, he wondered if the Marine wasn't just looking for some female companionship for the night.

Good. This will go easier if his mind is on something else.

He suspected the Marine was headed for one of the casinos flanking the highway on both sides just across the border into Nevada. He could prowl one of the many nightclubs at Bally's, Harrah's, Harveys, or the Hard Rock and return to the cabin with a girl drunk enough to think he was her ticket to a better life.

But the Jeep defied him and continued north on Highway 50.

The sounds of Tchaikovsky's "Winter Daydreams" filled the luxury sedan's cabin, and he reached down and massaged his aching leg as he settled in for a long evening. Continuing the drive was the last thing he wanted to do after nearly nine hours in the car earlier that day, but the Marine was crucial to their plan.

The symphony reached a crescendo, and he squinted at the Jeep's brake lights. "Where are you going, my friend?"

13

Victorville, California

Punky leaned against the black-and-white California Highway Patrol Chevrolet Tahoe, looking across a steaming cup of coffee at what remained of her classic Porsche. Police had cordoned off the intersection and set up floodlights for the crime scene investigators who were taking pictures from every conceivable angle, even though it was pretty clear what had happened.

"Your supervisor is almost here," an officer said, then nodded to her cup. "Need a refill?"

She shook her head. "Thanks, but I can't handle any more."

Her hands were still shaking. Hours after ventilating the Volkswagen Jetta, she was still riding an emotional roller coaster while battling to understand what had just taken place. First, she had followed Corporal Garett to the Miramar Reservoir, where she later found a dead Chinese operative. Next, she tailed the AWOL corporal leaving the San Diego area, which she believed was proof he was on the run and seeking refuge—with the Ministry or from the Ministry, she wasn't yet sure. Then there was this.

What the shit was this?

A dark Suburban with tinted windows exited the interstate and parked on the shoulder. Punky pushed herself off the Tahoe, smiling when she saw the door open and Camron jump out. They'd always had their differences, and she gave him more grief than she knew she should, but he was a good agent and always backed her plays. That he drove up from the Southwest Field Office in San Diego to personally check on her said a lot for his leadership.

"Punky . . ." Camron was breathless as he jogged across the street to confront her. "How the hell do you always find yourself in these situations?"

Her smile vanished.

"I told you—"

"*Surveillance*, Punky. That doesn't involve yet another car wreck and shootout."

She looked over at the CHP officer, saw the questioning look on his face, and shrugged. "This is only my third one." She turned back to Camron. "And, in case you forgot, I only returned fire."

She turned away from the Tahoe and stalked toward the twisted Porsche. She wasn't an expert, but she was pretty sure the frame had bent when the rear axle snapped in the collision. Among other reasons, she knew she wouldn't drive it again.

"Punky," Camron called after her. "Where are you going?"

She spun back to face him. "Did you suddenly forget that a Marine corporal has gone AWOL after an obvious clandestine meeting that left a Chinese intelligence operative dead?" She waved a hand at the Jetta she had turned into Swiss cheese. "Unless you plan on telling me *he* wasn't also Ministry, then I suggest you get the hell out of my way and let me get back to doing my job before something bad happens!"

Camron had silently turned to look at the dead body sitting in the Jetta's driver's seat while she delivered her rebuke. Once she finished, he turned back to her and spoke quietly. "We're pretty sure he *was* Ministry . . ."

"Thank you." Punky turned back to her ruined car, but a female crime scene investigator stepped in front of her to block her way. She glowered at the woman until she stepped aside, then ripped open the passenger door and removed her Osprey backpack. After fishing around in the car door pockets for several seconds, she stood and turned toward Camron. "I'm going after that bastard. Is that okay with you?"

"There's something you should know before you go," he said.

She had worked up a head of steam and recognized that she was ready to fight anybody for any reason. It was a character trait she had probably inherited from her father, and one she had worked her whole life learning how to overcome. But she hadn't missed that Camron appeared at least supportive of her decision to go after the Marine. She took a long, slow breath in through her nose and held it for a count of four before exhaling.

"What?"

Camron walked closer with his hands held open and low at his sides in an overt sign that he didn't want to fight. "After your . . . *accident*, I did a little more digging into Corporal Garett."

Punky sighed. She had done a complete background investigation on the Marine after seeing him for the first time at Fu Zan's house in San Jose. Something about him had set off alarm bells, which was why she began surveillance on him in the first place. But at first blush, his career in the Marine Corps appeared entirely unremarkable, and nothing jumped off the page as ominous.

"Yeah, Camron, I did a full workup on him."

"Then what did you make of his brief stint with the *Black Knights*?"

She cocked her head and wondered where he was going with this. According to official records, Corporal Garett had spent less than a year in the squadron before being transferred following non-judicial punishment for falsifying maintenance records. "He sucked at his job and was fired? What's your point?"

Camron sighed in obvious frustration, then looked around to see if any of the police officers or investigators were within earshot. "Does the *Abraham Lincoln* mean anything to you?"

"Yeah, it was the carrier the *Black Knights* deployed aboard. But Garett was already out of the squadron by the time the *Lincoln* went to sea."

"On deployment, yes," Camron said. "But not workups."

Punky squinted. "What are you saying?"

"I'm saying that while you were looking for a sailor, maybe you should've been looking for a Marine."

She opened her mouth to argue with him, then quickly snapped it shut as she laid out the sequence of events in her mind. She had glossed over Garett's time in the squadron because it hadn't aligned with the *Lincoln's* deployment cycle, but she hadn't accounted for all the times the carrier put to sea to participate in various exercises as part of its pre-deployment workup cycle.

"Are you saying . . ."

Camron nodded. "I'm saying, I think Corporal Garett is *KMART*."

"You can't be serious."

Camron turned and looked at the Jetta, taking in the aftermath of what she had endured. "It makes sense," he said.

She was stunned but not paralyzed, and she flung her pack across her back and made for the Suburban. "Then why are we just sitting here? We need to . . ."

Camron moved to block her way. "Punky . . ."

"Move, Camron."

"Listen to me."

She glared at him for a beat, then stepped aside to go around him.

"Punky, just hold on a second."

She wheeled on him, completely letting go of the thin shred of restraint she still held over her anger. "Why? So you can rub it in my face that the man I was following is the traitor I've been looking for all along? That I let him get away and now we have no idea where he is or what he plans on doing?"

"No, it's not . . ."

But she wasn't done. "It's not what? Like that? It's exactly like that, Camron! You should be coordinating a manhunt, not here reprimanding me and pointing out where I fucked up."

His face flushed at the accusation. "I would have been here sooner, but I was preparing an affidavit."

The admission caught her off guard, and she reined in her anger slightly. "A warrant?"

Camron nodded. "It wasn't easy since the attack on the *Abraham Lincoln* is still classified, but I got it."

They had ample evidence that the spy code-named *KMART* had been giving secrets to the Chinese related to the operational capabilities of the F-35 Joint Strike Fighter. And while she knew the communications had originated from the aircraft carrier, she'd always believed they had come from a sailor. Camron was right. She had completely ignored that the traitor could have been a Marine.

"And? Find anything useful?"

"We tracked his phone north to his family's cabin in South Lake Tahoe."

"Good work, Camron." Punky turned and started for the Suburban again.

"But he's not there anymore."

She stopped and hung her head, frustrated that he was keeping her from resuming her chase. Even if Corporal Garett wasn't on the run or up to no good, he was still the person she had dedicated the last several years of her life to finding. She needed to bring *KMART* in, once and for all. If for no other reason than that he was responsible for an attempted attack on the *Abraham Lincoln*.

"Where is he?"

"The Nugget Casino Resort in Reno."

Punky turned back to Camron. "Keys?"

"They're in the ignition," he said, nodding to the Suburban. "Now, go get your man."

14

Nugget Casino Resort
Sparks, Nevada

Colt opened his eyes and looked up at the ceiling, momentarily wondering why it tasted like a cat had used his mouth as a litter box. But one look around the hotel room told him everything he needed to know. He was sprawled out on one of the two queen-size beds, and from the snoring to his left, he was pretty sure he had ended up in Jug's room instead of his own.

He lifted his head off the pillow and the room spun violently. His stomach cramped at the sudden wave of nausea, and he stumbled out of the bed and lurched for the bathroom.

Jug's snoring rose to a violent crescendo, then abruptly stopped in a gasping fit as Colt bounced off the dresser against the far wall and hit his head on the bathroom door. But he managed to make it to his porcelain savior in time. His stomach heaved and expelled the poison he had consumed in copious amounts, and with each violent spasm, images from the night before flashed in his mind.

Beers at the Bug Roach Mixer. Rum and Cokes in the Adversary hospitality suite. Shots from an ice luge carved to look like a squadron mascot. More shots in the TOPGUN admin. Shots. Shots. Shots.

By the time Colt had rid himself of the liquor, he was left with a clammy, trembling body and a headache he knew would last until well after noon. He needed a shower, a cup of coffee, and two Extra Strength Excedrin before he had any chance of feeling close enough to normal to fall back to sleep for a few hours.

He flushed the toilet, then leaned his head under the sink and swished water around in his mouth to remove the litter box taste. Giving up, he returned to the bedroom and found the boots he had discarded before collapsing into bed, still fully dressed in his olive drab green flight suit. He sat at the desk and slipped on a pair of brown leather Red Wing boots, then bent over to lace them up, pausing every few seconds as waves of vertigo slammed into him.

As Jug's snoring resumed its normal relaxed cadence, Colt pushed himself to his feet and shuffled to the door. It took every ounce of strength he had to walk in a straight line, and he fixed his mind on the tasks he needed to complete to reach his goal. First, he needed to return to the parking garage and recover his duffel bag that held a toiletry kit with the two most important things in his mind—his toothbrush and the bottle of magic caplets that would at least blunt the full effects of his skull-splitting headache. Next, he needed to stop by the front desk and check in to receive a key to his dark, air-conditioned sanctuary where he could lick his wounds and crawl into bed for a much-needed nap.

Stepping into the hallway, Colt was again hit with uncertainty. He saw a glowing green exit sign and turned in its direction, stumbling down the hallway toward what he hoped was the elevator. His gamble paid off, and after several uneasy minutes where he thought he might throw up again, he reached a bank of elevators and pressed the down button.

When the doors opened with a metallic *ding*, he lumbered forward into the waiting elevator and pressed the button he thought would take him to the lobby. The ride down seemed to last forever as his stomach knotted up several more times and forced him to swallow hard to keep down the over-powering, sour taste of bile. It wasn't the first time Colt had imbibed to excess at Hook, and he knew he couldn't possibly be the only one suffering that morning.

Misery loves company.

The doors opened and Colt spilled out into the lobby. The sights and sounds assaulted his senses with a kaleidoscope of bright lights and a triumphant fanfare of bells, chimes, and electronic tones celebrating victory. He kept his head down in an overt admission of defeat, wishing he had only gambled away his life savings instead of consuming every drink put in front of him the night before.

On his way to the parking garage, Colt passed the stairs leading up to the convention floor, a front desk that was quickly filling with guests waiting in line, and a Bloody Mary bar that was teeming with aviators in similar states of disrepair. He ignored them all and recovered his duffel bag from the Bronco, after pausing only once to dry heave between two parked cars. Returning to the lobby, he allowed himself a moment of celebration—pleased that he had ticked off the first item on his to-do list and was well on his way to feeling right as rain. But he kept his eyes lowered and focused on putting one scuffed boot in front of the other.

When he reached the already-full queue snaking back and forth in front of the registration desk, he lifted his head to survey his surroundings. It was even odds that the people waiting in line were checking in or out, but it didn't much matter. Each one was an obstacle between him and the respite he desperately needed. He clenched his jaw and breathed slowly through his nose as he fought to tamp his frustration and quell his nausea.

Then, he saw him.

On account of the three wise men he had poured down his throat the night before, Colt thought he might have been seeing things. But as unlikely as it was, he was certain the man walking across the lobby floor with his head down was the Marine he had bumped into on the *Abraham Lincoln*—everything about that night was etched permanently into his brain. A flood of emotions overpowered him and erased the last vestiges of his hangover.

His eyes tracked the Marine as he rounded the corner and headed for the main exit on the south side of the hotel. Colt hesitated for a second, then stepped from the line and followed. He wasn't sure what compelled him to abandon the only thing that had mattered since waking up, but anything surrounding the night he had lost control of his jet and almost crashed into a guided missile cruiser seemed far more important than any other plans he had for that morning.

But Colt's equilibrium was still in question. He stumbled from the registration queue and bounced off a handful of other guests, barely noticing their angry shouts of, "Hey, watch it, buddy" or "Easy, pal." Each time, he mumbled an incoherent apology and kept his eyes fixed on the corner the Marine had retreated around.

He needed to catch up to him, because the Marine was another piece of the puzzle that still remained a jumbled mess of unanswered questions. Colt had learned that the Chinese Ministry of State Security had deployed an experimental weapon designed to hack into the fifth-generation stealth fighter and control it remotely. And he had been on the front lines when a Ministry operative took control of a jet—piloted by the man still sawing logs upstairs—in a daring plan to launch anti-ship missiles at the USS *Abraham Lincoln*.

But how they had managed such a feat was still a mystery. A mystery the Marine was a part of.

Colt rounded the corner and watched the Marine push through the doors and exit into the covered valet parking area. He followed without stopping, trading the sights and sounds of the lobby for the crisp, exhaust-filled air. The Marine hesitated for a second before turning right and walking out from underneath the overhang.

Colt adjusted his duffel bag's strap and set out to follow, increasing his pace to close the distance between them. With each labored breath, more and more memories flooded his mind, and he remembered seeing the Marine at a computer terminal in maintenance control when he had requested a copy of the technical data recovered from the computer system known as ODIN, or operational data integrated network.

"Hey, Marine," Colt shouted.

The man paused for a moment, then resumed his retreat from the hotel at a quicker pace.

"Hey, wait—"

A screech of tires pulled Colt's focus away from the speed-walking

Marine, and he turned just as a white Sprinter panel van came to an abrupt stop and blocked their path. Before he had a chance to process that anything was even amiss, the door slid open and three men in dark clothing and balaclavas jumped out and surrounded the Marine. Colt froze when he saw the AK-47 automatic rifles in their hands.

Not again.

Then the first gunshot rang out.

15

Punky had been parked on the street in front of the Nugget Casino Resort since arriving an hour after the sun rose above the hills east of Reno. She had driven through the night, carried onward by the unrelenting guilt that she had let *KMART* slip through her fingers. But the longer she sat in the Suburban's leather driver's seat, the more her fatigue took root and caused her resolve to waver.

She yawned and glanced up, squinting through the glare on her windshield as a white Sprinter panel van turned onto Nugget Avenue and drove toward her. Even early morning deliveries needed to be made in "the biggest little city in the world."

But then its engine roared, and the van surged forward and darted toward the covered valet parking area. Punky bolted upright in her seat and gripped the steering wheel with both hands as she instinctively scanned the driveway and sidewalk for potential victims standing in the path of the out-of-control van.

But when she saw the startled Marine, she knew it was no accident.

"Shit!"

She reached down and cranked the key to start the engine just as the panel van's brakes locked up and it skidded to a halt in front of the corporal. Forsaking the large government SUV, Punky opened the door and jumped out onto the street while her hand swept back to draw her service pistol in one crisp motion.

Though the van blocked most of her view, through its front windows she saw shadowed figures emptying onto the sidewalk and surrounding the startled Marine. She lifted her pistol and sighted in on the driver as her finger took out the trigger slack.

What the hell's going on?

But when she caught a glimpse of an AK-47 aimed at the Marine, she knew she hadn't stumbled onto another agency's operation or a prank gone awry. She pressed back on the trigger and broke through the wall, watching fire erupt from the barrel, followed by the side window shattering and the driver's head slumping forward against the steering wheel.

The Sprinter van's horn sounded in a pained bleat but was drowned out by the sound of her gunshot's echo off the casino tower. And the returning gunfire.

Punky ducked and darted across the street, diving behind a low stone wall that bordered a set of stairs descending to a casino entrance. She skidded across the crushed rock and slammed into a raised concrete utility access just as a second gunman sighted in on where she had taken refuge. She pressed her body into the ground to remain hidden behind the low stone wall as the machine gunfire intensified and high-velocity rounds ricocheted off the wrought iron railing above.

"Federal agent," Punky screamed, though she knew the shooters could care less.

Then she heard another, distinctly different gunshot echo off the casino's walls, causing a momentary lull in the gunfire that was keeping her pinned down.

This is my chance!

———

Colt's hangover was the last thing on his mind when the driver's side window shattered and a bullet caught the man in the temple, spraying blood across the panel van's interior. The driver slumped over against the horn, causing it to sound in one long, continuous blast that made his ears ring. But when two of the gunmen turned and opened fire on the unseen shooter, Colt's paralysis evaporated.

He dropped to a knee and flung his duffel bag onto the sidewalk at his feet. He rarely went anywhere other than the base without first arming himself, and he was thankful he had packed his SIG Sauer P365XL with spare magazine. He unzipped the duffel and reached inside for the holstered pistol, then ripped it free and brought it up to place the ROMEOZero red dot on the back of the nearest shooter's head.

No matter how much he had trained, Colt always hesitated before pulling the trigger. Growing up around guns in West Texas, he had been taught early on that a bullet was the one thing in life you couldn't take back. Once you pulled the trigger, it was gone for good. But just like on the streets of San Diego when a team of Chinese operatives closed in for the kill, Colt's hesitation was short-lived.

He pulled the trigger and watched a shooter drop to the ground like a marionette whose strings had been cut. He quickly shifted his aim to the second gunman but rushed his shot when his target turned and unloaded a long burst of gunfire. Colt's bullet missed high, and he dove to the ground and rolled into the driveway, hoping his maneuver had been enough to save him from being stitched from head to toe by the next burst.

When he came to a stop and looked up at the van, he saw the remaining gunmen dragging the Marine inside. He aimed his pistol again and fired several more rounds at the retreating shooters. But each one missed its intended target and only punched holes into the closing door.

The driver's door opened, and a body tumbled out onto the ground before another took his place behind the wheel. The door slammed shut, and the van's wheels spun briefly before it gained traction and backed into the driveway. It quickly reversed direction and sped out of the driveway and back onto Nugget Avenue.

Colt's headache came roaring back with a vengeance, and he pinched his eyes shut as his stomach lurched again. But when he heard the report of a pistol firing, he opened them to see a woman in a modified Weaver stance rapidly pulling the trigger and punching several more holes into the back of the fleeing van.

When it disappeared around the corner, the woman lowered her gun, then spun and turned toward Colt.

"You've got to be kidding me," he muttered.

Punky felt the slide lock back on her pistol and quickly thumbed the magazine release to let it fall to the ground while bringing the gun up into her workspace and reaching for her spare magazine. But when the van careened around the corner and disappeared, she slowed her movements and took her time indexing and seating the fresh magazine before sending the slide forward.

"That's twice," she said, frustrated she had let *KMART* slip through her fingers yet again.

Remembering the shooter who had disrupted the gunfight, Punky spun and saw a man in an olive drab green flight suit splayed out on the concrete with a pistol in his hand. She saw his sandy blond hair and crooked smile, and she groaned.

"You've got to be kidding me."

Looking away from Colt, she scanned the valet driveway and saw a handful of people poking their heads up from where they had taken refuge behind cars or podiums and concrete planters. Two men in suits with earpieces sprinted through the double doors and raced toward Colt, screaming at him to let go of the gun and remain face down on the ground. They were obviously casino security, which meant that the police had already been called and would be there shortly.

Holding her gun low at her side, Punky made her way around the sidewalk and approached the bodies of the slain gunmen. They were both dressed the same, dark jeans and long-sleeve shirts with black balaclavas pulled down to cover their faces. Both had been taken down with headshots, but she suspected she already knew what she would find when she peeled back their masks.

"Ma'am, stay where you are," one of the security guards yelled, holding a hand up to keep her from getting any closer.

Punky lifted her hoodie to reveal the gold badge clipped to her belt.

"Federal agent," she said, breathless with exhaustion. Then she pointed at Colt. "You can go ahead and release him."

"He's armed," the other guard protested.

She nodded. "I know."

Colt locked eyes with her and nodded, subtly thanking her for her intervention, then pushed himself off the ground and stood on shaky legs. She turned away and knelt next to the man who had been pushed from the driver's seat. Her bullet had entered the left side of his head just behind the eyes, but she figured she would still be able to make out his Asian features —all the confirmation she needed that the Ministry of State Security still had their fangs in Corporal Garett.

"You sure you want to do that?" Colt asked when she reached for the driver's mask.

"I need to."

She hooked a finger underneath the balaclava and tugged upward, peeling it back over the man's chin and exposing his face. She gasped when she saw the pale skin of a man who was clearly not Chinese. Even more surprising was the ink that stretched underneath his collar in either direction.

"No . . ."

Colt inched closer. "What is it?"

Punky quickly released the mask and moved to the second man—the one Colt had dropped with a well-placed shot at the base of his skull. She grabbed his shoulders and roughly rolled him onto his back, then ripped the balaclava off his head and stared in horror. Pale skin.

She tugged down on the collar of his shirt and saw an inked representation of domed towers peeking through.

"What the hell?"

16

Number One Observatory Circle
US Naval Observatory
Washington, DC

Vice President Jonathan Adams loosened his tie and sat down in the armchair to take full advantage of the few minutes he had allotted for himself in his busy calendar. He knew it came with the job. But he also knew that if he wanted to succeed beyond the upcoming election and survive his first term, he needed to take care of himself and pay attention to the classic signs that stress was taking a toll on his health.

"Mister Vice President," a disembodied voice said, its bearer remaining respectfully out of sight.

"What is it, Sam?" Jonathan asked, knowing his chief of staff wouldn't have disturbed him if it wasn't important.

Samuel Chambers ducked into the first-floor sitting room, hesitant to disturb his longtime friend and current boss. Jonathan knew Sam was fiercely protective of him and that blocking personal time on the VP's calendar had become something of a religion to his former college room-mate. "Sir, there's been an incident you need to be aware of."

Jonathan looked around the empty room, finished in a distinct glazed and lacquered peacock blue, then back to his chief of staff. "It's just us girls, Sam."

Sam took the hint and sat on the cream-colored sofa across from the tiled fireplace.

"Is it about your reporter friend?"

Sam shook his head. "No, he seems quite happy with the story we gave him."

"Good. I burned a lot of political capital by breaking my word to the president."

"We had no other choice—"

Jonathan waved him off. "I know that. But we're going to have to accelerate our plans and start building our coalition."

"That's why I'm here." Sam handed him a leather folder, then leaned back against the cushions as he waited for the vice president to review its contents. "It's about your first stop during your trip to Nevada."

"What about it?"

"Base leadership wants to use the visit as an opportunity to build support for one of their projects."

Jonathan read from the briefing. "Fallon Range Training Complex expansion?"

"It's a hot-topic item that will play well with military voters and give you a chance to demonstrate your leadership by addressing environmental concerns at the same time."

He rubbed his chin, unsurprised at the depth of thought that went into this decision. Sam had always possessed a shrewd political mind, and this was just another example of that. "So, what's the problem?"

"Chris called about an incident that took place this morning."

He stopped reading and looked up. "What incident?"

Sam gestured to the folder. "It's in there, sir. Apparently there was a shooting just north of the Reno airport at the Nugget Casino Resort that has drawn the attention of local, state, and federal law enforcement agencies."

Jonathan turned the page and read an executive summary that highlighted the key facts. He stopped reading halfway down the page and looked up at Sam. "Tailhook?"

His chief of staff's mouth curled up at the corner. "Completely unrelated."

Jonathan chewed on the inside of his lip. "Isn't Andy there?"

To his credit, Sam didn't seem surprised that his boss had remembered that the chief of naval operations had been invited to attend the symposium. Maybe it was because they were sitting in the house that had been the CNO's residence from 1923 until 1974, when Congress authorized transformation of the house into the official residence of the vice president. But more than likely, it was because Jonathan envied the popularity of the Minnesota native and fighter pilot and wished he could have attended Tailhook himself.

Though not a veteran, Jonathan had often sided with the veterans caucus—first, as a representative of California's 16th congressional district, then as a US Senator. His staunch advocacy for veteran causes led to him being endorsed by several prominent groups, including the Disabled American Veterans, Iraq and Afghanistan Veterans of America, Military Officers Association of America, and the American Legion.

Those endorsements were a key contributor in the president selecting Jonathan to serve as his running mate during the last election, and many thought it would be the veteran vote that pushed them into the White House at the top of the ticket the following year.

"Yes, sir. But early reports indicate that this incident had nothing to do with Admiral Peterson's presence or the convention itself."

"Does Chris have any reason to believe it's related to our visit?"

Sam shook his head. "Not at this time."

Jonathan slid the papers into the folder and handed it back to his chief of staff. "What about our other issue?"

"Nothing concrete yet," Sam replied. "But I'll take care of it."

The two locked eyes, and volumes passed between the men without a single word being spoken. They had a shared history that went back to their days at UC Berkeley. What had begun as a shallow friendship in the classroom had blossomed into a close one on the campaign trail for his first congressional seat. But it was the events they never spoke about that had bonded them closer than brothers—a bond that carried them into the Senate and Number One Observatory Circle.

And a bond that would carry them into the White House.

"If I haven't told you lately, I'm thankful you've stayed with me all these years, Sam."

"I've got your back, sir."

The vice president nodded, then glanced at his watch. His allotted personal time had come to an end, and he cinched up his tie and stood, smoothing out the wrinkles in his dress shirt before buttoning his suit coat. As Sam left the sitting room, Jonathan studied the bookcases on either side of the fireplace. On the top shelves were books about past vice presidents— good and bad—and he couldn't help but wonder what historians would say about his time at Number One Observatory Circle.

17

South Lake Tahoe, California

Mantis didn't need to recover the hidden key to unlock the cabin. Even if the front door hadn't been left unlocked, she kept a master on her keyring that worked for every door in the house. But she was more than a little concerned that she hadn't needed it. Especially since his Jeep wasn't in the driveway.

"Adam?"

Stepping into the foyer, she closed the door and locked the deadbolt while keeping her attention on the cabin's interior. She shuffled forward a step but paused when her toe kicked an overstuffed duffel bag resting on the floor. She stole a glance at the "USMC" and Eagle, Globe, and Anchor stenciled on the olive drab canvas, and knew it belonged to her adopted son.

"Adam, are you here?"

Keeping her back to the wall as she glided up the staircase, she suddenly felt uneasy in a place that had always been her refuge. Not because she had lied to her husband about driving up to the cabin, even though she had. Or because she was ignoring several key ongoing Ministry operations to check on her son's wellbeing, though she was doing that too.

As far as she was concerned, nothing was more important than Adam's safety, and Li Hu's reports about assassins and an NCIS special agent troubled her greatly.

Even more so now that Li Hu had gone silent.

"Adam," she called out again. "I'm coming upstairs."

For decades, Mantis had lived a life of suspicion and caution. As the Ministry of State Security's spy chief on the West Coast, she was responsible for coordinating agents and assets to support hundreds of operations spanning every aspect of American society. Academic, corporate, military. Not to mention local, state, and federal governments. Her reach was everywhere, and she knew that made her a target. And, by proxy, her son.

Taking her time, she moved silently from tread to tread while controlling her breathing and listening for sounds in the quiet house. Though fear battered at her composure, she hadn't risen to her station within the Ministry by succumbing to her baser instincts. And as much as her heart screamed to find and protect her son, she moved carefully and placed each foot deliberately.

When she reached the top of the stairs, she surveyed the kitchen and living room. Large windows bordered the wall to her right, and she looked out on a scene that had always brought her comfort. She tried to take solace in the placid deep blue waters of Lake Tahoe beyond the pine trees swaying gently in the breeze, but her mind still swam with fears for her son. Though she could sense his presence, she knew he was gone. She had been there enough times to know when the cabin was empty.

Picking up her pace, she moved from room to room, until finally making it to the one that had always been his. The bed was made, but the comforter was disheveled and the pillow was dimpled, as if somebody had been lying there. With rising anxiety, she swept through the house once more before satisfying herself that it was empty. Adam had been there, of that she was certain. But he wasn't now, and it looked like he had left of his own free will.

Stepping out onto the porch overlooking the driveway and the distant lake, she pulled out her cell phone and tapped on Adam's number. She listened to it ring with increasing frustration that she had spent nearly four hours in the car to be there for her son. But he hadn't even bothered to tell her where he was going. Not even a note. She ended the call when his voicemail picked up.

Switching over to her Signal application, she found Li Hu's contact and placed an encrypted call. But it too ended in disappointment, and she seethed as she pocketed her phone and gripped the railing. She was one of the most powerful women in the world, with almost limitless assets at her disposal, and the two people she wanted to talk to weren't even answering her calls.

"Breathe, Fu Zan," she said, reminding herself to remain unflustered with a composed mind.

She closed her eyes and felt the wind wash over her face, inhaling the fresh scent of pine she had always associated with peace. She listened to the gentle swaying of trees and the soft morning sounds of animals and insects facing another day of survival. The clipped buzzing sound coming from her pocket was entirely out of place, but she recognized it immediately. Her eyes snapped open and she answered the phone.

"Yes?"

"Hi, I need to reschedule my appointment," the man's voice said.

She pulled the phone away and glanced at the number. Mantis recognized it instantly and chastised herself for momentarily forgetting that one of her operations had reached a critical phase and demanded her attention. She brought the phone back to her ear to continue with the coded exchange. "Was this for heating or cooling?"

"Heating," he replied.

"Just one moment," she said, pausing to ensure she had captured the meaning of the call correctly. The man on the other end was a computer engineer for a major research laboratory that had been working on a project nearing completion at the Tonopah Test Range almost two hundred miles southeast of her.

The call to reschedule the appointment indicated that the final test of the weapon had been moved. Heating implied that it had been moved up, while cooling meant that it had been delayed. Neither option was particularly troubling to Mantis, except that moving up the test meant that the weapon might reach operational status sooner than expected. The question was, how soon?

"Okay," she said. "When would you like to reschedule?"

"Tomorrow," the engineer said.

Mantis swallowed. *Tomorrow?*

As much as Adam's disappearance bothered her, there was too much at stake to waste her efforts on finding him. Besides, he wasn't a boy any longer. He was a United States Marine. He would just have to fend for himself for a few more days.

"I'll pencil you in," she said. "What time?"

"After three?"

She grunted. "Three it is. See you then."

The call ended, and Mantis switched over to Signal to make one final attempt to reach Li Hu. She almost screamed when it predictably went to voicemail. Tucking her phone back in her pocket, she started to turn away from the railing.

But then she saw the approaching Mercedes sedan.

Their cabin was hardly isolated, so she wasn't too concerned that a car had turned off the road and onto the long driveway. More often than not, somebody had followed the wrong directions to their rental cabin and only used the driveway as a way of turning around.

But the Mercedes didn't appear to be lost.

The luxury sedan with dark tinted windows rolled silently up the shaded driveway and parked next to her Tesla Model X. Her heart thundered in her chest, but she remained stoic and peered over the railing at the S-class in rapt fascination. Whoever was behind the wheel had come to see her.

The driver's door opened, and a portly, middle-aged man with thinning gray hair stepped out and adjusted his sport coat before turning to face her.

"Fu Zan?"

Any surprise she felt that the man knew her name remained hidden behind an emotionless mask that covered her face. She nodded once in reply. "And who are you?"

He closed the driver's door and walked toward the front steps with an awkward limping gait. Remaining outwardly impassive, she studied him for any signs that were precursors to violence. She knew she held the high ground and still retained a position of strength.

The man stopped and looked up at her. He held his hands low at his sides and appeared almost relaxed. "Who I am is not important."

She studied the man carefully. "I'm not interested."

"May I come in?"

She gave a little shake of her head. "I think not."

His smile vanished, and she saw his eyes cloud over with surprising anger. "Very well. Shall I tell your son then that his mother isn't interested in doing a favor for a friend to save his life?"

18

The panel van's interior was spartan, and Adam pressed his face to the bare metal floor. Of course, the boot on the back of his head was ample encouragement to remain prone and avoid giving the impression that he was resisting. If he had any hope of surviving the ordeal, he needed to remain calm until the right opportunity presented itself.

And it would. Chen had prepared him for this. She had given him the knowledge and the tools he needed to make his escape.

Tools.

They had bound his wrists behind his back with zip ties, but he could still feel the cool metal bracelet of the watch Chen had given him pressing against his skin. His captors had made a mistake by not removing it, but he wasn't naive enough to think they would continue to make the same mistake once they reached their destination. He might only get a narrow window, but the steady pressure on the base of his skull was enough to remind him that the window hadn't yet opened.

Would anybody even notice?

He had fled San Diego, hoping to be free from his Chinese puppet masters. Now he hoped there were one or two strings left uncut and that they cared enough about him to follow through on Chen's promises.

Adam still remembered the morning she had given him the simple Tag

Heuer Carrera. At first, he thought it was payment for the intelligence he had provided on the F-35C Joint Strike Fighter. But, like most things with the Ministry of State Security, the watch was not what it seemed.

Like the modified Nintendo Switch she had given him to use for covert communications, she showed him the features of the watch and made him practice using it with either hand. And, like the Nintendo Switch, he'd demonstrated his proficiency with the tool she had given him but thought it silly and pointless.

It didn't seem so silly now.

The panel van hit a bump in the road, and Adam heard the sound of pebbles and other debris being kicked up and impacting the undercarriage. They jostled from side to side and swayed as the driver took them from the smooth pavement of the highway and city streets to what seemed like an unimproved surface. Adam knew there were many such roads in northwest Nevada, and it was pointless to even guess what direction they had fled. But it was still a clue. And Chen had taught him that clues mattered.

They hit another bump, and Adam's prone body became weightless for a moment before slamming back down. The boot on his head followed a split second later and added an exclamation mark to the impact. He cried out, but the boot only pressed harder.

"Quiet," a voice said.

It was one of the few things his captors had said since throwing him into the van and zip-tying his wrists and ankles together. The memory of the van screeching to a halt played on a loop in his head, but it was the moment before that really worried him.

As odd as it seemed, he was more concerned about the man who had called out to him moments before he was kidnapped. He hadn't turned to look, but the voice had a ring of familiarity to it.

He heard Chen's stern voice in the back of his mind. *"Do not delay. Once the dust has settled, they will strip you and search you."*

Adam took a deep breath through his mouth to avoid inhaling the stench of the soiled hood as he worked up the courage to activate the locator beacon. Maybe the Chinese wouldn't care enough to come. Maybe they would rescue him only to put a bullet in the back of his head for failing them. He had no way of knowing.

But he knew what would happen if he did nothing.

The van swerved right, then left, and vibrated with a brief but rapid series of bumps that taxed its suspension.

Cattle guard, Adam thought.

Another clue.

They hit another bump, and Adam's body came off the floor again. But instead of crashing down onto his face like before, he twisted and came down on his right shoulder with his back against the van's side. He couldn't see who else was in the van, or where they were positioned, but the boot's owner seemed to find his new position satisfactory and only pressed against his shoulder to pin him against the wall.

"Don't move," he growled.

With his back to the wall, Adam had the privacy he needed to activate the beacon and send up an electronic flare. Whether anybody came for him was irrelevant. Chen had taught him that his resistance was as much about maintaining a positive mental attitude as it was about actually escaping and making it to safety. No matter how grim things might seem, he always had control over his outlook.

They had bound his wrists with one over the other, but some gentle manipulation and articulation allowed him to angle his right hand toward his left wrist. It was a challenge, but he managed to get his fingertips onto the crown's knurled edges. Gripping it, he rotated the crown counterclockwise and unscrewed it from the locked position.

After several seconds, his effort was rewarded by the crown springing outward. The first detent could be used to adjust the date and the second detent allowed him to adjust the watch's hands and set the time. He pulled it to the second detent.

Each of his movements were slow and deliberate. Adam focused on his breathing and struggled to remain calm to avoid drawing attention to his subterfuge. He spun the crown and imagined the minute hand sweeping through the twelve o'clock position as the hour hand lagged behind. He could have guessed each time the minute hand passed through the twelve, but his watch had been designed with haptic feedback for just this purpose.

He counted almost nine full rotations before the single tap of the minute hand was accompanied by a double tap of the hour hand reaching its designated location at the six o'clock position. He stopped rotating the crown, reversed directions—felt the three distinct taps again for confirmation—then stopped. In his mind, he could see the watch's hands aligned straight up and down, just as Chen had shown him.

Adam took a few seconds to breathe, then pushed the crown in, past the first detent.

"What are you doing?" his captor asked.

"N-n-nothing," Adam stammered, adding a little dramatic flair for the sake of selling the performance.

He felt the boot's pressure abate on his shoulder, and he quickly screwed the crown into place. Once tightened, he knew the watch would begin emitting a distress beacon that Chen had assured him would be detected by Ministry resources. But unlike most Emergency Position Indicating Radio Beacons that broadcast in 406 MHz, his watch contained a locator beacon that broadcast in an ultra high frequency normally reserved for pagers.

A beacon only the Ministry knew to look for.

19

Nugget Casino Resort
Sparks, Nevada

Colt sat on an oversized sofa in the lobby and watched Punky navigate the crime scene among a growing sea of officers from the Sparks Police Department, Washoe County Sheriff's Office, and the Nevada State Police. Both uniformed and plain clothes detectives milled about while each agency bickered over jurisdiction. More than twice, Colt saw Punky throw her hands up in the air in obvious frustration.

If he wasn't still hungover and on the hook to answer questions surrounding his role in dropping one of the gunmen, he would have probably laughed at her misfortune. As it was, he didn't need the headache. Or at least the added contributor.

Colt leaned his head back against the sofa's thick cushion, propped his feet up on the coffee table, and closed his eyes. Punky had told him to remain in the lobby until she came for him, but the longer he waited for her to conclude her business out front, the more likely he was to ignore her order and sneak off to his room for that Excedrin, shower, and a nap. He felt his body sink deeper into the cushions as his fatigue reached up and drew him closer to sleep.

"Hey, Colt."

He opened his eyes and nodded respectfully at her. "Special Agent King."

She seemed exhausted but was just as beautiful as he remembered. "I think we've been through enough together to dispense with the formalities, don't you?" She gestured to the gold oak leaves embroidered on his shoulders. "Unless you expect me to call you 'Commander?'"

He cracked a smile, but there was no real humor behind it. "Colt's fine."

"Then it's just Punky," she said, taking a seat in one of the adjacent chairs and gesturing to his flight suit. "Congrats on the promotion, but what's with the getup?"

"Tied one on last night and haven't had a chance to change."

"You're staying here?"

He closed his eyes again and nodded.

"Why?"

He gestured to the sign perched on an easel next to the entrance.

She read the words printed there. "'Tailhook Association's Sixty-Seventh Symposium.' Wasn't Tailhook involved in some big scandal a few years ago?"

Colt felt his stomach knot up again, but he quickly burped to relieve some of the pressure. "A few decades, but yeah. That was the thirty-fifth symposium, in 1991. Things aren't nearly as wild now as they were then."

"Uh-huh," she replied. "Sure looks tame to me."

He opened an eye and studied her to see if she was being serious or merely giving him shit. Undecided, he sat up tall and rubbed his eyes to at least give the appearance that things weren't nearly as wild now as they were back then. "So, how does this work? Do you need to take me to the police station or something?"

Her impassive expression softened, and she smiled. "Relax, Colt. I was there, remember? I'll definitely take your statement, but it can wait a few hours if you need to ... get cleaned up."

He was almost certain she had been about to say, *if you need to sober up.*

"That might be a good idea," he said.

Punky reached into her pocket and removed a business card, then passed it across to Colt. "Wasn't sure you still had my number. But just text me when you're ready to talk."

Colt glanced at his watch and figured that a shower and a two-hour nap would be enough to make him at least coherent. But to be safe he added a buffer. "How about noon?"

Punky looked through the tinted front windows at the melting pot of boys in blue, scrambling around the crime scene and jockeying for their stake in the investigation. "Yeah, noon should work. I'll probably still be cleaning up this mess out there. But if not, look for me at the slots."

"I'll shoot you a text."

Colt pocketed her business card and leaned forward to begin the slow and painful process of getting off the sofa to take his place in line once more at the front desk. But his momentum came to a screeching halt when he heard Jug's annoyingly chipper voice.

"Well, fry me in butter and call me a catfish!"

Colt gave up trying to stand and sank back into the sofa. "I should've stuffed a sock in your mouth last night and called you quiet."

Punky rose and turned to the other pilot. "Hey, Jug."

"Don't tell me you came all the way here to see this joker," he said, pulling her in for a hug.

"Just a happy coincidence, I guess."

Jug took a step back and frowned at her. "What about me?"

She grinned and shook her head. "You too, Jug."

But he had already moved on and whipped his head toward Colt. "Hey, were you insinuating that I snore or something?"

"Something like that."

Either Jug hadn't imbibed nearly as much as Colt or his genes had mutated, giving him a superhuman ability to metabolize alcohol at an incredibly fast rate. Either way, he showed no signs of being lethargic or under-the-weather like his temporary roommate.

"Well, based on how you look, you might be onto something."

Colt grinned. "Are you insinuating that I look like shit or something?"

"Something like that."

Colt laughed as Punky shook her head and turned to look through the windows at the dwindling law enforcement presence outside. "Well, as much fun as it is listening to you two bicker like a couple sixth-grade school girls, I should probably get back out there before the sheriff tries throwing his weight around and pushes everyone else out."

Colt glanced through the window and saw a somewhat rotund man strutting like a cock in a henhouse. "If that's the sheriff, I'd be more worried about him *eating* everyone else."

The mischievous look on Jug's face faded away. "Wait a second . . ."

"It's probably better not to ask," Colt suggested, hoping to forestall the inevitable questions until after he had showered and taken a nap.

"What *the hell* did I walk into?" Jug asked.

Colt and Punky exchanged mirthless glances.

"I told you not to ask."

After Colt left, Punky spent a few minutes catching up with Jug in the lobby before she excused herself and headed back outside. As tired as she was, she couldn't ignore the investigation or what the apparent abduction of KMART on American soil meant for the Ministry of State Security.

But she needed to mend a few bridges first.

Despite her criticism of the local sheriff, Punky knew he was a competent professional. He had spent nearly twenty-five years in the Washoe County Sheriff's Office and worked his way up from deputy sheriff to assistant sheriff while gaining experience across a wide range of operations. From special weapons and tactics to hostage negotiations, Sheriff Haskin was the right person for the job and more than just a politician using it as a stepping stone to a bigger office. She wasn't looking forward to the conversation she knew they were about to have.

Ignoring the swarm of investigators angling to take photos of the two dead bodies in the driveway, Punky walked straight to the sheriff and tried to appear as contrite as possible given the circumstances. He saw her approaching and shifted his considerable bulk to confront her head-on.

"Mind telling me what the Naval Criminal Investigative Service is doing in Sparks?"

She knew she probably should have contacted his office and informed them of her presence in the county, but sometimes events had a way of spiraling out of control. And learning that Corporal Garett was likely the spy known as *KMART* demanded an immediate response.

"An ongoing counterintelligence investigation," she said, hoping the vague answer sufficed.

"Bullshit," the sheriff said. "We're plugged into the Northern Nevada Counter Terrorism Center and Northern Nevada Regional Intelligence Center, and we haven't gotten so much as a whiff that hostile actors were planning something like this."

If her suspicions about Corporal Garett were correct, then she wasn't surprised. "Be that as it may, I was following a suspect I have been after for several years."

"And he led you here?"

Punky nodded, looking beyond the sheriff at the two dead bodies in the driveway.

"Do you think your suspect was targeting the convention?"

She furrowed her brow, then suddenly realized he thought the slain bodies were shooters taking their orders from her suspect. But she still wasn't sure how much she should tell him about *KMART*. "Absolutely not."

Sheriff Haskin sighed. "Well, you made quite a mess here for me. I've got folks from the Regional Gang Unit and Northern Nevada Interdiction Task Force arguing that this was a hit fitting the profiles for several of the organizations they're investigating."

"Well, it's not. I can promise you that."

"It's not Bratva?"

Punky shook her head, though she understood his guess. The shooters' tattoos certainly looked like Russian prison ink, and she had sent several photos to Camron for confirmation. But she couldn't understand why Russian organized crime might want a Marine who sold secrets to the Chinese. "I really don't think so," she said.

"So, who is it then?"

This time, it was Punky who sighed. "I can't tell you that either, Sheriff. But I can tell you this wasn't a hit."

"Uh-huh." He glanced over his shoulder at the AK-47 rifles and spent shell casings littering the driveway, then at the gaggle of reporters that were being held back by several uniformed Sparks police officers. "Looks like I'm not going to have any answers to their questions."

20

Mantis rolled past the cordoned-off valet driveway on Nugget Avenue and craned her neck for confirmation of what the stranger had told her she would find. Her blood ran cold when she saw the horde of police officers, crime scene tape, and white sheets covering two bodies.

At the intersection with Pyramid Way, she made a U-turn and drove the Tesla Model X back toward the casino where she attempted to turn into the driveway before a uniformed valet stopped her. Rolling down her window, she feigned confusion and gestured at the throng of law enforcement vehicles. "What's going on?"

"There was an incident, but it's under control now," the young man replied.

"Was there a shooting or something?" She broke eye contact and studied the crowd of police officers and investigators from several different agencies, settling on the poised woman with dark hair she had come to find. She didn't look like the others—she wore jeans and a hoodie—but had a more commanding presence than the uniformed man with four stars on his epaulets. When she looked back to the valet, she could almost see the wheels turning behind his brown eyes.

"It's safe now," he said, giving her the response he had likely been instructed to use.

"Was it gang-related?"

He ignored her question. "Are you staying with us?"

"No, I just came to play pai gow."

The young man nodded and gestured to the garage on the east side of the casino. "If you want to self-park in the garage there, you're welcome to play."

Mantis thanked him, then reversed the electric SUV and made another U-turn to drive past the garage and enter on the far side. Not unexpectedly, it was full, but she found a spot reserved for EVs near the bridge leading across to the casino. As she walked inside, her mind was on the woman she had seen out front. If she was right, the woman was the Naval Criminal Investigative Service special agent who had been attacking her network for years.

She just hoped Special Agent King would make as formidable an ally as she did an adversary.

Walking inside, she was hit with the stench of stale smoke as each of her other senses were assaulted by the casino's sights and sounds. Neon and fluorescent lights of all shades and colors reflected off dark wood paneling and carpet that swirled in a kaleidoscope of reds and golds. She held her head high and walked with purpose as she scanned the faces she encountered, looking for just one in particular.

Her heart felt as if a hand had wrapped around it and squeezed slowly, applying just enough pressure to remind her what was at stake. She focused on breathing and centering her *qi*, putting aside her fears that she would be unable to rescue her son. Her husband had failed to protect Adam. She would not make the same mistake.

Mantis stopped in the middle of a sea of slot machines and listened to coins being inserted, levers being pulled, and wheels spinning as dozens of people held their breath. She heard collective sighs and moans, the triumphant chorus of electronic celebration and the soft plinking of another coin being dropped in defeat. The casino was both exhaustingly beautiful and depressing at the same time.

But Mantis cared little if the people surrounding her hit the jackpot or lost everything to their addiction. Her gaze settled on the dark-haired woman sitting at a table in the cafe and sipping on a steaming cup of coffee.

Mantis took a deep breath. She needed to sell this to make it work.

———

Punky set the cup down and looked at her watch again, regretting her decision to give Colt a few hours' reprieve before answering her questions. She knew he had only been a Good Samaritan in the wrong place at the right time—no matter how odd or coincidental it might have seemed—and likely wouldn't offer anything substantive to aid in her investigation. But she was tired.

She fished her phone from her pocket and called Camron again. Maybe it was her lack of sleep or her excessive caffeine intake, but she barely waited for him to answer. "I'm at a roadblock, Camron."

"Well, good morning to you too."

"Sorry, but I'm not really in the mood."

"Okay. First things first. We just got the forensics report of the shooting at the reservoir back from the lab," he said. "Though I'm not sure it's much help."

Punky rubbed her eyes. "Why? What's it say?"

"They think the bullet had a wedge shape for improved penetration and power."

"Wedge shape?"

"Does the . . ." She heard papers shuffling in the background. ". . . SP-16 round mean anything to you?"

"Should it?"

"Just that it's a wedge-shaped 7.62-millimeter noiseless ammunition developed by the Russians."

"The Russians?" The tattoos she had seen on the slain shooters immediately came to mind.

"It's not a very common round," Camron said. "As far as we can tell, it's only used in the PSS-2 silenced pistol fielded by the Russian FSB security agency."

Punky shook her head. "Do you think there's a connection with the tattoos?"

"I think your initial hunch might have been right. They look like Russian prison tattoos to me."

"But why would the Bratva do something like this? Kidnapping a US Marine in broad daylight?"

"They might be Russian prison tattoos, but that doesn't mean the shooters were Russian organized crime. Do you remember Dmitry Utkin?"

"The Wagner Group military leader?"

"He was a veteran of Russia's military intelligence division and had Nazi SS symbols tattooed on both sides of his neck. It's likely the tattoos you sent me have more significant meaning."

Punky shook her head. "Like what?"

"The dagger through the neck symbolizes that the bearer committed murder and was available to commit more for hire."

"Like an assassin."

"And a cathedral's domed towers most likely represent the number of sentences a prisoner has served over their lifetime. More domes indicate more time spent incarcerated."

"So, these are Russian prisoners."

"Or conscripts."

"Russian ammunition? Russian tattoos? Camron, do you think it's possible this is a turf war of some kind?"

"I don't know, Punky. We haven't heard anything even hint at this." Camron's sentiment was similar to what the sheriff had said, but it sounded different coming from him.

"Yeah, but do you think it's possible?"

"Sure, it's possible. What are you thinking?"

"I don't know," Punky replied honestly. "My focus has been on the Ministry of State Security, but what if another country is trying to step up their game on the West Coast? We need to figure out who's at play here, or this could blow up into something we can't control."

"We can't control it anyway," Camron said.

"Yeah, because we're just caught in the middle."

The supervisory special agent was silent for a few minutes as he thought about what she had said. "All the more reason why you should take a step back and hand this off to the FBI."

"Not yet." She looked at her watch again, then took another sip of coffee before answering. "I'm going to hang around here for a few more hours to run down a few leads first."

"Then what?"

"I don't know."

Punky hated the way it sounded, but it was the most honest answer. She doubted Colt was going to reveal some elusive detail that might give her a place to pick up *KMART*'s trail. But it was all she had to go on, and she wasn't ready to give up yet.

"Call me back when you figure it out," Camron said.

After ending the call, Punky set her phone down on the table and stared into the cooling black liquid inside her mug. This was the first time she could remember feeling completely rudderless and without a clear direction. Once she questioned Colt, she would be out of ideas and forced to return to San Diego with her tail tucked between her legs. After coming close to *KMART* and losing him—twice—she couldn't stomach the thought of returning home empty-handed.

"We're looking for the same person," a woman said from behind her.

Punky's heart bolted, and she spun while dropping her right hand to the holstered pistol on her hip. She had already drawn it twice in twenty-four hours and paused, locking eyes with an older Asian woman sitting at the table behind her with both hands placed palms down on the table. They stared at each other in silence for a few moments before Punky trusted herself enough to speak.

"Who are you?"

"My name is Fu Zan. Perhaps you've heard of me?"

Slowly, Punky rose from her chair and took the seat opposite the older woman. "I have. I've been to your house."

The woman's eyes flashed momentary surprise, but she quickly recovered and nodded as if she had already known. "Then I came to the right person."

Punky wasn't sure why the comment struck a nerve. "Why are you here?"

"Because my son has been kidnapped. And I need your help getting him back."

Punky's face flushed.

21

"Your what?"

Punky stared incredulously at the expressionless woman sitting across from her. She immediately discredited what she thought she had heard, though images flashed in her mind and corroborated everything that simple statement had implied. With her own eyes, she had seen the Marine arrive in the dead of night at a modest house in the suburbs of San Jose, only to be welcomed with open arms by the woman sitting across from her.

Welcomed like family.

"My son," Fu Zan said again. "My husband and I took him in as a foster child when he was a toddler, but we later adopted him and raised him as our own. I love him more than anything and will do whatever it takes to get him back."

Over the years, Punky had developed a pretty good nose for sniffing out bullshit, but everything the woman said rang true. Though if Adam Garett was the adopted son of Fu Zan and He Gang, she had to believe the Marine's treason was at least partially influenced by his parents. And that begged another question.

"Do you work for the Ministry of State Security?"

Fu Zan pursed her lips. "Yes."

Punky's heart bolted again. She might have suspected it, but she certainly hadn't expected the woman to confirm it. Least of all to a special agent with the Naval Criminal Investigative Service. "What do you do for them?"

Moving her hands for the first time since addressing Punky, Fu Zan slowly brought them together and interlaced her fingers before answering. "They call me Mantis," the older woman said, pausing to assess Punky's reaction to the name. "I run the Ministry's West Coast network."

Holy shit.

She had been mourning the loss of her connection to *KMART* but had just been approached by the one person Punky had hoped Garett's arrest would lead her to. Now she didn't have to find the Marine to get what she wanted—she was already sitting across the table from her.

Still, Punky was hesitant to take the woman's comments at face value, and she pressed to confirm her bona fides. "Was your son actively engaged in espionage?"

"Yes."

Punky's heart hammered faster. Even if Mantis had been forthcoming about her own involvement, Punky had at least expected her to shelter her son from probable prosecution.

If we ever find him.

The last thing she expected Mantis to reveal was that she and her adopted son were guilty of espionage. "In what ways?"

Mantis lowered her gaze and studied her hands. "He provided classified maintenance information on the F-35 Joint Strike Fighter that we used to develop a weapon capable of hacking into its secure network architecture and control it remotely."

Punky's mouth fell open. The older woman's statement confirmed everything that had happened to Colt when he had been a guest pilot in the *Black Knights* of VMFA-314 aboard the USS *Abraham Lincoln*. But her tone was so casual, she might as well have been telling her what she had eaten for breakfast.

"Do you still possess that capability?"

"No."

Mantis could have been lying. But given her candidness in answering

Punky's questions so far, she was inclined to believe her. But that didn't mean she trusted her. "What do you know about *SUBLIME*?"

The older woman's face cracked in a subtle smile. "You seem to know a great deal about my organization." She held up a hand when Punky opened her mouth to respond. "That is good. That will make this much easier."

"What will?"

Instead of answering, Mantis leaned back in her chair and nodded with approval. "*SUBLIME*. That was my husband's operation, and a foolhardy one at that. While I have dedicated my life to remaining in the shadows and gathering intelligence for my country, my husband has been intent on making a name for himself by taking unnecessary risks."

"So, you didn't play a role in attacking the *Ronald Reagan* with a synthetic bioweapon?"

Again, Mantis smiled. "No, I did not."

Punky leaned back in her chair, and the two women stared at each other in silence. For the last several years, they had been on opposite sides in a tepid war that had targeted two nuclear-powered aircraft carriers and caused violence to spill over onto the streets of Southern California. All Punky had to do was arrest this woman, and she could cripple the Ministry's network. It might not end the war, but she would be a hero.

Still, something prevented her from doing that.

"Why are you telling me this?" Punky asked.

"As I said, I want your help in getting my son back."

"You know he will be prosecuted and likely spend the rest of his life in prison," she replied. "And so will you."

Mantis nodded. "I'm hoping that what I have to offer will grant some leniency for my son."

"But not you?"

She shrugged. "I'm an old woman. You know who I am, and you know I can no longer do the job I was sent here to do. Help me get my son back, and I'll turn myself in and give you everything you need to dismantle the network I've spent decades building."

Punky narrowed her eyes, trying to decide whether to believe her. It would be the ultimate coup—arresting the traitor she had been hunting for years while simultaneously eradicating the Ministry's network on the West Coast. But her dad had always told her that when something seemed too good to be true, it probably was. Still, could she afford to let this opportunity slip away?

"I'm not sure that will be enough to let your son go free."

"I just want what any mother wants," Mantis said. "I want him safe."

Punky considered the woman's offer. As an accredited law enforcement officer, she had an obligation and duty to arrest the woman sitting across from her. But she was also a counterintelligence professional who understood that what the woman offered was the bigger win. It wouldn't be enough to simply remove the head of the network, because the Ministry would only replace her with another.

"You're willing to give up your husband to save your son?"

Mantis didn't flinch. "You're not a mother, are you?"

Punky pursed her lips. There was no way Camron would go for this and no way she could do it alone. But if she could pull it off . . .

"Can I count on your help?" Fu Zan pressed.

She made her decision. "How can I reach you?"

Mantis slid a phone across the table, then stood. "I'll call you when I find where they took him."

22

Harry Reid International Airport
Las Vegas, Nevada

The nineteen-passenger airplane shuddered as the four-bladed Hartzell propellers spun to a stop. Benjamin Hayes ducked his head and looked through the window at the passenger jets of various airlines taxiing on the east side of the parallel runways. He had always enjoyed watching airplanes fly and often wondered where their passengers were going. There was just something romantic about it.

Benjamin kept his face pressed against the plastic bulkhead until the passengers in front of him rose and gathered their things. Reluctantly, he stood and walked down the narrow center aisle while fishing for his cell phone to turn it on. Their time spent on the ramp, moving from the smaller turboprop to the larger twin-engine passenger jet, would be his last opportunity to have a connection with the outside world.

Not that he had anybody to connect with.

"I should have gone to fucking Google," he muttered.

Apple, Amazon, Microsoft, take your pick. He rotated the names on a continual basis, but the theme was the same—accepting an offer to work in Special Programs at Sandia National Laboratories had been a mistake.

After graduating summa cum laude with a degree in computer engineering from California Polytechnic State University in San Luis Obispo, he'd had his pick. And he'd chosen this lonely life of exile as an acceptable byproduct of clearing his conscience.

To his surprise, his phone vibrated almost immediately with the notification of a waiting message in Signal. He stopped walking, but a bump from the passenger behind him was enough to keep him moving.

"Let's go, Hayes."

Benjamin nodded. "Yeah, yeah. Hold your horses."

He tucked the phone back in his pocket and resumed his slow procession, giving every outward indication that he was just as bored and disinterested as he had been every other time his team landed at the Las Vegas airport. But this time his heart pounded with the sudden influx of adrenaline brought on by receiving a message from the only person who ever contacted him using Signal.

It all began when Benjamin had enrolled in a class on network security taught by one of the more popular teachers in the department. Benjamin quickly became enamored with David Wang and sought him out for career advice following graduation. Should he chase the money and go with one of the big offers? Or should he strike out on his own with a few classmates in a startup that gave him more control and had a huge upside?

But David surprised him and suggested an alternative. What if Benjamin did none of those things? What if he turned down the money to pursue something in research that gave him the opportunity to be on the cutting edge of technology—an opportunity to make a name for himself doing what others couldn't while satisfying his moral obligation to make the world a safer place?

Basically, Professor Wang had appealed to Benjamin's ego.

And ego carried the day.

At the front of the cabin, Benjamin turned left and descended the ladder on the left side of the plane, then stepped from the line of passengers walking across the tarmac to the waiting Boeing 737. He could hear the whine of the passenger jet's auxiliary power unit and knew its crew was already there and waiting on them to depart. He had limited time, but he couldn't depart Las Vegas for the electronic black hole without first finding out what his handler wanted. Their coded exchange earlier that day should have been their last communication.

Benjamin pulled out the phone again and quickly opened the Signal app.

Like most messages he received from his handler, it contained only a picture. But the subject of the picture was unimportant. What mattered was the metadata his handler had altered to convey her message. He saved the image to his phone, then opened his photos application and selected it. He tapped on the info icon and felt his stomach turn over when he deciphered the message.

At the top, the caption read, "DELIVER DRAGON LINE."

Immediately beneath that was a date and time that normally indicated when the picture had been taken. But that metadata had been altered too, and instead listed a date and time in the future.

Benjamin glanced at his watch.

Tomorrow?

The rest of the information indicated that the photo had been taken using an Apple iPhone 14 Plus Main Camera and delivered in High Efficiency Image Format. The remainder of the photograph's metadata—exposure, exposure bias, focal length, lens, and image size—was unimportant and unrelated to the message. But the map just beneath it pinpointed the location where his handler apparently wanted him to deliver the weapon.

He tapped on the map's thumbnail and pulled up a larger view of an airfield located northwest of the town of Gabbs—west of the Shoshone Mountains. It was only eighty miles in a straight line from where the Boeing passenger jet was preparing to take him. But it might as well have been on the moon for how impossible the task was.

Benjamin quickly switched back to Signal and tapped out a quick message: *UNABLE*.

The response was quicker than he expected, but even more pointed.

"Dammit," he muttered.

"You coming, Hayes?" a senior engineer asked when he saw Benjamin standing off to the side.

He heard the question but couldn't process its meaning. "Huh?"

Thomas paused his march and studied him. "You okay?"

The sudden show of concern snapped Benjamin out of his paralysis, and he looked up into the older man's eyes and nodded. "Oh, yeah. Sorry. Just got a text from my dad."

"Everything okay?"

If it wasn't for the fact that Benjamin just wanted Thomas to continue walking to the jet, he would have been thankful for the older man's genuine concern. He had always felt like an outsider since joining the team, but that simple act of compassion made him feel less alone.

And surprisingly guilty.

"Oh, yeah," he stammered. "He's just old."

Thomas gave him a funny look but kept walking. Although Benjamin was a proud American, he utterly despised the military-industrial complex and the companies who built weapons of war, then profited when politicians on their payroll took the nation to the brink. In his mind, diplomacy was dead. And the last thing he wanted was to be part of the problem.

"Dammit," he muttered again.

He tapped out another reply, unable to keep his disdain from dripping off each of the four letters: *FINE*.

He tucked the phone away and resumed his walk to the jet, eventually catching up to the line of passengers waiting to climb the Boeing's air stairs. When it was his turn, he turned off his phone and handed it to the attendant at the base of the stairs. What had originally almost been a deal-breaker in his employment with Sandia had become just another cost of doing business in the dark side of government contracting.

Their phones would remain in Las Vegas until after they returned from their short stint in the desert. But as he watched the attendant place his phone into the bin at her feet, he wondered if he would ever see it again. They were scheduled to return in five days, which was four days after he was supposed to deliver the weapon to his handler at the dirt airport in Gabbs.

What am I doing?

Benjamin pushed aside his communication with Mantis, just as he had done before every polygraph he had taken with the company. He buried each emotion that her message had evoked and took a deep breath before beginning his ascent into the passenger jet. With each step, he felt his stress and anxiety lessen as they were overtaken by a sense of purpose and adventure. After all, that purpose was the reason he had accepted Professor Wang's offer of recruitment.

Benjamin Hayes was an idealist who believed the United States had succeeded on the backs of other nations, just as the rich had done on the backs of the poor. Those who had amassed wealth had done so at the expense of men like his father—a man who had sacrificed everything for his son. Ending that disparity had become his purpose.

By the time Benjamin boarded the plane and found his seat, the only thing he could think about was stealing an experimental weapon from one of the most secure facilities on the planet and delivering it to an isolated dirt strip in the middle of nowhere. He had no clue how he was going to do it yet, but he would figure it out.

He didn't have a choice.

He had only one day.

23

Nugget Casino Resort
Sparks, Nevada

When Colt woke up from his nap, he felt like a new man. His mouth was dry—as much from the altitude and lack of humidity as from the drinking he had done the night before—but otherwise, he felt fine. He quickly showered and dressed in a pair of chinos and a gray button-down collared shirt from Pattern Ops featuring miniature FA-18 Hornets, stuffed his wallet and keys in his pocket, then left his room to face the music.

Riding down the elevator for the second time that morning was considerably less daunting than the first, and as Colt crossed the lobby for the cafe where Punky said he could find her, he wished that a hangover was the worst he'd have to contend with that morning. But a glance through the windows at the valet driveway on his right confirmed that it hadn't been just a bad dream.

Colt rounded the corner and saw Punky sitting at a table, staring into a coffee cup with a dazed expression. He sat down across from her and waved his hand in front of her face. "Earth to Punky."

She looked up but didn't appear startled. "Hey, Colt."

He had seen her drive a Corvette through the streets of San Diego to evade an SUV full of gunmen. He had seen her fly an experimental bush plane to an uninhabited island off the coast of California to take down a Chinese operative intent on sinking an aircraft carrier. And, just that morning, he had seen her confront a van full of AK-wielding gunmen with nothing but her service pistol.

This was out of character.

"You okay?"

She looked up at him, and her eyes immediately focused. "What if I told you I had an opportunity to dismantle the Ministry of State Security's West Coast network in one fell swoop?"

His interview and the lingering remains of his hangover forgotten, Colt leaned across the table. "I'd say it sounds too good to be true."

"Yeah, so would my dad."

"What's going on? Talk to me."

As if Punky suddenly realized they were sitting in a crowded cafe, she looked around and shook her head. "Not here."

"Okay. Where?"

"Let's go for a drive."

Without waiting for him, she got up from the table and began walking toward the casino's main entrance. He hesitated for only a few seconds, then got up and chased after her. Something definitely had Punky spooked, and Colt knew better than to try stopping her.

Despite the crystal-clear blue skies, it was surprisingly cool for late August in northwest Nevada. It was in the mid-seventies, and the weather forecasters expected it to remain dry and peak only in the mid to upper eighties for at least the next week. It was the perfect weather for driving with the top down, but Punky had led Colt away from his Bronco in the casino's garage to a government Suburban parked across the street. She gestured for him to climb inside, and he settled into the passenger seat as she put the SUV into gear and sped eastbound toward Interstate 80.

The Suburban was a far cry from the classic SUV Colt had modified with a three-and-a-half-inch suspension lift, front and rear sway bars, and fifteen-inch Pacer wheels wrapped in thirty-five-inch all-terrain tires. But the large Chevrolet SUV handled like a dream and hugged the road as Punky drove them into the hills east of Reno. He remained silent and waited for her to break the silence.

But after twenty minutes, Colt gave up. "Are you going to tell me what's going on? Or am I supposed to guess?"

Her eyes had been focused on the road in front of them, but she jerked her head in his direction before acknowledging his question. "Are you stationed in Fallon again?"

"Just moved back," he said.

"What's your job there?"

He opened his mouth to answer but hesitated. In his mind, he saw Master Chief Dave White leading him on a tour of the *Black Ponies'* hangar on the south end of the field, but he couldn't tell her about that. No matter what they had been through, the squadron was still classified, and his role in standing it up would have to remain a secret. "I'm on the staff at the Naval Aviation Warfighting Development Center."

She nodded, as if she knew exactly what that entailed. But she fell silent again.

"Punky, what the hell's going on?"

He glanced over at her and saw the creases in her forehead deepen with concern as she chewed on the inside of her lip. Just as Colt was about to demand she pull over and tell him what was going on, she answered.

"The man you saw abducted this morning was Marine Corporal Adam Garett, an Aviation Logistics Information Management Systems Specialist. He was assigned to VMFA-314 on the USS *Abraham Lincoln* while you were there."

"I thought I recognized him."

Punky took a deep breath before continuing. "But that's not all. Following the attack on the USS *Ronald Reagan*, I went to San Jose to conduct surveillance on a woman named Fu Zan."

Colt's heart beat faster at the mention of the *Reagan*.

"She claimed to be the grandmother of a little girl who was orphaned when we arrested her mother for being a spy."

"What happened to the girl's father?"

"The Chinese executed him for treason."

"Go on."

"I was watching Fu Zan's house when Corporal Garett showed up."

"What?" Colt shook his head as if to remind himself that this wasn't the opening act of a Mark Greaney novel.

"It seemed suspicious, at best. So, I began following him and witnessed him meeting with individuals I believed were agents of the Ministry of State Security—"

"Wait." Colt held up a hand. "So, you're saying this Marine—who was on the *Lincoln* at the same time as me—has met with people tied to Chinese intelligence? And you don't think he had anything to do with what happened to me?"

Instead of getting upset that he had cut her off, her face turned grim. "No, I *do* think he had something to do with it. We now believe that Corporal Garett is the spy we knew as *KMART*."

Colt's mouth fell open. Everything about the events surrounding the attack on the *Lincoln* came flooding back and filled him with a sense of despair. He had almost crashed into a guided missile cruiser and nearly shot down his best friend to prevent the unthinkable from happening. And the traitor had been under his nose all along.

"You can't be serious."

"There's more."

Colt shook his head in disbelief.

"Before you came downstairs, Fu Zan approached me—"

"At the casino?" His heart thundered in his chest, and he craned his neck to glance in the side-view mirror as if expecting an SUV full of Chinese gunmen to run them down. Owing to Punky's presence at the Nugget, he had already suspected the Ministry of State Security's involvement. But this was even worse than he had imagined.

"Yes, at the casino. She told me she runs the Ministry's West Coast network and that Corporal Garett is her son—"

His mouth fell open in surprise. "Her son?"

Punky remained silent but pulled the Suburban onto the shoulder and shifted into park.

"Who took him?" Colt asked.

She shook her head. "That's what I need to figure out."

Colt shifted in his seat and studied her. "Why do you need to figure it out? What's going on?"

"Fu Zan asked me to help get her son back. If I do, she'll turn herself in and give me everything I need to bring down the network she's spent decades building on the West Coast. This is the opportunity of a lifetime."

"So, what's the problem? What does your boss have to say about it?"

Punky flashed him a nervous look. "I haven't told him."

"Why not?"

"He'd never go for it." She paused. "But I can't do it alone."

Colt chewed on his lip as he considered the opportunity. It was way outside his wheelhouse, but they had been in some pretty tough situations before, and he knew he could trust the special agent's instincts. Punky was right. It was the opportunity of a lifetime. "I might have an idea."

24

The momentary elation Adam felt at successfully manipulating the watch to activate the locator beacon was blunted by the realization that it might have been a wasted effort. He knew Chen had disposed of him after getting what she needed, so it wasn't a stretch to think she might have lied to him about its utility. It might have been just a fantasy she used to placate him and keep him feeding her information.

And even if it was really a locator beacon, why would the Ministry lift a finger to help him? After they had reeled him back in and assigned a new handler to keep him under their constant control, Shi Yufei made it clear he was expendable. His value to the Chinese was only in what he could give them.

If they see the beacon, will they even care?

Adam knew it was a defeatist attitude, but he couldn't help himself. He had escaped San Diego and deserted the Marine Corps only to be shoved into a panel van at gunpoint, hogtied, and hooded. And he hadn't the faintest idea why.

"What do you want with me?"

His curiosity was rewarded with a boot to the back of his hooded head and a gruff reply. "Shut up."

He knew the Marine Corps wouldn't send a TRAP team aboard an MV-

22 Osprey to swoop in and rescue him from his kidnappers. His only hope was to believe what Chen had told him—even when everything else she had told him was a lie.

The *whoop whoop* of a siren behind the van halted his silent brooding, and the boot pressed him harder into the side of the van.

"Keep your mouth shut," his captor said.

"What do I do?" the driver asked.

"Pull over," a third man said. "But don't let him look in the back."

Adam felt the van slow and vibrate as it pulled off the road onto the shoulder. He still doubted the beacon was working as advertised, but maybe the Ministry had someone inside the police. Maybe this was what he had been hoping for all along.

I need to be ready.

As if reading his mind, his captor dug his boot deeper into Adam's back. "Don't. Move. A muscle," he breathed through gritted teeth.

Adam heard a car door open then shut, followed by the steady cadence of an officer walking alongside the van and approaching the driver's door. He heard a radio squawk briefly but couldn't make out the words.

As if the hood covering his head hadn't been enough, he suddenly felt a heavy wool blanket fall across his body as his captors attempted to keep him concealed from the police officer. Not that there was anything the officer could do about it. There were at least three men inside the van—all armed with automatic weapons—and Adam knew the officer was outgunned.

As the crunch of gravel stopped near the driver's door, Adam heard the electric whir of the window being lowered. "Afternoon, Officer."

"License and registration, please."

Adam wasn't sure, but he thought he detected a hint of fear in the officer's voice.

"Is there a problem?"

"Where you coming from?"

Adam tensed, worried that this line of questioning might lead his captors to assume the officer knew they had been at the Nugget Casino Resort. No matter how they answered, the question implied the officer thought they were guilty of something.

Please, just take their documents and call it in . . .

"Carson City," the driver replied. "Is there a problem?"

Adam felt the boot in his back ease up and heard shuffling as his captor inched closer to the rear of the van. He tried keeping his breathing calm, but the heavy blanket on top of the suffocating hood made him feel even more claustrophobic.

"Just a routine stop," the officer said. "Sit tight for me."

Adam almost whimpered with relief when the sound of footsteps retreated from the driver's door and back along the side of the van. He wanted to be rescued, but he knew that if the officer pressed them, it wouldn't go well for anyone. Most of all, him.

Suddenly, the footsteps stopped, and he heard what sounded like somebody touching the side of the van.

No. Keep going!

"What's he doing?"

"He's looking at something . . ."

"Shit," the man riding shotgun said. "He sees the bullet holes!"

Adam closed his eyes. In a matter of seconds, he knew his captors would spill out onto the street and gun down the unsuspecting police officer for being in the wrong place at the wrong time. And there wasn't a single thing he could do about it . . .

Wait.

His eyes snapped open.

Without hesitation, Adam jerked his body and kicked the side of the panel van as hard as he could. The sound reverberated through the interior, but his ears were trained beyond the thin metal wall and the sound of gravel scraping as the officer jumped back in surprise.

"What the . . ."

Adam listened to the officer's footsteps retreating at almost a jog, but the sounds coming from inside the van terrified him.

"Take him!"

The rear doors flew open, and Adam screamed when an AK-47 opened up and began spitting bullets at the police cruiser. He was frozen with fear by the chopping sound of automatic fire and the soft tinkling of spent cartridges bouncing across the metal floor.

When the police officer's service pistol barked and returned fire, both the driver's and passenger's doors flew open, bringing two more rifles to the gunfight.

What have I done?

Adam tucked his knees to his chest and curled into a ball as the firefight raged around him. When the AK-47 at the rear of the van went silent, he heard the shooter replace the empty magazine before dropping down onto the pavement. He heard the police officer shouting into his radio, but the words were drowned out by machine guns on either side of the van working their way back toward the police cruiser.

". . . officer down! I need—"

The officer's plea was cut short with one final burst of gunfire.

Then silence.

"Get back in the van," one of the men ordered.

Without objection, the others scampered back to their places, and the van rocked on its shocks as both the driver's and passenger's doors slammed shut. When the rear doors closed, Adam squeezed himself into a tight ball, knowing that it wouldn't take long for them to figure out what had happened. And when that happened, they would take it out on him.

The engine roared to life as the driver put the van into gear and sped away. Adam still had no idea where they were or where they were taking him, but he knew a police officer had just sacrificed himself to try stopping them. He had gotten a call out on the radio, but Adam wasn't holding out hope that the officer's pleas would result in his rescue.

He knew his reckless actions had probably doomed him.

On cue, his captor kicked him hard in the back of the head. "You idiot!"

"What happened?" the driver asked.

"He kicked the side and tipped off the cop."

"Now they'll be looking for us," the third man said. "We need to get off the road."

Adam still wasn't sure the beacon was working, but at least he'd given whoever came looking for him a place to start. Who that might be, and whether he'd live long enough to be rescued, was still up for debate.

What have I done?

25

Fernley, Nevada

A little over halfway between Reno and Fallon, Colt directed Punky to exit Interstate 80 in the town of Fernley and cut over to US-50. "You mentioned the attack on the *Reagan*. How did you know about that?"

Punky looked over at him and studied his face. For a moment, Colt thought she was going to deny any knowledge of it and recant her previous statement. But then she said, "That was you, wasn't it?"

His heart started pounding again. "Was *what* me?"

"Colt."

"What do you know about it, Punky?"

They had been through a lot together, but he wanted more reassurance.

She sighed before answering. "I was in San Diego, protecting a professor we thought was being targeted by the Chinese. They had killed her husband after he delivered secrets to one of our case officers . . ."

"Lisa," Colt said, remembering the battered woman who had been carried from the back of a Marine MV-22 Osprey to a waiting Agency Gulfstream business jet on the tarmac at Clark Air Base in the Philippines.

"So, that *was* you," Punky said.

Colt nodded. "I was on the Alert Five when the Chinese launched a pair of fighters and targeted our rescue forces. I was only doing my job."

Punky shook her head. "It was more than that. I read the full after-action report and know you shot down a Chinese fighter and helicopter before running out of gas. You could have saved yourself, but instead you went above and beyond to protect the rescue helicopter before punching out."

Colt shrugged. He knew others probably thought it was an incredible act of heroism, but he hadn't even considered the consequences. He knew what needed to be done, and he did it. To him, it was that simple. "Yeah, well, that's in the past now."

"Okay," Punky said. "So, what do we do about today?"

And that was the rub. No matter what they had done in the past, forces of evil continued to challenge the United States as a beacon of freedom in the world. This seemed like an opportunity that they couldn't ignore.

He pulled out his cell phone. "I have no idea how we're going to find a kidnapped Marine in the middle of the Nevada desert, but I know someone who might."

"Who are you calling?"

Colt scrolled through his list of contacts before selecting one, then brought the phone to his ear.

"Flyboy!"

"You still at work?"

"The skipper and I just finished briefing our flight. We're walking in about forty-five minutes. What's going on?"

Colt knew the time between briefing a mission and walking out to the aircraft was sacred to aircrew, and he didn't want to disrupt the Master Chief's rhythm. But he didn't know where else to go. "I'm on my way to the hangar. Can you let me in?"

"Aren't you supposed to be enjoying Tailhook or something?"

"Trust me, Master Chief, you'll want to hear this."

Dave chuckled. "I can't promise how much time I'll have for you. But call me when you're pulling into the parking lot, and I'll come let you in."

"Thanks, Dave." Colt ended the call and turned to Punky. "I'm going to introduce you to someone who might be able to help us with this."

"Who?"

"You'll see."

A few minutes later, Punky rounded the bend in Carson Road and steered the Suburban east toward Hangar 7. She had remained mostly quiet for the rest of the drive, but Colt could tell she was getting anxious to see who he planned on introducing her to.

"Where we going, Colt?"

At the end of the road, he pointed her north toward the flight line. "You'll see."

Punky gripped the steering wheel with both hands but angled her face away from him to demonstrate her perturbance. He almost chuckled at what he thought was an overtly feminine trait, but then remembered her competency with a pistol and willingness to use violence in solving problems.

As she made her way to the parking lot where Dave had taken him the day before, Colt pulled out his phone and placed the call.

"Took you long enough."

"We're almost there," Colt said, glancing across at Punky, who still seemed miffed.

"We?" Dave's naturally playful tone took a serious turn. "Who's with you?"

"You'll see."

Punky turned and fired daggers at him with her eyes. Apparently, it hadn't been lost on her that he had answered both their questions the same way. And it hadn't been lost on him that she was none too pleased about it.

But Dave only sighed on the other end. "I'll be right there."

When the line went dead, Colt tucked the phone back into his pocket and pointed to a spot in the parking lot closest to a turnstile set into the fence.

"Park there."

She did so, then shifted into park and set the parking brake before twisting the key to kill the engine. "What now?"

Colt shifted in his seat to face her. "There's something I need to tell you . . ."

"Flyboy!"

He closed his eyes and shook his head when he heard the SEAL's baritone voice carry across the tarmac.

"Is *he* the something you needed to tell me?" Punky asked.

Colt nodded. "Come on."

He opened the door and climbed down from the government SUV, then turned to see Punky staring through the chain-link fence at the bearded SEAL wearing a two-piece khaki flight suit.

"Whitey?"

"Punky?"

Colt looked up and saw a shocked expression on the Master Chief's face. "You two know each other?"

Dave pushed through the turnstile and walked up to Punky, then wrapped her in a massive bear hug. When he let go a few moments later, they looked at each other as if Colt wasn't even standing there. But he took it upon himself to make introductions anyway. "Dave, this is Punky . . ."

"Yeah, I know who she is. I've known her since . . . when? Middle school?"

Colt's eyes widened. "You went to school together?"

Punky laughed. "God, no! I'm not that old."

"Hey," Dave said, giving her a playful shove.

She shoved him back. "Whitey was a new guy in my dad's platoon at Team One."

"He was always bringing her around, and she pretty much became the platoon mascot." He turned to her with a somber expression. "I was sorry to hear about your dad. He was one of the finest."

"Long live the brotherhood," she said.

"Now, what are you doing mixed up with a guy like this? You know he crashes planes for a living, right?"

"Hey, you're the one who asked for me. Remember?" Colt tried to look like his feelings were hurt, but he knew Dave was only busting his chops. It had been a staple in their relationship since the very first time they met.

As if remembering that Colt had important news to deliver, Dave turned serious. "So, what's got your panties twisted?" He glanced at Punky. "Sorry, no offense."

"None taken," she said.

"Punky is a special agent with the Naval Criminal Investigative Service now. She and I have a history of running into Chinese spies together."

Dave gave her a skeptical once-over. "Was she involved in that one thing?"

"And the one before," Colt said.

"You know I'm right here," she said. "And I'd much rather talk about our latest run-in with them."

"When was that?" Dave asked.

"This morning."

26

Hangar 7
Naval Air Station Fallon
Fallon, Nevada

"I think you'd better start from the beginning," Dave said.

Colt looked to Punky for guidance on how to proceed, but she opted for the frontal assault. "The son of a senior Chinese intelligence operative was kidnapped this morning in Reno. That operative—code-named Mantis—approached me and offered to hand over her entire network if I help rescue her son."

Dave looked from Punky to Colt and back. The expression on his face said it all, and Colt didn't blame the SEAL for thinking the pair had lost their marbles. The situation was borderline insane. But given that Colt always seemed to find himself smack in the middle of one outlandish plot or another, Dave appeared to accept her statement at face value.

"Who has him?"

Punky shook her head. "We don't know."

"Where is he?"

"We don't know that either."

"Well, what *do* you know?"

"Not much."

Dave tilted his chin upward and let out an exasperated sigh, then pulled out his access card and swiped it against the control panel set into the turn-stile. He entered his four-digit PIN, waited for the light to turn green, then gestured for Punky to walk through. "Let's get you inside."

He repeated the process for Colt, then followed them onto the flight line before leading them to the hangar. After walking inside and coming face-to-face with the large *Black Ponies* mural, Dave guided them upstairs to a room furnished with a large conference table and several smaller couches and chairs set against the walls.

Colt took his time circling the room and looking at pictures showing OV-10 Broncos engaged in combat operations in Vietnam. Though he knew the history of the squadron and had already seen the mural and the plane in the hangar, Colt hadn't completely grasped what it meant to be part of such a lineage until that moment. He hadn't appreciated the gravity of the task they had entrusted to him.

Colt turned back to the center of the room where Punky sat in a chair at the conference table. Dave stood off to one side and glanced at his watch. "The skipper's waiting for me in the paraloft. Can I trust that you two will stay put until I get back?"

"Does that mean you're willing to help us find him?" Punky asked.

Dave shook his head. "I'm not making any promises. You don't know who has him or even where he is."

Punky rolled her eyes. "He was taken in broad daylight this morning at the Nugget in Reno."

"Which means he could be anywhere by now."

But Colt had a solution for that. "If only we had a plane purpose-built for intelligence, surveillance, and reconnaissance."

Dave leveled his gaze on Colt and shook his head. "No way, flyboy."

"Hear me out," Colt said. "I know some of the SIGINT equipment that was used during *Combat Dragon II* to find and track high-value targets down range—"

"We've got the improved versions on our birds," Dave said, confirming what he suspected. "But you know as well as I do that he's probably already dead. These things don't always pan out the way they do in the movies."

"But if we can find him—"

"Then what?" Until that moment, Dave's tone had been amused, as if he had only been humoring them. But it suddenly turned serious. "Listen, I know what this opportunity means to you—and, believe me, I'm all for taking down the bad guys—but this isn't something we can do without higher approval. There are rules about this."

"So, ask the skipper," Colt suggested.

Dave took a deep breath. "Just hang tight, flyboy. Wait for me to get back, and we can talk to the skipper together. I can't make any promises, but maybe he'll have a better idea how to go about this."

Colt didn't want to give up the fight so easily, but he didn't see that they had much of a choice. "We'll be here."

Punky watched the Navy SEAL Master Chief walk through the door, leaving them alone in the ready room. But whereas the Navy pilot seemed relaxed and at home in the space, she was uptight and unable to remain still. She popped to her feet and walked to the corner of the room where a wraparound desk had been constructed on a dais.

"What's this?"

Colt ambled across the room and stepped up onto the low platform to study the array of equipment stacked underneath the desk. "This is where the duty officer sits," he said. "At least in a normal squadron."

"I didn't know Navy SEALs flew in airplanes."

"They normally don't."

"What kind of squadron is this?"

He sighed. "The kind most people don't know about. Including me, until yesterday."

Punky cocked her head to the side. "What do you mean?"

While Colt fiddled with what looked like a portable radio of some kind, she stepped back and studied the photographs on the wall. It was apparent from the black-and-white and grainy colored photographs that the unit had a storied history, but the room had the look and feel of a brand-new car. It was the kind of juxtaposition that could only exist in an organization like the Navy.

Colt responded without looking at her. "Meaning that the existence of the squadron is a secret. But the Master Chief gave me his recruiting pitch yesterday."

"So, you're not at NAWDC?"

Colt's head popped up above the edge of the raised desk. "Officially?"

She shook her head. "Nevermind." A small speaker set atop the desk crackled to life with a warm static as Colt continued adjusting the radio's controls. "What are you doing?"

"If we have to sit here and wait until they get back, we might as well listen in on their flight's communications."

"Is that like a pilot thing?"

Colt shrugged.

"Whatever. Listen, I know you think Whitey's going to be able to help us, but I can't just sit here and hope for that. The clock is ticking on finding KMART, and if I don't come through for Mantis, I lose out on a major opportunity to take down their entire network."

"What's she doing while you're out looking for her son?"

Punky reached into her pocket and removed the cell phone the Chinese spymaster had given her, then unlocked it to check for missed calls or text messages. She cursed inwardly when she saw that she had neither. "I don't know."

"Don't you think she's already out there using her resources to find him?"

"I guess so. But I can't just sit and wait for her to do all the work."

The volume of the static changed as Colt fine-tuned the radio's receiver. "Yeah, I get it. You're only comfortable when you're solving the mystery and putting bad guys in the dirt."

"Or behind bars," she corrected.

"Just like I belong at the controls of a fighter jet and not sitting behind a duty desk while others go flying instead."

"Touché."

"So, use that investigator brain of yours and figure out where our kidnapped Marine might be."

Punky dropped back into the chair at the head of the conference table and closed her eyes. "You heard Whitey. He could be anywhere by now."

"Okay, so then just narrow it down to a smaller area."

"How?"

Colt stopped fidgeting with the radio and stepped out from behind the duty desk to join her at the conference table. "Well, when I punched out in the South China Sea, I had no idea how they'd find me. That's a huge area."

"How did they?"

"The Marine Osprey homed in on my emergency beacon—"

"Your what?"

"My beacon."

"If Corporal Garett really does work for the Ministry of State Security, then maybe they equipped him with one too," Punky mused.

"Do you think that's possible?"

Punky knew the Ministry employed state-of-the-art electronics for communications and data collection, but she didn't know the first thing about radio frequencies. She pulled out the cell phone Mantis had given her and dialed the only number listed in the contacts.

"Let's find out, shall we?"

27

Tonopah Test Range Airport
Tonopah, Nevada

Benjamin opened his eyes when the Boeing 737's main wheels touched down on the concrete runway. He gripped his armrests and tensed when the autobrakes engaged, and the pilot activated the thrust reversers. The passenger jet quickly slowed and rolled to the end of the 12,000-foot concrete runway.

Landing at the airport known to many as "Area 52" had lost some of its luster after his third or fourth trip, and it didn't have the same aura as its more famous cousin to the southeast near Groom Lake. Still, the airport had a rich history in the world of classified and covered aviation programs. In 1977, the Tactical Air Command established the 4477th Test and Evaluation Flight to assume the personnel and equipment of an undesignated unit at Groom Lake before moving the program to Tonopah.

For over a decade under a program code-named *Constant Peg*, the pilots of the 4477th TEF flew various models of Soviet-designed MiGs, including the MiG-17, MiG-21, MiG-23, and Shenyang J-6—the Chinese license-built version of the MiG-19. They exploited the capabilities of these aircraft and flew more than 15,000 sorties, providing dissimilar aggressor training in the Nevada desert.

But the US MiGs weren't the only secret aircraft operating in the northern reaches of the Tonopah Test Range.

Benjamin looked through the window on the left side of the plane as it turned onto a taxiway and saw rows of white canopies surrounded by security fencing. He knew the Air Force parked planes there that they wanted to keep hidden from the prying eyes of foreign satellites.

Thomas leaned over the seat in front of him. "We're not gonna have time to get settled at Mancamp, so just drop your gear in your room and meet out front."

Benjamin grimaced. He knew that meant the test directors had opted for expediency over secrecy and decided to run their tests in broad daylight. What that meant for his ability to steal the *DRAGON LINE* after the test and deliver it to Gabbs remained somewhat of a mystery to him.

"Did you hear me?" Thomas asked.

He glanced up at the senior engineer and nodded. "Yeah, I heard you. I'll be ready."

The plane came to a stop, and Benjamin heard the engines winding down as the pilots shut down in preparation to deplane their passengers. From experience, he knew there would be a bus already waiting to deliver them to their "home away from home" six and a half miles north of the airfield. Known as Mancamp, the compound contained fifty twin-level dormitories, an Olympic-size indoor pool, tennis courts, softball fields, and a recreation center with a bar, library, game room, and weight room.

It made living in the desert for days at a time at least somewhat bearable.

With the air stairs in place at the forward boarding door, the passengers began making their way to the front of the plane to disembark. Benjamin snatched his duffel from the overhead bin and followed the rest of his team out into the brilliant Nevada sunlight. He looked left toward the runway and saw the distinctive V-shaped tail of the airfield's other notorious resident—the F-117 Nighthawk.

"Come on, Hayes," said a voice behind him. "Keep it moving."

Based on the *Have Blue* technology demonstrator, the F-117 Nighthawk was developed by Lockheed's secretive Skunk Works division and gained notoriety for its combat use during Operation Desert Storm in 1991. Following the Gulf War, the Tonopah squadrons were transferred to Holloman Air Force Base in New Mexico until the platform's retirement in 2008.

Benjamin ambled down the steps as the first stealth fighter's General Electric turbofan engines roared to life and propelled the jet down the runway. Ten seconds later, the second stealth fighter began its takeoff roll, and Benjamin was momentarily transfixed. Though officially retired, he had yet to visit Tonopah without seeing one of the iconic fighters take flight. He just wished he knew what they were doing.

As the two jets disappeared into the distance, Benjamin followed the crowd to the waiting school bus and climbed aboard for the final leg of his journey. The trip had started with a short drive from his apartment in Livermore to the local municipal airport, and it would end with an equally short drive from a secretive airfield within Restricted Area 4809 to a temporary lodging facility.

But that's when the real work would begin.

He flopped down into a vinyl bench seat and tried ignoring the idle chatter surrounding him as the rest of his teammates geared up for the looming test. But his preference for blessed silence went unacknowledged as the bus pulled out of the parking lot and made its way north toward Mancamp.

"There she is," Thomas said, reaching forward to smack Benjamin on the shoulder.

He turned and saw what the senior engineer was referring to—an eight-wheeled Stryker armored vehicle that normally carried nine soldiers and a variety of turret-mounted weapons. But this one was different.

"The *DRAGON LINE*."

Previous versions of Strykers had been fitted with directed energy weapons in the 50-kilowatt class. Companies like Lockheed Martin and Raytheon had fielded smaller laser weapons for short-range air defense against smaller targets like drones or mortar rounds. But *DRAGON LINE* was the first to be armed with a 100-kilowatt class laser, capable of taking down larger targets at greater range.

"Yep. There she is," Benjamin replied, not feeling the same excitement as his peer.

The two men watched the idling Stryker retreat in the distance as they left the isolated airfield and headed north for the even more isolated living compound. Benjamin wasn't looking forward to spending any more time in the desert than he absolutely had to, but he'd be lying if he said he wasn't excited about the upcoming test.

"Think it'll work?"

Benjamin nodded. "I know it will."

There were few things in life of which he was absolutely certain, but his ability to modify the beam control system to account for atmospheric variations in temperature and density was one of them. It was ironic that the Chinese had recruited him to steal plans for a weapon that would have been completely worthless without his contribution.

Of course, now they wanted him to steal the weapon itself.

Thomas removed his thick glasses and used a microfiber cloth to clean them. "How can you be so sure? There's a lot riding on this test."

The project was well behind schedule, but Benjamin knew this would be the final test. After this, the *DRAGON LINE* would be ready for full-scale production if the warmongers in DC decided they wanted to bring yet another expensive weapon system online. That it was designed as a purely defensive weapon made it only slightly less repulsive in his mind.

Thomas moved to place his glasses back on his face, but Benjamin snatched them away and held them up to the window.

"Can you see without these?"

"Give them back." Thomas reached for his glasses, but Benjamin kept them just out of reach.

"You need glasses because of a refractive error that blurs your vision," Benjamin said, squinting through the glasses. "But how do you know what lenses will correct it?"

"I have a prescription," Thomas replied.

Benjamin handed the senior engineer his glasses back. "Well, now the *DRAGON LINE* has a prescription too."

"What do you mean?"

Benjamin inhaled deeply, trying not to get frustrated with the other engineer. Thomas's role on the project was ensuring an adequate constant power supply to the laser, so it wasn't unsurprising he didn't understand all that went into converting that power into directed energy that could be used to bring down a target aircraft. But it still annoyed him that he had to explain the genius behind his design.

"Just like you need those glasses to correct your vision, I figured out the prescription of the atmosphere to pre-distort the laser beam and programmed the beam control system to account for that. Now, as the beam propagates through the air, the atmosphere will counter the distortion and reach the target precisely."

"To what degree of certainty?"

That question was largely academic, but Benjamin answered anyway. "Complete."

Thomas eyed him skeptically.

"Imagine shooting a beach ball off the top of the Empire State Building from the San Francisco Bay Bridge."

The older engineer was quiet for a moment, then turned to face the front of the bus. "I hope you're right."

28

Reno, Nevada

Mantis looked at the clock on the Tesla's large central screen and knew her asset had arrived at Tonopah. With the wheels already in motion and no way of reaching him, she knew it was up to her to bring this all together. But if the NCIS special agent managed to come through for her, it might not even be necessary.

Then, as if she had somehow summoned the dark-haired special agent, the number for the burner phone she had given her appeared on the screen. She reached up and tapped on it to answer.

"Hello?"

"Fu Zan?"

The woman's voice had a trace of hope in it, and Mantis closed her eyes to picture her son's face. Not as she had last seen it, after already learning that her husband had allowed Chen to recruit their only son. But as it had been before he left home for the Marine Corps. He had been young and innocent and still looked at her with awe and wonder. She wanted more than anything for him to look at her in that way again.

But she knew it would probably never happen.

"Yes?"

"I don't know how to ask you this . . ."

Her heart suddenly pounded harder inside her chest. "Just ask."

The woman on the other end was silent for a moment, as if struggling to frame her query. Mantis grew impatient but was unwilling to break the spell, fearful of what the next few seconds might bring.

At last, the special agent spoke. "Are your assets given any form of personal locator beacon in the event they find themselves in distress?"

She inhaled sharply. Her first instinct was to deny the existence of any such beacons, knowing that if she unveiled those details, it would jeopardize the anonymity of hundreds of agents who placed their faith in the Ministry of State Security. But then she remembered she had already offered to provide the Americans with everything they needed to uncover their identities, making the secrecy of their beacons irrelevant.

Still, decades of lies and deceit were hard to overcome. "Such a device might exist."

"In the United States, average citizens can purchase personal locator beacons and register them in the NOAA SARSAT database so that their specific unit's distress signal is associated with vital personal information—like name, address, contact phone numbers—"

"I've heard of such things," Mantis said, though she didn't add that the Ministry had something similar to the National Oceanic and Atmospheric Administration Search and Rescue Satellite database. "But I cannot confirm that our agents have such a device."

The woman on the other end sounded frustrated. "Of course not. But maybe you'll look into it if you're serious about finding your son."

The call ended before Mantis could reply.

———

The panel van skidded to a halt not long after fleeing the gunfight, and Adam slid across the metal floor before his captor's boot pressed into him and pinned him in place. The movement torqued his shoulder, but he clamped his mouth shut to avoid crying out in pain. He knew they weren't happy with him for making noise and warning the police officer, and the only thing he could now do was remain quiet and compliant, and hope for the best.

The side door opened, and Adam tensed. He still didn't know why they had taken him, but he could only assume it had something to do with the work he had done for the Chinese. Over the soft puttering of the van's diesel engine, he heard a man outside issue a command in a language he didn't recognize.

Is he talking to me?

Fear gripped him as he waited to see if they would punish him for not answering. Sweat trickled down the side of his face, and he licked his lips while straining to hear anything else that might clue him in on his location. He heard the faint whistling of wind, the crunch of gravel under a heavy foot, and nothing else. Only his own heartbeat and quick, shallow breathing.

The man said something to him again. This time, more urgent.

"What?" Adam asked. "I don't understand."

Suddenly, a hand clamped down on his ankle and yanked hard. His body spun ninety degrees until his feet pointed at the door, then another hand joined the first and pulled him toward the opening. He barely had time to brace himself before he cleared the van and fell to the ground. His head slammed into the rocky ground, and he champed down on his tongue.

As the warm taste of metal filled his mouth, he felt even more hands descending on him, rolling him onto his back and pressing down on him.

"I'm sorry," he said.

Snip.

He felt the zip tie binding his ankles together break apart, but his captors' complete control over his every movement stymied his freedom. They ripped off his shoes, then his socks, and he heard them falling to the ground as if they had been tossed haphazardly to the side. He knew what was coming— Chen had prepared him for this—but it didn't help to ease his fears.

A pair of hands unbuttoned his fly and yanked downward, ripping his underwear and pants down his legs until he was left naked from the waist down. Under the hood, he pinched his eyes shut as if to stave off the embarrassment and barely noticed the sharp edges of rocks digging into his buttocks and legs.

After stripping his lower half, they rolled him onto his stomach. He couldn't stop himself from picturing the burly men violating him in the most barbaric manner, and he clenched his butt cheeks together and let out a whimper. The men encircling him laughed.

Snip. They cut the zip tie holding his wrists together.

His momentary reprieve from the fear of being raped was erased when he felt them undo his watch's clasp and yank it from his wrist.

Please keep it, he thought, hopeful they wouldn't want to throw away something of value. *Just put it in your pocket.*

But he heard what sounded like metal and glass impacting the ground a few feet away as his silent plea went unanswered.

Not wanting to remove the hood, they sliced the back of his shirt with a knife, then gripped his shoulders and pulled him up into a kneeling position. His torn shirt fell away, leaving him completely naked and more vulnerable than he had ever felt before.

His one hope of being rescued had just been stripped of him, along with the rest of his clothes and his dignity.

Dignity.

The thought made him want to laugh. He had tossed aside his dignity for the mere crumbs Chen had thrown his way. And now he was only getting what he deserved. He had expected life in prison in a federal penitentiary, but he thought being shot in the head and left as carrion in the Nevada desert was even more appropriate.

"I'm sorry," he said.

Then, he started crying.

His captors laughed when his bladder let loose, but he didn't care. He barely noticed when they yanked his arms behind his back and affixed another zip tie to his wrists before jerking him to his feet and pushing him face-first into the panel van. They shoved his legs inside, then slammed the door shut on his misery.

He was still alive. But without the beacon, he might as well be dead.

Reno, Nevada

Mantis glared at the Tesla's screen, chaffed by the woman's impetuous insinuation that she was withholding information from her. Of course, she was. But she didn't need to be reminded of that fact by an American law enforcement officer.

The woman's suggestion had merit, and she was somewhat surprised she hadn't thought of it first. Of course, she didn't know if Chen had even issued Adam a beacon he could use in the event he became captured or otherwise compromised. She had never wanted her son to become ensnared in a world of espionage and adept at tradecraft.

But now she hoped for the opposite.

Mantis hesitated for only a second more before placing an encrypted call to the regional operational center. A man's quiet voice answered after only one ring. "Authenticate."

"Mandate of Heaven," she said.

"Go ahead, ma'am."

"Are you receiving any distress signals on our satellite network?"

"Stand by," the voice replied.

She already had enough on her plate without giving in to hope that her son had somehow managed to activate a Ministry beacon that could lead her right to him. The last thing she wanted was to commit resources to something that would most likely turn out to be nothing but a wild goose chase. But, like it or not, the NCIS special agent's suggestion was her best bet at finding her son.

Right now, it was her only bet.

The voice returned. "There is a faint signal that just began broadcasting not too long ago."

"Do we have any assets unaccounted for in the area?"

There was a pause as the watch officer ran a correlated search. "No, ma'am."

It's him!

But she took a deep breath before responding. "Where's it coming from?"

"Ten miles south of Middlegate, Nevada."

This time, no amount of deep breathing or mindfulness could stop her heart from bolting with hope. She had no idea where Middlegate was, but she didn't think it was a coincidence. "How far is that from Reno?"

The watch officer hesitated. "Ma'am?"

"How *far*?"

She heard the rapid clicking of a keyboard in the background as the duty officer raced to find the information. "A little over one hundred miles," he said, his voice now hesitant and confused.

"Send me the frequency and current location immediately," she said. "And call me back if it moves or goes silent."

"Yes—"

She hung up before he could finish acknowledging her order.

A cascade of emotions descended on her as she considered the possibility. She didn't have any assets available to task with converging on the beacon's signal.

"Dammit!"

That meant it was up to her.

Mantis manipulated the map on the large screen in the middle of the Tesla's dash and tapped in Middlegate as the destination to let the navigation system provide guidance. She blanched when she saw the estimated time of arrival nearly two hours in the future—two hours Adam didn't have.

She swiped up on the side of the touchscreen and shifted the Model X into drive. She guided the electric SUV onto Interstate 80 and raced east away from Reno, hoping she was racing toward her son. Only then did she return the special agent's call.

29

Navy SEAL Chief Todd Lawson stepped out from behind the wheel of the Flyer 60 Advanced Light Strike Vehicle and shivered as he sighted through his rifle's ACOG at the target complex sprawling westward into Dixie Valley. It was at least ten degrees colder than it had been when they left the base several hours earlier.

"Should've brought a heavier jacket," he muttered.

Behind him, the external speaker mounted to the tubular roll cage squawked to life. "Mariner Nine, Pony One."

Todd lowered his rifle and turned back to the ground mobility vehicle just as Ron Parker pressed the push-to-talk to reply. "Pony One, this is Mariner Nine. Go ahead with your check-in."

"It's go time, boys," Todd said.

"Good," Graham McCarthy said from the rear seat. "Let's get this over with. I can already taste that burger."

Todd glanced at the third SEAL and shook his head. "Is that all you ever think about?"

His rebuttal was interrupted by the pilot who proceeded to deliver his check-in using the mnemonic *M-N Poppa*. "Mission number nine nine six. Single A-29. North ten at angels ten. Two by ELGTRs, code one six eight eight. Three zero minutes playtime. MX-15 multi-spectral sensor pod. Abort in the clear."

"The skipper doesn't sound like he's fucking around," Graham said.

"Yeah, so get your butt up there and be ready to lase this target for him."

Ron ignored the irreverent chatter as he copied down the pertinent data on the tablet resting in front of him. All three SEALs were qualified Joint Terminal Attack Controllers, but he was in the hot seat for the morning's evolution and wanted to give the squadron's commanding officer the best control possible. "Good copy, Pony One. Say when ready for situation update."

"Pony One, ready to copy."

Just like the check-in, the situation update used the standard mnemonic, *T-T Fac O-R*, and Ron delivered it with practiced precision. "Current surface-to-air threat is man portable air defense systems unlocated within the AO. Target is light armored company attempting to flank us to the south and two companies dug in six klicks to our west, break." He paused to give the skipper a chance to absorb the information. "Friendlies are a recon element on the high ground east of the one eighteen decimal two zero westing in the vicinity of Fairview Peak, negative artillery, break." Again, Ron paused. "Mariner nine has control. Plan on using your ELGTRs to disrupt the light armor. Winds on the deck are ten knots out of the west. Mariner is laser and IR capable. Advise when ready for game plan."

Over Ron's transmission, Todd began to make out the sound of a turboprop in the distance, and he scanned the horizon to the north for the dark gray airplane that would be executing the attack.

Pony 1
A-29 Super Tucano
Fallon South 1 Military Operations Area

Commander Andy "Freaq" Wood adjusted the Super Tucano's angle of bank as he orbited a piece of land ten miles north of the target complex east of Fallon. He glanced south toward the eight-thousand-foot peak in the Clan Alpine Mountains but couldn't see his SEALs on the ground.

"Your boys ready for this, Master Chief?"

"Easy day, skipper."

He keyed the microphone switch to transmit. "Mariner Nine, Pony One is ready for game plan."

"Deploying the turret," Dave said from the back seat.

"Roger."

The WESCAM MX-15 multi-sensor, multi-spectral targeting pod descended from the fuselage, and Dave quickly gained control and centered it on the airfield complex within the Bravo-17 light inert area. Constructed from plowed dirt and shipping containers, the "airfield" consisted of two runways, a parking apron, and hardened aircraft shelters on the north and south ends of the six-thousand-foot runway.

"Pony One, Type one, bomb on target. Advise when ready for nine-line."

Freaq grinned at the clinical efficiency of the SEAL on the other end of the radio. To the former Hog driver, the scripted back-and-forth between JTAC and attack pilot sounded like a beautiful duet. Like Sonny and Cher. Or Kenny Rogers and Dolly Parton. It was a love song with devastating results.

"Ready for nine-line," he replied.

There was a slight delay as the SEAL on the other end prepared to deliver the standard close air support brief. "IP Baltimore. Heading one eight zero. Offset east. One zero nautical miles." Pause. "Four four three zero feet. Light armored vehicles. North three nine degrees, one three decimal seven one six five minutes. West one one eight degrees, one four decimal four two six nine minutes." Pause. "Mariner nine will provide laser, code one six eight eight. East six thousand. Egress north to Baltimore above ten." Pause. "Laser target line two three zero degrees. Readback lines four, six, and restrictions."

Freaq finished copying the relayed information onto his kneeboard card before replying. "Standby."

"Got it," Dave said from the back seat.

Suddenly, the image on the right screen shifted as the SEAL Master Chief slaved their sensor pod to the coordinates that were passed to them. He cycled between electro-optical and infrared modes to make out the row of target vehicles arrayed to the southeast of the airfield complex. Freaq grinned again, feeling right at home at the controls of an attack aircraft poised to rain hate down on the enemy.

He keyed the microphone to read back the target elevation, coordinates, and restrictions. "Mariner Nine, Pony One copies four four three zero feet. North three nine degrees, one three decimal seven one six five minutes. West one one eight degrees, one four decimal four two six nine minutes. Laser target line two three zero degrees."

The reply was immediate. "Pony One, Mariner Nine good copy. Call when Baltimore inbound."

***

Bravo-17
Fallon Range Training Complex
Fallon, Nevada

"You ready up there?" Ron asked.

Graham sat in the Flyer's gunner's seat where the team's AN/PED-1 Lightweight Laser Designator Rangefinder, or LLDR, was mounted to the vehicle. He panned and tilted the device until it was aimed at the mock convoy located on the valley floor beneath them. "Good to go," he said.

Todd lifted his rifle and sighted through the ACOG again, eager to see how their squadron's new toy performed. Granted, the tactical situation was static with ideal conditions, but he was still excited about the possibilities of what a dedicated light attack squadron could do for Naval Special

Warfare. He sighted in the lead vehicle in the convoy just as the speaker squawked again.

"Pony One, Baltimore inbound."

"Pony One, continue," Ron replied.

Todd risked a glance over his shoulder and saw Graham's face pressed against the latest version of the LLDR. In a real-world engagement, they would have put down covering fire to give Graham some breathing room to keep his focus on the device that would guide the Super Tucano's bomb to the target. But now all he had to do was validate their tactics and sign off the SEAL as a current and qualified JTAC.

"Pony One, in heading one nine zero."

Todd returned his focus to the convoy in the valley as Ron stared into the sky north of their position to spot the attacking turboprop. "Pony One, cleared hot."

"Pony One, op away, time of fall thirty seconds."

"Mariner Nine," Ron replied.

"My stomach is growling," Graham said.

"Don't you fuck this up," Ron said. "I don't want to have to come in on Sunday too."

"Relax, boss. I'm ready."

The sound of the turboprop grew louder as it screamed high above their heads and hurtled an Enhanced Laser Guided Training Round at the lead vehicle in the target convoy.

"Pony One, ten seconds."

"Ten seconds," Ron echoed.

"Laser on."

Graham's hunger apparently forgotten, he shouted, "Lasing one six eight eight."

Ron echoed his call to their skipper in the attacking aircraft, "Mariner Nine, lasing one six eight eight."

Todd again sighted through the ACOG as he counted down the final ten seconds in his head. He shivered when a gust of wind cut through his thin thermal layer and again lamented his decision to leave the heavier GORE-TEX parka back at the squadron.

Thump.

Though the ELGTR was designed to mimic the performance of the Paveway II Laser Guided Bomb, the ninety-pound training round had a disappointingly small impact that only showered the lead truck with dirt. But had it been a real five-hundred-pound bomb, the target vehicle would have been totally destroyed.

"Direct hit," Ron said.

"Pony One, off safe," the pilot replied.

"Pony One, proceed Baltimore and reset."

"Great," Graham said. "Can we go get that burger now?"

30

Antelope Lake
Ten miles southeast of Tonopah Test Range Airport

"Alright folks, look alive," the test director said.

Benjamin groaned and set his worn paperback copy of Tom Clancy's *The Cardinal of the Kremlin* onto the workstation in front of him. The book had been published before he was even born and reminded him that the idea of using lasers in combat wasn't a new undertaking. But while the novel prominently featured the Strategic Defense Initiative—otherwise known as *Star Wars*—the real-world program had failed to produce technology that rendered nuclear weapons obsolete.

But research in directed energy weapons continued throughout the 1990s and beyond.

In 2003, the Army deployed a specially configured Humvee to Afghanistan to counter the threat of improvised explosive devices. The system, known as the High-Energy Laser Ordnance Negation System, or HLONS, used a laser named *Zeus* to destroy more than two hundred objects. Despite the challenges associated with using lasers in cloudy, dusty, or similarly obscured conditions, federally funded research labs continued evolving the technology to develop a weapon that could be consistently deployed.

"Target track one zero six four, bearing one nine zero for sixty, thirty-nine thousand feet," the operator two stations to his left said.

Benjamin brought up a screen showing the radar picture of the airspace surrounding them, provided by datalink from an orbiting E-3 Sentry on loan from the 966th Airborne Air Control Squadron at Tinker Air Force Base in Oklahoma. Not surprisingly, the air picture surrounding the Tonopah Test Range was clear. All commercial traffic remained north and west of them on approved jet routes.

He hooked the target with his cursor to bring up additional information on the target. The Beechcraft MQM-107 Streaker was designed as a reusable, turbojet-powered, target-towing drone that had been used in various surface-to-air and air-to-air missile tests, including the FIM-92 Stinger, MIM-104 Patriot, AIM-9 Sidewinder, and AIM-120 AMRAAM. For this test, the drone had been launched from Groom Lake and was being controlled remotely to represent the flight profile of a tactical strike aircraft.

"Four hundred knots ground speed," Benjamin said, tapping on a key to feed initial target data to the beam control system.

Previous versions of mobile laser weapon systems had fielded relatively low-power weapons and were designed to negate smaller targets at closer ranges. During the 2016 Maneuver Fires Integrated Experiment, or MFIX, at Fort Sill in Oklahoma, the Army unveiled the Mobile High Energy Laser that utilized a two-kilowatt laser. A year later, an upgraded version employed a five-kilowatt laser to burn up commercial quadcopter- and hexcopter-style drones. The year after that, the laser had improved to ten kilowatts.

"Engage the TILL," the test director said.

"Engaging," the operator to Benjamin's left replied.

He glanced over at the Advanced Dual Optical Tracking System monitor on his right, showing the target drone centered in the screen. A beam of light instantly appeared, stretching from the lower right corner of the screen to the target drone over fifty miles away. Known as the TILL, the target illuminator laser was used for engagement-quality tracking of targets and fed information back to the computer system Benjamin had designed.

"Receiving atmospheric data," he said, as information from the BILL, or beacon illuminator laser, measured the beam's distortion and applied corrections to the main laser's adaptive optics.

While others watched the target screen pensively, Benjamin scanned the raw data being processed through the beam control system that would result in a "prescription" for the HEL, or high energy laser. His eyes darted across the screen, evaluating the values for air density and temperature that were having an effect on the BILL. As thousands of incremental corrections were applied, the beam appeared to sharpen and focus more clearly on the target.

"Solution complete," Benjamin said triumphantly, less than three seconds later.

"Engage target track one zero six four," the test director said.

"Firing."

Other than the hum of the power supply providing energy to the laser, the interior of the Stryker armored fighting vehicle was silent. All eyes were fixed on the infrared display, showing a white-hot underbelly where the drone's single Microturbo TRI 60 turbojet engine was affixed. Slowly, a white spot appeared on the nose and blossomed as the laser bored a hole in the target.

"Target track one zero six four, bearing one nine zero for forty-five, thirty-nine thousand feet."

Suddenly, the drone pitched down and wobbled in the air as the laser severed the datalink connection with its human operator.

"Target negated," the test director said with a smile, prompting a chorus of cheers and fist bumps from the engineers who had made it all possible.

But Benjamin didn't smile. Had it been a real engagement, the laser could have been used to target a human pilot in the cockpit, an engine, or any other critical component. To him, it wasn't just a drone that now floated harmlessly under a parachute to be retrieved once back on solid ground. It wasn't just a target that had been neutralized after months of hard work by every member of his team. To Benjamin, the *DRAGON LINE* represented a weapon that would end a person's life.

Despite the celebratory atmosphere inside the Stryker, Benjamin couldn't help but feel that he had just helped bring to life a weapon that wouldn't just be used to take down drones or cruise missiles. Like it or not, he was now complicit in murder, and his only hope was that the Chinese intended to use the technology for something noble—something that would save his soul from eternal damnation.

"You were right," Thomas said with tears in his eyes and a smile on his face. "You did it."

Benjamin faked a smile and nodded.

But what did I do?

31

Pony 1
A-29 Super Tucano
Fallon South 1 Military Operations Area

Freaq banked the light attack turboprop and looked over his shoulder as the second of his ELGTRs impacted the trail vehicle in the convoy. He grinned, as much from his ability to put warheads on foreheads with deadly accuracy as from the quality control his SEAL JTACs had provided.

"Another direct hit, skipper," Dave said.

"Did you expect anything less?"

As the Super Tucano banked left over the target area, Freaq scanned the terrain east of the target area. He was looking for the Ground Mobility Vehicle and the three Navy SEALs who had driven out to the Clan Alpine Mountains to provide terminal control for the mission. Of course, even when they wanted to be found, it would have been hard to pick them out against the rugged wilderness backdrop.

"Pony One, Mariner Nine, request panel check our position."

His grin grew wider.

"Panel check?" Dave asked.

"Can you get me their position?"

"What's a panel check?"

"You'll see," Freaq said, then keyed the microphone switch to reply. "Mariner Nine, Pony One, copies. Setting up for panel check."

He rolled out and pointed the Super Tucano north while Dave continued manipulating the sensor pod to find the three heat signatures representing the SEALs. ". . . like trying to find a needle in a haystack," he muttered. But Freaq took it as an opportunity for the Master Chief to exercise the A-29's sensors and become more familiar with each of its unique capabilities. If they were going to use the plane in combat, they needed to know what it could do.

"What luck?"

Fortunately, the Master Chief was no slouch. After only a few more seconds, the cursors on his display centered on three heat signatures staggered around a five-place all-terrain vehicle with tubular frame and integrated roll cage. "Got 'em!"

"Well done, Master Chief," Freaq said, then quickly rolled the Super Tucano onto its back and yanked the stick into his lap to reverse direction in a modified split-S aerobatic maneuver. He keyed the microphone switch. "Mariner Nine, Pony One, inbound from the north for panel check."

"Pony One, continue," the JTAC replied.

"One thousand feet . . . what are we doing, boss?"

Freaq pointed the turboprop's nose at the computer-generated diamond in his HUD that represented the ground force's location, then eased forward on the stick to bring them even closer to the ground while keeping the throttle forward against the stops. "Visor down," he replied, then reached up and pulled his dark visor down to shield his eyes. A glance in his mirrors showed that Dave had followed suit.

"Pony One, Mariner Nine is visual. Continue."

Whoop! Whoop!

The radar altimeter sounded to let them know they had descended beneath the designated floor for the exercise.

"Five hundred feet," Dave said.

But that was the whole point of a panel check. He continued descending closer to the earth while heading south and paralleling the mountain range off his left wing. The SEALs were about a third of the way up the slope, in higher elevation related to the target complex, but low enough that the mountains already towered above them.

"Ten seconds," Freaq said, continuing to fly closer to the ground.

"Two hundred feet."

"Nervous, Master Chief?"

"Easy day, skipper," Dave replied. Though Freaq thought he detected a slight tremor in his voice. "One hundred feet."

Through his heads-up display, Freaq began to make out the Flyer 60 Advanced Light Strike Vehicle and three camouflaged individuals waving their arms above their heads. He jinked the nose to the right and planned on taking them down the left side as close to their elevation as possible. In his mind, if he could brush the tops of their helmets with his wingtip, it would be the perfect pass.

"Fifty feet."

Freaq's eyes were padlocked to the approaching vehicle while his hands and feet danced across the controls and brought the light attack airplane to within mere feet of the SEALs. Within seconds, they raced by in a blur, and he chuckled when each of the bearded frogmen ducked. Freaq returned his attention to his forward windscreen and eased the nose upward to begin a climb away from the mountains.

"*That* was a panel check," he said.

"Pony One, Mariner Nine," the JTAC said. "*Ho-ly shit!*"

"Guess they liked it," Dave replied.

"Enjoy your burgers, boys," Freaq said. "We'll see you back at base."

Hangar 7
Naval Air Station Fallon
Fallon, Nevada

The burner phone rang, and Punky quickly answered it. "Hello?"

"You were right," Mantis said. "It appears there's a Ministry emergency beacon broadcasting in the area."

Punky exhaled loudly, pleased that they seemed to have finally caught a break. Colt saw the relief etched on her face and moved to take the seat next to her. He produced a pen and a sheet of paper and set it on the table in front of her.

"Okay. Give me the location," Punky said into the phone.

"Do you know where Middlegate is?"

Punky looked up and scanned the room for a map or a chart of some kind. She spotted one laminated and hanging in front of a whiteboard against the far wall and gestured for Colt to retrieve it for her. He nodded that he understood and quickly jumped to his feet.

"I can find it," she said. "Is that where you are?"

Mantis hesitated. "No. I'm just east of Reno."

"Are you going after him?"

Colt returned with the chart and placed it on the table in front of Punky. She scanned the chart until she found Middlegate—barely more than an intersection located along US-50 almost forty miles east of Fallon. She tapped on it with her finger and made eye contact with Colt to let him know that was where the beacon was broadcasting.

"I have . . . other business to attend to," Mantis replied.

Punky thought it a strange comment, given the urgency she knew the spymaster had felt to recover her son from his kidnappers. But she finally had a lead, and she didn't want to spoil the moment. "Okay, I've found Middlegate. It's not far. But I need you to send me the beacon's coordinates and frequency."

Mantis hesitated for only a moment. "North three nine decimal one three one four, west one one eight decimal zero two eight seven."

Punky scribbled the coordinates down. "And the frequency?"

"Nine three one megahertz."

Punky wrote down the frequency and circled it several times. With that information, they ought to be able to find *KMART*. "Where will you—"

Mantis ended the call.

"What did she say?" Colt asked.

Instead of answering, Punky said, "This is only about thirty miles away. Let's go."

The pilot chewed on his lip in thought, then sprang to his feet and raced for the duty desk in the corner of the room. "I have a better idea."

"What are you doing? We need to go."

Pony 1
A-29 Super Tucano
Fallon South 1 Military Operations Area

Dave leaned back into the ejection seat and rested his forearms on the canopy rails on either side. He felt a little more relaxed now that the skipper had climbed to a safer altitude, and he was enjoying what had turned into a leisurely flight. Because it was Saturday and most of the base's jet jockeys were in Reno for the annual Tailhook convention, they had almost the entire airspace to themselves. And the skipper was taking his time making their way back to the base.

"Dave, it's Colt. You up?"

He leaned forward with a start and made eye contact with the skipper in the mirror before reaching for the radio transmit switch. "I'm up."

"Got a priority tasking for you," Colt replied.

"Who's this guy on my frequency?" Freaq asked Dave over the intercom.

Dave sighed with frustration. "Colt Bancroft," he said. "He's been working with a special agent from NCIS to take down a Chinese intelligence operative."

"Okay, but what's he doing on my frequency?"

Colt grew impatient and broke in again. "Dave, you copy?"

He keyed the microphone switch to reply. "Yeah, I copy, flyboy. I told you to hang tight."

"Listen, we have a location on the individual we told you about. Any chance you can use your fancy new toy to put eyes on for us?"

"What individual?" Freaq asked.

Dave shook his head. His frustration at being caught in the middle was beginning to boil over into anger. He ignored the skipper and focused on the TOPGUN pilot who had hijacked their radio. "Listen, Colt. We're on our way back to base and can sit down and hash this out when we get there."

"Where are you?"

"Dixie Valley."

"You're not far. Just take a quick look for us. Please."

The skipper broke his silence. "Master Chief, what's going on?"

But Dave made up his mind. "What's the location?"

"Middlegate."

32

Middlegate Station
Middlegate, Nevada

It wasn't much to look at from the outside. The Middlegate Station had a dilapidated appearance that belied its history as a stop on the Pony Express. But the large neon sign proclaiming "BAR" and the Can-Ams and other dusty off-road vehicles parked out front told a different story.

Then there was the sign.

"You see this?" Todd asked, gesturing to the wooden sign bolted to the building's weathered exterior.

"Welcome to Middlegate," Graham read. "The middle of nowhere. Elevation forty-six hundred feet. Population eighteen . . . no, seventeen." The number eighteen had been crossed out and replaced, probably due to a wild coyote attack or other unfortunate incident that could only befall a citizen of Middlegate.

"This really where you want us to eat?" Ron asked.

Graham nodded and opened the door, leading the other two SEALs inside the dimly lit establishment. The interior was just as rustic as the outside, with heavy wood beams adorned with various souvenirs of a bygone era in the Silver State. Antique rifles, lanterns, handcuffs. Every square inch of the ceiling was covered in autographed dollar bills, making the decor more valuable than the building itself.

"This is it," Graham said, pointing to the menu. "Check this out—the *Middlegate Monster Burger.*"

"Some kind of challenge?" Ron asked.

"Yeah, a triple-decker beast. One and one-third pounds of Angus beef on a sourdough bun, piled high with lettuce, tomatoes, red onions, pickles, cheese, peppers, and olives."

"Doesn't sound too bad."

"*And* a gargantuan heap of fries."

Todd shook his head but tuned out the other two SEALs when he heard a soft, warm static filling the miniature earpiece inserted deep in his left ear canal.

"Mariner Six, Pony One," Dave's voice said.

"Heads up," Todd said to his teammates, gesturing for them to follow as he rose from the table and made for the door.

"But I wanted to try the Monster," Graham said.

"Another time, bro."

Todd stepped outside and reached into his pocket to key the push-to-talk. "Pony One, this is Mariner Six."

The other two SEALs took up position on either side of him, their disappointment at being forced to leave without completing the food challenge painted plainly on their faces.

"Listen Mariner Six, we've got some priority tasking. Are you near Middlegate?"

Todd scrunched up his face. "We were just about to sit down and scarf down some burgers."

"Good copy. We need you to head south on Nevada three-sixty-one and standby for further instructions."

Todd still didn't know what was going on. But he knew the Master Chief and knew when to take him seriously. "Roger that."

Pony 1
A-29 Super Tucano
Fallon South 1 Military Operations Area

Freaq banked the Super Tucano right and turned south over the town of Middlegate. He looked down on the intersection of Highway 50 with the state highway stretching south to Gabbs.

"Deploying the turret," Dave said from the back seat.

"I hope you know what you're doing, Master Chief."

Dave gained control of the WESCAM MX-15 targeting pod and aimed it at the largest structure beneath them. "Middlegate Station," he said.

Freaq nodded and glanced at the multifunction display on his right just as the crosshairs centered on the Flyer 60 ground mobility vehicle parked in front of the dive bar. "There's our boys."

He rolled the plane out heading south and trimmed it for level flight, then watched as three men climbed into their seats and quickly backed out from their parking spot in the gravel lot. Looking up from the display, Freaq turned his head to the right and saw Fairview Peak at the north end of a ridgeline between them and the Bravo-17 target complex.

"Well, we've got all our assets in place," Freaq said. "Might as well find out what Colt wants."

"Roger that, skipper." Dave keyed the microphone switch to transmit on the base frequency. "Colt, it's Dave."

"Go ahead." His voice sounded like they were communicating through soup cans attached with a length of string.

"Nearing the coordinates you gave us. What frequency should we be scanning for?"

"Stand by."

Freaq could barely make out the V-shaped mock runway made with plowed dirt and the individual DMPIs—desired mean points of impact—that looked like surface-to-air missile sites. The simulated light armored convoy they had just decimated was even harder to see.

Colt's voice echoed again over the radio. "Nine three one megahertz."

"Copy."

"Now what?" Freaq asked.

"Now, we scan along that frequency until we get a hit."

With nothing to do other than fly the plane, Freaq scanned the horizon in either direction, as he would on a real combat sortie. The desert land-scape had an almost ethereal appearance, as if it had been painted using a palette of khaki, dirty olive green, and red-brown. Up ahead, a large gath-ering of vehicles with flashing police lights drew his attention down to the only paved road in the area. Freaq took control of the sensor pod to zoom in for a better look.

Dave noticed the shifting display. "What do you see, skipper?"

He centered the crosshairs on a silver Nevada Highway Patrol Ford Explorer, sitting immobile on the side of the road with flattened tires and a splintered windshield. Just to the left of the open driver's door was what looked like a body covered by a tarp.

"Looks like there was a shootout of some kind," he said.

"Out here?"

"Yeah, that's definitely not normal."

Dave whistled as the sensor panned across a half dozen other police vehicles. "That's some heavy law enforcement presence. Wonder if it's related to our missing person."

Freaq looked at Dave in the mirror. "Who *exactly* is missing, Master Chief?"

"That's a long . . ." He paused. "Bingo! Clear as day."

Freaq reached down to the audio control panel and turned on the channel to listen in on the frequency band Dave had been scanning for. Immediately, he heard the high-pitched tone of a locator beacon emitting an omnidirectional signal.

"Can you lock in on it?"

"Already did," Dave replied.

Freaq glanced down at the multifunction display just as the sensor's crosshairs panned across the desert and centered on a spot west of the road. Dave manipulated the pod through each of its electro-optical and infrared modes, and Freaq banked right to adjust his heading and point at the target locator mark.

"Is that . . ."

But Dave's transmission cut him off. "Mariner Six, Pony One, standby for updated target coordinates."

Ten miles south of Middlegate, Nevada

As the sun dipped lower in the sky, Todd reached down and turned on the Flyer's headlights. The Advanced Light Strike Vehicle resembled a miniature Humvee with a tubular space frame that left its occupants exposed to the elements. But with four-wheel coilover shocks, heavy duty suspension, and thirty-seven-inch tires, it was purpose-built for unmatched all-terrain capability. And, based on the coordinates Dave had just passed them, it looked like each of those features were about to come in handy.

"Make a right up here," Ron said from the passenger seat.

Because the Flyer lacked a windshield, the SEALs wore goggles pulled down over their Ops-Core helmets and communicated using an intra-team radio connected through their Peltor headsets that helped block out wind noise.

Todd took his foot off the gas as he looked for a good place to turn off the paved road. The headlights reflected off two raised markers on either side of a dirt road, and he coasted until he passed the first, then steered the Flyer between them. It wasn't completely dark yet, but he wanted every advantage to keep them moving toward the objective, so he flipped another toggle switch and activated the floodlights mounted wide on the front bumper.

"Let there be light," Graham said.

Dave's voice boomed in their headsets. "Mariner Six, Pony One, the signal is coming from a turnoff approximately nine hundred meters from your present position."

Todd brought the microphone up to his mouth to reply. "Copy. What are we looking for?"

"You should see a distant rock outcropping directly in front of you."

Though dusk was settling over the desert landscape, he could still clearly make out a jagged rock formation jutting into the sky beyond the more immediate hills. "Contact."

"That's your objective," Dave replied.

"What exactly is our objective?" Ron asked.

"A personal locator beacon."

Todd scrunched up his face as he steered the Flyer carefully along the winding dirt road. He heard Ron and Graham inserting magazines into their M4 carbines and couldn't shake the feeling that they were heading into combat—the last thing any of them expected in the Nevada desert. "Any heat signatures?"

"Negative. The location appears cold."

Graham racked his charging handle to chamber a round. "I'm still going in hot," he said.

Ron apparently agreed, because he did the same.

As the road bent to the left and they neared the rock outcropping, Todd let the light tactical vehicle slow to a crawl. Even though the Master Chief was above them and using the Super Tucano's infrared sensor to scan the area, he wasn't about to race up on a target location without using at least some caution. Especially when he hadn't the faintest idea what this was about.

"Turnoff in one hundred feet," Dave said.

Todd saw the dirt track split, and he steered right onto the turnoff.

"Target in ninety feet."

He slowed even more and leaned forward to scan the ground in front of them for anything amiss. Out of the corner of his eye, he saw Ron doing the same thing.

"Fifty ... forty ... thirty ... on top of target," Dave said.

Todd pressed on the brake pedal and brought the Flyer to a halt.

"What do you see?" the Master Chief asked.

Todd shook his head in dismay, then keyed the microphone switch again. "Nothing. Nada."

33

Near Main Lake
Seven miles northeast of Tonopah Test Range Airport
Tonopah, Nevada

Benjamin sat in the back of the eight-wheeled Stryker armored vehicle as it bounced along one of the many roads east of Cactus Flat, linking the various sites within the Tonopah Test Range with the airport and Mancamp. He only had a general idea where they were but knew it was isolated enough that if he kept off the main roads, he could reach Highway 6 without being spotted.

What happened when he left the test range would be the real issue.

"Stop the car!" he yelled, bending over at the waist and clutching his stomach.

Thomas leaned down in the seat next to him. "What is it?"

"I'm going to be sick."

Thomas put a comforting hand on his back and turned to look at the back of the driver's head. "Driver! Stop!"

The Caterpillar C7 industrial diesel engine roared as the driver forced the Allison MD3066 automatic transmission to downshift when he stomped on the brakes. The passengers in the back lurched forward, but

Benjamin bolted for the rear of the vehicle, where he flipped up the guarded switch and pressed down on the toggle to actuate the hydraulic motors that lowered the ramp.

"Hayes, you okay?" Thomas called out.

But he didn't answer. Before the ramp had completely opened, he leaped out and spun away from the troop entrance to the side of the vehicle. Adrenaline flooded his veins as he reached the moment when he knew the very next thing he did would have lasting consequences. The looming decision had been at the forefront of his mind since they left Mancamp in the back of the armored vehicle, but his stomach still twisted into knots now that the moment was upon him.

He heard the senior engineer's feet pattering on the ramp behind him, then drop to the desert floor alongside the armored vehicle. Still clutching his stomach, Benjamin bent forward and vomited, surprising himself that he hadn't needed to fake it. He had agreed to work for the Chinese to *stop* the violence—not perpetrate it.

"Hey, are you okay?" Thomas said from behind him.

Why couldn't you have taken the bus?

Benjamin pinched his eyes shut and felt another wave of nausea slam into him when he realized his time was up. He could either wipe his mouth clean and climb back aboard the armored vehicle for the remainder of the short drive to Mancamp, or . . .

He drew the concealed knife tucked inside his waistband, then spun toward Thomas and thrust the blade into the man's paunchy gut. The senior engineer exhaled in a surprised cough and stared at Benjamin with wide, pleading eyes.

"I'm sorry," Benjamin whispered.

They stared at each other in a silent standoff for several seconds before the instinctive will to live took over and filled Thomas with surprising strength. With both hands, he clamped down on Benjamin's wrist and pushed the blade clear of his body. His face turned red from both anger and exertion, and red-tinged spittle bubbled at the corners of his mouth.

"Why?" he croaked.

"I'm sorry," Benjamin repeated, feeling his stomach again knot up with an overwhelming guilt. But he had made his decision. There was no turning back now, and there was only one way out of this. "I'm so sorry."

With a sudden burst of energy, Benjamin yanked his hand free from Thomas's grip. The sharp blade sliced through the man's fingers, releasing even more crimson droplets onto the desert floor. The senior engineer instinctively drew his hands into his body to protect them, but Benjamin had crossed the point of no return, and he exploded in a violent frenzy. With quick and erratic stabbing motions, he plunged the knife several more times into the older man's stomach, then ended the brief melee with a slashing motion across his neck.

Still beet-red in the face, Thomas dropped to his knees, letting his bloody hands dangle at his sides and lowering his jowls to his chest in defeat. Benjamin's breathing was shallow and panicked. And an odd feeling of detachment settled over him, as if he were observing the scene from a short distance away.

"What's going on out there?" the driver asked from his hatch on top of the Stryker.

Benjamin planted his foot into Thomas's chest and shoved, toppling him to the ground. "There's something wrong with him!"

The driver climbed down and started running when he saw the senior engineer motionless. Benjamin waited until the driver had passed him, then reached up and wrapped his fingers across the man's face. The driver flinched, but it was too late. Benjamin brought the blade up into the man's lower back and repeatedly stabbed upward into what he thought was the kidney.

But, unlike Thomas, the driver wasn't willing to go down without a fight. Even as he gasped in shocked pain, he slammed his left elbow back and caught Benjamin in the ribs. The blow did little damage, but it temporarily halted his attack.

"What the fuck!" The driver spun toward Benjamin with a snarl and instinctively held his hands out in front of him in a defensive posture.

"I'm sorry," Benjamin said. "She's making me do this."

"Who?"

But he wasn't interested in answering questions. He had already killed the only person on his team who had shown him any kindness. Now, he needed to finish off the driver and get off the roads before another vehicle came along. He stepped forward and slashed at the air in front of the driver's face, but the man leaned away from the blade and demonstrated a proficiency in the martial arts Benjamin lacked.

He slashed again. And again, the man avoided the blade.

But his face contorted in pain as the shock of the initial stabbing attack wore off, and his brain finally processed the agony radiating from his lower back. Benjamin stepped forward and thrust the blade toward the man's stomach, hoping to finish him off the way he had Thomas. But the driver deftly parried the blow, slipped to the side, and sent a wicked left hook into the side of Benjamin's face.

Stars ringed his vision as he wobbled into one of the Stryker's thick tires. But he bounced back and slashed blindly with the knife, hoping to prevent another punch.

Unfortunately, the driver was quicker. He stepped back to remain out of reach, then quickly darted in and delivered a jab and cross combo to Benjamin's face.

Crack.

His eyes snapped shut as his nose splintered underneath the man's knuckles. But, somewhere in the recesses of his brain, he registered that the punches hadn't been as powerful as that first hook. Opening his watery eyes, he blinked quickly to clear his vision and slashed left and right with the blade. He knew he had lost the upper hand, but all he needed to do was outlast his opponent.

The driver's weaving became slower. His parries had a little less force. Benjamin recognized the shifting tide and set his jaw to finish what he'd started. With blood running down his face, he stepped in and grasped the man's shirt with his free hand. He yanked him close while stabbing the knife at his midsection.

Parry. Parry. Strike.

The driver moaned when the blade sank into his gut, and Benjamin quickly withdrew it and plunged it into the man once more. Again and again, he stabbed without skill or precision, barely registering the weakening blows that connected first with his head, then his shoulder and arm. He held onto the driver's shirt with a death grip, treating it like it was the only thing that could see him clear of this mess. He just needed to hold on.

"I'm sorry," he said again. "I'm sorry. I'm sorry. I'm sorry."

The driver let out a weak cry for help. With each thrust of the knife, his cries became softer. His punches stopped. His defiant posture fell into a slump, and Benjamin withdrew the knife one last time, then slashed it across the man's throat.

Like Thomas, the driver's neck opened up and spilled blood down the front of his body. His hands lowered in defeat, and he looked at Benjamin with sad and accusing eyes. He opened his mouth, but no sound came out.

Why?

"I'm sorry," Benjamin whispered. "I'm so sorry."

When the driver's legs buckled, he released his grip on the shirt and stepped back to let his body collapse to the desert floor only feet from the senior engineer. Gasping for breath, ears ringing, and his adrenaline-fueled heart pounding mercilessly in his chest, Benjamin released his grip on the knife and let it also fall to the ground.

"What have I done?"

He brought his hands up in front of his face and saw the blood covering them, but he felt detached from what had just taken place. It was how he had pictured it and nothing like what he had expected, at the same time. He knew she hadn't given him a choice and had left him with only this one opportunity to meet her demands. But until that moment, he hadn't been certain he would be able to do it. Now he had blood on his hands.

He looked up and turned toward the setting sun. A little over two miles away, the white sands of the playa known as Main Lake were barely visible. The dormitory structures of Mancamp even less so in the heat haze rising from the desert floor. He scanned left and right, searching for another vehicle that might happen upon the idling Stryker, then looked up and wondered if the stealth fighters he had seen take off were overhead and bearing witness to him standing over two dead bodies.

Benjamin swallowed.

He had done what he hadn't thought possible. But this was only the beginning.

Stepping over Thomas's body, he ran to the ramp and climbed inside, then reached up and flipped the toggle to actuate the hydraulic motors. He spun for the driver's seat at the front as thick chains pulled the ramp closed.

Unlike normal Stryker combat vehicles, the one used as the *DRAGON LINE* test platform had been configured with a row of workstations along the starboard side, opposite jump seats on the other. There were places for three, but he and Thomas had been the only two who volunteered to return to Mancamp in the back of the armored vehicle. The others had opted to take the air-conditioned bus.

"Why couldn't you have taken the bus?"

Guilt consumed him, but he quickly suppressed the all-too-familiar emotion and worked his way forward past the commander's and gunner's stations. It probably would have been easier to slip into the driver's seat from the overhead hatch, but he had been in the same place for too long already. He didn't know how long it would take for somebody to notice the Stryker missing, but he didn't want to be sitting around when that happened.

Benjamin contorted himself into position behind the wheel and looked at the screen in front of him in dismay.

34

Hangar 7
Naval Air Station Fallon
Fallon, Nevada

Punky paced back and forth in front of the duty desk, occasionally glancing at Colt, who sat on the dais, clutching the radio's handset as he waited to hear back from Dave. She was unaccustomed to sitting on her hands and letting others follow up on a lead. But she admitted it was far better to have an airplane purpose-built for intelligence, surveillance, and reconnaissance out searching for the beacon than for her to be stumbling around the desert at night.

"What's taking so long?" she asked, staring over the top of the desk at Colt.

"Patience, Punky," Colt replied. But his own was beginning to thin, and he adjusted the squelch until the speaker again emitted a warm static.

She pulled out the burner phone Mantis had given her, hoping to see a message or missed call or anything else she could use to continue her search for the kidnapped Marine. As it was, she was beginning to feel that searching for the personal locator beacon was something of a Hail Mary. If they came up empty on this, she would be back to square one—searching for a needle in a haystack.

"What are we—"

The speaker crackled and the static was replaced with Dave's baritone voice. "Colt, it's Dave."

Punky spun back toward the duty desk as Colt lifted the handset to his mouth and pressed the switch along its side to transmit. "Go ahead."

"We have a mobile team on site at this time, and they're conducting a sweep of the area."

Punky darted around the edge of the desk and stepped up on the dais to crowd over Colt at the radio. "What does that even mean?"

Colt held up a hand before replying. "Copy. So, you found the beacon?"

"Affirm. We picked up the signal south of Middlegate, right where you said it would be. But when we vectored our ground team into position, there was nobody around."

Colt exhaled loudly and dropped his chin in defeat. "So, it was a dry hole."

"Afraid so, flyboy. It looks like the beacon was transmitting from a Tag Heuer watch, but it had been discarded along with some torn clothing."

Punky leaned forward and placed her hands flat on the duty desk as she processed the new information. It made sense that *KMART*'s abductors had stripped him of his personal belongings. They probably suspected he had some type of tracking device. It had been a long shot to begin with, but now it seemed like they were truly back to square one.

"Copy that," Colt said. "What's the plan now?"

"We're getting close to bingo, so we're going to depart station and RTB."

Punky glanced over at Colt. "RTB?"

"Return to base," he replied. "It means they're coming home."

"Empty-handed," she muttered.

But Colt ignored her. "Copy that, we'll be standing by to recover you. Need anything from us?"

There was a healthy pause on the radio, and for a moment Punky thought they had lost reception with the airborne Super Tucano. "Our guys on the ground are going to continue their site exploitation for a while longer before returning to Fallon. Either way, if they come up with anything, you should be able to have it within the hour."

"Roger that," Colt said, his tone clearly indicating his disappointment.

"Hey, Colt . . ."

He keyed the microphone switch again. "Yeah, go ahead."

"It might be nothing . . ."

Punky's head whipped up, suddenly clinging to hope that the airborne crew had found another thread—thin as it was—for her to follow. Despite trying to temper her expectations, her heart started beating faster.

"What is it?"

"Just north of where we found the beacon transmitting, we flew over a pretty large law enforcement presence. We had the sensor on it for a few minutes and saw what looked like a Nevada Highway Patrol vehicle that had been shot up pretty bad."

Her dim glimmer of hope suddenly flared bright. "Did he say *shot up*?"

Colt held up a hand again to silence her. "What else did you see?"

But Punky had heard enough. She walked away from the duty desk and pulled out her personal cell phone to place a call to Camron. Before he even picked up, she had already built her own narrative around the shooting. All she needed was to confirm it for herself.

"Hey Punky, did you decide what you're going to do?"

For a moment, she had forgotten that she promised to keep him apprised of her plans related to the investigation into *KMART*. She had been so caught up in her meeting with Mantis and the potential opportunity to bring down the entire Ministry of State Security West Coast network, that she hadn't bothered bringing him up to speed on what she was doing.

"Listen, I need to stay up here a while longer. There've been some developments that I need to run down. But I could use backup."

"What do you need?"

"It sounds like there was an officer-involved shooting on Nevada State Route 361 south of Middlegate, and I need help getting in touch with the officer running the investigation."

"Do you think it's related?"

Punky didn't have anything other than a hunch to go on, but she didn't believe in coincidences. "Yeah. It's definitely related."

Her supervisor sighed. "Alright. Let me make some calls, and I'll get back to you."

She ended the call and turned back to the duty desk. Colt stood when he saw her approach and looked down at her from the dais. "There are at least a half dozen police cars on the scene right now, but Dave doesn't have any reason to think it's connected to *KMART's* abduction."

She shook her head. "Of *course* it's connected. I need to get out there to find out what happened."

Colt opened his mouth as if he was about to argue, then snapped it shut. After several seconds, he finally nodded and picked up the radio handset again. "Dave, you still up?"

"Go ahead," the SEAL replied.

"I won't be here when you get back. Punky and I are going to drive out to Middlegate to look into what happened. Can you pass me the coordinates?"

"Copy that," Dave said, then read off the latitude and longitude, which Colt hastily scrawled on a sheet of scrap paper. "Be safe, flyboy."

"You too. Colt out." He dropped the handset and stepped off the dais. "Alright, let's go."

"Thank you," she said.

"Don't mention it."

Together, they left the ready room and turned down the hall for the staircase at the end of the hangar. Punky took the steps two at a time as they descended to the ground floor where they exited into the crisp, evening air. Though the warmth of the day had retreated with the setting sun, she felt a fire inside her that kept her moving forward. They might have struck out with the radio beacon, but something told her that the officer-involved shooting was related and would give her the break she needed.

Colt remained one step behind as they crossed the tarmac to the turnstile set into the chain-link fence, exited the flight line, and made for the government Suburban. As he climbed into the passenger seat, Punky jumped into the driver's seat, started it up, and quickly backed out of her parking space. But before she could shift the large SUV into drive, her phone rang and she quickly answered.

"Talk to me, Camron."

"I'm going to text you the name and number of the officer running the crime scene, but it sounds like you might be onto something. A trooper was gunned down during a traffic stop made on a white panel van—"

"That's it," she said.

"Punky..."

"I'll be careful."

"The trooper's cruiser was riddled with seven six two."

She shifted the Suburban into drive and quickly stomped on the gas. She couldn't explain it, but she knew they were only fifty miles away from uncovering a detail that would lead them straight to *KMART*.

Then she could shut down the Ministry's operations for good.

35

Tonopah Test Range
Tonopah, Nevada

Once Benjamin got the Stryker moving, he left the paved surface, informally known as Perimeter Road, and traveled cross-country almost due north to what had once been referred to as Gate 12. Though the actual test range perimeter extended well beyond this point, the direction gave him the best chance of disappearing into the desert with the *DRAGON LINE* weapon before anybody could stop him.

How he got it to Mantis at Gabbs Airport was another matter altogether.

Passing the old Boundary Patrol Road, he steered the armored vehicle northeast and paralleled the Warm Springs Short Cut into a wash west of Kawich Peak. It was a relatively gradual climb, and the Stryker handled it with ease. But Benjamin was sweating with exertion by the time he again turned north and descended back to the desert floor.

He was driving blind in more ways than one. The small monitor in front of the steering wheel gave him a two-dimensional view of the three-dimensional world around him, but even that began to erode and left him almost completely blind. Benjamin braked the eight-wheeled vehicle and came to a stop as he screamed at the screen in frustration.

He leaned his head against the steering wheel and closed his eyes. The whole thing almost felt like a bad dream. From his professor preying on his pacifist tendencies and recruiting him to accept a job with Sandia National Laboratories, to forsaking his beliefs and murdering two of his co-workers to steal a multi-million-dollar high-tech laser weapon system. He still believed it was for the greater good. But the blood was real. The cries were real. The consuming guilt was real.

Benjamin took a deep breath.

He could continue to beat himself up for doing what needed to be done. Or, he could use the brain God had gifted him with to get himself out of this mess—the same way he had used it to get out of his dead-end hometown.

Opening his eyes, Benjamin stared at the image on the screen and saw several shapes that appeared washed out. He leaned in close and could tell that what he was seeing was a product of what was known as the AN/VAS-5 Stryker DVE, or Driver Vision Enhancer. They had provided the entire team with an information sheet on the Stryker used as the test vehicle, and he had memorized every detail—like he did with everything else.

The Stryker DVE was a compact, lightweight, uncooled, passive thermal imaging system designed for use during periods of darkness or degraded visibility caused by smoke, dust, haze, fog, and rain. It had a field of view of thirty degrees in elevation and forty degrees in azimuth and was focused from five meters to infinity, providing thermal images to the driver.

"Thermal images," he said, feeling just the tickle of an idea at the back of his mind.

The longer he stared at the screen, the less washed-out the shapes appeared. Then, it hit him.

"Of course." He popped the hatch above his head and looked out into the darkened sky. At some point after commandeering the Stryker, the sun had set. "Thermal crossover."

He shook his head at himself as he recalled learning about the two short periods each day known as "crossover periods" when most natural objects were essentially the same temperature—in the early morning when they heated up and again when they cooled down at night. Being roughly the same temperature during these periods, thermal imaging systems like the Stryker DVE had difficulty distinguishing separate objects and washed out the image, leaving the driver temporarily blind to the environment outside the armored vehicle.

Benjamin ducked back inside and looked down at the screen. Already, the objects were cooling to the point that he was able to make out some of the larger terrain features. He breathed a sigh of relief, closed the hatch, and resumed his drive north. The sooner he was clear of the test range, the better.

Once clear of the wash, Benjamin again steered northeast to parallel a road that led all the way to Highway 6—the Grand Army of the Republic Highway. He was traveling lights-out, so unless somebody had a thermal imaging system—another Stryker, perhaps—he should be able to clear the range and begin making his way toward Gabbs.

"Then I can finally be done with this mess," he muttered.

Suddenly, a bright object appeared on his screen, moving from right to left, just beyond what appeared to be a depression in the earth. Benjamin stomped on the brakes and brought the Stryker to a halt, his heart pounding inside his chest as he watched what looked like a truck racing across his path to block him.

Have they seen me?

The truck came to a stop, and he watched as several bright figures exited the vehicle and descended into the depression.

"Shit!" he exclaimed.

Had the Stryker been operational, it would have been armed with an M240 belt-fed 7.62mm machine gun. But this was only a test, and he was deep inside one of the most secure test ranges in the country. There should have been no need for armament.

Then again, he was the one who had stolen the multi-million-dollar armored vehicle with an experimental directed energy weapon. *He* was the one they needed to defend against.

As the heat signatures of three dismounted personnel rose from the earth and ascended the near side of the depression, Benjamin sprang into action. He wasn't a soldier and didn't know the first thing about combat. But he was an engineer who knew exactly how the laser weapon worked.

Benjamin scrambled through the tight passage from the driver's seat into the Stryker's main cabin and took up position at the same workstation where he had sat during the final test. His fingers flew across the keys and switches needed to power up and activate the *DRAGON LINE*. It was the only weapon he had available to him, and his only chance of eliminating what he thought was a threat.

As the screens flickered to life and broadcast images from the Advanced Dual Optical Tracking System, he wondered if what he was attempting to do was even possible. He knew that previous vehicle-mounted directed energy weapons had been used to destroy roadside improvised explosive devices, but the *DRAGON LINE* had been designed as an air defense weapon. He didn't even know if the laser would tilt low enough.

"Come on, baby," he muttered. "Let's see what you can do."

The vehicle hummed as the power supply system began feeding the necessary energy to the HEL. He reached for the joystick and depressed a button to assume manual control, then panned the sensor forward to where he had seen the truck and dismounted personnel. When the sensor reached the approximate azimuth, he pressed forward on the stick and tilted it down until several white-hot thermal images appeared in the center of the screen—the largest being the truck, blocking his path.

"There we go."

He made several more minor adjustments and shifted the sensor through its various optical and thermal modes to sharpen up the image and make heads or tails of who these people were. After several seconds, he saw what appeared to be rifles in the dismounts' hands. He didn't want to take another human life—he already had two stains on his conscience— but he couldn't allow them to stop him from completing his task.

A mournful sob rose from deep within as he steadied the crosshairs on the nearest of the three security guards.

Unlike when they had tracked the target drone, the beam control system didn't need to account for atmospherics to complete an intercept. For such a short distance, it didn't need the use of the target or beacon illuminator lasers. All he needed to do was squeeze the trigger and send one hundred kilowatts of directed energy through another human being.

"I'm sorry," he whispered.

Benjamin squeezed the trigger.

He knew what would happen. But even armed with that knowledge, he wasn't prepared for what he witnessed. Almost instantly, a narrow beam of invisible light twenty million times stronger than a typical laser pointer punched a hole through the closest guard. The *DRAGON LINE* power output was one hundred times greater than the energy needed to melt steel, and it completely eviscerated the unsuspecting man.

What remained of his body fell to the ground in an unrecognizable heap as the other two continued their advance, unaware that something had happened to their comrade.

Benjamin ignored the bile rising in his throat and shifted the crosshairs to the next target. "I'm so sorry."

36

6 miles south of Middlegate, Nevada

The road in front of them seemed to disappear into the horizon. Only the glow of flashing red and blue lights against the hills on either side of the road told Punky they were nearing the location Dave had passed to them. But as they drew closer, her anxiety wrapped around her like a cloak, and she eased her foot off the gas.

Colt glanced at her from across the cab. "We're going to find him."

She nodded but didn't take her eyes off the road. "I know. But something about this doesn't seem right."

They crested the hill, and Punky pulled the Suburban in behind a blue Nevada Highway Patrol cruiser on the shoulder. She squinted through the strobing red and blue lights at several more police vehicles parked in the road and officers milling about and shining their flashlights across the ground.

"Nothing about this seems right," Colt said. "Why would somebody kidnap *KMART*, drive out to the desert, and gun down a police officer? I saw what those guys were capable of at the Nugget, and they didn't strike me as anything but professionals. They didn't shoot up the place indiscriminately and were almost clinical in the way they took him."

She had thought the same thing. Whoever took *KMART* had done so for a very specific reason. But she was no closer to figuring out what that was than she had been when Mantis approached her . . .

"Mantis," she said.

"What?"

Punky shifted the Suburban into park and turned to face Colt. "This has to be related to Mantis somehow."

She could tell by the confused look on Colt's face that he wasn't following her logic.

"Think about it," she said. "If Mantis runs the Ministry's West Coast network, that makes her valuable to almost any other organization that wants to conduct espionage in the area. It's no mystery that China has infiltrated almost every facet of American society—especially in California, which has an abundance of targets in academia, technology, military, and government. If somebody wanted to leverage the Ministry's resources, they could do so by controlling only one person."

"Mantis," Colt said.

She nodded. "And what's one surefire way of gaining leverage over another person?"

"By kidnapping a loved one."

"Like a child," she said.

Colt remained silent, but Punky could already see the truth in her theory. Aside from the Joint Strike Fighter maintenance data the Marine had provided to the Ministry, there was no indication he even had access to anything of value. And after Colt helped stop a Chinese attack on the USS *Abraham Lincoln,* Punky's investigation into *KMART* had largely centered around a Marine corporal who continued to meet with Ministry operatives but provided nothing substantial.

Almost as if somebody was keeping him close to protect him.

But protect him from who?

Before she could run down that line of thinking further, her phone rang. She shook away her thoughts and answered. "Special Agent King."

"This is Lieutenant Moore from the Nevada State Police," the caller said. "I understand you might have some information related to a trooper's murder."

Though Punky had been in law enforcement her entire adult life and had lost several people close to her—including her father's best friend—hearing the words "trooper's murder" put things into perspective. As much as she wanted to find *KMART* and bring down the Ministry's West Coast network, she couldn't ignore the fact that a trooper had lost his life trying to keep his community safe from criminals.

"I'm sorry for what happened to your trooper."

"Thank you."

"I have reason to believe it might be related to an active counterintelligence investigation I'm currently working," she said. "My partner and I just arrived on the scene. Are you here?"

Through the windshield, she saw an officer in plain clothes with a phone to his ear look up and turn in their direction.

"Dark Suburban?" Lieutenant Moore asked.

"That's us."

"Come on out."

The call ended and Punky slipped the phone back in her pocket. With one more glance at the burner phone Mantis had given her, she opened the door and gestured for Colt to join her. Stepping out on the paved highway, she looked around and absorbed the vastness of the surrounding desert. They were in the middle of nowhere, and she felt more isolated than she had ever felt before.

"Is that our guy?" Colt asked after walking around the front of the SUV to join her.

The lieutenant she had spoken to walked toward them with his head lowered and hand resting on the holstered pistol on his hip. His demeanor screamed for retribution and vengeance against those who had perpetrated what he saw as a senseless act of violence.

"Looks like it," she said.

"Special Agent King?" the lieutenant asked as he neared.

Punky held up her credentials, though she knew introductions had already been made through Camron and the lieutenant's captain. "Again, let me express how sorry I am for what happened to your trooper."

The lieutenant nodded curtly, but his jaw muscles flexed as he clenched his teeth in anger. "What do you have for me?"

She gestured to Colt standing next to her. "This morning, my partner and I witnessed an abduction at the Nugget Casino Resort in Sparks."

"I'm aware. It was the description of the panel van that caught my trooper's attention and precipitated the traffic stop. Do you think the perpetrators of that abduction were the ones responsible for this?"

"I think it's likely," she said. "Have you reviewed the trooper's dash camera footage?"

The lieutenant nodded. "It looked like an ambush, plain and simple."

"May we have a look?"

Again, he hesitated, but gestured for Punky and Colt to join him at another cruiser idling in the road. They followed him in silence. The lieutenant opened the driver's door and gestured inside at an open laptop resting above the center console with a video already cued. "You'll see three separate individuals—the driver, passenger, and a third man from the rear —who engaged my trooper with AK-style automatic rifles."

"The same kind used in the abduction at the casino," Colt said.

Lieutenant Moore pursed his lips. "I read the report. What do you know about these men?"

Punky slipped into the driver's seat. "Unfortunately, not much. But I'm hoping this video will give me an idea of who's involved."

The lieutenant stepped back and folded his arms across his chest while Colt knelt and watched the screen over Punky's shoulder. She clicked on the laptop's trackpad and the video started playing.

At first, it looked like a normal traffic stop. The panel van had its emergency flashers on but sat idle on the shoulder. Punky looked up from the laptop and through the patrol car's windshield at the vacant patch of concrete where the van had been only a few hours earlier. Her eyes lowered to the screen again as the trooper approached the driver's window. She easily read the nerves in his body language.

"He clearly had his radar up," Colt said over her shoulder.

She nodded in agreement. The video had volume, but she couldn't make out the words that were exchanged as the trooper collected the driver's documents. A few seconds later, he began walking back to his vehicle. But as he walked alongside the van, something caught his attention, and he paused.

"What's he looking at?" Colt asked.

"I don't know..."

The trooper reached out and touched something along the side of the van, but his body seemed to tense. Suddenly, he jumped back away from the van and dropped his hand to his holstered service pistol.

"Rewind that," Colt said.

Punky tapped on the icon to rewind the video ten seconds, then pressed play.

"Can you turn the volume up?"

She dragged a slider along the bottom of the screen to the right and watched as the trooper again reached out and touched the side of the van.

Thump.

He jumped back and reached for his pistol.

"What was that?" she asked, looking over her shoulder at the lieutenant.

"We don't know. But whatever it was, it got his attention and alerted him that something wasn't right."

As the trooper drew his pistol and scampered back toward the safety of his vehicle, the rear doors flew open and a gunman wielding an AK-47 began spitting bullets into the Explorer. The dash camera's footage became obscured as the windshield splintered and spiderwebbed from the impacting bullets, but it was still clear enough for Punky to see the trooper return fire with his service pistol.

"Did you see inside the van?" Colt asked.

Again, Punky tapped on the icon to rewind the video ten seconds. She leaned closer to the screen as the rear doors flew open.

"Pause it," Colt said. The image froze with a gunman bringing an AK-47 to bear. But Colt pointed at a spot deeper inside the van. "What's that look like to you?"

She squinted at the image and was just barely able to make out the shape of a man curled in the fetal position. She pulled her cell phone from her pocket and placed a call.

"Hey Punky, did you get in touch with—"

"Camron, I'm going to send you screenshots of three individuals and a license plate. Whoever shot the Nevada trooper also kidnapped *KMART*.

We've got dash cam footage of him tied up in the back of their van. I need to find out who these people are."

37

Between Tonopah and Gabbs, Nevada

Benjamin's stomach still lurched every time he thought of what the laser had done to the hapless security personnel. The first two had been obliterated before the third finally caught on that they had even been spotted. There was no sound. No visible indication that they were taking fire. Only his comrades' decimated bodies dropping to the desert floor.

But even after the third man realized what was happening and reversed direction to retreat to the safety of his truck, Benjamin didn't spare him. He directed the *DRAGON LINE* at the security vehicle and watched it punch a hole through the thin sheet metal. And the human body inside.

He pinched his eyes shut to quell the sudden nausea, then took several ragged breaths before resuming his slow trek toward Gabbs.

After clearing the test range and crossing Highway 6, Benjamin steered the Stryker to parallel Nevada State Route 376 north into Ralston Valley. He continued following the highway's meandering path westward until it turned north into Big Smoky Valley, then he cut west around Toiyabe Range. But because it was dark and the Stryker DVE only gave him a narrow and fixed field of view, he couldn't see Arc Dome—the highest point in the range at just under twelve thousand feet.

Stuck inside the cramped cockpit, Benjamin turned north on the west side of the Humboldt-Toiyabe National Forest and drove up the Reese River Valley until he was almost exactly abeam where his handler had instructed him to deliver the weapon. He still had no idea what awaited him at Gabbs Airport, but after cutting the throats of two men and liquifying three more with a laser, he figured things couldn't get much worse. He just needed to deliver the weapon and disappear into peaceful obscurity.

He brought the Stryker to a stop just south of Nevada State Route 844 and popped the hatch above his head. The wind whistled as it swept down the valley and over the eight-wheeled armored vehicle. Benjamin took a deep breath and inhaled the fresh air, enjoying the way its coolness washed over him and chilled him to the core. It felt refreshing after being trapped inside the Stryker. But it was the openness of the Nevada night sky that brought him the truest sense of peace.

Mountain ranges stretched skyward on either side of him and framed a wide tapestry of stars. He easily made out the faint outlines of Buffalo Mountain and Grantsville Ridge to his east, and Sherman and Paradise Peaks to his west. It was between the last two where State Route 844 cut through the Paradise Range and descended the western slope into Gabbs—an unincorporated town in Nye County and the most distant community in Greater Las Vegas.

His stomach knotted up again as he thought of the first security guard collapsing to the ground like a figure from a wax museum caught in an inferno. But he choked back the sour bile and slid back down into his seat. He needed to put this day behind him. He needed to flush these memories from his mind and start over.

Benjamin pulled the hatch closed over his head and put the Stryker back into gear. He had remained clear of paved roads since leaving the Tonopah Test Range, but he was in the middle of nowhere and had only one final stretch to go. The chances of encountering another vehicle deep in the Nevada desert at this time of night were slim to none.

And there's always the laser . . .

He shook away the thought, refusing to believe that ending another human life was an acceptable course of action. No, he had taxed his conscience enough and would be plagued by nightmares for the rest of his life as it was. He didn't need to add another notch in his belt.

He pulled out onto the two-lane asphalt road and turned west, letting the Stryker's powerful engine propel him up the hill. The deeper into the mountains he went, the more rugged the terrain. Even if he had wanted to stay off the main road, he didn't see how that would have been possible. Jagged rocks had been blasted and cut away to make room for the road, and a sheer drop into a ravine on his left caused him to subconsciously hug the narrow shoulder on the opposite side.

After several minutes of winding back and forth through the forest, he rounded a bend to the right and spotted the Gabbs Valley stretching out in front of him. Smaller hills and distant mountains broke up the smooth landscape, but like a fatigued marathoner who had spotted the finish line, Benjamin pressed his foot into the floor and spurred the armored vehicle faster down the hill.

Almost there.

Following one last hairpin turn to the south, he eased off the gas pedal and slowed to a crawl as the guardrail ended and exposed empty desert to his right. Leaving the smooth asphalt surface, he again pushed the Stryker to the limits of its off-road capability and bounded over low mounds of dirt and shrubs as he pointed its nose at the remote airfield. This was the final stretch. He had rounded the last curve and was in the straightaway to the finish line.

Don't fuck up now.

The desert floor sloped gently toward one final narrow ravine, and he took care in navigating the uneven terrain. He had made good time reaching the rendezvous point, and the last thing he wanted to do was give up his advantage by stumbling into an ambush. He would remain hidden and survey the area before exposing himself.

And if things didn't look right, he wouldn't hesitate to turn and run as far and as fast as he could with the fuel he had remaining. Then he would abandon the Stryker and keep running until he found someplace where Mantis would never find him.

Ever.

Gabbs Airport
Gabbs, Nevada

Mantis stood in front of the dilapidated hangar on what could only be described as the airport's parking apron. In truth, the "airport" was really nothing more than two intersecting swaths of tamped dirt, with the east-west "runway" the longest at just under six thousand feet. She wasn't a pilot and didn't know what kind of airplane might land there, but over the several hours she had been surveying the skies overhead, she hadn't seen much more than a kettle of vultures circling above.

As the sun set and night deepened around her, she sank back into the darkest shadows and listened to the sounds being carried on the wind. Nevada State Route 361 was far from a bustling interstate, and she had passed fewer than five automobiles—each of them some version of a farm truck—on her way south from Middlegate. But now, the road stretched in either direction devoid of cars that might portend disaster.

She lifted the night vision monocular to her eye again and scanned the eastern horizon.

Still nothing.

She had no idea when her asset would deliver the *DRAGON LINE*—or even if he had succeeded in stealing the top-secret experimental weapon and escaping the sprawling Tonopah test range. All she knew was that it was the one thing she could possibly use as leverage against the men who had kidnapped her son. Without it, she would have no choice but to place all her faith in the NCIS special agent in hopes that the Americans could somehow track down his captors and rescue him.

But based on how deeply she had managed to infiltrate the American government, she didn't think that likely.

No, it was up to her to get Adam back.

Lowering the monocular, Mantis leaned back against the hangar's corrugated metal siding and checked her watch. She would wait all night if she had to. Like most things, whether her asset came through for her was entirely beyond her control. If he did, she just hoped he delivered the weapon with enough time for her to put the wheels in motion on her plan to recover her son.

She knew her position within the Ministry made her a target. But it also gave her the tools and resources she would need to eradicate those who had threatened her. She checked her watch again, growing increasingly anxious to take receipt of the *DRAGON LINE* and go on the attack.

It will be my greatest achievement.

38

Near Gabbs Airport
Gabbs, Nevada

As capable as the Stryker DVE was, it lacked the ability to scan over far distances. Had he thought ahead, Benjamin might have brought with him a pair of binoculars or something else he could have used to surveil the isolated airport. But he hadn't, so he was left with only his trusty Mark 1 Mod 0 eyeball as tool of choice. He sat atop the armored vehicle and shivered with each gust of wind that blew down the slope at his back—just one more reminder of how inhospitable the desert could be. The days were hot with a brutal and relentless sun, but the nights were bitterly cold and dark.

And suffocatingly lonely.

After seeing nothing suspicious during an hour spent in the foothills east of the airport, Benjamin decided he had waited long enough. He climbed through the hatch and lowered himself into the driver's seat, fired up the Caterpillar C7 engine, then sealed himself inside. He adjusted the contrast on the Stryker DVE display in front of him before resuming his slow procession down to the valley floor.

"You're almost there, Benny boy," he said. As he thought about crossing the highway and delivering the weapon to Mantis, he felt the tightness in his chest ease up for the first time since he had boarded the Boeing in Las Vegas. All he needed to do was make it through the next few minutes, and he could be free of the guilt. "Mission accomplished," he added, mocking the preternatural arrogance of the former president who claimed victory in Iraq.

Leaving Craig Canyon, Benjamin found a gravel road and steered the Stryker onto its relatively smooth surface. He ignored his fears and pressed his foot harder into the floorboard to bring the armored vehicle up to speed. The more distance he put between him and the Tonopah Test Range, the more confident he felt that he was still alone in the middle of nowhere.

He drove past what looked like a wellhead and reached Nevada State Route 361. He paused long enough to open the hatch above his head and scan the highway in both directions, then proceeded across onto a dirt road his map showed as leading to the southern perimeter of the airfield—or what passed as an airfield in that isolated patch of Nevada desert.

"Almost there," he said again.

The finish line was in sight. All he had to do was drive another mile. After all the miles he had put behind him and all the obstacles he had overcome, this last one would be the easiest.

Then the Stryker hit a large pothole, and Benjamin bounced off the thick steel above him, as if to remind him he wasn't out of the woods yet. But even the stars ringing his vision and the knot forming on the crown of his head weren't enough to erase the shit-eating grin that had crept onto his face. At long last, he had made it.

Nothing can stop me now.

Then, his screen went blank.

Mantis heard the Stryker's diesel engine straining long before she saw it. She stepped forward into the night and lifted the night vision monocular to her eye again, sweeping across the horizon to spot a growing cloud of dust following a rapidly approaching vehicle from the east.

That has to be him.

She was about to lower the monocular in triumph and prepare for his arrival when a dark shadow settled over her narrow field of view as if someone had turned off a nearby floodlight. Puzzled, she squinted at the green-hued image of the armored vehicle rumbling along a gravel road on the opposite side of the highway. She watched it pause momentarily, then cross over onto the dirt road leading to the airport's southern perimeter.

But still, something about it seemed off. Shadows shifted across the ground in unnatural ways as if something other than the moon was illuminating the Stryker. Puzzled, she lowered the monocular and scanned the horizon with her naked eye but saw nothing out of the ordinary.

What the hell?

She stepped away from the metal hangar, thinking that maybe her position just inside the open doors had somehow distorted her view of the approaching vehicle. Maybe it was a trick of the mind or a byproduct of her already heightened paranoia.

But she hadn't reached her position within the Ministry by being cavalier with seemingly unrelated pieces of intelligence just because she couldn't understand them. The odd view through her night vision monocular had provided a clue of . . . *something.* Just because she wasn't sure what that was yet didn't mean she could simply dismiss it and act as if nothing was amiss.

Believing that exhibiting caution would be the prudent course of action, Mantis turned away from the encroaching darkness and strode inside the hangar where she had parked her Tesla Model X. She opened the awkwardly shaped cargo compartment at the front of the SUV known as a "frunk," unzipped a canvas duffel, and removed something she had never had cause to use in her role as spymaster before—a suppressed Heckler & Koch MP7 personal defense weapon.

Even though she had never before resorted to using the machine pistol, she was more than skilled in its use. Mantis extended the buttstock and flipped down the forward grip before yanking the charging handle back to chamber the first of thirty 4.6 x 30mm cartridges. She snatched up a backpack containing several more thirty-round magazines and other tools she might need if things went south, slammed the frunk closed, and returned to the expansive parking apron in front of the hangar.

Feeling the first trace of anxiety, she turned south toward the dirt road just as the Stryker came to a screeching halt and kicked up a cloud of dirt that spiraled into the air. Confused by its sudden stop, she paused and lifted the monocular to her eye once more and trained it on the immobile armored vehicle.

What she saw sent a shiver down her spine.

A brilliant wide beam of infrared light—visible only through other night vision devices—illuminated the Stryker while several smaller, sharper beams zigzagged through the dusty air like a Pink Floyd laser show. She dropped the monocular and let it dangle from its tether around her neck, then raised the MP7 and aimed it in the direction of the nearest shooter.

Benjamin was still confused by the Stryker DVE screen going blank when he heard the first gunshot. He froze, at first not understanding what it was he had heard. It had been little more than a distant muffled *pop* through the armored vehicle's thick steel walls, but something about it struck a familiar chord that gave him pause.

Are they shooting at me?

But when several more followed the first in rapid succession, there was no question what it was. He had never fired a gun before, but he had played enough video games and watched enough movies to know he didn't want to be on the receiving end. He reached for the hatch above his head—almost compelled to investigate where the shots had originated—when another gun joined the fight and added its own distinct reports to the cacophony. When a third gun opened up, his heart lurched with sudden fear.

Relax, he told himself. *You're in an armored vehicle.*

He moved his hand away from the overhead hatch and listened to the gunfight raging outside, the curious part of his brain wanting to know who was doing the shooting. Security forces from Tonopah? Local police? The Chinese? But the practical part of him didn't really care, as long as they weren't shooting at him.

If he could only get the DVE to work again, then maybe he could navigate his way back into the mountains and escape the crossfire. He fiddled with the controls on the monitor, trying to regain some semblance of a picture he could use. He knew that if he tried moving without it, he would only dig himself deeper into an already deep pile of shit.

"Dammit!" he cursed, slamming his palm against the steering wheel.

He could use the laser to dispatch whatever threat resided in the darkness outside the Stryker's armored walls, but he already knew what that would look like. He didn't want to add any more gruesome images to the carousel of horror that already plagued his subconscious. But he didn't have much of a choice.

"Dammit! Dammit! Dammit!"

He contorted his body, preparing to squeeze once more through the narrow passage into the rear of the vehicle where the laser's controls were located, when the first rounds impacted the armor plating. It sounded like someone had repeatedly hit the side of the Stryker with a ball-peen hammer, and his ears rang with the deafening sound.

"Fuck this," Benjamin exclaimed, then dropped once more into the driver's seat.

He shifted the armored vehicle into reverse and stomped on the gas pedal. It wasn't nearly as quick to accelerate in the opposite direction, but the sudden jolt of movement caused him to fly forward and impact the steering wheel with a grunt. But he quickly recovered and strained to make out anything on the blank Stryker DVE display. The image flickered once, then quickly returned to its frustrating canvas of nothingness.

It's like someone tossed a blanket over the periscope.

But he didn't have time to dissect that thought. A loud *boom* shook the vehicle just as the Stryker slammed into something hard and came to an abrupt stop. The momentum caused his head to whip backward in a painful snap and flood his limited vision with stars.

39

Mantis dropped the first shooter with a lucky shot and quickly shifted aim to the next shadow converging on the stalled armored vehicle. She emptied the rest of her magazine and released it to fall away while sprinting headlong into the darkness. With her support hand, she reached into the backpack for a fresh thirty-round magazine, then inserted it into the pistol grip.

Though she didn't have the advantage of a night vision device, her eyes had adapted to the darkness, and she saw half a dozen dark shapes closing on the Stryker from her right. She quickly resumed laying down covering fire while silently pleading for her asset to reverse the armored vehicle and escape the ambush before she lost the element of surprise. She could hold them off, but she wasn't sure for how long.

Keep moving.

But the returning gunfire abruptly put an end to her hope, and she dove to the ground to avoid the rounds snapping over her head like a swarm of angry wasps. Mantis rolled to one side, aimed her MP7 in the direction of another shooter, and squeezed the trigger without any real chance of hitting her intended target. Without thought, she emptied her second magazine and performed another emergency reload with one eye trained on the motionless Stryker.

Come on! Move, dammit!

She was growing frustrated with what she saw as a dangerous situation slipping beyond her control and becoming even more dire. If she allowed them to get their hands on the Stryker, she would lose the only leverage she had over his kidnappers. Then, Adam was as good as gone.

In a desperate attempt to keep the *DRAGON LINE* from falling into their hands, she pushed herself up onto one knee and took aim at the Stryker. Maybe her asset needed a little encouragement to make his escape. With the determination possessed only by a mother whose child was endangered, Mantis gritted her teeth and squeezed the trigger to empty her third magazine into the vehicle's thick plating.

Sparks flew as the rounds ricocheted off the Stryker's armor and the sound of metal plinking on metal echoed across the flat desert but fell on deaf ears. With the last round spent, she held her breath and waited to see if her Hail Mary had paid off.

One second passed.

Then another.

She felt her spirits sink like a life raft that had been punctured too many times to stay afloat. But then the diesel engine roared to life, and the Stryker sped away in reverse.

Breathing a sigh of relief, Mantis reached back for her last magazine when she saw the armored vehicle veer off the dirt road and head into the desert. Still, it had backed off the X and cleared the ambush, giving her the breathing room she needed to further distract them while her asset made his escape. What happened to her after that was of no consequence—just as long as they didn't take the *DRAGON LINE*.

"Fucking pigs," she muttered, then completed her final reload.

After chambering a round, she removed a fragmentation grenade from her backpack and pulled the pin. Pushing herself up to her feet, she cocked her arm back and, with a giant crow-hop in the direction of the shooters, let the grenade fly and sent it sailing through the air. Without waiting for its detonation, she pulled the MP7 up into her shoulder and resumed her frantic assault on the enemy position. Only this time she forced herself to be more discriminate with her shots, taking her time to aim at the moving shadows while waiting for the perfect time to strike.

BOOM!

The grenade detonated harmlessly between two groups of enemy fighters, but she hadn't expected it to do any real damage. She had only wanted to use it as a distraction to keep their heads down while she crossed as much open ground as possible to get within the submachine gun's effective range.

Now.

Sweeping the MP7's suppressed barrel in short arcs from left to right, Mantis sprinted toward the retreating Stryker while dodging clumps of brush and large rocks strewn across her path. But when the armored vehicle slammed into something solid and came to a jarring halt, she almost stumbled and lost half a step.

What the...

Her ears rang with the sudden onset of silence, and she slowed her advance to carefully pick her way across the battlefield while continuing to scan for unseen threats. The armored vehicle's crash seemed to have momentarily stunned the attacking force, but as the seconds ticked by, she heard their frantic, hushed voices begin coordinating a response.

One by one, dark shadows rose up from the ground and began moving again toward the Stryker. She shifted her aim but didn't pull the trigger. She needed more information before she opened Pandora's box again. How many were there? Where were they? What were they trying to accomplish?

As usual in her line of work, the decision was made for her. Suddenly, the hatch on top of the Stryker opened, and her asset willingly gave up his one advantage.

"No..."

But it was too late. She stared in disbelief as the silhouette of a man emerged, followed quickly by a single gunshot. Mantis watched in horror as her asset's body jerked backwards and fell as still as the armored vehicle he had stolen from Tonopah.

Such a stupid move.

With one careless mistake, he had taken away her only chance. Now, there was nothing she could do. Nothing to stop them from climbing into the armored vehicle and disappearing into the night. Nothing to stop them from putting a bullet in her son's head.

"No!" she shouted.

As dark shapes swarmed the eight-wheeled armored vehicle, she aimed the MP7 and pulled the trigger. Mantis rushed her shots and several plinked into the Stryker's armor, but a few reached their intended targets. One by one, the shadowed human shapes fell to the ground. But despite her withering fire, more still climbed up onto the vehicle.

One of the men plucked her asset from the hatch and tossed his body over the side onto the hard ground. When he disappeared, she shifted her aim and squeezed the trigger at an advancing soldier, dropping him with an errant shot that severed his spine.

When the bolt locked back with her final round spent, she released her grip and let the MP7 dangle at her side from its sling, then reached behind her for another party trick she had stowed in her backpack. As her fingers fumbled for purchase on its smooth shape, a searing pain blossomed in her right shoulder and spun her away from the Stryker.

Mantis gasped as her knees buckled and dropped her to the ground, still clutching the grenade. She winced and pushed herself up, but another enemy bullet found her still form and punctured a hole in her chest. A third round found its mark and toppled her onto her back.

Stunned, she blinked her eyes rapidly as if to clear her vision of the pain that enveloped her and opened and closed her mouth in an attempt to breathe. She turned her head to the right and noticed the shadowed figure of a man approaching. She looked left and was unsurprised to see the same thing. Barely audible over the sound of blood pulsing in her head and the distant rumble of the Stryker's diesel engine, she heard the men converging on her position and plotting her demise in hushed voices.

She knew she had lost the battle and likely the war. They had taken the DRAGON LINE from her and no longer had a reason to keep Adam alive. In a morbid way, she was thankful she wouldn't have to live in a world without her only son.

"Adam . . ." she croaked.

One of the men heard her whisper and bent over her. He said something she didn't understand, then raised his rifle and aimed it at her head.

Closing her eyes, she relaxed her grip and felt the grenade's spoon release with a faint *tang*.

The man leaning over her had heard it too, and he recoiled with a sharp gasp.

"*Ty Suka . . .*"

Mantis closed her eyes and prepared for the inevitable. If he didn't shoot her and put her out of her misery, her final party favor would do the trick. Despite her failures and the tidal wave of agony crashing over her, her mouth turned up at the corners in a tight smile. She had failed the Ministry and failed her son, but she welcomed death.

There was honor in that.

40

Hangar 7
Naval Air Station Fallon
Fallon, Nevada

Punky parked the Suburban in the same parking spot they had vacated only hours earlier, then climbed down from the driver's seat, feeling more fatigued than she had in a very long time. She stared blankly across the flight line at the rows of fighter jets sitting dormant in front of the hangars north of them.

Colt walked over and stood next to her near the front of the SUV. "You okay?"

"I'm just tired. Tired of chasing people who willingly sell out their country. Tired of always looking over my shoulder or seeing hidden assassins in the crowd."

Colt nodded and placed a comforting hand on her shoulder. "I get it. But what would you do if you weren't out there chasing bad guys?"

She glanced over at him and gave him a sour look.

"No, I'm serious," Colt said. "People like you—"

"What do you mean, 'people like me'?"

Colt removed his hand from her shoulder and held it up defensively. "I didn't mean that in a bad way. I'm just saying that you were born to be one of the good guys. People sleep peacefully every night because you're out there keeping our nation's enemies at bay."

"Yeah. Well, so are you," she countered.

He nodded. "And so are all the other people on this base. Or Miramar and North Island. Or the *Abraham Lincoln* and *Ronald Reagan*. Face it, Punky, you might not wear the uniform, but you were born to be a guardian of freedom. To stand up for what's right."

"I never wanted it," she said. And she meant it. After her mom had died, she placed the blame at her father's feet. As a teenager, she blamed the Navy, the SEAL Teams, and his numerous lengthy deployments. The last thing she wanted was to put on a uniform and carry on the family legacy of selfless sacrifice.

"Yet, here you are," Colt said. "Right where you belong."

She knew he was only trying to make her feel better about the choices she had made that led her to sacrifice a real life in favor of hunting spies or traitors and cleansing the corruption in her father's Navy. In truth, she didn't know how she ended up becoming a special agent with the Naval Criminal Investigative Service. But she knew it had always felt like the right choice.

"Damn you," she muttered, just as Dave appeared from the hangar's side entrance.

"You know I'm right," Colt said.

She ignored his comment and turned to wait for the SEAL Master Chief to permit them access through the turnstile and onto the secure flight line. She chewed on the inside of her lip as Colt passed through the gate. But before it was her turn, she felt her phone vibrating in her pocket.

Punky quickly fished it out and answered. "Talk to me, Camron."

"Looks like you were onto something. Facial recognition identified two of the three men from the dash camera footage."

She felt a stir of hope. "Known operatives?"

"*Sluzhba vneshney razvedki.*"

"Russia," she exclaimed. "I knew it."

Colt turned and appraised her with a worried look etched on his face.

"Based on this and what you discovered this morning in Reno, it looks like the Russian foreign intelligence service kidnapped *KMART*. For what reason, we still don't know."

Punky again debated telling him what Mantis had shared with her in the casino's cafe, but she knew he wouldn't understand. He was a good special agent, but he would approach the situation from a law enforcement angle. Had he been in her shoes, Camron would have arrested Mantis on the spot and taken the victory, no matter how small. But she had approached it like an intelligence operative and viewed the opportunity through the lens of countering espionage, weighing the risks against the potential benefits.

Camron would never have signed off on letting Mantis go. He never would have agreed to help recover her son in exchange for permanently dismantling the Ministry's West Coast network. Camron would have played it safe. She had gambled.

And now she wondered if that had been a mistake.

"Punky, you still there?"

But she was already thinking about her next move. Gamble or not, this was far from over. "Yeah, I'm still here."

"There's been another development you should be aware of . . ."

"What now?"

"I doubt it's even related, but our office was notified that an experimental directed energy weapon has gone missing from the Tonopah Test Range. The only reason this even came to our attention is because the program was sponsored by the Office of Naval Research in partnership with several other defense contractors, and they wanted us to look through the personnel assigned to the program to see if any stood out as potential compromises."

This was exactly the kind of information Mantis had promised to provide if Punky helped recover her son. "There are probably hundreds of people connected to the program—"

"Yeah, but only one person is missing."

Though she couldn't possibly see how this was related to *KMART*'s abduction, her natural curiosity got the better of her. "Who's the missing person?"

"His name is Benjamin Hayes. He's an engineer with Special Programs at Sandia National Laboratories." Camron paused for a beat. "He graduated summa cum laude with a degree in computer engineering from California Polytechnic State University in San Luis Obispo."

Her heart bolted with sudden fear. "You've got to be kidding me."

"Didn't you identify a professor at Cal Poly as having ties to the Ministry of State Security?"

"Yeah, Professor David Wang," she said. "He was a computer science professor who helped modify the waveforms used to hack into the F-35 Joint Strike Fighter."

"It makes sense that he was also recruiting."

Punky had to agree, but she didn't see how that changed anything. Maybe if she succeeded in rescuing *KMART* from the Russians, she would get all the information she needed to hang Benjamin Hayes for stealing an experimental weapon from Tonopah.

"I'll look into it," she said. "But I need you to do something for me first."

"What?"

"I'm going to send you the coordinates for where the trooper was shot, and I need you to look at the cell towers in the area and identify what phones connected to it around the time of the shooting."

"There will probably be hundreds, if not thousands of phones, Punky."

She shook her head. "I don't think you realize just how isolated it really is out here. Please. Just do this for me."

He sighed heavily on the other end. "I'll see what I can do."

When she ended the call, she swapped out her personal phone for the burner phone Mantis had given her. Ignoring Colt and Dave—who were standing off to the side and waiting not-so-patiently for her to fill them in—she placed her call and waited for the Chinese spymaster to answer.

No answer.

She hung up and tried again.

No answer.

"Dammit," she muttered.

"What's going on?" Colt asked.

Punky scrunched up her face. "A lot. It looks like the Russians kidnapped *KMART*—"

"The Russians?"

"Yeah, and I have a hard time believing Mantis didn't know that. She was in charge of the Ministry's largest network in the United States Bureau. There is *no way* she didn't know the Russians were behind this."

"Did you say something about the JSF?" Colt asked.

She looked at the TOPGUN pilot as if confused, then remembered that he had been piloting the fifth-generation stealth fighter when the Chinese attempted hacking into it. "Yeah, it appears a student of the professor responsible for that hack has gone missing. Along with an experimental directed energy weapon."

"Directed energy?" Dave asked.

"A laser," Punky said.

"Like Star Trek?"

"Something like that." But her mind wasn't on the missing computer engineer or futuristic laser weapon. She needed to track down the Russians and bring down the Ministry's West Coast network once and for all. Punky switched back to her personal phone and dialed Camron's number again.

He answered after one ring. "Forget something?"

"Actually, yeah." She opened the burner phone and read him the phone number she had been using to reach Mantis.

"What am I supposed to do with this?"

"When you get the list of numbers that connected with the cell towers in that area, cross-reference it with this number."

If she couldn't find *KMART* or the Russians, then maybe she could find Mantis.

41

Vice President's Ceremonial Office
Eisenhower Executive Office Building
Washington, DC

It was already late when Vice President Jonathan Adams walked into his expansive office in the Eisenhower Executive Office Building and sat behind the mahogany pedestal desk to review the itinerary for the next day's trip to Nevada. Colloquially known as the Theodore Roosevelt desk, it had an understated design with elegant, masculine lines and brass pulls.

Jonathan pulled out the center drawer and looked at the signatures of the desk's previous users. Nelson Rockefeller, Walter Mondale, George H.W. Bush, Dan Quayle, Al Gore, Dick Cheney, Joe Biden, and Mike Pence. Even Presidents Harry S. Truman and Dwight D. Eisenhower had added their names following the desk's use in the Oval Office from 1945 to 1961. He traced his finger over the looping signatures and felt a part of the lasting legacy that began when the desk had been modified to conceal a recording device during Nixon's presidency.

A device that had played a role in his downfall.

His chief of staff walked across the carpeted floor and stood in front of his desk before clearing his throat. "Sir, I thought you might want to know

that Secretary Short and General Tilley are on their way to the White
House to speak with the president."

Jonathan set down the itinerary and looked up at his longtime friend.
"Do you know why?"

Sam shook his head. "My source at the Pentagon didn't know. He just
said everyone is really worked up about something and that they left in a
hurry."

The vice president leaned back in his leather executive swivel chair and
massaged his chiseled chin. He had spent a considerable amount of time
cultivating relationships within the Department of Defense and gone to
great lengths to be seen as the military's champion in the administration.
Normally the Secretary of Defense or Chairman of the Joint Chiefs of Staff
called him directly before bothering the president with minor issues. That
they hadn't done so this time spoke volumes about what their visit
portended.

"Keep working on your sources," Jonathan said. "I can't afford to be
frozen out. If something big is going on, I need to be a part of it."

It was more than just boastful arrogance or the embodiment of his
thoughtfully crafted persona that compelled him to be in the same room
with the three most powerful men in the world. It was his unwavering
sense of duty. Though he had spent his entire adult life in service to the
country, part of him regretted never taking the opportunity to serve in the
military. It was that part of him that drove him to pour his efforts into
supporting the men and women in uniform.

But if his country was under attack, he needed to be included in the
decision to hit back.

"Yes, sir," Sam said, then ducked back through the door into the
adjoining room where he kept his office. Jonathan looked across the expansive and ornately decorated room bathed in soft light from chandeliers that
were replicas of the turn-of-the-century gasoliers that formerly adorned the
room. Aside from the history scribbled into his desk's center drawer, he
knew the room had once been the office of sixteen secretaries of the Navy
when the executive office building had been home to the State, Navy, and
War Departments.

He picked up the phone on his desk and pressed the button that connected him directly to Donald Livingstone, the assistant to the president for national security affairs—a role more commonly known as the national security advisor. The call picked up after one ring.

"Mister Vice President."

"Don, what the hell's going on? Why are Frank and Bart on their way to the White House?"

The president's national security advisor sighed heavily as if burdened by the knowledge he was being asked to provide. "A minor matter. Nothing more."

"Bullshit," Jonathan said. His tone was playful but cut with a shard of truth.

"That's all I'm at liberty to say."

"Is he going to call the council together?"

Established by the National Security Act of 1947, the National Security Council was the president's principal forum for national security and foreign policy decision making. Chaired by the president, regular attendees included his chief of staff, the vice president, attorney general, national security advisor, the US representative to the United Nations, the administrator of the US agency for international development, and the secretaries of state, treasury, defense, energy, and homeland security. The chairman of the joint chiefs of staff and the director of national intelligence rounded out the advisors for military and intelligence matters.

Jonathan knew he had undercut the president by allowing Sam to leak his intent not to run for a second term. But he didn't think it so grievous that the president would exclude him from sitting on the council if convened.

"I don't know yet," Don said.

Jonathan didn't like not being in the know. He had built relationships and forged coalitions to prevent that from happening, and he bit back a sharp retort before responding. "Well, find out. I'm on my way over right now."

"Mister Vice—"

He hung up the phone and looked down at the mahogany desk, wondering if any of its previous users had been shut out by the president. Then again, Sam's reporter friend hadn't done him any favors.

"Sam!" he bellowed as he pushed himself to his feet.

"Yes, Mister Vice President," his chief of staff replied from the adjacent room.

"I'm going across the street."

Sam knew what he meant and strode into the room, ready to accompany his boss and longtime friend across West Exec to the Oval Office of the White House.

Two hours later, Jonathan burst from the White House onto West Exec and strode purposefully across the parking lot toward the Eisenhower Executive Office Building. Sam was only two paces behind, but he hurried to catch up and pull even with the vice president.

"Sir, we need to postpone your trip," Sam said.

Jonathan shook his head. If there was one axiom he had always used to guide him, it was that he never allowed another person to dictate his actions. When he had received an unsolicited acceptance letter to his estranged father's alma mater of Stanford, he promptly shredded it and sent it back to the elder Adams with a handwritten note proclaiming his intent to go to cross-bay rival, Cal. When a San Diego–based defense contractor had offered to contribute handsomely to a war chest for his Senate bid in exchange for favorable votes, he outed the company in a public statement that made it clear he could not be bought. And when a reporter from the Washington Post had asked questions about something that would ruin his political career if made public, he hadn't thought twice about offering him a more appealing story.

There was no way he was going to allow the theft of an experimental directed energy weapon to deter him from demonstrating his commitment to supporting the American fighting man and woman. If he wanted to be seen as a strong leader and capable of donning the mantle of commander-in-chief, he needed to stand firm in the face of this uncertainty.

His chief of staff gripped his elbow and pulled him to a stop.

He whipped around, jaw clenched in barely constrained anger. "Do not forget your place, Sam."

"This *is* my place, Jonathan," his chief of staff said, holding up his hands in a calming, placating gesture.

The use of his name instead of title—as his friend normally insisted—instantly cut the tension between them. Jonathan closed his eyes and lowered his chin to his chest in obvious defeat. "I'm sorry. You're right."

Sam placed both hands on the vice president's arms as he spoke. "Until we know who has the weapon and what they intend on doing with it, we can't risk having you fly into Nevada and knowingly put yourself in danger. I know you want to be seen as brave and unafraid, but your image will be useless if you're dead."

He opened his eyes and saw the earnestness etched on his friend's face. "You heard Frank. There's no reason to think whoever stole it has any intention of using it."

"Jonathan—"

"I know you mean well, Sam, but the answer is no. We're leaving on time." Jonathan looked at the black Rolex Daytona on his wrist, as if to watch the minute hand sweeping them ever closer to their planned departure the next morning from Andrews Air Force Base. "We have twelve hours to find out who has it."

Sam took a deep breath and straightened his back to stand tall in front of his friend. "Yes, Mister Vice President."

42

Old Ebbitt Grill
Washington, DC

A short while later, Samuel Chambers darted across the sidewalk on the corner with G Street and purposely avoided looking at his watch. Like most nights, he was arriving well into the iconic tavern's second daily happy hour but had texted ahead and placed an order for a dozen Jack's Point oysters and a tin of Conservas sardines from Spain. That and a few rounds of Gin Balalajkas, and he might be able to catch a few hours of sleep before boarding Air Force Two for their trip out west.

He swept in through the revolving door and turned left to head upstairs for the Corner Bar. Even though it was well after midnight, Washington's oldest saloon was still teeming with politicos. Doffing his light overcoat, he ignored the polite nods of recognition from other White House and Congressional staffers and weaved through the crowd to the open seat waiting for him at the bar. It was open and waiting for him each night.

"Thought you were never gonna make it," Teddy said.

Sam didn't bother with an explanation and reached for the highball and his first drink of the night. He tipped the glass back and sighed as the gin concoction passed his lips and slowly descended into his empty stomach. The drink—named for a Russian stringed instrument from the eigh-teenth century—paired well with oysters and caviar. Or, in Sam's case, the Conservas sardines he thought of as his guilty pleasure.

Teddy watched Sam drain the first glass and gesture for the bartender for a second round. "Long day?" he asked.

Sam shook his head. "Not any longer than the others."

Of course, the second drink on the way argued that point. "Uh-huh."

The Conservas were served with crusty bread and whipped salted butter, and Sam put a sardine on a chunk of bread and popped it into his mouth before finally taking his seat next to Teddy. He savored the taste while letting the stress of the day fade away with each bite.

"You're flying out to Nevada tomorrow, aren't you?"

A sour look crossed Sam's face. "Against my objections."

Teddy took a sip of his gin martini and nodded in agreement. "You know he'll poll well in Nevada. Maybe you should capitalize on the buzz surrounding the news by visiting a base in a swing state instead. It might give you more bang for your buck."

"It's not that . . ."

But he stopped himself from saying more. As much as he wanted to explain that it had nothing to do with polling or potential votes, he had to remind himself that not everybody was privy to the knowl-edge that an experimental directed energy weapon had gone missing from the Tonopah Test Range. But even if that knowledge wasn't clas-sified or being held close within the president's inner circle, he couldn't very well discuss it with one of the least discreet men in Washington.

Even if Teddy had his uses.

Like leaking Jonathan's intent to run for president.

Teddy eyed him suspiciously as if looking for a hidden meaning that might give him the scoop on a story. But Sam shook his head. "There's not a story here. I promise."

"Like Aurora Holdings?"

Sam gave his friend a hard glance. "Let's not go there tonight."

The reporter shrugged, took another sip of his martini, then nodded at the bartender who set a drink in front of Sam.

Sam reached for the highball without looking but stopped just shy of lifting it. "I think you gave me the wrong drink."

After the day he'd had, the last thing he wanted to do was explain to his regular bartender how he intended to have his usual drink made with gin, orange juice, and Schweppes Russchian—tonic water with a hint of berries, carrot, and hibiscus. But the drink in his hand was not that.

"No, sir. This is courtesy of the gentleman at the end of the bar."

Sam eyed the drink dubiously, then craned his neck out to look beyond the throng of people to where the bartender had gestured. But he didn't see anyone he recognized.

"What is it?"

"From Russia with Love."

Sam's heart skipped a beat, but he forced himself to act nonchalant and nodded in thanks to the bartender. He had no idea who would have sent him the drink—or why—but just the name alone was enough to send a chill down his spine.

"I'll be right back," he said to Teddy, scooping the highball off the bar and sliding off the stool.

It was nearing one a.m., but the crowded bar showed no signs of thinning out. Contrary to popular public opinion, most deals in Washington weren't made during normal business hours. And Old Ebbitt Grill had seen more than its fair share of back-room handshakes.

Sam weaved through the patrons who were packed like his Conservas sardines, firmly moving aside the ones not observant enough to see the vice president's chief of staff approaching. With a racing heart, his eyes fell on a man who sat hunched over at the end of the bar. He was rail thin, wore a bespoke suit that set him apart from even the more finely dressed regulars, and had a full head of silver hair that made him appear dignified.

Despite the unsolicited and unnerving drink.

Sam wedged himself in between the older gentleman and a young woman who was probably an undergraduate student at Georgetown. She started to protest, but Sam shot a look at the young staffer she had been talking with, and he wisely guided her off the stool and away from the bar. Sam took the vacant seat and set the highball in front of him.

"Do I have you to thank for this?" he asked, staring at the unfamiliar face.

He noticed that the man hadn't splurged on a fancy cocktail for himself and instead sipped clear liquid from a shot glass while staring straight ahead without emotion.

"It got your attention, didn't it?"

Sam had never been gifted with the ability to ferret out specific accents, but the stranger's was so obviously Russian that he wasn't at a disadvantage. Of course, based on the drink that had been foisted on him, he could have guessed that even before confronting him.

He slid the highball in the man's direction. "Thank you, but I'm not much of a vodka drinker."

The stranger tipped his own glass back and drained the remaining vodka. "Shame."

Sam stared at the man—who hadn't even bothered looking in his direction—and grew impatient. "Was there something you wanted to say to me?"

Taking his time, the stranger reached into his tailored suit jacket for a wallet and removed several crisp hundred-dollar bills. He set them on the bar, then placed the empty shot glass on top. He returned the wallet to his inside breast pocket, then fished around for a few more seconds before removing a photograph and laying it face down on the bar.

Sam saw a phone number scrawled on the back of the photograph, but he resisted the urge to snatch it off the bar and turn it over. As much as he wanted to know what the old man had brought him, he didn't want to give him the satisfaction of knowing he was terrified. So, he did what he always did. He plastered a smug smile on his face and acted as if he was in complete control.

At last, the man turned and stared at him.

Sam's smile faltered, but he prevented himself from recoiling. The stranger's right eye was a prosthetic, tickling a memory he had tried to bury long ago, but his good eye bored into him and saw right through his facade. Without mirth or satisfaction, the stranger studied Sam in a way that conveyed his utter contempt.

"Call me," he said. "*Before* you leave for Nevada."

Sam opened his mouth to reply but couldn't find the words. The vice president's itinerary wasn't entirely secret, but it unnerved him that the stranger knew who he was and where he was going. The din of the crowded bar faded into the background, leaving him with only the sound of his beating heart and panicked breathing. Still, he tried to present a calm outward demeanor, even if his insides twisted and knotted up with total fear.

The stranger slid off the stool, buttoned the top button on his suit jacket, then placed a matching felt fedora on his head. He rested a calloused hand on Sam's shoulder and gave it a squeeze, applying just enough pressure that Sam felt the notable absence of the outer two digits.

"*Before* you leave," he said again, then brushed past on his way to the exit.

Sam remained stock-still for several seconds to calm his breathing, but when he reached for the photo, his hand trembled. As his fingers rested on the glossy backing, the walls he had built around a particular memory came crashing down. He had even begun to think he had succeeded in burying it for good—that his influence in Washington had given him some semblance of immunity.

But when he turned the photo over, he knew he had been wrong.

It had made him a target.

43

Thomas Jefferson Memorial
Washington, DC

Sam woke early on Sunday with the taste of Gin Balalajkas still on his breath, but his hangover that morning had more to do with the stranger who had approached him at the bar than with consuming copious amounts of alcohol. Whatever the reason, he had tossed and turned most of the night, and he yawned while standing on the walking path and staring across the placid tidal basin at the towering obelisk of the Washington Monument on the other side.

What am I doing here?

He lifted his wrist to look at the time again—bemoaning how little he had remaining until he was supposed to be at Andrews Air Force Base—then turned and put his back to the water and made for the first set of marble-stepped terraces leading up to the memorial.

During his time in office, President Roosevelt had ordered the pruning of every tree between the White House and the Jefferson Memorial. Since then, there existed a direct line of sight from where he stood to the office he hoped his boss and longtime friend would occupy in a little over a year.

As long as this unexpected meeting didn't put a kink in those plans.

But as Sam began climbing the steps to the memorial, he couldn't help but feel as if he was turning his back on both his friend and the White House by even entertaining this.

I shouldn't be here.

He looked up at the circular, open-air structure featuring a shallow dome supported by a colonnade composed of twenty-six Ionic columns. It had been crafted from white Imperial Danby marble from Vermont, and rested on a wide terrace flanked by granite buttresses on either side of the granite and marble stairs. He thought it a grand memorial for the American statesman, diplomat, lawyer, architect, philosopher, and Founding Father.

It was still early and the grounds surrounding the memorial were largely devoid of visitors, giving Sam the impression that he had the entire place to himself. But, of course, he knew that wasn't the case. After debating the decision for much of the night, Sam had called the phone number scrawled on the back of the photograph and received a very simple set of instructions to follow.

Jefferson Memorial. Eight a.m.

It was ten minutes to eight when Sam climbed the last of the steps leading to the north portico and stepped inside, refusing to make eye contact with the bronze statue of his political hero standing atop a pedestal of black Minnesota granite. He even avoided looking at the scroll in the statue's left hand—a representation of the Declaration of Independence—feeling as if the words it contained were a silent indictment of his past actions.

But that didn't mean he could ignore them.

He was startled by a voice behind him. "That whenever any Form of Government becomes destructive of these ends, it is the Right of the People to alter or to abolish it."

Sam turned just as the frail-looking older man from the night before stepped out from behind a column and stared at him with his one good eye. "I've read it," he said, his mouth suddenly dry.

But the Russian continued. "And to institute *new* Government."

Sam held his gaze. "I said I've read it."

"Then you understand why those words have significance to this moment."

Sam swallowed back the fear he had felt since first confronting the stranger the night before. "Who are you?"

"I'm not surprised you don't remember me. It's been a long time since we last met." He removed the black leather glove covering his right hand—the one missing two digits—and held it out in greeting. "My name is Viktor Drakov."

Sam recoiled. The name did more than tickle a faint memory, and his heart suddenly raced with worry that his worst fear had finally come to light. The man was right. It *had* been a long time since they last met. Almost two full decades.

"Are you behind what happened in Nevada?"

Viktor shrugged. "If I knew what you were talking about, I might be able to answer."

Memories of dealing with a younger Viktor and several of his Russian SVR operatives came flooding back, and he suddenly remembered their knack for doublespeak. "The experimental weapon?"

Again, the older man shrugged. But Sam thought he saw a sparkle in his eye.

"Why are you here? What exactly do you want from me?"

Viktor let his hand dangle in the air between them, then finally lowered and slipped it back into his glove. "I've come to ask a favor from an old friend."

"An *old friend*?"

Viktor smiled. "What else should I call the person who asked for my help many years ago?"

Not for the first time, Sam regretted the brashness of his youth. He had only been trying to help Jonathan out of a situation that would have derailed his political career before it even began. Of course, Jonathan knew. Not all the details, but enough to make it clear they were bonded together for life—that Sam would do anything to protect Jonathan and that he expected the same loyalty in return. It was one of the many secrets the two had shared for nearly twenty years. But it was the only one they never talked about.

And the one Teddy had come a little too close to uncovering.

That realization hit Sam like a sledgehammer. "Did you put him up to it?"

Viktor had mastered the ability to look genuinely confused and innocent of the implied accusations. "Put *who* up to *what*?"

"Teddy Miller," Sam replied.

"Your reporter friend?"

"Did you tell him about Aurora Holdings?"

But the Russian shook his head. "*Nyet.* If Teddy is starting to ask questions, it only means you have become careless. Maybe you thought the past could remain buried and that the sins of your youth would be forgotten? That you could simply accept my help and walk away?"

Sam's heart hammered in his chest, and he suddenly felt light-headed. "Are you threatening me?"

"Threatening?" Viktor shook his head and made a soft clucking sound. "*Nyet.* I am not threatening you. I am merely asking you for the same courtesy I gave you all those years ago."

Sam swallowed. "Then why the picture?"

Viktor's smile was tight. "Just a reminder."

"Of what? A mistake that was made twenty years ago?" The longer he stood under the shadow of Thomas Jefferson, the more certain he was that it had also been a mistake to come today. He should have simply ripped up the picture and pretended none of it ever happened. "Is this some sort of shakedown?"

Again, the older man didn't appear fazed by Sam's indignation. "As I said, I came to ask a favor from a friend. I have no intention of exposing your secrets—"

"He's not the same person he was back then," Sam said. Then, almost as an afterthought, he added, "And neither am I."

"That's why I'm asking for your help."

A light gust of wind could have knocked Sam over. For almost twenty years, he had convinced himself that a simple business arrangement in the form of Aurora Holdings would keep them safe. From the California State Legislature to the US House of Representatives—from Sacramento to Washington, DC—Sam had lived with the belief that what he had done to promote Jonathan to the second-highest position in government would remain buried in the past.

And now Viktor had come to threaten that belief.

Sam chewed on his lip. But what if Viktor *hadn't* come to threaten it? What if Viktor had come to offer him an opportunity to bury the secret once and for all? What if this was his chance to ascend Jonathan to the White House without a dark cloud hanging over them—a dark cloud that possessed the power to take down one of the most popular political figures in American history. What if this was an opportunity?

Like everything in politics, Sam owed it to his boss to evaluate what the Russian had to offer. It was the only reason he had taken this detour to meet with the former intelligence operative.

"What's the favor?"

Then, Viktor told him.

Hangar 7
Naval Air Station Fallon
Fallon, Nevada

Punky opened her eyes and stared up at the ceiling tiles, groaning at the stiffness in her neck caused by sleeping on a sofa in the *Black Ponies* ready room. She pushed herself upright and swung her feet out onto the floor, instantly regretting her decision not to get a room at the Navy Gateway Inns and Suites. But it had been late when they returned to the hangar, and like she had told Colt, she was utterly exhausted.

The ready room door opened, and Colt walked in carrying two cups of steaming hot coffee. "Thought you could use a little pick-me-up," he said, setting one of the cups on the large conference table in the middle of the room.

Punky yawned, then stood from the couch and stretched her arms high while rolling her head from side to side. "Thanks. It wasn't the greatest night of sleep, but I definitely needed it."

Colt pulled out a chair and sat down. "Do you think the missing laser weapon is somehow related to all this?"

Punky reached for the cup of coffee and took a sip, wincing as it scalded her tongue. "Maybe. Maybe not. But I'm not sure it really matters."

But the look on Colt's face made her think he didn't agree.

"Why? What are you thinking?"

He slid a sheet of paper across the table. At the top was a header that read, "UNCLASSIFIED/CUI."

"CUI? What's this?"

"Controlled Unclassified Information. It means the information was created by the government and not classified but still requires safeguarding. In this case, it's the flight schedule for the Naval Aviation Warfighting Development Center."

Punky picked up the sheet of paper and scanned it, not seeing what had Colt so worked up. "What am I missing?"

"Look at the notes."

She scanned the document that was dated for that day and listed information such as the Julian date, sunrise, and sunset, and several rows she suspected were for the scheduled flights. At the bottom, she found the block labeled "Notes" and read the first one.

"Twelve to fourteen hundred, field closed for VIP movement." She looked up at Colt. "What VIP?"

"I wondered the same thing, so I called the duty officer."

Her coffee forgotten, Punky had an uneasy feeling she wasn't going to like what Colt found out. "And?"

"It appears that the vice president is coming to visit today." He pointed to one of the scheduled flights. "And the admiral wants me to take him flying."

She shook her head. "But the laser . . ."

"That's what has me worried too. We now know the Russians abducted *KMART* and moved him somewhere into the Nevada desert. The head of the Ministry's West Coast network asked for your help to recover him, and now you can't reach her. You don't think they're using him as leverage over her?"

Punky nodded. "I do think that. But for what?"

"The Russians have threatened Mantis. Somebody with ties to a known Chinese operative at Cal Poly has gone missing with an experimental weapon. And the vice president is coming for a visit. That's three major events happening at the same time."

Punky understood exactly what Colt was driving at, and she admitted it made a lot of sense. Even before learning that the vice president was coming to visit Fallon, she knew *KMART's* abduction by the Russians was somehow tied to the laser weapon. But she didn't know for what purpose.

"So, what are we going to do about it?" Colt asked.

Before she could answer, Dave walked into the ready room wearing a khaki-colored two-piece flight suit. "I assume you two are talking about the VP's visit later today?"

"What do you know about it?" Punky asked.

Dave leaned over Colt's shoulder and stole his cup of coffee. He took a sip and winced. "Where'd you get this sludge?"

"Seriously, Dave. Do you think the vice president's visit is a good idea considering what's been going on?"

The SEAL Master Chief set the cup back down on the table. "No, actually I don't. And neither does the skipper. That's why he called back to the Beach and had them elevate our concerns through JSOC."

"What does JSOC have to do with this?" Punky asked.

Colt and Dave traded glances before the SEAL replied. "This squadron falls under the operational control of the Joint Special Operations Command Naval Special Warfare task force. Our bosses back in Virginia Beach have a direct line to the JSOC commanding general who can elevate our concerns directly to the secretary of defense."

"And what was their take?" Colt asked.

"The SecDef and chairman of the joint chiefs met with the president last night. The skipper called me this morning and let me know that we've been tasked with finding the missing weapon and neutralizing the threat before the vice president's arrival."

Punky's jaw dropped open in shock. "But we don't even know where to look."

Her cell phone rang before Dave could dismiss her concerns, and she fished it out to answer.

"Please tell me you found something, Camron."

The NCIS supervisory special agent sounded tired but relieved. "I cross-referenced that phone number like you asked and got several hits on nearby cell towers, but none were on the highway at the time of the trooper's shooting."

She groaned, feeling like she had hit another roadblock. "So, we're back to square one."

"Maybe not," Camron said. "That cell phone is still pinging a tower near the town of Gabbs."

Punky jumped to her feet, feeling like she had just been given the information she needed to break the case wide open. "Thanks, Camron."

She ended the call and quickly summarized for Colt and Dave what she had learned. Out of all the assets they had available at their disposal, the squadron's Super Tucano was ideally suited for locating and neutralizing the experimental laser weapon. But they still needed to put boots on the ground to locate the Russians.

"So, what are we going to do?" Colt asked.

"I need to get out to Gabbs," Punky said.

Dave agreed. "I'll have Todd and my boys take you in our Flyer 60 while we jump in the Super Tucano and track down this laser weapon."

"We?" Colt asked.

"Well, it ain't gonna fly itself, flyboy."

Thirty minutes later, Colt returned from the NAWDC hangar with a flight suit and parachute bag containing his flight gear and met Dave in the squadron's paraloft to get dressed for their flight. Though he hadn't flown the A-29 Super Tucano in several years, the process of putting on flight gear —whether for training or for combat—felt like the most natural thing in the world.

The two men donned their gear in silence, then exited the paraloft for the cavernous hangar. The massive doors were open, exposing the squadron's only airplane to the Nevada sunlight. Though it was Sunday— and most of the pilots assigned to the base were still enjoying Hook in Reno —it still felt oddly blasphemous to expose their top-secret squadron to the rest of the base.

Dave turned to Colt. "You ready for this?"

"I was born ready," he replied. Though a kaleidoscope of butterflies raced around his stomach, he knew they would calm once the plane's wheels broke free from the ground. Regardless of branch or aircraft, every pilot felt at home in the sky. It was his natural habitat where instincts and training took over—where he executed his mission without the unrelenting fear or worry that gnawed at him when confined to the earth.

He slapped Dave on the back and turned him toward the A-29 Super Tucano sitting idle in the middle of the hangar. He suspected they would have normally towed the plane onto the ramp before the flight, but without even a skeleton crew to get the plane ready, most of the preflight preparation had fallen on the Master Chief. Even so, Colt and Dave conducted the preflight inspection as a crew.

Colt started forward of the wing on the port side and walked toward the nose, looking for anything that hinted the plane wasn't ready to fly. Things like missing panels were obvious and easy to spot, but fluid leaks were often harder to catch. When he approached the large Hartzell propeller, he stepped outside the prop arc and ran a hand along the leading edge of each blade, looking for nicks or other damage. It didn't matter that the plane was practically brand-new—habits were habits.

Colt glanced over at Dave, who had started in the same place but worked his way along the port wing to inspect the FN Herstal M3P machine-gun barrel protruding from the leading edge inboard of the first hard point. Then he dropped into a squat and examined the GBU-12 Paveway II five-hundred-pound laser-guided bomb mounted there.

"You really think it's going to come to that?"

"You never know. But we'll be ready no matter what."

Colt nodded and knelt to inspect the bomb's twin on the starboard side, then the LAU-68 2.75-inch rocket launcher carried on the outer hard point. As a former Hornet driver, Colt had trained with rockets before, but this would be the first time employing the Mk4 Folding-Fin Aerial Rockets tipped with WDU-4/A anti-personnel warheads—each containing 2,200 20-grain flechettes.

The Super Tucano carried far less ordnance than the Hornet. But two 500-pound bombs, fourteen rockets, and four hundred rounds of .50 cal were more than enough to neutralize any threat that Punky and the SEALs on the ground might encounter.

Colt gave Dave a serious look. "All set?"

"Let's do it, brother."

He waited for Dave to open the canopy and climb into the back seat before he stepped up onto the wing. With one more glance at the eerie calmness enveloping them, he stepped over the rail and lowered himself into his ejection seat, where the first of his butterflies fell dormant.

He was in his element.

45

Adam sat on the edge of the cot with his head buried in his hands, wishing he could wake from the nightmare that had consumed his life for the last several years. Though his captors had stripped him of his clothes and left them somewhere in the desert, they'd given him a pair of simple gray sweatpants and a sweatshirt to wear while he waited for whatever was supposed to happen to happen.

He had no idea where he was, though he suspected he was in just another rundown shithole homestead deep in the middle of nowhere. He should have been relaxing in his family's upscale cabin in Tahoe, but instead he'd done the absolutely wrong thing and dug himself an even deeper hole. Like always.

"Why me?"

Frustrated, he rose from the cot and paced the dirt floor of the shed they had locked him inside. It had been freezing cold at night and surprisingly hot during the day, but at least they had left him alone for the most part.

Six paces. Stop. Turn.

Back and forth, Adam walked the worn path he had cut into the dirt while replaying the events of the last several years in his mind. He hadn't joined the Marine Corps intending to be a total fuck-up, but within the first forty-eight hours of boot camp, he knew he wasn't like the other young men and women who had enlisted to be like the steely-eyed killers they saw on recruiting posters. He didn't enjoy running—or any other physical activity for that matter—and he sure as shit didn't get a hard-on by yelling "ooh-rah" every few minutes.

Six paces. Stop. Turn.

So, it seemed like a natural progression for him to fall into the welcoming arms of a woman like Chen. She had made him feel important. Like he mattered. By the time he realized he wasn't important and didn't matter at all to her, he was already too far in to back out. Chen had only used him to get what she wanted. Now the Ministry had him by the balls, and there wasn't a damn thing he could do about it.

With a heavy sigh, he started pacing again but stopped short when he heard someone rattling the chain that kept him locked inside the shed. He turned to face the door and shuffled back several paces while he waited to see who it was. Not that it mattered. None of his captors had abused him or tortured him. Hell, they hadn't even talked to him other than to issue an occasional curt command.

Adam heard the chain fall away and tensed for the door to open. When it did, the sudden daylight stunned him, and he squinted against its brilliance to see an imposing figure standing in the doorway.

"Back against the wall," the voice commanded.

It wasn't quite as brutish as the others but carried far more authority. Feeling like a new recruit responding to the commands of a drill instructor, Adam scurried away and pressed his back against the corrugated steel wall. But his eyes never left the man who stepped into the shed with a limping shuffle and stared at him with thinly veiled amusement.

"It is time we had a talk," he said.

Adam had so many questions. But after only one night of captivity, he had already lost what little spine the Chinese had allowed him to keep. So, he kept his mouth shut and waited for the stranger to speak.

"My name is Nikolai Voronov." He paused as if assessing whether Adam had heard the name before. "I work for the Foreign Intelligence Service of the Russian Federation."

Adam swallowed.

"We have been watching you for some time."

"Why? I'm nobody."

Voronov sat on the cot and gestured for Adam to join him. Fearing this was some sort of trap or ploy to keep him off guard, he hesitated before lowering himself onto the stretched canvas.

"You don't realize how important you are," the Russian said, echoing the same sentiment Chen had used to recruit him to spy for the Ministry of State Security.

Adam shook his head. "Even if the Chinese didn't already have their hooks in me, I'm worthless to you. I went AWOL from the Marine Corps and will only be arrested when they catch me."

Voronov chuckled. "Yes, you will be arrested. That is part of our plan."

Adam's mouth fell open, unsure of how to respond to that. For years he had fed Chen secrets on the F-35 Joint Strike Fighter, and the Ministry had used those secrets to build a weapon that allowed them to hack into the fifth-generation stealth fighter. That mistake had almost cost him his life. And now they wanted him to get arrested? It wasn't much of a sales pitch.

"I don't understand," he said.

"As of this moment, you no longer work for the Chinese," Voronov said.

Adam didn't really see how he had much of a choice. But he still didn't know how they could possibly use him, now that he no longer had access to secrets the Russians might find useful.

"Won't they come looking for me?" Adam thought of the emergency beacon he had activated only to have it stripped from his person and left in the desert.

Voronov more than chuckled at that. "Let's just say we have come to an agreement with the person in charge—the woman known as *Mantis*. Nobody will come for you. You belong to us now."

Adam had never heard the name before, but he had always known there was somebody above Chen and Shi Yufei. His shoulders slumped, and with that, the Russian stood and looked down at him. He placed a heavy hand on Adam's head like a priest offering a blessing and muttered something he couldn't understand. Then, he limped through the door and closed it behind him.

Adam waited until he heard the chains being locked together, then he flopped back onto his cot and cried.

———————

Nikolai walked across the barren ground while thinking about the curious young man he had locked inside the cramped shed. Halfway between the shed and the house where the rest of his men were waiting, Nikolai removed a satellite phone from his pocket, unfolded the bulky antenna, and turned it on. He waited until it had established a connection with the satellite constellation overhead, then dialed Viktor's number from memory.

After waiting for the signal to travel halfway around the world, his call was answered. "Yes?"

"He doesn't know," Nikolai said.

"Are you certain?"

He thought of the blank expression on the Marine's face and how his pupils had maintained their shape—neither constricting or dilating in shock or confusion. He thought of the young man's respiratory rate and pulse, both of which had remained constant, and knew without a doubt. "He doesn't have a clue that his adopted mother was a Chinese spy who ran the Ministry's West Coast network."

"*Was?*"

Viktor didn't miss much.

"She *intervened* last night when we recovered the *DRAGON LINE* and had to be put down." He said it with such little emotion that anyone who might have overheard would have thought he had just informed his boss that he had killed a rabid stray dog. But Nikolai couldn't have cared less whether she lived or died. To him, she had only existed to ensure her asset stole the weapon and delivered it someplace where they could get their hands on it.

Of course, he had known she would try to double-cross them. He would have been more than a little disappointed in the Chinese spymaster if she hadn't.

After a moment Viktor said, "We can still use her, yes?"

Nikolai smiled. "*Da.*"

Viktor never failed to impress Nikolai with his shrewd and cunning mastery of the espionage game, though this went well beyond simply stealing secrets from their enemy. With both the Marine and the weapon in their possession, they now had everything they needed to usher in a new era of global Russian dominance.

And the best part was, nobody would ever know who was behind it.

46

Air Force Two
Boeing C-32A

Two hours into the flight, Sam rose from his wide leather executive chair and followed Jonathan aft through the center aisle to the rear cabin where thirty hand-selected members of the press sat in business-class seats. It was common practice for the vice president to hold an informal briefing known as a gaggle, and Jonathan never missed an opportunity to push his agenda on those chosen to accompany him.

"How's everybody doing?" Jonathan asked, stepping into the press area with a wide smile on his face.

Most of the reporters were busy tapping away on laptop computers set on the tray tables in front of them, and a few were reclined, watching news broadcasts from miniature TVs set into the cabin bulkhead. But when they heard Jonathan's voice, they all sat up and looked in his direction.

"The pilots assured me we're going to have a smooth ride the whole way, but a wise person once told me you can always tell when a pilot is lying because his lips are moving."

The reporters chuckled politely, but Sam looked at Teddy and saw the Washington Post reporter roll his eyes. The vice president's infamously unfunny jokes were a common topic of discussion at their near-nightly happy hours at Old Ebbitt Grill.

"I won't take up much of your time," Jonathan continued, knowing full well they were at his beck and call for the duration of the trip. "But I think it's important to let you know why you're here. And I don't mean why you're here on Air Force Two with me—we all know it's to make me look good . . ." There were more chuckles. "But why it's important for me to visit Nevada. And why I wanted *you* to see it."

The reporters who didn't already have their notepads out lifted their cell phones to record the vice president's impromptu remarks. From Teddy, Sam knew that several members of the press had been questioning the impetus for a trip to Nevada—a state whose six electoral votes had gone to the president and would likely go to Jonathan in the next year's election. What could he possibly gain from the visit?

"You've probably seen the state flag of Nevada, but have you ever really looked at it? It's made from a field of cobalt blue with the state emblem in the upper left corner. The emblem consists of two sprays of green sagebrush with yellow flowers, framing a silver star that represents the state's rich history in silver mining that led to its prosperity in the late 1800s.

"Following the discovery of the Comstock Lode in 1858, Nevada quickly became a hub of silver mining that resulted in Virginia City becoming the wealthiest city in the world. The Mackay Mansion—home of Comstock mine owner John Mackay—is still an example of opulence. The downstairs parlor is adorned with a gold chandelier, an original Tiffany window, and a mirror made from crushed diamonds."

Jonathan smirked as he looked from one reporter to another. "And you thought the infamous Pentagon gold toilet was wasteful spending."

Sam shook his head, but he grinned despite himself.

But the vice president had already worked up to the point he wanted to make. "Atop the silver star on the state emblem is a golden scroll emblazoned with two words. Anybody know what they are?"

A reporter from the Wall Street Journal answered without looking up. "Battle Born."

Sam didn't think it was possible for Jonathan's smile to grow any bigger, but he was wrong. Instead of acting like he just had his punchline snatched away from him, he nodded his head eagerly. "That's right. The Silver State joined the Union a week before the presidential election in 1864, after telegraphing the Nevada Constitution to Congress—the largest and costliest transmission ever by telegraph."

Jonathan leaned against the forward bulkhead in a pose that seemed to strike a balance between John F. Kennedy and Hugh Hefner. "Where's my New York Times reporter?"

A slender blonde woman in her mid-forties gave Jonathan a timid wave, though she already knew the vice president knew who she was. He winked at her in thanks for playing along. "One day later, on November first, *your* newspaper published an article stating, 'Nevada is probably the richest state in the Union.' In the midst of the Civil War, a rising star in the United States was born. Battle born."

Sam's eyes darted across the members of the press pool, surprised to see they all seemed enthralled by the vice president's history lesson. He had long been a firm believer in Jonathan's ability to rise to the top of the political elite, and the charisma on full display aboard Air Force Two was the main reason why.

"The recent National Defense Authorization Act granted more than five hundred thousand acres of public land for bombing ranges and military exercise areas belonging to Naval Air Station Fallon. But despite the increased threat to our national security from aggressors like China and Russia, there has been opposition by environmentalists and politicians on both sides of the aisle to this expansion."

Jonathan looked at his watch.

"In just over two hours, we will be landing at Naval Air Station Fallon, where you will get an opportunity to meet the brave American men and women who stepped up and answered the call to defend our great nation. And you will get an opportunity to see why the state that was 'Battle Born' has once again answered the call of a nation embroiled in war."

Sam felt the hairs on the back of his neck stand up with sudden pride for the man he was certain would become the next president of the United States—the man who had been his best friend for two decades.

"Ladies and gentlemen, thank you for being here to bear witness to the future of our national security."

As Jonathan basked in the afterglow of his rousing speech, Sam remembered with sudden clarity the favor Viktor had asked of him. And the feeling of pride was instantly replaced by gnawing anxiety and guilt at what he had done.

"Sam, a word?" Jonathan asked once they had returned to the front of the plane.

Sam hesitated before taking his seat across the table from the vice president, who was already back at work preparing for the upcoming base visit. With the press content now that he had given them something to work with, his focus had turned to studying up on each of the people he was scheduled to meet once on the ground.

"Yes, Mister Vice President?"

He held up a sheet of paper. "You added a person to the reception guest list?"

Sam swallowed. He knew the addition wouldn't go unnoticed, so he had already thought of a plausible explanation for the last-minute change. "Yes, sir. I was made aware of a young man who hails from your home district."

Jonathan looked up from another sheet he was reading. "From San Jose?"

Sam nodded. "Yes, sir. The Willow Glen neighborhood."

The vice president set the paper down and leaned back in his chair, turning to look through the window at the azure blue of the sky beyond. "We've come a long way, haven't we?"

"Yes, sir. We have."

"Do you really think it's wise for me to appear as if I'm playing favorites to my home state? As commander-in-chief, I will be responsible for all soldiers, sailors, airmen, and Marines. Not just the ones from California."

Sam had considered this argument too. "I don't think it's wise for you to play favorites to your home state. But I do think it's a good look for you to spend a few moments with a Marine corporal when most of your visit will be spent with senior military leaders. It shows that you care about all of

America's sons and daughters, not just the ones who have the influence and power to do something for you."

"A leader of the people," Jonathan said.

Sam nodded. "Your entire political image is centered on being approachable. You weren't born with a silver spoon in your mouth like your most likely opponents. You were raised by a single mother with a modest upbringing and fought to earn your place. At Cal. In the state legislature. Congress." He paused. "The White House."

The vice president turned and made eye contact with him. "If you think this is best."

Sam swallowed. "Yes, sir. I do."

But truthfully, Sam didn't think it was best at all. He didn't know what Viktor had planned, but Sam knew the Russian didn't have Jonathan's best interests in mind. It seemed like such a harmless, inconsequential favor. But the former intelligence officer had asked him to add Adam Garett's name to the list for a reason.

He just didn't know what that reason was.

47

Naval Air Station Fallon
Fallon, Nevada

The butterflies were completely gone by the time Colt turned the page in his checklist to the engine start procedure. Though he had several hundred hours in the A-29 Super Tucano and could have completed each step from memory, he took his time and ran his finger down the checklist to make sure he hadn't missed anything.

Within minutes, the Super Tucano's engine turned the large propeller, and the plane vibrated like an anxious pony. Dave was quiet in the back, working to align the Inertial Navigation System and verify satellite coverage that would tighten their location through the Global Positioning System, then tuned the radios to the channels they would use to communicate with Punky and the SEALs on the ground.

"Mariner Six, Pony One, check SAT," Dave said over their satellite communications network.

"Pony One, Mariner Six," Todd said. "We read you five by five and are en route to the target at this time."

"Good copy, Mariner Six. We'll be airborne in five mikes." Dave ended the transmission before speaking over the intercom to Colt. "All systems green."

"Let's do this, then." Colt released the parking brake and advanced the throttle slowly. The A-29 Super Tucano rolled through the wide hangar doors and out onto the tarmac, where they were struck by the brilliant late morning sun.

He pulled down his dark visor and looked around. Their hangar sat at the southern end of the base, segregated from the large ramps to the north by a short east-west runway that was rarely used by the fighters monopolizing the base. Rows of Hornets, Super Hornets, and F-16N Vipers sat dormant on the TOPGUN flight line.

He looked right and watched a section of F-35C Lightning II Joint Strike Fighters take off from one of the longer parallel runways. He felt a pang of longing for the fifth-generation fighter, though he would have been lying if he said he wasn't excited about flying the Super Tucano again.

"You okay up there, flyboy?" Dave asked over the ICS.

"All good."

Colt tested the wheel brakes by tapping on them, then let the plane accelerate to fifteen knots. He stepped on the right pedal to swing the nose in the direction of the taxiway and the departure end of Runway 25. Their plane crept toward the hold short line, where Colt gently brought them to a stop.

"Fallon tower, Pony One, takeoff runway two five," Colt said.

The tower controller's response was delayed and laced with confusion. "Pony . . . uh . . . One?"

"Affirm."

His answer was met with silence.

"Hey Dave, did you let them know we were going flying?"

"Was I supposed to?"

Colt groaned, but he couldn't expect the Master Chief to understand the intricacies of operating a squadron from a base like Fallon. Then again, until that morning they hadn't planned on going flying. So, it was probably his fault as much as it was Dave's.

"Nevermind," he said, then switched back to the primary radio. "Fallon tower, Pony One is an add-on to the schedule and will be VFR to the east."

The confused controller's voice was replaced by one that sounded confident. "Pony One, winds two one zero at seven, cleared for takeoff runway two five."

Colt echoed the takeoff clearance, then released the wheel brakes and taxied onto the runway. With his nose aligned with the runway centerline, he again pressed on the brakes and advanced the throttle to the firewall while checking for warnings and cautions that might prevent them from going flying. When he released the brakes, the thrust was almost instantaneous. Aside from the violent spinning of the five blades in front of him, he almost felt like he was in a jet.

"Yeeee-haw!" Dave howled from the back seat.

Colt broke into a smile behind his oxygen mask and waited until the plane had reached 100 knots before pulling back on the stick to break free from the earth and return the plane to its natural habitat. He kept his nose five degrees above the horizon and allowed the speed tape in his HUD to increase to 120 knots before reaching forward to raise the landing gear and flaps.

"Pony One airborne," Dave said over SAT.

"Mariner Six," Todd replied.

Colt craned his neck to the left, then banked to enter an ascending spiral over the runway. They leveled off at ten thousand feet and pointed east into the vastness of the Nevada desert. Somewhere beneath them, a lightweight and highly mobile ground mobility vehicle carried three SEALs and an NCIS special agent to an isolated dirt strip in the town of Gabbs.

Jason 11
Navy F-35C
Fallon Range Training Complex
East of Fallon, Nevada

Lieutenant Commander Bill "Jug" McFarland rolled out heading almost due east and looked over his right shoulder to watch his squadron's training officer maneuver into position one mile abeam. It was the Sunday of the annual Tail-hook Symposium, and Jug had opted to give the squadron's junior officers the morning off to recover. But that just meant he had to suffer through a basic fighter maneuvering sortie against Lieutenant Carlton "Cubby" Elliott.

Sour stomach and all.

"Jason, reference zero nine zero, accel, G-warm."

Jug advanced the throttle and added a little forward pressure on his control stick to level off with his nose pointed at the Stillwater Mountain Range. He listened to the jet hum as it accelerated through the dry air and watched his airspeed jump in his Helmet Mounted Display. He glanced right and saw that Cubby had matched his speed and was both even and level with his jet.

This is going to hurt.

"Jason, ninety right, go."

Without hesitation, Jug twisted his wrist and applied side pressure to the control stick to command the fifth-generation fighter in a roll to the right. Once he had banked almost ninety degrees, he added back pressure to the stick and began tracking his nose across the horizon while he craned his neck upward to sight in on Cubby's jet. He strained against the rising G-forces as they pushed him down into his seat.

Three . . . three and a half . . . four Gs.

Jug eased and allowed the displayed number in his helmet to remain steady at four, then held it there until his nose pointed due south. He quickly released the back pressure and snap-rolled the JSF upright almost exactly one mile behind Cubby's jet. With practiced hands, he cycled through his various radar modes to acquire a targeting solution on the other fighter, then tested the infrared seeker on his captive air training missile and listened to the immediate rise in tone as it locked onto the other jet's hot exhaust.

"Jason, resume."

With a sharp inhale, he braced himself for another ninety-degree turn, then rolled left and quickly snatched back to six Gs before relaxing the pull to hold four Gs until both fighters had turned back to the east. Even though he had taken most of Saturday to recover from the Bug Roach Mixer, his internal gyro still tumbled in a natural response to his body maneuvering through the air in an unnatural way.

He leveled his wings heading east, then quickly rolled inverted and added a little forward pressure on the stick to induce negative G-forces and check for loose objects in the cockpit that might pose a hazard during an engagement. Satisfied when nothing floated "up" toward the canopy, he returned his jet upright, then began climbing again into the training airspace.

"Jason One One, fenced in, eighteen point oh."

Cubby's response was immediate. "Jason One Two, fenced in, seventeen eight."

With the G-warm maneuver complete, they had successfully evaluated their individual performance to combat the stress of high-G maneuvers while simultaneously preparing their bodies for the upcoming fight. Jug glanced at his moving map display as they crossed into Dixie Valley, on the other side of the Stillwaters from Fallon.

"Jason, tac right."

He immediately banked right to come up on a wing and began pulling his nose across the horizon while Cubby continued flowing east. When his nose pointed at Cubby's jet, he watched his wingman replicate the maneuver by banking right and executing his own pull to the south. When he rolled out heading toward the Fallon South 2 Military Operating Area, they were once again one mile abeam, but had swapped sides.

His stomach still churned, and he wasn't looking forward to being abused by the guy who had bested Colt Bancroft on Friday. But what was the worst that could happen? It wasn't like the Chinese had hacked into his jet and were going to use it to conduct an attack against an American aircraft carrier off the coast. He was still in control of the F-35C Lightning II —not just along for the ride while Colt tried shooting him down.

His body shuddered at the memory, but he shook it off and focused on the mission at hand. "Alright, the first set will be an abeam set at fourteen thousand feet, one mile abeam, and three hundred and fifty knots." He paused and glanced over at Cubby's jet to verify he was in position. "Jason One One, speed and angels on the right."

"Jason One Two, speed and angels on the left."

"Three . . . two . . . one . . . Fight's on!"

48

Twenty miles west of Gabbs, Nevada

Nikolai Voronov checked his watch, then stepped out from the Stryker armored vehicle to look up into the deep blue sky. He couldn't see it, but he knew the blue-and-white Boeing C-32A was up there somewhere, preparing to make its descent to the naval air station in Fallon.

He spun back to the open ramp at the rear and ducked inside the darkened vehicle to hover over the men sitting at the weapon's consoles. "Do you have a targeting solution yet?"

The men didn't bother turning to look at him and instead focused their efforts on the screens in front of them. None of them had used the system before, but their own asset inside Sandia National Laboratories had provided them with a complete set of rudimentary procedures to operate the directed energy weapon. They had all seen the results of the live fire testing done at the US Army's High Energy Laser Systems Test Facility at White Sands Missile Range in New Mexico and knew what it was capable of.

"I cannot hold a lock long enough to pass telemetry data to the TILL," the man at the radar console said.

Nikolai glanced at the next monitor over to view the images provided by the Advanced Dual Optical Tracking System. He could tell a jet was centered on the screen, but its image wasn't stable. The operator in control of the target illuminator laser attempted tracking the target, but it again seemed to shift and move across the screen of its own accord.

"I can't get a track," the operator said, obviously frustrated.

"Does it have some defensive capability we aren't aware of?"

Instead of answering, the men continued manipulating the *DRAGON LINE*'s controls to lock onto the targeted aircraft. Nikolai watched his men working for a few moments longer, then stepped back out into the bright sunlight and stared up into the sky again, feeling the weight of the moment settling over him. There was a lot riding on what happened in the next several minutes. But if they were successful, the Americans would believe the Chinese were responsible for stealing the weapon and targeting the frontrunner to be the next president of the United States.

Beautiful.

Air Force Two
Boeing C-32A

Sam reclined in the wide leather seat with his eyes closed, but his mind raced with worry. Normally, a trip on Air Force Two was an uneventful affair that saw Sam managing only the mundane tasks related to the vice president's schedule. When they arrived at their destination airport, the Secret Service would be waiting with vehicles to take them wherever they needed to go. The large muscle movements were already taken care of, leaving him with not much to do.

But this trip seemed different.

He knew it was probably the favor Viktor Drakov had asked of him. Or maybe the missing experimental laser weapon. Or, more likely, it was both. Whatever the reason, he found that he couldn't rest like normal and would remain anxious until they had returned to Washington.

They hit a pocket of turbulence, and Sam's eyes shot open as he clutched the armrests of his chair and braced himself. He wasn't a nervous flyer, but his nerves were already shot.

I'm losing my mind, he thought.

Clenching his jaw in frustration, Sam unbuckled his seat belt and rose to make his way to one of the lavatories available for use by the vice president and his staff. He opened the door, stepped inside, and gripped the counter as he stared at himself in the mirror. Deepening wrinkles at the corners of his eyes reminded him that he was no longer as young as he had been when they set out on this journey.

"But we're not done yet," he told his reflection.

He ran water in the sink and splashed it into his face. The cool water instantly refreshed him and washed away some of the anxiety that had prevented him from truly resting. He repeated the process several more times, feeling more and more like the young idealist who had latched on to a rising political star and permanently joined their futures. For better or worse, he had followed Jonathan into politics, and he would follow him wherever this journey led.

"We're going to the White House."

Sam ignored the bags under his eyes while he dried his face and slicked back his hair. He knew they were already in their descent into Naval Air Station Fallon, and he needed to bury his anxiety and be the chief of staff his best friend needed. Though Nevada was as close to a sure thing as they could get, this would be Jonathan's first appearance as an official candidate for the highest office in the land.

Sam opened the door and stepped out of the lavatory to return to his seat. He smiled and nodded at the staffers who looked in his direction, then lowered himself once more into his wide chair. He buckled his seat belt again, then leaned forward to look through the window and down on the desert landscape beneath them.

It was barren and desolate for as far as he could see.

Then, he saw a flash on the ground that made his stomach drop.

Nikolai heard the whir of machinery over his shoulder, and he turned to see the domed turret on top of the Stryker turning and pivoting as the operators inside aimed the laser at a target in the sky. He glanced back up into the air, tracing an imaginary line from the weapon to its target, but he still couldn't make out the jet against the vastness of blue. But when the air around him reverberated with a low humming sound, his heart jumped in excited anticipation.

The humming of energy grew louder, and Nikolai sprinted for the opening at the rear of the Stryker. "Do you have him?"

"Engaging TILL," the first operator said, his voice laced with nerves.

Nikolai looked at the screen for the Advanced Dual Optical Tracking System and saw the infrared image of a jet centered in the crosshairs. He was so consumed by what was about to happen that he had to consciously remind himself to take a breath. Years of planning had led to this moment, and he was honored Viktor had chosen him to be on the front lines and bear witness to its aftermath.

"It's working," another operator said, almost breathless with excitement. "We are receiving data."

Nikolai knew the basics of what was happening. He understood that the second laser in the system measured distortion caused by the atmosphere and fed that information to a computer to correct the high energy laser's beam. But to anybody without knowledge of how the system worked, it would appear like nothing was happening at all.

In a matter of seconds, the computer had crunched the data through a program created by the Chinese asset and returned a solution to the operator with a simple message that the system was ready to engage the target. "Ready to fire," the first operator said, keeping his eyes fixed on the image of the aircraft centered on the display.

Nikolai remained still, frozen in place as he waited to see what would happen. Slowly, each man turned to look at him in anticipation, and he realized they were waiting for him to issue the command. All their years of waiting in the shadows had finally culminated in this moment.

He shook himself free from the momentary paralysis and looked at each operator in turn. Their eyes betrayed a myriad of emotions, ranging from resolute determination to abject horror. Nikolai knew that each man understood the consequences of what they were about to do, and he didn't take lightly the responsibility they had bestowed upon him.

He cleared away the lump in his throat. "Fire."

49

Jason II
Navy F-35C

In the skies above Gabbs, Jug twisted in his seat and braced himself against the canopy to look over his shoulder as the other F-35C maneuvered to take a shot. He had a narrow window to reverse—too early and he would only forfeit his control zone to Cubby, but too late and he would take a make-believe missile up his tailpipe. Even if it wasn't real, his ego was, and he counted silently and waited patiently for the right moment to act.

Now!

Jug pressed forward against the stick to unload his wings, then quickly slapped it to the right. Unlike the Hornet or Super Hornet, which had a control stick positioned between his legs that he could move in all four quadrants, the Joint Strike Fighter utilized a side stick that only afforded about one quarter-inch of movement in any direction. Instead of jamming it against his thighs, he only had to put pressure on the side of the JSF's stick to actuate the flight control logic.

But even though it felt unnatural, the jet responded almost as if it was wired directly to his brain. Still looking over his shoulder, he barely registered the horizon swapping sides as he went from turning left to right. His head whipped around to maintain sight of Cubby's jet over his other shoulder, but he groaned when he recognized that the former TOPGUN instructor hadn't made the mistake of pressing his attack.

By reversing, Jug had complicated Cubby's geometry and instantly forced him to make a choice. He could either continue driving toward Jug's jet for a fleeting shot opportunity and overshoot in the process, or he could break off his attack and preserve his offensive advantage by continuing to pull toward Jug's control zone.

"Fox two."

Cubby was too smart to allow an overshoot, and it grated on Jug that he had absorbed yet another heat-seeking missile and was about to lose his third engagement.

"Fox three," Cubby said as he maneuvered into lag, letting Jug know he had simulated firing again—this time, an active radar missile.

Jug cursed inside his mask but continued straining against the G-forces as he waited for his opportunity to reverse again. Even if Cubby never made a mistake, he had to stay in the fight. In the real world, staying alive longer meant giving your wingman an opportunity to maneuver for a shot. Staying alive longer meant giving the enemy more chances to fuck up. And staying alive longer meant staying alive longer.

Again, he recognized the cues, unloaded his wings, and reversed directions.

"Fox two."

Again, Cubby was too smart and refused to make a careless mistake.

"Fox three."

Dammit.

"Knock-it-off, bingo," Cubby said, letting Jug know he was ending the fight because he had run out of gas and needed to return to the air station in Fallon.

"Knock-it-off, knock-it-off," Jug said. "Jason One One, knock-it-off."

"Jason One Two, knock-it-off."

Jug leveled his wings and pressed forward on the stick to accelerate to three hundred knots, then eased back and began a gentle climb toward

Fallon. They were running out of time before the airfield closed for VIP movement, and Jug was thankful Cubby knew what he was doing as he maneuvered his jet and gradually closed the distance between them. With their mock engagement over, they were once again on the same side.

But Jug was still pissed.

No wins, three losses.

Jug looked over his shoulder as Cubby maneuvered his jet into a tight parade formation on his left side. He lifted his hand above the canopy rail with his thumb and forefinger extended in the shape of a pistol. Wagging his thumb, he gave Cubby the signal to conduct a battle damage check—a visual inspection of his aircraft to ensure their mock engagement hadn't caused any real damage to his jet.

Cubby nodded, then dropped low and crossed underneath to inspect the underside of his jet. Once on the other side, Jug would pass him the lead before repeating the process for the other fighter. But for now, all he had to do was fly straight and level and let his wingman do his job. He unclipped his mask and let it dangle to one side as he took several breaths of the cockpit's stale air, enjoying a few moments of respite after the beating he had just endured.

"Jason, switch Approach," Jug said, reaching up to select the appropriate frequency for Fallon approach control.

"Two," Cubby replied.

Out of the corner of his eye, Jug saw his wingman's jet crossing under to the right side, and he turned to watch the stealth fighter maneuver wide and complete the battle damage check. Even feeling tired after a few days at Hook, he grinned when he thought about how lucky he was that Uncle Sam paid him to fly such an amazing machine. He keyed the microphone switch to say as much to Cubby, but the words never came out.

Without warning, a hole appeared in the top of Cubby's jet behind the canopy and seemed to lengthen outward to his left side, as if the stealth fighter was being cut in half.

"What the . . ."

Instinctively, Jug banked away, but his eyes remained glued to his wingman's jet.

"Something's wrong," Cubby said, apparently unaware of the fissure growing less than six feet behind his head. It looked as if he had initially tried turning to follow Jug before his jet faltered. "It's not responding. The electronics are going haywire."

Not again.

"You have the lead on the right," Jug said. Falling back on his training, he passed Cubby the lead. Flying in formation was the last thing the stricken pilot needed to worry about while dealing with whatever this was.

"Lead right," Cubby replied, but his nose continued falling away.

"Level your wings, Cubby."

"I'm trying."

Every emotion he had felt when his jet had been hijacked by the Chinese off the coast of California came roaring back. Impotence. Fear. Anger. Disbelief. He knew this was a different kind of threat—the sudden appearance of a hole was proof of that—but it was close enough.

As Cubby's jet continued rolling slowly to the right, its nose fell closer to the nadir, and Jug glanced at their altitude as he spiraled down to keep sight of the stricken jet. "Twelve thousand feet," he said.

Cubby didn't reply, and Jug knew he was probably frantically trying anything he could think of to regain control of the stealth fighter and level his wings. But the jet continued rolling onto its back and its nose dug deeper, gaining speed as gravity overcame the aerodynamic forces of lift and pulled it ever closer toward the desert floor.

"Eleven thousand feet."

Cubby's nose was pointed straight down, and Jug saw the other jet's exhaust cool as his wingman pulled the throttle back to idle and removed thrust from the equation. But it didn't seem to matter. The Joint Strike Fighter continued rolling as it raced downhill.

"Ten thousand feet, Cubby. Get out of there."

Again, the other pilot didn't reply. For a moment, Jug worried that maybe he had been incapacitated somehow and couldn't eject. But before that thought could take hold and root around inside his brain, the canopy disappeared in a sudden flash of blossoming light and smoke, and the ejection seat rocketed away from the stricken jet.

"Shit," Jug said.

He leveled off as Cubby's parachute canopy inflated, then immediately fell back on his training. He didn't have enough gas to establish a persistent presence over the crash site, so he dropped a waypoint for his location and noted the latitude and longitude rescue crews would need to reach the downed aviator.

"Mayday, mayday, mayday," Jug said over the military air distress frequency. "Jason One Two has gone down. Position thirty-nine degrees, four point seven minutes north. One eighteen degrees, twenty-five point four minutes west."

He didn't know if anybody would even be monitoring UHF Guard on a Sunday, but his entire focus was on following the parachute as it descended onto a relatively flat piece of land between Gabbs and Fallon. Out of the corner of his eye, he saw the pilotless F-35C crash into higher terrain east of the valley floor and explode in a brilliant fireball. Fortunately, it looked as if Cubby would touch down well away from the crash site.

"Mayday, mayday, mayday," he repeated. "Jason One Two—"

"Emergency aircraft transmitting on Guard, say your callsign," a calm voice said, cutting him off.

Jug glanced at his fuel state and cursed, then banked left and pointed his nose at the naval air station in Fallon. "This is Jason One One. My wingman has crashed approximately two seven miles southeast of Fallon."

"Any chutes?"

"One," Jug said, thankful the voice on the other end of the radio was taking him seriously. Until 2022, search-and-rescue services in the Fallon Range Training Complex had been provided by a unit known as *Longhorn SAR*. But due to cost-saving measures, the Navy reassigned its active duty personnel and transferred three MH-60S Knighthawk helicopters to San Diego. Now, the Naval Aviation Warfighting Development Center was tasked with picking up the slack.

"Copy," the voice said. "We are spinning up SAR now. Can you remain on site and assume on-scene commander?"

Jug bit his lip and again checked his fuel. "Negative. I'm on fumes."

"Copy."

He dipped a wing and looked down at where Cubby had landed. He didn't have much fuel to play around with, but he had just enough to let his wingman know he wasn't alone. Rolling onto his back, Jug pulled down in a descent to the valley floor and leveled off a scant one hundred feet above the desert. He pointed his nose at the collapsed multi-colored orange, white, and green silk parachute, and raced overhead while rocking his wings left and right.

"Hang in there, Cubby."

50

Pony 1
Navy A-29 Super Tucano
Fallon Range Training Complex

Whether it was a single-engine turboprop or a multi-engine jet fighter with afterburners, Colt belonged at the controls of an airplane. As he and Dave flew east over the Nevada desert, he felt right at home.

"Pony One, Pony Base."

He glanced in his mirror at Dave in the back seat. "Freaq knew we were taking the plane, right?"

But Dave ignored his question and responded to the query. "Go ahead, Base."

While he waited to hear if he was going to be brought up on charges for the theft of government property, Colt focused his attention on the landmarks that passed underneath them. He had spent so much time in the airspace east of Fallon that he knew exactly where they were without even consulting a map.

"NAWDC is spinning up their search-and-rescue helicopter," the *Black Ponies* skipper said.

Dave glanced up and they made eye contact.

"For what?" the SEAL asked.

"A Joint Strike Fighter went down in the training range."

Colt jumped in. "Where?"

"Twenty-seven miles southeast of Fallon."

Colt didn't need to look at his moving map to know that was in the vicinity of Gabbs, where Punky and the other SEALs were headed in a Flyer 60 Advanced Light Strike Vehicle. According to Punky's supervisor with the Naval Criminal Investigative Service, the phone number attributed to Mantis had been stationary in the vicinity of Gabbs for some time. His stomach dropped when he realized there was a very real possibility the crash was caused by more than a simple accident. It could have been the work of an enemy attack.

He banked the plane right to point their nose in that direction. "Tell NAWDC we're en route. And find out what frequency I can reach their SAR crew on."

"On it," Freaq said, not bothering to remind Colt that *he* was the ranking officer.

"Colt . . ." Dave seemed as if he was about to argue but trailed off when he came to the same conclusion. "Do you think it's related?"

"I don't believe in coincidences anymore."

Dave apparently agreed and switched the SATCOM channel. "Mariner Six, Pony One."

"Go ahead, Pony One," Todd said.

"NAWDC is launching a search-and-rescue operation for a Joint Strike Fighter that went down southeast of Fallon," Dave said.

"Near Gabbs?"

"Close enough. Standby for updated coordinates and further instructions, but I'm betting this was a hostile act."

"Copy all," Todd said. "We'll be ready."

In the distance, Colt saw a dark cloud of billowing smoke, and he adjusted their heading yet again to fly toward the crash site. He had a hard time believing that the fifth-generation stealth fighter had been brought down by enemy action, but the proof was in the pudding. With the Russians, Chinese, and a missing experimental weapon all in the same place at the same time, an intentional hit seemed like the only plausible explanation.

"Pony Base, Pony One is visual smoke and proceeding to crash site," Dave said.

"Roger," Freaq replied. "The SAR helo should be launching in the next ten minutes."

Colt shook his head. If the F-35 had been brought down by a hostile act, ten minutes was far too long for the pilot on the ground to be without air support overhead. "Get me a frequency yet?"

"They said you can reach Strike Two Four on cheerleader. I'll switch over to SAT."

"Copy."

"Cheerleader?" Dave asked from the back seat.

Colt punched the frequency into the keypad on his Integrated Control Panel. "Two four six eight," he answered.

"Who do we appreciate," the SEAL said, finishing the popular cheer.

Freaq knew they would be busy coordinating with air traffic control on their primary radio and the SAR crew on their secondary. Fortunately, their Super Tucano came equipped with a dedicated channel for satellite communications that afforded them the ability to maintain constant contact with Punky and the SEALs on the ground as well as their skipper in the squadron ready room. With the rising terrain between their hangar and where the JSF had likely gone down, it was an advantage Colt knew they would need over normal line-of-sight communications.

He continued climbing over the dried lake bed south of the air station and pointed his nose on a course that would take them through restricted airspace surrounding two bombing ranges. He selected the secondary radio and toggled the switch on his throttle to transmit. "Strike Two Four, Pony One on two four six decimal eight."

There was a pause, but then he heard a calm voice reply in a choppy cadence caused by the helicopter's rotor blades beating the air into submission. "Go ahead, Pony One."

"We are a special operations A-29 and are assuming on-scene commander."

"Copy," the helo pilot replied. "Do you have eyes on the survivor at this time?"

"That's a negative. We are five mikes out. But be advised, we have reason to believe that the aircraft was brought down by enemy fire."

The pause was a little longer this time. "Uhhh . . . say again?"

Dave beat Colt to the punch and answered in the way only a Navy SEAL could. "He said shit just got real. This ain't no joke, flyboy. We've got a truck full of shooters on their way to secure the crash site on the ground, so get your head on straight and be ready for a hot exfil."

Twenty-seven miles southeast of Fallon, Nevada

Cubby pushed himself off the desert floor and looked up in time to see Jug rocking his wings as he raced north over his position. He watched his wingman disappear toward Fallon, knowing that the *Argonauts* operations officer had probably already coordinated a search-and-rescue effort before returning to base. Even knowing that, he fumbled to remove his AN/PRC-149 rescue radio and turned it on.

Although he had been required to complete aviation physiology and water survival training every four years that included a refresher on the various rescue radios he might fly with, it took him a few minutes to remember how to select the right channel to broadcast in both VHF and UHF Guard frequencies. No matter how many times he had trained for this scenario, nothing could have prepared him for the utter chaos of being launched from his jet on a rocket-powered seat.

"Any station, this is Jason One Two on Guard," he said, then released the push-to-talk and pressed the volume up switch while listening to the static grow louder. After several seconds of trembling with nervous anticipation, he attempted making contact again. "Any station, any station, this is Jason One Two on Guard."

This time, when he released the push-to-talk, the static only lasted for a few seconds before a voice he recognized responded. "Hey Cubby, it's Jug. Good to hear your voice, brother."

Despite having seen Jug fly over and rock his wings as a visual signal that he had spotted Cubby and that help was on the way, it still felt good knowing he wasn't alone. From horizon to horizon, he saw nothing but clumps of dirt and scrub brush, distorted by heat shimmering off the desert floor. But the trembling stopped, and he felt comforted by Jug's voice.

"You too, Jug. I assume you woke up the SAR bubbas, and I should just sit tight?"

Another voice responded when he released the button to transmit. "Jason One Two, switch twenty-eight, twenty-eight."

Cubby bit off a sardonic reply, frustrated that the new voice wanted him to switch over to a NATO frequency that combined voice and direction finding. Despite knowing it was commonly used by search-and-rescue assets, it was just one more hoop he had to jump through.

"Copy."

He lamented not paying closer attention during his refresher training, then flipped the radio over and read the instructions before toggling the mode select switch to transmit and receive in 282.8 MHz. He listened for a few seconds before pressing the push-to-talk again and holding the radio to his mouth. "Jason One Two is up twenty-eight, twenty-eight."

Cubby continued scanning the horizon when movement atop a hill several miles to his southeast drew his attention. It was little more than a dark speck against the brown and gray backdrop, but based on the cloud of dust following in its wake, it appeared to be an approaching vehicle.

"Jason One Two, this is Pony One."

Cubby had never heard the callsign before, but he thought it might belong to the NAWDC SAR helo. "Go ahead, Pony One."

"We are approaching your position at this time and have a ground force mobilized to secure your location. Recommend you hunker down and remain out of sight until we arrive."

Ground force? Remain out of sight?

"Say again?" He squinted at the approaching vehicle, increasingly certain that it had spotted him and was making its way across the desert terrain to reach him. "I think I see your ground force vehicle approaching in the distance..."

There was no hesitation in the reply, and the pilot's voice cut like a blade. "That's not a friendly force. Find someplace to hide. *Now!*"

51

Pony 1
Navy A-29 Super Tucano

Colt felt the hair on the back of his neck stand on end when Cubby told him he saw a vehicle approaching. If he hadn't already had the throttle pushed all the way forward, he would have tried coaxing a few more ponies from the already straining Pratt & Whitney Canada turboprop. As it was, all he could do was keep his nose pointed at the distant cloud of smoke and spur the Super Tucano onward.

"Deploying turret," Dave said from the back seat.

Colt heard an electric whine and felt the disturbance of airflow as the MX-15 sensor pod descended from its housing near his feet. With the drag caused by the laser-guided bombs and rockets mounted under each wing, he was pushing the limits of the airframe at over three hundred knots of true airspeed.

"Copy," Colt replied.

Knowing that the SEAL was already manipulating the sensor and guiding it to find the source of the smoke, Colt kept his eyes outside the cockpit and scanned the horizon for signs of incoming fire or another hostile act, though he had no clue what he might see if he was being targeted by a directed energy weapon. If Cubby had been brought down by enemy action, he had to assume the threat still existed and that they were flying into harm's way. But if there was ever a plane built for the mission they were about to undertake, it was the A-29 Super Tucano.

And Colt was just the guy to fly it.

"Got it," Dave said.

Colt knew Dave had the electro-optical image pulled up on his center display in the aft cockpit, so he manipulated his left multi-function display to bring up a repeater of the MX-15 sensor pod's video. Glancing down, he saw the crosshairs centered on a dark spot in the rugged terrain where Cubby's jet had crashed after he ejected.

"See the pilot yet?" Colt asked, though he was seeing the exact same thing as the SEAL in the back seat.

"Standby."

As they neared the crash site, Colt resisted the urge to nose over and approach from low level. While that might have prevented hostile forces from spotting him and engaging him with surface-to-air gunfire or shoulder-fired missiles, it would have limited their ability to use the pod to locate the downed aircrew. Without that critical piece of information, they would have no way of providing effective covering fire when Punky and the SEALs or the NAWDC helicopter finally arrived to retrieve him.

"Got a vehicle," Dave said. "Not our guys."

Colt felt his heart thump in his chest, and he stole another glance at the MFD to see for himself. "Shit."

"Definitely a tango."

Centered underneath the crosshairs was an eight-wheeled armored vehicle.

Just like the one carrying the experimental weapon that had gone missing at the Tonopah Test Range.

Colt reached up to ensure the Super Tucano was in air-to-ground master mode, then selected the first of two GBU-12 Paveway II five-hundred-pound laser-guided bombs slung under his wings. "We need to put an end to this thing. Right here, right now."

"I'm with you, flyboy."

As the minutes ticked by following his ejection, Cubby felt new aches and pains pop up across his body. But he scrambled away from the flat piece of ground where he had left his multi-colored parachute fluttering in the breeze and found a shallow depression to crawl in. It was barely enough to keep him hidden from view if he flattened himself out, but it was the best he could do with the barren terrain.

"Jason One Two, say your position," the approaching pilot said.

Cubby groaned. How was he supposed to answer that? Did he want a latitude and longitude? A bearing and range from where his fifth-generation stealth fighter had been relegated to a smoking hole in the desert floor?

But the pilot seemed to recognize his gaffe and clarified. "Relative to the approaching vehicle."

Cubby lifted his head over the lip of the depression he had burrowed himself into and squinted through the heat shimmer to spot the approaching vehicle. Rolling onto one side, he rummaged through the pockets of his survival vest until he found what he was looking for. He removed the lensatic compass, unfolded it, and aimed it at the armored vehicle while sighting through the lens to gain a bearing.

Dropping the compass, he picked up the rescue radio and pressed the push-to-talk. "My bearing to the approaching vehicle is one three four degrees. You can do the math."

"Copy. Range?"

Not surprisingly, it wasn't the first time Cubby wished he was on the golf course. Had he been, he might have been able to use his laser rangefinder to give the pilot an accurate distance from the vehicle. But without it, he was left with nothing but his naked eye and a lifetime of experiences to guess how far away he was.

"I don't know . . . one mile?"

"Copy. Standby."

Cubby ducked back down and buried his face in the dirt as he waited for whoever was on the other end of the radio to give him some good news. It was hard to believe that he had just been having the time of his life— beating up on one of his squadron's department heads in the Navy's most advanced fighter—and now he was in the middle of nowhere being hunted by an unknown enemy.

"Tally ho, Jason One Two. I see you." the pilot said. "Keep your head down while we maneuver to engage."

Engage?

Cubby couldn't help himself. He poked his head back above the edge of the depression and scanned the sky overhead for whoever was talking to him on the radio. He suspected the pilot had used a sensor of some type to find him, but the only sound he heard was the wind whipping through the surrounding scrub brush and the faint hum of a distant turboprop airplane. No jet noise. No thumping helicopter rotor blades.

Definitely nothing that could *engage* the vehicle a mile distant and racing closer.

He dropped his head in despair just as a blur of dark gray raced overhead.

Pony 1
Navy A-29 Super Tucano

After designating the Stryker as a target, Colt nosed over and approached the valley at low altitude from the north. Nearing what he expected was the limit of potential small arms fire, he banked right while Dave worked to spot the pilot based on the bearing and range he had given them.

"Got him," Dave said. "He's hunkered down outside the blast radius."

Colt let Cubby know they saw him, then told him to keep his head down. Even though he was beyond the effective blast radius of the five-hundred-pound laser-guided bomb, the last thing Colt wanted was for a stray piece of shrapnel to injure the pilot while he waited to be rescued. Something like that would only make his bad day worse.

"I'm popping," Colt said. "Keep that laser steady."

Colt raced over Cubby's head, then snatched back on the stick and pointed his nose skyward, banking to preserve some separation from the Stryker. He waited until the weapon's delivery symbology in his HUD indicated that he had flown into what was known as the "basket"—an arbitrary piece of sky that accounted for the multitude of variables that affected a weapon's delivery. Samples of his altitude, airspeed, and G-forces, as well as environmental conditions like wind, were all taken into consideration when calculating a viable release point.

"Releasing in three, two, one," Colt said. "Op away."

The plane lurched as it suddenly became five hundred pounds lighter.

"Laser on," Dave replied from the back seat.

Colt looked down at the display and watched the crosshairs flashing, indicating that the MX-15 sensor pod was sending an invisible beam of light at the Stryker armored vehicle that gave the Paveway II laser-guided bomb something to aim for. Though he couldn't see the bomb falling toward the target, he knew its seeker had locked onto the laser energy and was providing guidance to the bomb's control surfaces to keep it pointed at the target.

"Ten seconds," Dave said.

Colt echoed the call, letting Cubby know that a bomb was inbound and to keep his head down.

It was disorienting to watch the target shift on the screen as he banked the Super Tucano away, but his entire focus was on ensuring that he didn't inadvertently gimbal the sensor and break the laser track at the last second. Using what was known as "bang-bang" guidance, the Paveway II laser-guided bomb relied on full deflection from its control surfaces to zigzag across the laser beam until reaching the target. If it lost radar energy in the final seconds of flight, a lack of input to its guidance system would cause it to either fall short or fly past the target.

Neither would be preferable. But falling short would put Cubby at even greater risk.

"Three, two, one . . . impact."

A blur raced into the pod's field of view and detonated directly underneath the crosshairs. In a split second, the Stryker armored vehicle disappeared in a brilliant flash of light.

52

Pony 1
Navy A-29 Super Tucano

Thirty minutes later, Colt had established a low-altitude orbit overhead while Dave worked the airplane's sensors and intelligence-gathering equipment from the back seat. Directly beneath them, a black smear on the desert floor and burning pile of scrap metal was all that remained of the Stryker armored vehicle, but Colt had a hard time believing it was the only threat in the area.

"Anything?"

"Nada," Dave replied.

Again, Colt glanced down at the valley floor and struggled to accept what had just taken place. Less than forty-eight hours earlier, he had been piloting a Super Hornet in a mock dogfight against the pilot who was now waiting for a rescue helicopter to come pick him up—after being shot down by an enemy that was now just a smoking hole. The contrast between their experiences a few days before was stark, and he could hardly believe it was real life. The word *surreal* came to mind.

"Here comes the rescue bird." Dave gestured at the MH-60S

Knighthawk painted in a brown-and-tan desert camouflage pattern as it maneuvered at low level just above the desert floor.

Colt continued in his left-hand orbit and passed overhead the helicopter, glancing down at the helicopter's open doors and twin GAU-17/A miniguns jutting out into the air. He cracked a mirthful grin, pleased to see that the NAWDC search-and-rescue crew had taken their comments about flying into danger seriously. It would have been such an easy thing to dismiss, considering they were in the middle of Nevada and hundreds of miles from the coast.

"Strike Two Four, Pony One on twenty-eight, twenty-eight," Colt said.

"Go ahead."

"The threat has been neutralized, and the landing zone is clear."

The helicopter pilot hesitated before answering, apparently finding the moment just as surreal as Colt. "Copy all, Pony One."

Not to be left out of the conversation, Cubby's voice spoke up. "Strike Two Four, I'm popping smoke at this time."

"Copy."

Colt pulled his eyes away from the helicopter just as a bloom of red smoke wafted into the air and billowed upward before the wind carried it away. Activating the smoke marker served several purposes, not the least of which was to guide the rescue pilots' eyes onto the survivor's location. But it also gave them a good assessment of the surface winds and conditions surrounding the landing zone.

"Strike Two Four is visual," the pilot said.

On the surface, it looked like everything was coming together nicely. The Joint Strike Fighter pilot who had been shot down by an experimental weapon had been rescued. The Stryker carrying that weapon had been destroyed. But Colt circled above the whole thing with growing unease that it was far from over.

Despite the lack of a continued enemy presence.

"It's too quiet," Dave said, again demonstrating his uncanny ability to read Colt's mind.

"I was just thinking that."

Colt glanced down at the screen showing video from the MX-15. Even after destroying the Stryker, the SEAL Master Chief had remained vigilant and continued scanning the surrounding area for additional threats. He had been in combat too many times to believe that the battle was over just because the shooting had stopped.

"Mariner Six, Pony One," Dave said.

"Go ahead, Pony One."

"What's your current posit?"

"Approaching the crash site from the northeast," Todd said. "We have eyes on the survivor's red smoke."

Colt watched Dave slew the sensor's crosshairs from the Stryker's wreckage across the valley to the northeast, where he centered it on the Flyer 60 ground mobility vehicle. "Copy, Pony One is visual."

They hadn't had time to dress out in full combat fatigues, but each SEAL wore some variation of what they normally wore when down range—a pair of denim jeans or Kuhl pants, plaid button-down shirts with lightweight Arc'teryx softshell jackets, and Solomon trail shoes. Only Punky stood out in her Vans and red USC Trojans hoodie.

"Tally ho," Graham said from the front passenger seat, pointing across the valley at the billowing red smoke.

"I see it," Todd replied, steering the nimble five-place all-terrain vehicle toward the downed pilot.

The SEALs had insisted Punky wear a helmet and goggles despite her protests, but she was thankful for the ability to communicate with them over the AN/PRC-148 Multiband Inter/Intra Team Radio, or MBITR, connected to her Peltor headset. It allowed her to speak with the Flyer's other occupants while also monitoring communications between the other assets supporting them. In this case, that included the *Black Ponies* A-29 Super Tucano and NAWDC MH-60S Knighthawk helicopter.

"What's that over there?" she asked, pointing at the dark smoke and burning wreckage not far from the helicopter's intended landing zone.

But before anybody could answer, Dave's voice broke in again over the radio. "Mariner Six, Pony One."

"Go ahead," Todd replied.

"Proceed from present position to the destroyed armored vehicle and conduct SE. How copy?"

"SE?" Punky asked.

Ron turned to look at her. "Site Exploitation. It means he wants us to extract as much potential intelligence as possible from the site in hopes the data might lead to other enemy targets."

"He knows we're in Nevada, right?"

"He just wants us to document what we find and exploit any materials we uncover."

"Good copy," Todd said, cranking the wheel over to aim the Flyer at the smoldering wreckage. "What are we looking for?"

Punky reached back and felt for the pistol holstered on her hip before noticing that both Ron and Graham had inserted fresh magazines into their individually customized SOPMOD M4 carbines. Despite their unorthodox attire, all three wore olive drab plate carriers configured with an assortment of pouches containing their tools of the trade—spare magazines, radios, individual first aid kits, and other accoutrements they might need if things got hot.

And based on what they had heard from the squadron's Command Master Chief in the orbiting Super Tucano, things had definitely gotten hot.

"The armored vehicle should have been outfitted with an experimental laser weapon," Dave said. "I need you to provide confirmation that it was destroyed with the vehicle."

"Copy all. Any hostiles in the area?"

"Negative," Dave replied. "Looks cold."

Graham racked his charging handle to chamber a round. "I'm still going in hot," he said.

"Whoa," Ron said. "Déjà vu."

Punky leaned to one side and looked over Todd's shoulder at the rescue helicopter as it dropped low and flared near the landing zone, causing thin tendrils of red smoke to swirl and dance in the air. Then she leaned to the other side and saw what remained of an armored vehicle after Colt and Dave dropped a five-hundred-pound laser-guided bomb right on top of it— less than a mile from the downed fighter pilot.

But like their eyes in the sky had said, there were no hostiles in the area. *How is that possible?*

The Flyer 60 jostled over the uneven terrain as Todd kept his foot on the gas and raced for the wreckage. Punky turned her attention back to the helicopter, where a Navy aircrewman jogged across the desert floor to render aid to the downed pilot. Even through the smoke and haze, she could tell the fighter pilot wasn't badly injured and only needed a ride home.

"Strike Two Four, Pony One, our ground force is visual and proceeding to secure the wreckage."

"Copy all," the helicopter pilot replied. "We're recovering the pilot now."

Dave double-clicked the microphone transmit switch in acknowledgment before shifting his focus back to Punky and the SEALs. "Mariner Six, Pony One, we've got eyes on. The target area is clear."

"Copy," Todd said.

They bobbed and weaved across the undulating terrain and veered around several larger rocky outcroppings before Todd brought the vehicle to a stop. They were still over a hundred meters from the smoldering Stryker.

"Why are we stopping?" Punky asked.

Todd jumped out from behind the steering wheel and lifted his carbine to scan the horizon for unseen threats. "With it still smoking, there's a fifty-fifty chance any unexpended ordnance still on board could detonate. We'll continue the rest of the way on foot."

The other SEALs seemed to accept the explanation and dismounted to take up their positions on either side of Todd. She climbed down from the all-terrain vehicle and fell in behind the frogmen, keeping her pistol holstered but her hand on its grip. Like the SEALs in front of her and the Master Chief in the back seat of the light attack plane circling overhead, she knew better than to let her guard down.

The sound of the Knighthawk's rotor blades reverberated in her chest as they advanced on what remained of the armored vehicle. Punky watched Todd's barrel carve the air in a lazy eight as he glided across the uneven terrain in a rolling heel-toe movement. Without looking, she knew Ron was scanning their left flank while Graham covered their right. But she was focused on doing her best not to slow them down.

"Mariner Six, you are seventy-five meters from the objective."

Without missing a step, Todd reached up for the push-to-talk on his plate carrier. "Copy."

They neared the charred remains of one of the most technologically advanced fighting vehicles on the planet, and Todd slowed his pace to take in their surroundings. Punky's mouth was already dry from the physical exertion and thin desert air, and the taste of acrid smoke irritated the back of her throat and only grew worse as they moved closer. The sound of the helicopter had been replaced by the hollow sound of wind whipping across the exposed landscape and the occasional echo of rotor blades thumping in the distance. The horizon on either side of the Stryker's charred remains was devoid of anything living and gave credence to Dave's assertion that the area was clear.

"Fifty meters," the Master Chief said from his perch in the sky.

The scent of burning rubber, plastic, and lubricants grew stronger with each step, and the rocky ground underfoot felt a little warmer. Todd stopped to adjust the keffiyeh he had tied around his neck and brought it up to cover his nose and mouth. The other SEALs did the same thing, so Punky pulled the collar of her hoodie up to mimic them as best she could.

Hesitantly, Todd took another step toward the wreckage, then stopped. Punky squinted through the smoke still wafting upward and swallowed back the sour taste building in the back of her throat.

"Is that . . ."

With a heavy sigh, Todd reached up for the push-to-talk on his plate carrier.

"Pony One, Mariner Six. At the objective."

The bodies were burned but not disfigured. She could see two of them and was almost certain one of them belonged to a woman. Her body had been scarred with several wounds that looked like they were made by shrapnel—wounds that were notably absent on the other corpse. But both were riddled with what looked like bullet holes.

What the hell's going on?

"Mariner Six, do you see the weapon?"

"What does it look like?" Todd asked.

"I'm not entirely sure, but I imagine it would be mounted on a turret of some kind on top of the vehicle."

From her vantage point, Punky couldn't see a turret on top of the Stryker. But Todd's reply told her why.

"Looks like the turret might have been removed," he said.

53

After being locked in the shed again, Adam fell onto the cot and fought against his rising anxiety. Despite his panicked, labored breathing, he attempted sleep and tossed and turned for several hours until the temperature rose and reminded him of his hopeless situation. He eventually gave up on falling asleep, just as he had given up on the slim hope that the Chinese would come rescue him and return him to an uninspired life of mediocrity. He belonged to the Russians now, like an abused pet passed from one cruel owner to the next.

It was well into morning when Adam heard footsteps approaching, and he suspected his captors had come to serve him breakfast. Despite their demonstrated affinity for violence, they had treated him remarkably well since locking him in the shed. He sat up and swung his feet to the dirt floor, neither fearing the footsteps nor holding out hope that they portended an imminent release from his prison.

Whether he liked it or not, being a pawn in the game of global espionage had become his lot in life.

Instead of standing when he heard the chains rattling, his shoulders sagged, and he slumped forward with his eyes fixed on the ground. He knew he was defeated and relegated to do their bidding. The door opened, and a large figure again blotted out the muted late morning sunlight. Adam looked up, unsurprised to see Nikolai standing there.

Neither spoke for several seconds, and Adam briefly wondered if the Russian had come to end his misery and put a bullet in his brain. He had done plenty in his life to deserve it, but he suspected Nikolai finally recognized what a mistake taking Adam had been. Maybe he had come to accept that Adam had been telling the truth when he said he was of no use to them.

"Come with me," the Russian said at last, then turned and started walking away.

Adam remained glued to his cot, frozen by indecision as he watched the SVR operative limp-shuffle away from the shed. *It's a trap*, he thought. *He'll shoot you the second you set foot through the door.*

But Nikolai didn't hesitate or even look over his shoulder to see if the Marine was following. His gait was consistent as he steadily walked away from the shed and made his way across the barren desert floor.

Maybe it's not.

Adam felt a faint flicker of hope that maybe the Russians had no intention of ending his miserable life after all. Maybe they had been right in believing he could be useful to them. Or maybe the Chinese had come through for him and negotiated his release. He shook his head.

Not possible.

Adam stood and crept closer to the threshold, his ears straining to detect the sounds of hidden assassins lying in wait on either side of the door. His eyes darted from one shadow to the next with waning unease. He took another hesitant step forward but froze when Nikolai stopped to look over his shoulder and grunted.

"Come. We don't have all day."

Adam waited to see if the order was followed by an ultimatum, then tossed aside his caution and stepped out into the sunlight. He squinted and brought a hand up to shield his eyes as he scanned his surroundings, but his brief elation at being paroled was replaced by a feeling of despair settling over him. Even if he wanted to take this opportunity of being free from the shed to make his escape, there was nowhere to go. The terrain was flat and barren, with only one other structure in sight—a dilapidated building that was the larger cousin to the shed he had been locked inside.

I'm trapped.

His shoulders sagged as he again accepted his fate and set out to follow Nikolai.

It was time to do his master's bidding.

Naval Air Station Fallon
Fallon, Nevada

Colt glanced down at the gear position indicator lights to verify that all three were illuminated green. A wise old aviator had once told him that there were two types of retractable gear pilots—those who had landed gear up, and those who would. His subconscious recalled that advice and brought it to the front of his mind each time he rolled into the groove and prepared to land.

"One hundred and fifteen knots," Dave said from the back seat.

Colt adjusted power until the flight path marker in his heads-up display dropped three degrees below the horizon bar while keeping the number representing his angle of attack within the acceptable range.

Eleven degrees.

It had been a while since he had flown the A-29 Super Tucano, but he could still fly a three-degree glide path at the optimum AOA for landing. As the light attack plane neared the runway, he eased back on the stick and increased the angle of attack another two degrees while pulling power and letting the airspeed bleed off.

"One hundred and five knots."

The main wheels touched down on the two-hundred-foot-wide asphalt runway, and he abruptly chopped the power while lifting the nose in an aerodynamic brake, letting the airplane roll out on the runway centerline. For not being proficient in the plane, his landing was almost textbook, and he grinned behind his oxygen mask in silent self-adulation.

"Amazing," Dave said from the back seat.

His smile grew wider.

"You managed not to crash."

His smile disappeared.

As they cleared the runway on Taxiway Echo, Colt looked to the right at the expansive parking apron in front of Hangar 2 and saw the distinctive shape of a twin-engine Boeing passenger jet.

Flown by the 89th Airlift Wing at Andrews Air Force Base in Maryland, the Boeing 757-2G4 was a variant of the mid-size, narrow-body twin-engine jet airliner, modified for VIP travel. Known as the C-32A in the military, the plane dedicated to fly the vice president of the United States had been altered to accommodate a 45-passenger interior and included upgraded military avionics. Painted in blue and white livery, vertical stabilizer flag, and prominent "UNITED STATES OF AMERICA" cheatline markings, there was no mistaking it for anything else.

Air Force Two.

The base had obviously pulled out all the stops to accommodate the vice president's visit and had cleared a space for Air Force Two to park on the ramp in front of Hangar 2. Colt brought the Super Tucano to a stop as Dave keyed the microphone. "Ground, Pony One clear of the active, taxi to Hangar Seven."

"Pony One, taxi to Hangar Seven via Alpha, Delta, cross Runway Two Five."

Dave read back the instructions as Colt released the brakes and inched the plane forward, turning south on the main parallel taxiway. At Taxiway Delta, he steered the single-engine turboprop onto the parking apron and made for the open hangar doors. He crept through the opening and brought the plane to a stop in the middle of the massive building.

Colt set the parking brake, then moved the throttle to CUTOFF to kill fuel to the Pratt & Whitney Canada engine. The plane shook as the Hartzell propeller spun to a stop, and Colt swept his hands around the cockpit to complete the shutdown sequence from memory. After turning off the strobe light and beacon, he rotated the knob to shut off the embedded GPS-aided inertial navigation system, or EGI. When he turned off the master avionics switch and battery, the two men were plunged into an eerie quiet.

Dave opened the canopy, and Colt took a moment to appreciate what had just happened. He had gone flying in the Fallon Range Training Complex to locate a stolen experimental directed energy weapon. But he had ended up acting as on-scene commander for a combat search-and-rescue mission. And the weapon was still missing. In the Nevada desert.

Unbelievable.

"You going to just sit there all day, flyboy?"

Colt shook his head, then quickly unstrapped from his ejection seat and followed the Master Chief out onto the wing before dropping down to the concrete floor. With a little more than idle curiosity, he watched the SEAL move around the airplane to safe and pin the remaining ordnance, then he turned for the doors and stared across the ramp at the blue-and-white tail of Air Force Two sticking up prominently above rows of dormant fighter jets.

"What're you thinking?" Dave asked.

Colt shook his head. "Something doesn't feel right about this."

Dave slapped him on the back. "About what? We caught the Chinese red-handed and made sure the vice president landed safely. I'd say that's a pretty successful Sunday morning, wouldn't you?"

Colt knew there would be plenty of Monday morning quarterbacking after this, but he couldn't help himself from asking one simple question.

"Yeah? So, where's the weapon?"

54

Nevada desert

Adam sat at a small wood table in the kitchen of the dilapidated house while the Russian stood silently to the side and watched him shovel scrambled eggs into his mouth. After finishing the eggs, he went to work on the bacon and hash browns, pausing just long enough to wash it all down with orange juice and a sip of coffee. It almost felt like a dream, and as the plate of food slowly disappeared, he slowed his pace to prolong it and avoid waking up back in the shed.

But the coffee. *Ahhh...*

With each sip, Adam felt the caffeine shoot straight to his weary brain. It energized him and allowed the nearly extinguished flicker of hope to burn just a little bit brighter.

"When you are done, you will shower and shave and get dressed," Nikolai said.

Adam bobbed his head eagerly. It had only taken twenty-four hours of captivity to condition him to behave like a brand-new recruit and follow orders without question. But even if he hadn't responded like an abused dog, the prospect of a hot shower was such a heavenly thought that he would have jumped at the chance.

"What will I wear?" Adam asked, in between bites of bacon.

Nikolai didn't answer at first, then disappeared into a room around the corner. When he returned, Adam froze with a strip of bacon halfway to his mouth. "What's that?"

The Russian held up a freshly pressed outfit in a clear garment bag. "Your uniform."

The bacon fell back to the plate, and Adam shook his head. "I'm not going back."

Nikolai gave him a sad smile as if to remind him of his station in life. He didn't need to point out that he was eating breakfast sitting at a table instead of on his cot in the shed. He didn't need to proclaim that Adam was alive only because the Russian allowed it. If he wanted Adam to wear the uniform, he would wear the uniform. It was that simple.

"You will wear this today."

Adam swallowed the half-chewed bite of bacon as his eyes traced across the dark blue coat featuring a scarlet-piped mandarin collar—legendarily created to protect the wearer from sword strikes. Both sleeves were adorned with matching twin chevrons over crossed rifles that represented his rank of corporal. And he didn't have to see the sky-blue trousers to know they were also adorned with the "blood stripes" worn by commissioned and non-commissioned officers to pay silent tribute to the fallen from both cadres at the Battle of Chapultepec.

"I already told you, they'll arrest me," Adam said with a trace of fear and anxiety creeping into his voice. "I'm a deserter now and no good to you."

Nikolai hung the uniform on a hook set into the wall and leaned against the counter to appraise Adam with tired eyes. "Oh, but that's where you are wrong. You will serve a very important purpose. One you were born for."

Adam's eyes shifted from the Russian to the uniform and back. The Marine Corps dress blues uniform traced its history to the American Revolution and was the only uniform in the United States military to incorporate all three colors of the American flag. But they were only worn for ceremonies with foreign dignitaries, visits with US civil officials, and formal social functions attended in an official capacity. He had no idea which of those the Russian expected him to attend, but he doubted such an event existed in the Nevada desert.

"Where do you want me to wear this?"

"Naval Air Station Fallon."

"Why?"

"The vice president of the United States is visiting the base."

Adam swallowed but said nothing.

"Take your shower. Shave. Make yourself look like a respectable Marine. We leave in one hour."

Adam didn't know how to tell him he had never been a respectable Marine and hadn't the foggiest idea how to go about making himself look like one. So, he just bobbed his head and agreed to pretend.

"Yes, sir."

Gabbs, Nevada

Punky's knee bounced nervously up and down in the back seat of the Flyer 60 as she tried to process everything that had taken place. She agreed with Todd and the other SEALs that someone had gone to great lengths to make it look like the Chinese spymaster had been killed when the *Black Ponies* Super Tucano bombed the Stryker armored vehicle. The shrapnel wounds and bullet holes just didn't add up.

Between that and the missing directed energy weapon, Punky knew something else was going on. She just didn't know what.

Ron leaned over and tapped her leg. "Tell me again why we're going out to Gabbs when we already know Mantis was killed?"

Everything she had uncovered since following Corporal Garett from San Diego pointed to Russian involvement. She had concrete evidence that Russian SVR operatives kidnapped him at the Nugget Casino Resort, and her best guess was that they intended to use him as leverage over Mantis to turn over the experimental directed energy weapon.

But then they used the weapon to shoot down a Joint Strike Fighter and staged the Stryker to make it appear as if the Chinese were behind the attack. Why? Where was the weapon now? What did they intend to use it for?

"Her phone is still pinging at the Gabbs airfield, and we still don't know how the Russians factor into this," she shouted over the wind. "Maybe we'll find something there that will unveil what the Russians have planned."

"Maybe it was all a ruse," Todd said from the driver's seat. "Have you considered that maybe Mantis lied to keep you off her trail while she stole the weapon and moved it into position to take down Air Force Two?"

"Then where's the weapon now?"

None of the SEALs replied to her rhetorical question, but she knew it unnerved them just as much as it did her. They all wanted things tidied up and wrapped neatly with a bow. But the real world didn't work like that.

"Can't you go any faster?"

Todd shook his head. "Relax, Punky. Whatever's there isn't going anywhere."

That wasn't what worried her. She was worried about not finding it in time—that she would be too late to stop whatever the Russians had planned. She glanced at her watch, then stared over the nose of the ground mobility vehicle at the vast nothingness in front of them. She found it hard to believe they would uncover something at the airport to make sense of it all. But it was all she had to go on.

There has to be a reason her phone is still pinging there.

Her silent brooding continued until Todd slowed the Flyer 60 and turned off the highway onto a dirt road. The Advanced Light Strike Vehicle's off-road shocks handled the undulating terrain with ease, but Punky's knee took a back seat to her entire body bouncing with each dip in the road.

"What are we looking for?" Graham asked from the front passenger seat.

"I have no idea," Punky said, then squinted through the dust and pointed at a distant building. "Does that look like a hangar to you?"

Todd nodded. "As good a place to start as any."

They continued down the dirt road until reaching a wide swath of land in front of a corrugated metal structure. The ground appeared to have been cleared and groomed for vehicles and was probably where visiting airplanes parked. Though why somebody would want to visit the dirt strip was a mystery to her.

"Let's check it out," Punky said.

Todd came to a stop in front of the weathered building, and they all climbed out of their seats as Punky reached back and drew her service pistol, subconsciously aware that the others held their SOPMOD M4 carbines at the low ready. She followed Todd, who took control of the tactical situation and prepared to clear the hangar. He hadn't said a word, but she could tell he was switched on and acutely aware of his surroundings. She took up a supporting position just behind his right shoulder as he spun into the hangar and pivoted left to clear the open space. Punky confidently stepped inside and turned right.

"Clear left," he said.

"Clear right."

Though neither had completely relaxed, they both stared at the Tesla Model X with California license plates sitting idle in the empty hangar.

"Was this what you were hoping for?" Todd asked.

"Maybe."

Punky walked over and opened the frunk, naively thinking it possible the experimental laser weapon could have been hidden inside. When she saw that it was unsurprisingly empty, she pulled out her cell phone and dialed Camron, letting it ring a half dozen times before he answered.

"What's going on, Punky?"

"Need you to run a plate for me."

"Okay, give it to me."

She read him the license plate number, then waited patiently for him to enter it into the database. He whistled softly when he got the results, and she waited with bated breath for him to share his discovery.

"The vehicle belongs to Fu Zan of San Jose, California."

"Mantis," she said, though she had already suspected as much. "I was afraid of that."

He was quiet for a moment. "Punky, I've been on the phone with the vice president's security detail. They knew about the missing directed energy weapon before he landed at Naval Air Station Fallon."

"Then why did he still come?" She shook her head. "It doesn't matter. It looks like the Chinese used it to shoot down a Navy Joint Strike Fighter this morning before he arrived."

"The Chinese?"

"Well, we found the bodies of who we believe are Mantis and the computer engineer who stole the weapon from Tonopah."

"But what about the Russians?" Camron asked.

Ron yelled to her from outside the hangar. "Punky! Come see!"

She turned to look over her shoulder at the Navy SEAL, hesitant to believe he'd found something useful. "I've got to go, Camron."

"Wait a second. Just one more thing. I gave the Secret Service your information and assigned you to liaise with them—"

"You what?"

"I needed someone who was up to speed on everything that's been happening."

"I don't have time for this, Camron. The laser—"

"Make time," Camron said. His tone made it clear he wasn't entertaining objections.

Punky sighed. "Fine. Send me the details of the vice president's visit."

"On its way."

"But, Camron, this isn't over. I think the vice president is still in danger."

"He's on the ground, Punky. He's safe."

"I'm not so sure." She ended the call and slipped the phone back into her pocket before jogging through the hangar doors to where Ron squatted in the bushes just off to the side of the cleared area.

"What'd you find?"

Ron held up his hand, and she saw the faint glint of a metal object pinched between his thumb and forefinger. "Shell casings," he said. "Lots of them."

She stopped and studied the ground. He was right. It was littered with what looked like a relatively fresh supply of spent brass. And Punky couldn't help but think back to the bodies they had found in the destroyed Stryker that were riddled with gunshot wounds. Was this where they had been shot? Ron brought the one in his fingers to his nose.

"Pretty fresh, too," Ron said.

What the hell happened here?

Punky's phone chirped with an incoming message, and she pulled it out to scan the email she had just received from Camron. It contained several attachments, including a formal instruction that identified who was responsible for each specific task during the vice president's visit, an abbreviated itinerary, and a list of personnel who had been granted access.

"We need to get back to Fallon," she said.

Ron stood. "But what about this?"

Punky turned and looked at the Tesla hidden in the hangar's shadows. She shook her head. "Something tells me Mantis wasn't playing it straight with me."

"What does that mean?"

How could I have been so stupid?

"It means we've been following the wrong threat."

55

Nevada desert

Adam stared at himself in the dirty bathroom mirror and felt like a fraud. Even before he deserted, he hadn't been an ideal Marine. In truth, he wasn't sure he'd ever been. From boot camp on, he had pretty much been a fuck-up. He lacked drive and initiative—at least according to Sergeant Narvaez —and he had been more interested in doing Chen than his actual job.

But the Marine Corps dress blues did a pretty decent job of covering that up.

"Are you ready?" Nikolai asked.

Adam tugged on the hem of his coat and smoothed the front of his uniform, wishing he had put more effort into taking care of his physical appearance. Even if he hadn't been a good Marine, he could have at least taken the opportunity to look like one. "Yeah," he called.

He opened the door and stepped out into what he guessed was the master bedroom. The floor was littered with blankets, but he doubted Nikolai or any of his other captors actually slept there.

The Russian studied him like a drill instructor, circling him slowly and looking for even the slightest mistake in the uniform's wear or appearance. "This will do. This will do nicely."

"For what?"

Nikolai stopped in front of Adam and looked down at him. "Air Force Two has landed at Naval Air Station Fallon. We have arranged for you to have a private audience with the vice president."

His mouth fell open. "How did you manage that?"

Nikolai grunted as if he found it amusing that Adam even cared. "At one time, he was the congressman for your home district. Let's just say that he has *fond memories* of his time there."

However the Russian had managed it, Adam didn't really care. But he was terrified to learn what Nikolai expected him to do once he was alone in a room with the vice president. Adam swallowed. "What do you want me to do?"

The corners of the Russian's mouth curled up in a close approximation of a smile, but his eyes couldn't hide his enjoyment at seeing the Marine squirm. Corporal's chevrons or not, blood stripe or not, the uniform didn't make him feel brave. And he definitely didn't feel worthy of the uniform.

"Nothing."

Adam recoiled in shock. "Nothing?"

The Russian's smile grew wider, but he turned away and reached for a cigar box resting on the counter. Nikolai picked it up and inspected it reverently, then turned and presented it to Adam. "All I want you to do is give him this."

Adam reached up to take the box, but Nikolai pulled it away.

"Not yet. When the time is right, you may have it. And you will give it to nobody other than Vice President Jonathan Adams. Is that clear?"

Adam swallowed again. "Yes, sir."

Naval Air Station Fallon
Fallon, Nevada

Colt was surprised to learn that the downing of an F-35C hadn't deterred base leadership from continuing with the vice president's planned visit. But the Secret Service had been alerted to the potential danger and apparently didn't think it warranted additional security measures. So, he borrowed Punky's government Suburban and drove from the *Black Ponies* hangar to the Fleet Training Building to prepare for the VP's orientation flight.

Ours is not to reason why . . .

After parking in the lot in front of the secure compound, Colt walked through a set of outer doors into an anteroom filled with stacks of security lockers on either side. He powered down his phone, locked it away, then walked through the inner doors and handed his Common Access Card to the security guard behind the desk.

"Guess you're here for the dog and pony show?"

Colt shook his head and accepted the offered security badge. "Somebody's got to do it."

"You heard he's running for president next year, right?"

He clipped the security badge to his Velcro name tag before replying. "Yeah, but it honestly makes no difference who the commander-in-chief is. We just follow our orders."

Even though the security guard was a contractor and not a uniformed service member, Colt knew he needed to be careful how he responded. He gave the obviously apolitical answer through gritted teeth, but the truth was he had heard good things about the vice president and hoped he succeeded in winning the election. Washington could use more guys like Jonathan Adams.

"Well, if you're taking him flying, try to remember he could be your boss one day."

Colt smiled. He didn't have to be a genius to read between the lines. "Don't worry, I'm not going to get him sick or make him black out."

"That's what they all say."

Colt winked at the guard, then turned for the hallway leading away from the lobby. The Fleet Training Building—home to the US Navy Fighter Weapons School, better known as TOPGUN—was one of the few places Colt felt at home. Walking the halls of the FTB came second only to being at the controls of a high-speed fighter jet or low-speed light attack plane.

But today it was eerily quiet.

Normally, the building's classrooms or briefing rooms were full of students eager to absorb the knowledge from the cadre of instructors. With it being the Sunday of Hook, it was as close to a ghost town as Colt had ever seen it. Maybe not as quiet as Austin or Middlegate, but it came close.

"How'd I know they'd bring you in to do this?"

Colt stopped mid-stride and backed up, ducking his head into the briefing room he had just passed. He squinted through the darkness and was surprised to see his friend and former test pilot sitting in a ready room chair with an ashen look. "Hey, Jug. What are you doing here?"

"The VP's orientation flight?"

Colt furrowed his brow. "They have you flying in the event too?"

The former test pilot nodded. "It was supposed to be Cubby, but . . ."

Colt flipped the light on and appraised the other pilot carefully. "Wait. Were you the one flying with him?"

Jug nodded.

"What the hell happened?"

"I don't know. We just finished a BFM set and were doing battle damage checks before heading back to base, when . . ."

Again, Jug trailed off, and Colt understood exactly how he felt. He remembered how shell-shocked he had been in the hours after his F-35C Joint Strike Fighter refused to respond to commands and rolled inverted in an attempted kamikaze attack on a guided missile cruiser. Things like that weren't supposed to happen.

Not in the warning areas off the coast of California.

And not in the training ranges in the heart of Nevada.

"Is he okay?" Colt asked.

The simple question seemed to shake Jug free from his maudlin, and he looked up at Colt. "Yeah, just banged up. He's over at the clinic right now getting looked at."

"Good," Colt said. "That's good."

"But I still don't understand what happened."

Colt took a seat next to him. "What'd you see?"

Jug shook his head. "It sounds crazy—"

"Try me."

"It looked like somebody took a scalpel to his jet and cut it in half. Right behind the cockpit."

Colt had no idea what the damage from a directed energy weapon might look like, but he imagined it could look something like that. But if the laser weapon had brought down Cubby's JSF, then why hadn't Punky found it among the Stryker's wreckage?

Jug turned and looked Colt in the eyes. "I sound crazy, right?"

Colt shook his head. "No, Jug. You don't."

"But—"

Colt reached over and placed a hand on Jug's shoulder. "Listen, there's something going on that I can't even begin to explain. But what happened to Cubby was no accident."

His eyes grew wide. "It's the Chinese, isn't it?"

Colt wished he could say yes. But knowing the Russians were somehow mixed up in things, he wasn't willing to put money on that. "Honestly, I don't know. But I believe he was brought down by an experimental directed energy weapon that went missing from Tonopah yesterday."

"How . . ." Jug trailed off, but Colt could see in his eyes that he was reliving the moment Cubby's jet was torn apart. "How's that even possible? Where's the laser now?"

"I don't know," Colt replied honestly.

"So, is taking the VP flying even a smart idea right now?"

Colt took a deep breath. "I don't know, man. I just don't know."

56

Sam stepped out of the trailing Suburban and watched the one-star admiral in charge of the Naval Aviation Warfighting Development Center greet Jonathan in front of the Fleet Training Building. His team of Secret Service agents surrounded them and turned outward, looking for approaching threats. That wasn't likely on a military base like the Naval Air Station, but it wasn't in their nature to let their guard down.

The admiral gestured for Jonathan to join him Inside, and Sam followed the group as they made their way up the walkway to the front of the building. Even on military bases, some locations and buildings were more secure than others, and this was one of them. He felt even more relaxed as the group passed the security guard stationed in the lobby and turned down the hall.

"We have something special in store for you," Sam heard the admiral saying. "We wanted to give you the best chance of seeing how our training ranges are used and why the expansion and modernization is needed."

Jonathan placed his hand on the admiral's back in a reassuring gesture one might expect a father to give his son. But it looked odd for a man his age to do so to one ten years his senior. "Admiral, you know I'm a huge supporter of our military and believe in giving the warfighter every tool they need to succeed. You don't need to convince me of that."

The admiral stopped walking and turned toward Jonathan with just the hint of a smile on his face. "Does that mean you don't want one of my instructors to take you up in a Super Hornet?"

Sam wasn't sure if Jonathan's reaction was an act or genuine, but he looked like a kid on Christmas morning who had just opened a present containing the one thing he had asked for. "Take me up? Like, in the air?"

The admiral's smile grew. "Yes, Mister Vice President. One of our most skilled pilots will take you up in the back seat of a Super Hornet. Then you'll get a chance to see firsthand how we prepare the warfighter to protect America from its enemies."

"I'd be honored, Admiral."

This time, it was the older man who placed a reassuring hand on the other's back. Jonathan might have been the second most powerful man in the world, but he had just stepped into the admiral's domain. And there was no question who was in charge.

"Great, then let's introduce you to the man who will take you up." Gesturing to a briefing room on the left, the admiral followed Jonathan inside. "Attention on deck."

Colt came to attention when he heard the admiral's voice and stood ramrod straight, even as his thoughts still swirled around the question Jug had asked.

Is taking the VP flying even a smart idea right now?

"At ease, please," the vice president said. He walked across the room to shake Colt's hand.

"Lieutenant Commander Colt Bancroft, Mister Vice President," he said.

"Pleased to meet you, Colt." The vice president smiled warmly, then turned to Jug. "And you are?"

"Lieutenant Commander Bill McFarland, sir."

"Pleased to meet you, Bill." They also shook hands, then the vice president turned to look at the admiral. "So, these are the *best of the best*, Admiral?"

The NAWDC commander puffed out his chest and nodded. "Yes, sir.

Colt was an instructor here at TOPGUN before going out to Air Wing Five in Japan for his training officer tour." He paused and gave Jug a furtive glance. "You might recall an event that happened last year in the South China Sea?"

Colt felt his cheeks flush but saw that the vice president did indeed recall the event. He turned back to Colt with a beaming smile and slapped him on the shoulder. "Of course I do, Admiral. He's a real American hero."

Colt cleared his throat. "All due respect, Mister Vice President, but I was just doing my job." Then, as if to forgo any further showering of praises, he glanced at his watch and gestured for the vice president to take the seat next to Jug. "Sir, if you're ready, we can get started with the brief."

"Spoken like a true professional," the vice president said.

The admiral locked eyes with Colt. "Take care of him, Mother."

"Aye aye, Admiral."

"Mother?" The vice president looked confused.

"It's my callsign, sir."

"Dare I ask why?"

As if the admiral had found the topic mundane and beneath him, he spun from the room and closed the door, leaving Colt alone with Jug, the vice president, and a short, dodgy-looking man standing in the corner. Before Colt answered, he addressed the stranger.

"Would you like a seat, Mister . . ."

"Chambers," the dodgy man said. "Sam Chambers. I'm the vice president's chief of staff."

Colt nodded and gestured to a seat in the back row. "You're welcome to join us for the brief, Mister Chambers. Please, make yourself comfortable."

As Sam lowered himself into the vacant ready room chair, Colt turned back to Jonathan. "The dormitory at the US Naval Academy is known as Bancroft Hall, named after former Secretary of the Navy George Bancroft."

"Any relation?"

"Not that I know of," Colt said.

"So, why Mother?"

"All four thousand midshipmen live in Bancroft Hall. There are over seventeen hundred rooms and almost five miles of corridors, covering thirty-three acres of floor space. And the midshipmen who live there lovingly refer to her as 'Mother B.'"

"Mother Bancroft," Jonathan said.

Colt grinned. "That's my name, sir."

The vice president shook his head. "I'll never understand you aviators."

Strike 1
Navy FA-18F Super Hornet
Fallon, Nevada

A short while later, Jonathan took a deep breath of the stale air and tried reminding himself to relax and breathe easy. The admiral had told him the Navy lieutenant commander at the controls of the two-seat Super Hornet was one of the best. And Colt Bancroft had assured Jonathan that this was just another day at the office for him. All he had to do was sit back, relax, and enjoy the ride.

But that was easier said than done when you were unaccustomed to having your face covered by a bulky piece of rubber and plastic and forced to breathe air through a one-inch-diameter rubber hose.

"How you doing, sir?" Colt asked.

Jonathan took another deep breath, then exhaled slowly and tried to calm his racing heart. He held a thumb up for the pilot to see in his mirror, not trusting himself to press the button to toggle the intercom system and answer using actual words. For a man accustomed to high pressure situations, sitting strapped to an ejection seat in a seventy-million-dollar fighter jet was a humbling experience.

"Okay, sir. We're next to go," the pilot said. "So, we're going to run the takeoff checklist and arm our seats, okay?"

"Roger that," Jonathan said, feeling like it was the appropriate thing to say.

They had started up on the TOPGUN ramp and taxied to the hold short for one of the long parallel runways where Lieutenant Commander Bill

McFarland met them in an F-35C Lightning II Joint Strike Fighter from VFA-147.

"Watch your knees, sir."

Jonathan looked down as the control stick moved forward and back and side to side, making a boxlike pattern as Colt verified their jet would be safe to fly.

"Okay. Controls are free. Wings are spread and locked. Trim is set, flaps are half, hook is up. My harness is connected eight points in the front . . ."

Jonathan remembered this part of the brief. He looked down at the straps connected around his ankles and upper thighs, then felt for the lap belt and shoulder harnesses to make sure he was strapped in properly to the ejection seat. Even though a contractor assigned to NAWDC had crouched just outside the canopy to make sure he was, it was still his responsibility to make sure he was ready to go flying.

"Eight points in the rear," Jonathan said.

"Warning lights are out, and nose wheel steering is in low. I'm ready to arm in the front."

"Ready to arm in the back."

Jonathan heard a click as Colt rotated the lever to arm his ejection seat. "Armed in the front."

He reached for the lever near his right leg, squeezed the locking mechanism, and rotated it toward him to hide the word "SAFE" painted in black on a field of white. That left only the black and yellow striped face with the word "ARMED" painted on its surface.

"Armed in the back."

Jonathan had been so engrossed with the entire experience of briefing the flight, being measured and fitted for flight gear, and strapping into the fourth-generation fighter, that he had almost forgotten what was about to happen.

"Ready, sir?" Colt asked.

Jonathan shook away his thoughts and gave the pilot a thumbs-up.

"Fallon Tower, Strike One, flight of two is ready for takeoff."

"Strike One flight, Fallon Tower, cleared for takeoff three one left."

Jonathan looked up and saw the pilot grinning at him in the mirror, then clip his oxygen mask into place. Within seconds, he had the engines spooled up and they began rolling forward to taxi in front of the Joint Strike Fighter and line up on the far side of the runway.

Jonathan leaned his head back against the ejection seat and closed his eyes as his stomach turned somersaults. But his eyes snapped open as Colt pushed the throttles forward to the stops. He felt the Super Hornet slowly moving down the runway, then quickly accelerate once the afterburners ignited and pushed him back into his seat.

57

Thirty miles east of Fallon, Nevada

Punky sat in the back seat of the Flyer 60 ground mobility vehicle while trying to reconcile everything that had happened. Each event that followed *KMART*'s kidnapping from the Nugget in Reno pointed to the Russians as the likely culprits. And nothing she had found contradicted that theory.

Yet here she was. Trying to make sense of the evidence.

"Do you really think the vice president is still in danger?" Todd asked.

Punky reached up and adjusted her headset's volume. "The laser's still missing, isn't it?"

Graham turned and made eye contact with her. "He's not in danger as long as he's on the ground, right?"

Punky nodded. "The weapon was designed for air defense, but your guess is as good as mine whether it can be used against a land-based target. Either way, I think the safest course of action is to get to Fallon, brief the Secret Service on the threat, and recommend the vice president remain on the ground until the weapon has been located. Don't you think?"

The SEALs apparently agreed because nobody offered an alternative.

"How far away are we?" Punky asked.

"Thirty minutes," Todd said. "Where will he be when we get there?"

Punky was upset she had momentarily forgotten the email Camron had forwarded to her. She pulled her phone out of her pocket, opened her inbox, and tapped on the message containing several attachments pertaining to the vice president's visit. Her leg bounced anxiously as she waited for the email to download—no easy feat given the poor cellular coverage east of Fallon.

Todd glanced over his shoulder. "Punky?"

"I'm waiting for it to download," she said.

The SEAL chief didn't seem nearly as anxious over the lack of 5G service in the Nevada desert. "Well, I'm guessing he'll probably meet with the admiral first. We'll just go straight to the NAWDC headquarters. He should be safe until we get there."

"I hope you're right."

When the email finished downloading, Punky felt a momentary reprieve from her frayed nerves. She scrolled to the bottom where the attachments were located and tapped on the PDF labeled "Itinerary_VP." She almost screamed when her phone's screen went blank while attempting to download all forty kilobytes.

"You've got to be kidding me . . ."

Graham glanced at her over his shoulder. "What?"

She just shook her head in frustration while trying to keep her blood pressure from soaring into stroke territory. Like it or not, she was at the mercy of electromagnetic radiation and packets of data being transmitted from a cellular tower to her smartphone. She didn't know how wireless connections really worked. Just that they had never failed her before.

"The cell service here is . . ."

She trailed off as the document appeared on her phone's screen. Pinching on the image, she zoomed in to read the text and scrolled to the top of the page. Her heart stopped when she saw Colt's name.

"Oh, shit."

Strike 1
Navy FA-18F Super Hornet

Colt glanced in his mirrors and grinned when he saw the vice president's wide eyes and white knuckles gripping the straps above his upper Koch fittings. He snapped the control stick against his thigh and rolled the Super Hornet upright after completing the inverted FOD check. It was common practice before any tactical sortie to apply negative Gs and check for Foreign Object Debris that could become lodged in the flight controls and compromise the safety of the flight.

But if you were unaccustomed to being upside down and hanging in your straps, it was disconcerting to feel yourself floating away from your ejection seat with nothing but the earth filling the canopy. More than one guest rider had reached for something to hold onto and inadvertently pulled the ejection handle.

That was part of the reason Colt had instructed the vice president to hold onto the straps at his shoulders when he felt uncomfortable. His white knuckles were all Colt needed to see to confirm he had crossed that particular threshold.

"Doing okay back there, sir?"

Almost as if Jonathan sensed that Colt was watching him, he relaxed his grip and nodded. "Just fine," he said. But his words carried a slight tremor to them.

Colt had taken plenty of people flying before. Normally, they were junior enlisted sailors who had earned the opportunity through sustained superior performance, flight surgeons who avoided actual work and pretended to be pilots, or other aviators who just couldn't get enough. But this was the first time he had taken a civilian flying.

A powerful civilian maybe, but still one unaccustomed to danger.

"Okay, then. We're going to do a little tail chase. You ready?"

The vice president's eyes flashed with fear as if trying to recall whether Colt had briefed him on the maneuver. "A little *what?*"

Colt smiled. "Tail chase. It's very benign. Jug will break away, and a few seconds later we will follow and fall in trail about a mile to a mile and a half behind him."

"Okay . . ."

"Then he'll start to maneuver, and we'll follow him through the sky. There's nothing to it, and we won't be pulling many Gs. This is just a fun way for us to practice visualizing pursuit curves in a 3D environment."

The vice president gave a little shake of his head as if trying to make sense of Colt's explanation. It was clear the politician wasn't comfortable being strapped to an ejection seat, but that didn't mean he couldn't still have fun.

"You ready?"

"I guess."

Colt keyed the microphone switch. "Strike One is set."

"Strike Two set," Jug replied.

"Three . . . two . . . one . . . Go!"

Twenty miles east of Fallon, Nevada

Punky angrily stabbed at the button to end her call, upset with herself for forgetting that Colt had told her he was on tap to take the vice president flying. "It's going straight to voicemail," she said.

"They're probably already in the air." Somehow, Ron knew precisely what not to say. And he said it anyway.

"Well, there has to be something we can do!"

She wanted to throw her phone as far as she could, even though it didn't deserve the focus of her scorn. It was an inanimate object and an easy target for her to project her frustrations onto. Even if her own failures were the source of those frustrations.

"We've all seen what Colt can do," Todd said. "If the vice president's in his back seat, he's in good hands."

"Not good enough," she spat, though she was the first to admit she didn't have a clue what else they could do to keep the vice president safe. If the laser weapon was still in play—and she had no reason to think otherwise—then they needed to get Colt and the VP on the ground as soon as possible.

"I have an idea," Graham said.

Punky looked at him riding shotgun next to Todd but remained quiet as she waited for him to explain. He chewed on the inside of his cheek as he worked through the plan in his mind, then he quickly reached for the backpack on the floorboard between his feet.

"You going to keep us guessing?" Todd asked.

"TADIL," he replied.

"Tattle?" Punky asked.

"No, TADIL. Tactical Digital Information Link."

"Okay . . ."

But it was apparent the other SEALs already understood where he was going with it, and Todd's voice sounded hopeful. "Dude, that's brilliant. Set it up."

"I'm working on it."

While Punky looked on in open-mouth bewilderment, Graham removed a Toughbook laptop from his backpack and powered it on. Resting it on his lap, he again reached into his backpack and began removing a tangled mess of cables that he connected to the computer and to another device that looked like a handheld radio.

"Somebody want to explain to me why this is so brilliant?" Punky asked.

Ron was the first to speak up. "TADIL is a communication system that supports information exchange between tactical command, control, communications, computers, and intelligence systems. The radio transmission and reception component is known as JTIDS, or Joint Tactical Information Distribution System—"

"Can you skip to the good part?"

If Ron was offended by her brusquely cutting him off, he didn't let it show. "Right. Well, the Super Hornet uses its successor, known as MIDS— an ultra high frequency and line of sight communication terminal that provides secure digital data exchange."

"Meaning what exactly?"

Ron smiled. "Meaning we can send his jet an encrypted text message."

58

Ten miles east of Fallon, Nevada

Todd kept his foot to the floor, and the Flyer 60 ground mobility vehicle drove westward—racing against an invisible clock and uncertain threat. But they all felt it. Graham hunched over the Toughbook laptop perched on his knees, but Punky's eyes were glued to the mess of wires connecting it with several other nondescript boxes he had scattered throughout the vehicle's cockpit.

"How long's this gonna take?"

Instead of answering, Graham briefly held a finger up, then resumed the hunting and pecking that had occupied his time since he first suggested TADIL as a possible solution. Punky threw her hands up in the air in frustration, then folded them across her chest as she leaned back in the uncomfortable seat and waited for the Advanced Light Strike Vehicle to reach the Navy base where she might be able to do some good.

But Ron took pity on her. "Relax, Punky. He knows what he's doing."

"Oh, I'm sure he does—"

"Datalink isn't as simple as picking up a phone and dialing a specific number. For example, TADIL uses a digital modulation technique known as TDMA, or Time Division Multiple Access."

Punky just stared at him with her lips parted in stunned silence.

Ron didn't seem to notice. "This TDMA scheme provides twelve-second frames divided into over fifteen hundred time slots that can be used for data transmission. This means that each of the many possible nets is using the same fifty-one frequencies in a different hopping pattern to communicate over a single network."

"I have no clue what any of that means," Punky said.

"Before he can send a message and even hope for Colt to be able to read it, he has to make sure they are both using the same cryptovariables. For Colt's jet to even receive the message, they both need to use the same transmission security. But then for him to *read* the message, they both need the same message security."

"Crypto-what?"

"Got him!" Graham shouted, then turned to Punky with the faint flicker of hope dancing brighter in his eyes. "Cryptovariables. It means I needed to figure out what decoder ring he's using before I sent him the message."

"Makes perfect sense," she said, then turned to Ron. "Why couldn't you have just said that?"

But Ron ignored her. "So, you found him?"

The other SEAL nodded. "Our flyboy's the only participant in the network. So, what do you want me to tell him?"

Punky scrunched up her face for a moment, then told him what to type.

Strike 1
Navy FA-18F Super Hornet

Colt looked left of the canopy bow at the descending F-35C Joint Strike Fighter. He had promised the vice president relaxed and gentle maneuvering, but it looked like Jug was trying to make him work for it. He rolled right —away from Jug's jet—and parked his nose high to preserve separation. Then after several seconds of feeling almost suspended in the air, he rolled inverted and pulled straight down.

As their nose passed through the nadir, Colt glanced up in his mirrors and saw the vice president's eyes wide but focused, tracking the fifth-generation fighter across the desert landscape beneath them. At only a mile of separation, the jet was still relatively easy to see. But it took some getting used to tracking another object in the three-dimensional environment, where up wasn't always up and the earth and sky frequently swapped places.

At least he didn't look uneasy.

"Still doing okay back there, sir?"

Colt pulled back on the stick and gradually increased the G-forces as he brought his nose up to track Jug's jet. Had they been engaged in a mock dogfight—or a real one like they had been over the Pacific—the test pilot wouldn't have waited for Colt's nose to point at him before maneuvering. But he had meant what he said—tail chase was a more relaxing evolution and perfect for giving the vice president a taste of how the jets performed.

"I'm doing great," Jonathan said. "This is amazing!"

Colt smiled. "Hey Jug, let's—"

His train of thought was interrupted by the flashing letters "MSG" in his heads-up display that indicated he had received a message over the datalink network. Without thinking about it, he reached up and navigated his left display to the Multifunctional Information Distribution System, or MIDS, page and read the message with growing unease.

"What the . . ."

His heart started beating faster, and he read the message twice more, before glancing in his mirrors at the vice president in the back seat. The second most powerful man in the country appeared relaxed, taking advantage of the momentary straight and level flight to drop his mask and drink a sip of water.

"What do want to do now, Colt?" Jug asked.

He glanced back at the message and read it a third time.

"Hey Jug?"

"Yeah?"

"Did you get that message?"

"What message?"

Colt looked at the vice president again as icy tendrils of fear spread across his body. He knew Punky and the SEALs hadn't yet found evidence that the laser weapon had been destroyed when they bombed the Stryker. But had they discovered it was being used to target the vice president?

The man sitting in his back seat?

Oh, shit.

"Follow me," Colt said, then snapped the stick into his left thigh and rolled nearly inverted before pulling it back into his lap and rapidly increasing the Gs. In his mirrors, he saw Jonathan nearly lose his grip on the water bottle but scramble to clip his mask into place.

"Where we going?" Jug asked.

He didn't need to look over his shoulder to know that the test pilot had maneuvered his F-35C into trail and was following Colt toward the desert floor. "We need to get back to Fallon," Colt replied. "*Now.*"

He knew the vice president hadn't read the message, and the last thing he wanted to do was to scare him. But he wasn't willing to take a chance with his safety, either. The admiral had trusted Colt to take care of him, and he intended to do just that.

"What's going on, Colt?" Jug asked.

"Not now," he said, then spoke over the intercom to the vice president. "Sir, if you could lower your visor, we're going to go low altitude."

Unlike Jug, Jonathan seemed content with simply following instructions, and he lowered his visor to shield his eyes, then gripped the straps like Colt had shown him in the brief. Colt returned his focus to the rising terrain and pushed the throttles forward to spur the Super Hornet through four hundred knots.

He glanced once more at the message.

VP IN DANGER. LASER IN PLAY. LAND ASAP.

This can't be happening, Colt thought.

As they descended through one thousand feet, Colt pulled back on the stick to shallow out his descent and race for the desert floor. Flying on the deck in the Fallon Range Training Complex was almost second nature to Colt, but this was the first time he had felt like he needed to push the boundaries of his comfort and get as low as possible.

"Colt—"

"Just stay on my six, Jug."

They were in the Gabbs North Military Operations Area, south of

Mount Moses and east of Dixie Valley, and were at most ten minutes from reaching the naval air station. Colt turned their formation west as his eyes scanned far ahead of them. He had no idea what he was looking for, but he figured it was safest to avoid farms or roads and cross over the Stillwater Mountain Range to approach Fallon from the north.

"What's going on?" Jonathan asked.

Colt didn't dare take his eyes off the ground whipping by at over five hundred miles per hour. Like his former instructors used to say, the ground had a one hundred percent probability of kill, and complacency had killed more fighter pilots than enemy action. "We just need to get you back to base, sir."

They crossed Dixie Valley and headed west, where the terrain rose up in front of them and loomed large in Colt's windscreen. The valley floor was less than one hundred feet beneath them, but almost four thousand feet in elevation. The mountains ahead of them topped eight thousand feet and appeared like a giant wall stretching up to block their path from horizon to horizon. Colt aimed the Super Hornet at a notch, then pulled back on the stick and began a climb to match the slope of the rising terrain.

When they reached the apex, Colt rolled the Super Hornet inverted and pulled the stick back into his lap to bring their nose down on the other side. He grunted from the G-forces, but before he could roll the Super Hornet upright, he heard a single tone from his Radar Warning Receiver.

A single tone that quickly turned into a high-pitched warble.

Colt's stomach dropped.

"I'm spiked!"

59

"Sorry, that was me."

Colt let out a long exhale. "Dammit, Jug. You almost gave me a heart attack."

"What the hell's going on?"

Colt rolled upright and guided the Super Hornet back down to the deck over Lone Rock—the dried lake bed north of Fallon on the western side of the Stillwaters. Even at their low altitude, he could see the naval air station thirty miles away, and he turned to point his nose south as Jug maneuvered his Joint Strike Fighter onto his right side.

"You're telling me you didn't get that message?"

"What message?" Jug asked again.

"Let's talk about it on the ground." Colt shook his head. He had no idea what was going on, but if somebody had sent him an encrypted message over MIDS, then it was in his best interest to take it seriously. "Switch Fallon approach."

Click. Click.

Colt reached up and dialed in the Fallon approach control frequency and checked in, letting the controller know that they saw the airfield and were proceeding direct to the initial. Normally, they would compete with other tactical aircraft coming back from the Fallon Range Training

Complex to be first for the initial. But as the only two jets airborne, they owned the sky.

"Strike One, Fallon Approach. You are number one for the initial. Switch tower."

Colt acknowledged the handoff and again twisted the knob to select the tower frequency as he guided their formation south on the east side of the airfield. On his left, Colt saw a break in the rugged terrain of the Stillwaters where the Sand Mountain Recreation Area was located, idly wondering if that was where the laser weapon was located. He swallowed back his fear, then started a right turn to the airfield.

With the throttles still pushed up, the Super Hornet hummed through the dry air and continued gaining speed as they raced closer to the runway for the carrier break. Colt glanced in his mirror to make sure Jug had closed the distance between them and collapsed into a parade formation. Just over his shoulder, he caught a glimpse of the vice president craning his neck to watch the fifth-generation stealth fighter maneuver into position.

"Tower, Strike One. Initial."

The air traffic controller's response was immediate. "Strike One, report the numbers."

"Strike One."

Colt leveled his wings with the long parallel runways directly in front of him, offset just slightly to the right. His eyes never stopped scanning the horizon in every direction, and he prayed to just make it through the break and get the vice president on the ground safely.

"Okay, sir," Colt said over the intercom. "Remember in the brief when I talked about the carrier break? We're going to make a hard left turn and pull four to five Gs, so be ready with your Anti-G Straining Maneuver."

The vice president gave him a weak thumbs-up, but at least he was still conscious and aware of what was going on. The Super Hornet bobbed in the turbulent air, but Colt kept his nose level with the horizon and didn't fight it.

As they passed even with the approach end, he keyed the microphone. "Strike One, numbers."

"Strike One, break left."

"Here we go, sir." Colt momentarily let go of his control stick and brought his hand to the side of his face, giving Jug a "kiss off" gesture. Then he reached down for the stick, slapped it into his left thigh to roll up on a wing, and pulled it back into his lap as the G forces pressed him down into the seat.

"Strike One, breaking."

After passing through the main gate on Churchill Avenue, Punky looked up and felt the knot of tension in her shoulders ease just a smidge when she saw a Super Hornet arcing across the sky in a turn to downwind. A Joint Strike Fighter followed less than four seconds behind, and she watched as the two jets rolled out heading south.

"Did he get the message?"

Graham shrugged. "I can't tell if he read the message, only that it was sent. But if that was him, I'd say there's a good chance it was the reason he returned to base early."

Punky looked up as they passed the Silver State Club and saw a white Ford Explorer across the road with "CNRSW Police" in bold letters on the side. Its lights were on and the uniformed police officer from Navy Region Southwest stood outside, directing traffic on Churchill Avenue to stop.

"Keep going," she said.

But Todd moved his foot from the gas pedal to the brake and slowed the Flyer 60 to a crawl. "Punky, I can't just run a police barricade for no good reason. If you want to get the Secret Service's attention, that'll do it. But I don't think you're going to like the outcome."

After they came to a stop, Punky opened her door and jumped out. Her movement caught the uniformed officer's attention, and he raised a hand, gesturing for her to stop from coming any closer while resting his hand on the butt of his pistol. But she had expected it. She unclipped her gold badge from her belt and lifted it high above her head.

"Federal agent," she yelled.

The officer seemed to relax, but she still kept her movement slow and deliberate to avoid spooking him. The last thing she needed was a jumpy base police officer thinking she was a threat to the vice president and deciding to shoot first and ask questions later.

"Can I help you, ma'am?"

"Why are you blocking traffic? We have an urgent need to get to the Fleet Training Building."

"All traffic is halted. The vice president is landing right now."

Punky could no longer see the two fighter jets, but based on how much time had passed, she assumed they had already touched down. "I think they just landed, and I've been assigned to his detail from NCIS. I need to speak with the special agent in charge."

The officer's radio squawked, and he held a hand to the earpiece in his ear to listen in on the tactical communications channel. "Ma'am, I just received confirmation that they landed . . ."

"Yeah, I just said that."

". . . and if you return to your vehicle, traffic will be allowed to resume in a moment."

She looked over his shoulder just as a light gray Super Hornet rolled by on the runway in the distance. "Thanks for your help," she said. Then she turned back to the team of SEALs waiting in the ground mobility vehicle.

Colt felt both relief and frustration when he exited the runway and guided the Super Hornet south on taxiway Alpha to return the jet to the TOPGUN ramp. He was relieved that an invisible laser hadn't cut his jet in half or burned a hole through the vice president. But he was frustrated that somebody had sent the urgent message without providing any amplifying information.

"Strike One, taxi to Mat Five via Alpha," the ground controller said.

He read back the instructions before switching to his tactical frequency. "Jug, you're cleared to detach."

Click. Click.

The F-35C Joint Strike Fighter turned into Mat Two where a team of sailors from the *Argonauts* waited to greet him. But Colt's eyes were drawn to the blue-and-white Boeing passenger jet that occupied most of the ramp space.

He looked up at the mirror and locked eyes with the vice president. "Well, sir? Did you have fun?"

He gave Colt two thumbs up. "Thanks for taking me, Colt. I don't think I'll ever look at a fighter jet the same."

Colt turned the Super Hornet onto the TOPGUN ramp and came to a stop in front of a gaggle of sailors who verified his nose and captive air training missile were pinned and safe, then checked his brakes for excessive heat. After successfully passing inspection, they sent him on his way to taxi to a parking space directly in front of the hangar.

Colt saw a crowd of military personnel, Secret Service agents, and a host of men in suits he suspected were part of the vice president's entourage. Nobody looked overly concerned, but he knew looks could be deceiving.

"It was my pleasure, sir," Colt said.

60

After shutting down the Super Hornet, Colt unstrapped from his ejection seat and crouched on the LEX while contractors rolled a set of stairs up to the side of his jet. Normally, aircrew used a built-in ladder to climb down from the cockpit, but he didn't think the admiral wanted to see the vice president take a tumble and had ordered the stairs for an easier egress.

Jonathan Adams paused to shake Colt's hand before taking the steps down to greet a crowd of military officers led by the NAWDC commander. Each of them beamed from ear to ear and gave no indication that they thought the vice president had been in mortal danger. Even the dodgy Sam Chambers seemed happy to see his boss return to earth in one piece.

What the hell's going on?

Colt watched the crowd of senior officers disappear inside the hangar, then returned to his normal post-flight duties. He might have just flown the second most powerful person in the world, but he was back to the reality of being just another lieutenant commander who the Navy trusted to fly a seventy-million-dollar fighter jet. And it was his job to make sure he put her to bed correctly.

Colt took his time walking around the jet, trying to ignore the nagging voice in the back of his head that told him he had somehow cheated death. He was lost in his thoughts when a golf cart pulled up and Jug hopped out.

"Mind telling me what the hell that was all about?"

Colt shook his head in disbelief. "I received a message over Link-16 that the laser was still in play and the vice president was in danger."

Jug stared at Colt like he had two heads. "What? Who sent it?"

"I have no idea."

Together, the two pilots turned and looked at the hangar where the crowd of officers and Secret Service agents surrounding the vice president had disappeared. "Well, he's safe now."

"Is he?"

Colt couldn't shake the nagging feeling that something bad was about to happen.

Despite her best efforts to remain calm, Punky gripped the Flyer's tubular frame as Todd turned off Churchill Avenue onto the road fronting the NAWDC headquarters. But they barely made it one hundred feet before a throng of base police vehicles and a host of security personnel stopped them from advancing further.

"Looks like this is the end of the line," Todd said. He shifted the Flyer 60 into park and lifted his hands, palm out, at the police officer who turned in their direction.

This time, Punky didn't just jump from the back seat. She watched as a caravan of vehicles pulled to a stop in front of the headquarters building and emptied several Secret Service agents who surrounded the vice president's car. She leaned to the side to look around Todd as one of the most popular political figures in recent history stepped out into the Nevada sunlight wearing a flight suit. The admiral walked up to him and guided him inside.

"Looks like he's doing just fine," Ron commented.

"Yeah," she said, though something still gnawed at her.

The uniformed police officer assigned to Navy Region Southwest cradled his M4 carbine and casually walked up to Todd, who had his elbow propped up on the sill and leaned into the door while keeping both hands visible. Ron and Graham also kept their hands well away from their

SOPMOD M4s, though it was clear by how they were dressed that the men were ready for battle.

"Better get ready to flash that fancy gold badge of yours again," Todd said.

"For all the good it'll do me," she said.

"Help you?" the nervous officer asked, glancing only momentarily in Punky's direction before fixing his gaze back on Todd.

"I'm just the driver, man." He thrust a thumb over his shoulder in Punky's direction. "She's the boss."

The officer glanced at Graham in the passenger seat, then Ron in the back, and finally Punky. "Ma'am?"

She held up her gleaming gold shield. "Special Agent Emmy King with NCIS. I've been assigned as liaison with the Secret Service, and I need to speak with the SAC about a time-sensitive issue."

Her reference to the special agent in charge didn't do much to put the officer at ease, but he at least lifted the radio clipped to his tactical vest and spoke quietly into the microphone. Punky was antsy and looked beyond the Flyer's nose at the men who were gathered there to protect the vice president. She saw each of them react to the officer's message and turn to look in their direction. But none appeared too eager to speak with her.

"Somebody will be along shortly, ma'am," the officer said.

"This really can't wait." She reached for the door handle to let herself out. "We don't have . . ."

The officer stepped back and raised the M4. He didn't point it at her, but he made it clear that he took her reaching for the door as an overt act of hostility. "Remain in the vehicle."

"Easy, son," Todd said. He hadn't flinched as the barrel of the carbine came within inches of his head, but his tone was as hard as iron. "We're not a threat to you. But if you point that thing in my direction again, it won't go well for you."

"Is that a threat?" The cop's voice rose in pitch.

Punky recognized the telltale signs of heightened stress, and she reached forward to place a hand on Todd's shoulder. "Easy, Chief."

"I just said we're not a threat," Todd said in a calm but firm voice.

Unlike Todd and the other SEALs, the cop seemed unsure of himself and on edge. "I said somebody will be along shortly. Remain in the vehicle."

Punky held a hand up and gestured in a calming manner. "We'll stay right here. But could you *please* stress that this is time sensitive?"

"They'll be along shortly," the cop repeated, as if that reassured her that they were taking her request to speak with the SAC seriously.

Punky bit her tongue from saying more and leaned back against the uncomfortable seat to focus on her breathing. Though she had managed to remain calm during the encounter, her heart rate was elevated, and she knew she was under more stress than was useful for the situation. After several slow inhales and exhales, she felt it dip to a more comfortable resting heart rate.

"Well, what now?" Todd asked.

"Now, we wait."

He turned to look over his shoulder. "We wait?"

"Well, what the hell else can we do? Deacon Jim over there's likely to empty an entire magazine into us if we dare move."

Todd smirked and glanced at the nervous cop from the corner of his eye. "He's just doing his job. Even if his muzzle awareness is a little lax." He said the last part loud enough for the uniformed officer to catch the admonishment.

Punky pulled out her cell phone and opened her recent call history.

"Who are you calling?"

"Colt. Maybe he has some pull with the base bubbas." But the call went straight to voicemail. She tried his number several more times and got the same result. "Dammit."

"No luck?" Ron asked.

She shot him an irritated look. "You know, you could do something to help."

"Right now, I'm just trying not to get shot."

She went back to her call history and dialed Camron's number. Unlike Colt, he picked up on the first ring.

"Punky?"

She didn't bother with niceties and jumped right into her impassioned plea. "I don't have time to explain, Camron. Right now, I need to speak with the SAC, and one of Navy Region Southwest's finest is stonewalling me. Can you get in touch with somebody at the Secret Service and help expedite things?"

"Where are you? Right now, where are you?"

After she described the Flyer 60 ground mobility vehicle and their location on the base, Camron promised to make some calls and hung up. Her knee started bouncing again with the same nervous tic that had propelled them back from Gabbs, but her eyes never stopped scanning the crowd gathered in front of the NAWDC headquarters.

"How long are we going to sit here?" Todd asked.

"As long as it takes, I guess."

But Graham was growing impatient too. "The longer we sit here, the more time the Russians have."

To do what?

She opened her email inbox and again tapped on the message Camron had sent her containing the base instruction for the VP's visit. She was about to open the attachment containing the schedule again when she saw the one labeled *Cleared Personnel.*

Intrigued, she tapped on it and waited for it to open.

61

Adam came to attention and stared straight ahead at the stage, aware of the people descending toward the front of the auditorium on his left side. He tried to harness the discipline the Marine Corps had failed to imbue in him and keep his eyes firmly "in the boat." But as the admiral and vice president neared the stage, he couldn't help himself, and his eyes darted to the side.

"Take your seats, please," the vice president said.

Adam sat in his theater chair toward the front of the auditorium and reached underneath the seat to remove the cigar box Nikolai had given him. Despite the comfortable temperature they kept the building, he was sweating inside his dress blues, and the mandarin collar chafed at his neck. But he kept his face passive as he looked up at the man wearing a flight suit who the Russians had sent him to meet.

"Thank you all for taking a few minutes out of your day to come see me," the statesman said. "I understand we've set aside some time for each of you, but I wanted to tell you all how incredibly fortunate I am to serve as your vice president. And, God willing, next January as your commander-in-chief."

Adam had been forced to sit in the audience for visiting senior officers and dignitaries in the past, and each one had given him the impression they were just checking off a block on some checklist. His leadership had always ensured each Marine was properly dressed and represented the command well, but he knew he was nothing more than window dressing. The visitors never really cared about the enlisted Marines. They never cared about Adam.

But this man seemed different.

"I never served in the military, but I have the utmost respect for those who did." The vice president looked each person in the eye—from the lowest seaman to the admiral—and tugged on the flight suit with a grin. "Even more so after today, I have the utmost respect for *you*. And it means a lot to me that you are here with me today. Thank you."

Before the admiral could call the assembled sailors and Marines to attention, they all popped to their feet as the vice president walked off the stage. Adam clutched the cigar box in his hand, wondering again what it contained and why the Russians had gone through such effort to have him deliver it. Deep in the recesses of his brain, a part of him believed it contained some type of explosive—that Nikolai expected him to martyr himself for their cause.

And, if he was being honest, that same part of him was okay with it. Not because he hated the vice president or aligned himself with the Russians. He was okay with it because it was a just end to the life he had wasted.

"Take your seats," a voice called out.

Adam dropped back into his theater chair and looked over at the admiral's aide walking in front of those assembled in the auditorium. He eyed the lieutenant with envy, taking in his gleaming gold pilot wings and blue-and-gold braided double loop on his left shoulder.

The lieutenant addressed the group. "When your name is called, I will escort you to the admiral's office. There, you will have your picture taken and have no more than five minutes with the vice president. Please remember your courtesies as you represent your commands."

Who do I represent? Adam thought.

———

Punky's knee jackhammered up and down as she waited for the attachment to open. She wasn't sure why, but something about it made her uneasy. And if all she could do was sit in the SEALs' ground mobility vehicle and wait for the special agent in charge, she might as well pull the thread and unravel the sweater.

"What's that?" Ron asked, looking across the cab at her growing angst.

"It's a list of cleared personnel."

The attachment opened, and she squinted and zoomed in on the list of names. It was broken up by tenant commands and listed the points of contact for each stop as well as each person who had been cleared by the vice president's staff to spend time with him. Her knee stopped bouncing when she saw Colt's name as the point of contact for the Fleet Training Building.

"Anything good?"

She shook her head. "Almost all military personnel. He's with the admiral now, and they've cleared commanders and seamen and almost every rank in between."

"This is about the safest place in the world right now."

Punky looked up again and glanced at the group of special agents waiting outside the headquarters building for the vice president to move on to his next stop. They were in the middle of nowhere, on a secure military base, and surrounded by military personnel.

"I know you're right. It's just . . ."

Her heart dropped when she saw his name.

Corporal Adam Garett.

"Punky?"

But she wasn't listening. Without thinking, she opened the door and almost tumbled onto the ground with the fear of what was happening inside the headquarters building spurring her onward. She ignored the startled shouts of the uniformed police officer or the three SEALs she had surprised by suddenly springing into action, and she looked beyond the throng of Secret Service agents who seemed to come alive with her sudden movement. Her entire focus was on the front doors and what she feared awaited her on the other side.

They had been stopped less than two hundred feet from the main entrance, but it might as well have been a mile. Police cars and up-armored

SUVs lined the street as their occupants converged on the unhinged dark-haired woman who sprinted through the gauntlet.

"Punky! Stop!"

Todd's voice had taken on the grizzled commanding tone only a Navy chief could summon. But still she ran. She shoved past two more stunned uniformed police officers but was knocked off balance by a master-at-arms petty officer who hadn't been shocked into inaction by her sudden sprint for the secure building.

One hundred and fifty feet.

She twisted and regained her footing, stepping up onto the sidewalk to resume her advance. She didn't know what was happening inside. But she knew that if *KMART* was inside with the vice president, it couldn't be good. The Russians hadn't kidnapped him and killed Mantis for nothing.

One hundred feet.

Punky's vision narrowed as fear propelled her onward. She felt hands reaching for her, but she spun and twisted and narrowly escaped from their grasp. She heard men shouting at her to turn back. To stop. To drop to the ground. She heard the fear in their voices—their determination to protect the vice president from every threat, no matter the cost.

Seventy-five feet.

Suddenly, a force slammed into her left side and knocked her off her feet. She flew through the air and came down hard on her shoulder in the desert landscaping. A weight crashed down on top of her, and she was only partially aware that a body clad in the green camouflage navy working uniform was smothering her and keeping her pinned to the ground.

"Don't . . . move," the breathless voice gasped.

Even as her surroundings came into focus, she struggled to get up. But the master-at-arms was stronger and kept her face pressed into the rocks. There was no malice in it. No anger or hatred. Just the calm and detached professionalism of a sailor doing his job.

"He's . . . in danger," she said through gritted teeth. She could barely breathe, and her voice came out as little more than a whisper.

"Stay still."

"But. . ."

"You're not *listening* to me," the sailor hissed. "They're going to shoot you."

Her eyes darted up at the men converging on her, and she saw something she hadn't expected. To them, *she* was the bad guy. *She* was the person who posed a threat to the vice president. She wasn't a hero, racing into battle to avert disaster, but the enemy who needed to be stopped at all costs.

Only, they were looking outward for the snake when the snake was already inside.

"Adam Garett," she said, still struggling to make herself heard.

The sailor eased off her just enough to let her breathe. "What?"

"Corporal Adam Garett," she said. "He's the threat."

She felt the master-at-arms react to her words, but he still kept her pinned to the ground as more hands descended on her to keep her immobile. "Who's that?"

Though she had been able to take several ragged breaths, she still struggled to speak. "He's a spy."

"Corporal . . ."

Another voice cut off the sailor's response. "What *the hell* is going on here?"

She twisted and made eye contact with a stocky Secret Service agent with a silver high-and-tight haircut. "He's in danger," she said.

He seethed at her and stepped closer. "Who are you?"

"Special Agent King. NCIS."

"Chris Albanese," the man replied. "I'm the SAC."

"You need to stop him."

"Who?"

"Corporal Adam Garett."

62

Sam held the door open and waited until the petty officer had left the office before closing it behind him. He returned to the chair next to where Jonathan lounged in his flight suit, looking more relaxed than he had in a very long time.

"Did you know about the Super Hornet flight?" Jonathan asked.

Sam lowered himself into the chair. "No, sir. I think that was all the admiral's doing."

The vice president looked around the office, taking in the photographs and lithographs of various Navy fighter aircraft that represented the admiral's career. Sam knew his longtime friend wasn't easily impressed, but it was hard not to be by somebody who had spent decades flying high performance fighter aircraft in defense of their nation.

"We'll need to do something special for him to show our appreciation."

Sam nodded. He had already made a mental note to do just that. But knowing how much his boss appreciated the gesture made it all the more important. "Did you have something in mind?"

"Not yet. I'll think on it." He clasped his hands together and leaned forward in his chair. "Okay, let's wrap this up."

Sam scanned the list of names, and his heart lurched when he saw the one he had added at the last minute at Viktor's behest. He cleared his throat. "There's just one more, sir."

"Great," Jonathan said, his mood exuberant since returning from his back seat ride. "Tell me about him."

Sam swallowed hard, though his mouth felt as dry as the air outside. "Corporal Adam Garett."

"A Marine."

"Yes, sir. He's the one I told you about who grew up in your home district."

Jonathan nodded. "Ah yes, I remember now. How long has he been here in Fallon?"

Sam should have expected the question. He had given the vice president a brief summary of each person's background and their current assignment before their meeting. It was one of the things that made the vice president special—he always made the effort to make the other person feel special. It didn't matter if they were an admiral or a corporal.

"Not long, sir. I think this one can be wrapped up pretty quick."

At least, he hoped so.

Jonathan nodded, then stood and smoothed out the front of his flight suit, adjusting his zipper to look as dignified as the fighter pilots who normally wore the outfit. If the men and women who took time out of their schedules to greet him had to look good in uniform, then so did he.

"Let's bring him in, then."

Sam wasn't sure why, but he suddenly felt lightheaded. He stood and cracked the door open to call out to the admiral's aide. "Lieutenant, can you bring in Corporal Garett?"

A host of conflicting emotions washed over Adam when the lieutenant finally called his name. He rose from his theater chair, straightened his uniform, and gently picked up the cigar box and tucked it under his arm. He was relieved it was finally his turn, putting an end to the agonizing wait. But he was terrified of what the next few minutes might bring.

"Is that a gift for the vice president?" the lieutenant asked when Adam joined him at the auditorium exit.

"Yes, sir."

The admiral's aide held out his hand. "You can give it to me, and I'll make sure he gets it."

Instinctively, Adam turned to put the box further away from the lieutenant, remembering what Nikolai had told him. *You will give it to nobody other than Vice President Jonathan Adams.*

"If it's all the same, sir, I'd prefer to give it to him myself."

The aide shrugged as if Adam snubbing his offer of assistance wasn't worth a second thought. "Suit yourself."

Without another word, the lieutenant turned and led Adam away from the auditorium and through the hall toward the admiral's office. The building was eerily silent, but Adam wasn't sure he would have been able to hear a marching band over the pounding of his heart. He knew the Russians had kidnapped him for a reason. He knew they had arranged for his name to be added to the list for a purpose. He wasn't walking through the hallways at NAWDC in his dress blues for no reason.

And he had a feeling the cigar box tucked tightly under his arm *was* that reason.

"When we reach the admiral's office, you will remain in the waiting area while I check on the vice president to make sure he is ready to receive you. It won't be long, so remain standing, but make yourself at ease."

Adam swallowed hard against the lump in his throat. "Aye, sir."

"When I call for you, walk into the office, stand at attention in front of the vice president, and announce your presence."

He cleared his throat. "Aye, sir."

The lieutenant turned and studied him. "Nervous?"

"Yes, sir," he croaked.

The aide grinned. "Don't be. The vice president's a good guy. Just be respectful and polite, and it'll be over before you know it."

He readjusted his grip on the cigar box and nodded. He wasn't sure he trusted himself to say much more than his name or one of the seven basic responses the Marine Corps had drilled into him. "Aye, sir."

They reached the admiral's office and walked through the outer doorway into the anteroom. The room was empty, but Adam could tell it was normally occupied by the admiral's inner circle—his aide and secretary among them. He stopped in front of an uncomfortable-looking sofa while the lieutenant crossed to the closed door to the admiral's inner office. He knocked, then cracked the door open.

"Mister Vice President, I have Corporal Adam Garett here to see you."

"Bring him in."

Adam's stomach lurched as the lieutenant turned and called for him. *Here goes nothing.*

The special agent in charge looked down at her with a look that alternated between anger and amusement. Punky could tell he was accustomed to knowing every single person who entered his sphere of influence when he was on the job. Probably even when he wasn't.

"Sit her up," Chris said.

The Navy master-at-arms climbed off her, then gently helped her into a seated position. It was only then when she realized she had attracted the attention of nearly every person who was a part of the vice president's entourage. Secret Service, uniformed Navy Region Southwest police officers, masters-at-arms, and several reporters who had been required to remain outside the NAWDC headquarters building.

"Where are your creds?" Chris asked once she was upright.

"My back right pocket." She didn't make a move to reach for them. With as amped up as the gathered law enforcement officers seemed, she didn't want to increase their stress any further.

Chris nodded at the master-at-arms, and he reached into her jeans and removed the billfold where she kept her NCIS credentials. He handed it to the SAC and waited to see if it passed muster. To his credit, the Secret Service special agent nodded with reassurance before handing them back to the sailor to return to her pocket.

"I assume you're the reason his flight was cut short?" Chris asked.

Punky clenched her jaw in frustration, embarrassed that her mistake about the laser weapon had put a wrinkle in the vice president's itinerary.

But she didn't want to back down. "I had reason to believe a directed energy weapon would be used against him."

"And now you don't?"

Honestly, she wasn't sure. They still didn't know where the laser was. But she knew where *KMART* was. And she knew he couldn't be trusted. "I'll tell you anything you want to know, but you need to protect the vice president. *Right now.*"

Chris studied her for signs she was trying to deceive him, then lifted his hand to speak into the microphone he had concealed there. Punky couldn't hear the response, but it was clear from the SAC's reaction that he had just confirmed that the vice president was alive and well.

"We've got him covered," he said. "But why should we believe you now?"

"I followed Corporal Adam Garett from Marine Corps Air Station Miramar after he deserted. I watched him get abducted by a van full of Russians in Reno yesterday . . ."

"How do you know they were Russians?"

"Because I shot one in the head."

They locked eyes, and she could tell the SAC was at least beginning to take her seriously. Everything she was telling him could be easily verified. Later. Right now, she needed him to stop *KMART* before he took out the vice president and party hopeful to be the next commander-in-chief.

Chris said nothing, then lifted the microphone to his mouth again. This time, he didn't bother to conceal his transmission, and she heard him say, "I need a location on Corporal Adam Garett. Possible threat to *GOLDEN BEAR.*"

Punky didn't recognize the callsign but assumed it was the one the Secret Service had assigned to the vice president. She didn't have to wonder long, however, because Chris's eyes went wide at the response. He and every other Secret Service agent turned and sprinted for the front doors.

63

Jonathan grinned when he saw the nervous Marine enter the office and come to attention in front of him. The military did strange things to people. He always found it fascinating that bits of gold thread or silver emblems affixed to their collars made one man forget he was simply in the presence of another. In his case, his uniform had only a NAWDC patch opposite a name tag adorned with the embossed seal of the vice president.

"Mister Vice President," the corporal said, staring at a spot six inches above his head as if making eye contact was as dangerous as staring at Medusa. "Corporal Adam Garett, United States Marine Corps."

Jonathan took a step forward and held out his hand. "At ease, Marine."

Adam glanced down at the offered hand and blanched. It was obvious he had never been treated with the level of courtesy Jonathan found normal between two adults. The vice president didn't normally wear the uniform and would never expect the Marine to salute him, but he also didn't see himself as anything other than just another American citizen.

He let his hand hang in the air between them before Adam awkwardly shifted the cigar box from under his right arm to his left while he shook Jonathan's hand.

"Thank you, Mister Vice President."

"So, I understand you're from the Bay Area."

When Jonathan first entered the political arena, he had made it his goal to learn how to put people at ease. Whether they were on the same or opposing side of an issue, he always made the effort to find a neutral ground from where they could build rapport. One of the easiest ways was to find something the two had in common. In this case, the opportunity had been served up to him on a silver platter—hailing from the same hometown was a natural unifier.

"Yes, sir. San Jose."

"I graduated from Willow Glen High School," Jonathan said. "Class of 1991."

The Marine released Jonathan's hand, but his entire body seemed to deflate with relief. "Class of 2019, sir."

Jonathan stepped back and gestured for Adam to take one of the chairs arranged in front of the admiral's desk. "Please, have a seat. I'd love to hear how a kid from Willow Glen ended up in Fallon, Nevada."

Adam hesitated, then took a seat in one of the offered chairs.

Sam stepped forward and addressed him quietly while keeping his gaze fixed on the Marine. "Sir, we have a schedule to keep and should probably move this along."

He nodded respectfully, then gave Sam's upper arm a squeeze before taking his seat next to Adam. "I think we can carve out another five minutes with our hometown hero here. Don't you think so, Corporal?"

Garett seemed to stumble over his words. "I'm no hero, sir. Just doing my job."

But the issue had been settled. Sam had made his objections, and Jonathan had made the decision to ignore his argument and press on ahead with what he saw was his responsibility as vice president—a responsibility that would become even more important once he became commander-in-chief.

"And what is your job, Marine?"

"I'm a sixty-six, ninety-four, sir."

Jonathan shook his head in confusion. "A what?"

The corporal pursed his lips as if chastising himself for speaking to a civilian in terms only another Marine would understand. "I'm sorry, sir. That's my MOS—my Military Occupational Specialty."

"Oh, of course." He nodded, then let his smile grow wider. "And what exactly does a sixty-six . . ."

"Ninety-four," Adam offered.

"What does a sixty-six, ninety-four do?" Jonathan asked, committing the MOS to memory.

"I'm an Aviation Logistics Information Management Systems Specialist," Adam said.

Despite the impressive-sounding title, Jonathan could tell it wasn't one the Marine was overly fond of. Again, not having served in the military himself, he felt he was at a disadvantage with understanding what role a title played in a service member's identity. He smiled at Adam to convey his thanks for entertaining his curiosities, then turned to Sam.

"Any idea what that is, Sam?"

"No, sir," his chief of staff replied.

Jonathan looked back to the Marine, who seemed almost humiliated that he would have to explain what he did to serve their country. But instead of acting insulted, he smiled sheepishly. "It's okay, sir. My own mom doesn't understand what it is I do."

"Enlighten me?"

The Marine fidgeted with the cigar box on his lap and nervously shifted it from one knee to the other. "I'm responsible for a broad spectrum of network infrastructure and information systems operation, installation, and maintenance."

Jonathan stared at him with a blank look of amusement.

"I basically operate the computer systems our squadrons rely on to put aircraft in the sky."

"I can barely operate my iPhone," Jonathan said. He hadn't the foggiest what encompassed the corporal's daily responsibilities, but he knew enough to know it was a job he wouldn't have been successful in. "Thank God we have men and women like you who take on the challenge."

Adam lifted his head, and Jonathan almost thought he looked more confident in himself than he had when he first walked through the door. His eyes dropped again to the cigar box in the corporal's lap, and he wondered about its importance.

"What's that?"

Adam pulled the box closer to his body as if to protect it from Jonathan's probing eyes. "It's just a gift."

"For me?"

"Yes, sir."

Jonathan leaned forward in his seat in anticipation of the Marine handing the cigar box to him. But Sam stepped between them and held his hand out. "May I?" he asked Corporal Garett.

"Sam..."

"No!" Adam snapped, his eyes darkening with sudden anger. "It's for him."

Maybe it was the way the Marine's mood seemed to shift in an instant, but Jonathan recoiled back into his seat. He had never been gifted with the innate ability to sense danger, but he had built his political career on his ability to read people. And he suddenly disliked what he read on Adam's face.

"What's in the box?"

64

Jonathan stood and looked down on the Marine. Adam's face had morphed from anger back to nervousness, and he shrank away from the vice president as he loomed over him. Jonathan clenched his fists and champed his teeth together as if preparing for a fight.

"Give it to me."

"Jonathan . . ."

He fired a look at his chief of staff and cut him off. "Now."

With trembling hands, Adam lifted the cigar box from his lap and held it out for Jonathan to take. He hesitated for only a second, then carefully plucked it from the corporal's fingers. The Spanish cedar cigar box had a polished black exterior and smooth edges with a simple gold clasp. An ornate rectangular logo in gold framed the name "Regius" in red.

"What's in the box?" he asked again. When Adam didn't answer, he looked up from the box. "I asked you a question, Marine."

Gone was the smiling politician who earned points by treating everyone as equals. Gone was the man who thought of himself as just an average American. Jonathan felt like he had been played, and he was itching for a fight.

"I . . . I don't know," Adam said.

"Maybe you shouldn't open it," Sam said.

Jonathan shot him another look. "*You're* the one who put him on the list, Sam!"

"I only..."

"Shut your fucking mouth."

The longer he stood there with the box in his hands, the more his blood boiled at what he felt was a betrayal of the worst kind. Sam had been with him since the beginning. They had been roommates and best friends at the University of California, Berkeley. They had canvased neighborhoods for local, state, and national elections. And they had agreed to ride the wave of politics as far as it would carry them. Together.

Sam took a step back, but Jonathan shook his head. "Don't you move. If this thing blows, you're going with me."

He reached down for the gold clasp and released it. Carefully, he cracked open the lid, hesitating for a moment as if expecting the box to release some form of noxious gas or a deadly viper. When nothing happened, he snapped the lid open the rest of the way and stared in horror at what was inside.

San Jose, California
November 2000

Jonathan Adams sat on the park bench and looked up into the gray sky. It wasn't raining, but the clouds hung low enough that he felt like he could reach up and touch them. It was a fitting scene to accompany his foul mood, and he brooded in silence.

Saint James Park was a large green space on the north end of downtown San Jose. During the day and in warmer months, it wasn't uncommon to find young families playing on its grass or having a picnic lunch and enjoying the mild Bay Area weather. But at night it was mostly empty, except for a handful of vagrants who sought a safe place to unroll a sleeping bag and catch a few hours of sleep. In November, the park was even more barren. It was the perfect place for Jonathan to escape the noise.

In truth, it should have been a night for celebration. After an early projection that gave Democrat Al Gore a victory in Florida was retracted, Republican George W. Bush received the state's twenty-five electoral votes. Even closer to home, Jonathan had stunned pundits and defeated his incumbent opponent in a landslide victory that gave him a seat in the California State Assembly as representative from District 25.

"There you are."

Jonathan looked up and saw Samuel Chambers—his best friend and closest confidant—shuffling toward the park bench. He wore a heavy wool overcoat and a scarf cinched tight around his neck to keep the cool mist from finding its way under his clothes.

"Hey, Sam."

Sam stood in front of Jonathan and scanned the dark park around them. "What are we doing out here? Everybody's waiting to celebrate with you."

When Jonathan didn't answer right away, Sam lowered himself onto the bench and shrugged his shoulders to tuck his neck deeper inside his coat. The clouds overhead glowed brighter as a jet on approach to the international airport descended lower. Both men looked up as the diffused light became crisper and more defined, and the roar of the jet's engines broke apart the silence surrounding them.

They waited until the jet's noise subsided before turning back to the issue at hand. "Seriously, Jonathan. You can't sit here all night. You're the new assembly-member for District Twenty-Five. You have a staff to build and need to start thinking about the year ahead."

Jonathan shook his head. "It's Mila."

Sam turned his head slowly as if he hadn't heard him. "It's what?"

"Mila. She's pregnant."

Sam groaned. They had been best friends since freshman year at Cal when they had shared a dorm room on Clark Kerr Campus—a Spanish mission–style residential complex named for the American economist and the first chancellor of the university. They had sought out female companionship in and out of bars along Telegraph Avenue and taken them to concerts at the iconic William Randolph Hearst Greek Theatre. Jonathan knew his best friend believed he was prone to falling in love, but even he knew Mila had been a mistake.

"When did you find out?"

"Tonight."

Sam shook his head. "I know you don't want to hear another lecture from me, but we've come too far. I told you that girl was a mistake and only wanted to latch on to you before you made it big. I told you she would be your downfall and end your political career before it even began."

"I know, Sam," Jonathan snapped. "You were right. You're always right."

Sam placed a comforting hand on his shoulder and squeezed. "I'm not always right, but you need to listen to me if we're going to end up in the White House one day."

Jonathan thought about all the times they had shared their mutual dream of reaching the pinnacle of American politics. In truth, it was Sam who had the strongest desire for the top spot in the land. But Jonathan had the looks and the charisma that would take him to the Oval Office. If they joined forces and worked together, they could go from the California State Assembly to the House of Representatives and then the Senate. And, eventually, the White House.

"I know I let you down," Jonathan said.

Sam chuckled. "It's hardly the first time a politician got a girl pregnant."

Jonathan pinched his eyes shut against the tears that began to blur his vision. He shook his head. He needed to own his mistakes and stop running from them. He needed to stop relying on Sam to get him out of trouble.

"Not one who's underage," he whispered.

"Oh."

Jonathan winced at the response. Of course, Sam had met Mila. They had spent an evening sipping cocktails in a hot tub during a ski trip to Lake Tahoe. They had toured wineries in Napa. Of course, Sam thought Mila was of age— Jonathan had even thought so until a month into their relationship. But by then, he had already fallen for her, and it was too late to back out.

"I need to own this," he said.

"No."

He whipped his head in Sam's direction and saw a look he never thought he'd see plastered on his best friend's face. Disappointment.

"What?"

"I'm not letting you fuck this up for me."

"Sam—"

"I'm going to take care of this for you. And you're never going to ask me about it. Do you understand?"

Jonathan felt a glimmer of hope trying to break through the soul-crushing *feeling of despair that had spiraled him into a deep depression. "What are you going to do?"*

Sam suddenly stood and whirled in his direction. "I'm going to make sure Mila doesn't ruin my chances of making it to the White House. I'm not going to be left standing around with my dick in my hand just because you can't keep yours in your pants."

They'd had frank conversations in the past, but this was the first time Sam had talked to him in that way. Jonathan opened his mouth to say something, but snapped it shut when Sam turned and stormed away. He had no idea what his best friend was going to do, but he owed it to him not to ruin their dreams because of his selfish behavior.

"I'm sorry, Sam," he whispered.

"What did you do, Sam?"

Jonathan looked up from the cigar box and stared his best friend in the eyes. The look he saw there horrified him, and he suddenly remembered that night in San Jose after winning his seat in the California State Assembly. It had been a low point in his career—in his life—but, like always, Sam had taken it upon himself to solve the problem.

And he hadn't looked back.

"I did what I said I'd do," Sam said. "I took care of the problem."

Jonathan looked back down into the cigar box at what was one of the most expensive cigars on the planet. The Regius Double Corona was almost a gimmick—a cigar that represented an experience more than the smoke itself. Priced at over $50,000 and sold worldwide in places like Davidoff of London and Mandarin Oriental in Hong Kong, it offered the purchaser an opportunity to be a part of the brand's history.

But it wasn't the expensive cigar that caused Jonathan's heart to race. It was the baby blue silk ribbon tied around the cigar and affixed to a card with a simple phrase.

It's a boy.

Underneath the card was a photograph of a woman who, for two decades, had only lived in his memories. Her pale blue eyes stared back at him, and he felt his heart race with fear and anxiety at what had become of her.

"Sam," he said, his voice quiet and vibrating with violence. "*What* did you do?"

Before Sam could answer, the door flew open, and a sea of Secret Service agents flooded into the room. Several homed in on the seated Marine corporal, tackling him from the chair and pinning him to the floor. But the rest rushed at the vice president, grabbed him, and practically carried him from the room.

"What's going on?" Jonathan asked, though he felt deflated and allowed them to guide him from the admiral's office toward the front of the building.

"Not now, Mister Vice President," Chris said.

He was the special agent in charge, and if he felt there was need to remove him from the admiral's office and place him someplace safe, he wasn't going to argue. But his mind was still reeling from what had been in the box. Underneath the photograph was a handwritten note on a folded sheet of paper. He hadn't had a chance to read it yet, but he held it with a death grip in his hand as the agents ushered him to the exit.

He felt light-headed. Blindsided. Betrayed.

And he knew the truth—whatever that was—was written on that paper.

65

After the Secret Service agents disappeared inside the headquarters building, the Navy master-at-arms helped Punky stand but cautioned for her to remain well away from the entrance. Even though it appeared like she had saved the day, she knew that could turn in an instant. And if she was in the wrong place at the wrong time, they wouldn't hesitate to put her down.

Even after the SAC and his fellow agents rushed GOLDEN BEAR from the NAWDC headquarters and to the waiting up-armored Suburban, she knew enough to remain back with Todd and the other SEALs. Together, they watched the Secret Service rush the vice president from the NAWDC headquarters building to the caravan that would take him to Air Force Two that was waiting to depart.

"What do you think happened?" Todd asked.

Punky shook her head. She had been hunting KMART for so long that she could hardly believe it had ended like this. What had started as a disgruntled service member giving up secrets to the Chinese in exchange for sex had ended with him spending time one-on-one with the fron-trunner to become the next president of the United States of America.

But Jonathan Adams was safe.

He was alive.

Punky straightened when she saw the doors open and several Secret Service agents leading a handcuffed Marine in dress blues to a waiting police cruiser. She knew her job was far from done. Camron would want her to question Adam Garett to get to the bottom of whatever had taken place behind closed doors. But at least he was finally in their custody.

"Where do you think they're taking him?" she asked.

"Probably to the precinct," the petty officer said.

Punky made a mental note to have Camron arrange for her to have access. She needed to sit down across from him, look him in the eye, and let him know that she was the one who brought him down. She was the one who had followed him from San Diego and put an end to his treachery once and for all.

As the cruiser pulled away, Punky turned to the master-at-arms. "Thanks for not shooting me."

He grinned sheepishly. "I knew you were just trying to do the right thing."

"What now?" Todd asked.

KMART might be in custody. Mantis might be dead. But the United States of America would always be a target to those who resented what the red, white, and blue represented. And men and women like Colt Bancroft and Punky King would always step up to prevent their adversaries from causing harm.

"Back to work," Punky said.

Todd shrugged and turned back to the Flyer 60. She knew the chief and his fellow SEALs would be at the tip of the spear for whatever conflict came next. But it was her job to stop it.

A few minutes later, Air Force Two rolled down the runway, lifted off, and immediately banked away from the populated area of Fallon to put as much distance between them and whatever threat they were leaving behind. Jonathan didn't think he was still at risk, but he knew enough to trust the Secret Service and allow the Air Force pilots to follow their protocols. They were the experts and had his best interests in mind.

But the events in Fallon had proved that wasn't the case for everyone.

He leaned back in his chair and looked through the window at the vast emptiness of the Nevada desert beneath them. He still wore the olive drab green flight suit and looked far braver than he felt. But his thoughts were consumed by more than appearances, and he swallowed as he thought about the gut-wrenching betrayal.

The Boeing jostled as it passed through a thin layer of clouds, and Jonathan cleared his throat. In a matter of days, he had gone from being on the precipice of realizing his lifelong dream to fearing for his life and believing everything he had worked for was at risk of being taken from him. His most trusted advisor—his best friend and confidant—had gone behind his back and put him in the same room with somebody the Secret Service now believed was a threat.

Why? Why, Sam?

As the passenger jet continued climbing away from the turbulent desert air, Jonathan replayed the events in his mind. The Marine was scared, that much was clear. He didn't want to be in the admiral's office with the vice president. Somebody had forced him to put on his dress blues and hand deliver the cigar box. Was it a gift? A message?

Jonathan remembered the handwritten note underneath the cigar and reached into his flight suit pocket where he had hidden it. It had become crumpled in the ensuing chaos as Chris and his team of agents rushed him to the safety of Air Force Two, and he carefully unfolded the note.

He stared in horror as he read the words.

The Marine is your son. We'll be in touch.
From Russia with Love,
Viktor Drakov

Declared Hostile
BATTLE BORN #4

A treasonous plot. Clandestine actors. World order hanging in the balance.

Elite NCIS investigator Emmy "Punky" King, seasoned in global espionage, uncovers the edges of an intricate international conspiracy following the arrest of a U.S. Marine. Relying solely on her sharp intuition, she starts peeling back layers of a complex mystery that links the U.S. president to a clandestine corporation. As she navigates the corruption, Punky finds herself deep in an escalating game that threatens more than just national security.

Halfway across the world in Eastern Europe, Colt Bancroft and the Black Ponies are thrust into a high-stakes mission to prevent nuclear weapons from falling into the hands of rogue Russian operatives. But when their operation spirals into chaos following an ambush by an unexpected adversary, Colt finds himself navigating the deadly terrain of enemy territory, fighting for survival.

Although separated by continents, their missions are fatally intertwined. Colt must battle against overwhelming odds while Punky races against time to uncover the traitor behind it all—both unaware that if either fails, the world will plunge into chaos.

**Get your copy today at
severnriverbooks.com**

ACKNOWLEDGMENTS

Writing the Battle Born series has been a dream come true for me, and none of it could have been possible without the constant encouragement of my wife, **Sarah.** Her patience and understanding are unmatched, but our three amazing children, **Tre, William,** and **Rebecca** come close. I can only hope to repay them by demonstrating the importance of following your dreams.

My circle of fellow authors has continued to grow over the years, and I can't possibly thank all of them for their friendship and mentorship. But I am forever in their debt, and they can bet I will be calling when my travels bring me to their neck of the woods. My bar tab is always open for them.

Although this is a work of fiction and the characters are not real people, they feel like it to me. Colt, Punky, and Dave embody the spirit of the men and women I served with for over two decades. I hope I have made my shipmates proud, and I hope you enjoyed getting to know them.

To my amazingly talented super-agent, **John Talbot,** I am thankful for your patience and guidance as I navigate the publishing world. To **Andrew Watts, Cate Streissguth, Randall Klein, Cassie Gitkin,** and the unsung heroes behind Severn River Publishing, thank you for giving me a home and helping to mold this story into a finished product I am incredibly proud of.

Lastly, to you, my readers. Thank you for continuing to give up your most precious commodity to spend time with Colt and Punky. I hope you enjoyed their adventure and look forward to the next one. I know I look forward to delivering it to you.

I'm out.

Farley

ABOUT THE AUTHOR

Jack Stewart grew up in Seattle, Washington and graduated from the U.S. Naval Academy before serving twenty-three years as a fighter pilot. During that time, he flew combat missions from three different aircraft carriers and deployed to Afghanistan as a member of an Air Force Tactical Air Control Party. His last deployment was with a joint special operations counter-terrorism task force in Africa.

Jack is a graduate of the U.S. Navy Fighter Weapons School (TOPGUN) and holds a Master of Science in Global Leadership from the University of San Diego. He is an airline pilot and has appeared as a military and commercial aviation expert on international cable news. He lives in Dallas, Texas with his wife and three children.

Sign up for Jack Stewart's reader list at
severnriverbooks.com